JUST BECAUSE

THE COMPLETE SERIES

MARI CARR

BECAUSE OF YOU

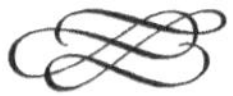

This one is for the gals at work who keep me sane and laughing during the day so I can spend my nights lost in fiction. Your encouragement and support of "my second job" makes all the difference. Thank you, Nan and Lisa!
And for my editor, Lindsey. You may have made me rewrite this book 37,504 times and I wasn't always happy about it, but I have to admit, I really like Caleb and Jessie's story now! Thanks for not giving up on them....and me!

CHAPTER 1

"I don't understand why you can't tell me who he was meeting with," Jessie Warner said, her hands shaking with frustration. She'd tried for two weeks to get her late husband's partner to agree to see her, but to say the man had been evasive was an understatement.

"Client confidentiality, Jessie," Rex replied so smoothly she wanted to reach across the desk and ram her fist through his smug face.

"You're an accountant, Rex. Not a fucking priest or psychologist. It's not like I'm going to grill them about their back taxes. All I want to know is which clients Tommy met with the day he died."

"Why?"

Jessie sighed, perfectly aware that this discussion was going to end like every other conversation she'd had regarding the night of her husband's death.

"I just want to talk to them. See if they noticed anything strange in his demeanor that day."

"Why?" Rex repeated, and for a moment Jessie was struck

by the fact that the man was no longer looking at her with annoyance, but rather with pity in his eyes.

Shit.

She hated pity. She'd seen it on the faces of too many people lately and it only made her angrier, more frustrated. She was tired of being treated like she was weak, and she was sure as hell tired of being treated like she was crazy.

"Forget it," she said, rising quickly. "You aren't going to tell me a fucking thing. You know it and I know it. Thanks for nothing, Rex."

"Dammit, Jessie, don't leave like this. I know you think Tommy's death wasn't an accident, but believe me when I say it was. It's been seven months since he died. You've got to let this go."

An accident. She'd read the police and coroner's reports and she knew what they all believed. They'd said it was an accident, but she couldn't shake the idea that it wasn't—despite the fact she had no proof to the contrary. Tommy had fallen on the ice and hit his head. It seemed to be an easy answer for everyone—everyone but her.

Shortly after his death, she'd begun probing into the details a bit more—asking the police and hospital workers questions, but so far everyone she had encountered had been less than helpful. They thought she was some silly, grieving widow who had watched one too many episodes of *CSI* and had decided to create a crime out of thin air.

Apparently Rex was no different. He'd ignored her phone messages until finally she'd decided to take the direct approach. Her spur-of-the-moment, "oh I was just in the area" visit had been a surprise to him. She knew he was too wrapped up in appearances to throw the widow of his former partner out on her ass in front of an office full of employees. She'd seen in his face that he wasn't pleased about being shanghaied into this visit. No doubt he'd heard the rumors that she was chasing shadows and had hoped to avoid this conversation.

"I can't let it go, Rex," she said quietly as she reached for the door. At one point, she'd considered the man a friend, but nowadays she found it harder and harder to reconnect with the people she'd known before Tommy's death. Aside from her best friend Todd, she'd drifted away from everyone else in her life. "Please help me."

The man shrugged sadly. "I'm sorry, Jessie, but I can't."

"There's a world of difference between *can't* and *won't*. I think you have them confused," she said, storming out. She closed the door loudly behind her and sighed heavily. She'd known when she left the house this morning it would be a wasted trip. She'd been a fool to think that Rex would offer her any sort of help. Hell, the man had avoided her calls like she was a telemarketer.

"Jessie? Is that you?"

"Jordan." She smiled at the older man in the foyer as he leaned down to hug her. Jordan Scott had been a good friend to Tommy in addition to being one of his biggest clients. He'd always been kind to her as well. He'd never forgotten to send a birthday card or his traditional bottle of champagne Christmas gift. They'd dined at his penthouse apartment on more than a few occasions. Neither she nor Tommy had been close to their families, and in some ways Jordan had taken on the role of a beloved uncle. One they didn't see often, but with whom they were always happy to reconnect.

"What a nice surprise," she said as he released her. Always dressed to a tee, he was an extremely attractive gentleman in his mid-fifties, with salt-and-pepper hair and expressive deep blue eyes. She had often questioned him about why he'd never married. She couldn't imagine a whole generation of women letting Jordan slip through their fingers. He was handsome, rich and charming.

"I haven't seen you since—" He paused and Jessie nodded at the silence that followed.

"Since Tommy's funeral," she finished for him.

"How have you been, my dear? I meant to call, but I'm afraid a problem at work pulled me out of the country for a few months. I've only just returned from Italy this past week."

"I'm fine," she answered, the lie a familiar one. She hadn't been fine for seven months. Not since the night she'd found her husband's dead body.

"What brings you to the firm?" Jordan asked. "I thought Rex said you'd sold Tommy's half of the business to him."

"Oh, I did," she said. She looked into Jordan's compassionate face and found her suspicions, her fears falling from her lips. "I've had this feeling since Tommy passed away that something was wrong and I wanted to know which clients Tommy met with the day he died. I was hoping to speak to them, hoping one of them could help me understand his frame of mind that day."

Jordan's puzzled look gave her a moment's pause. "Frame of mind?" he asked.

"I don't think his death was an accident."

"You don't?" he asked in such a way that for the first time, she felt a glimmer of hope that someone actually understood.

She shook her head.

"I met with Tommy the day he died, Jessie."

Jordan's confession stopped her short. She'd anticipated another pitying look, another pat on the head, another condescending comment about being foolish. She hadn't expected an answer. "You did?"

"We met earlier that morning about the audit he was performing for my company. Rather run-of-the-mill stuff. I can assure you his behavior was perfectly normal. I wish I'd known then that I'd never see him again. So many things I would have liked to have said to the dear boy." The older man looked away and Jessie could see the glimmer of tears at the corner of his eyes. When he turned back toward her, the look of sadness was replaced with one of concern. "What's going on, Jessie? Why don't you believe it was an accident?"

The tightness in her chest that never left eased as Jordan spoke. For the first time in months, someone was listening to her, answering her questions, taking her seriously. "Tommy called me earlier in the afternoon, the day he died. He said something that made me think—" She paused, uncertain how to word her concerns.

"Made you think?" he prodded.

She paused and shrugged, her thoughts were traveling a different direction. Jordan had seen Tommy, spoken to him that day. She couldn't focus on anything other than that fact. "Was Tommy acting strangely that day? Did he seem preoccupied, overwrought, worried?"

"Not at all. What did he say on the phone, Jessie?"

"Nothing specific." Tommy hadn't said anything at all really. Perhaps it was his tone more than his words that had sparked her suspicions.

"I suppose you've spoken to the police about this," he said.

She nodded and sighed. "Yes, for all the good it's done me."

"I take it they don't share your belief that there was foul play involved?"

She shook her head. "No. I sort of get the impression they think I'm insane."

Jordan laughed lightly at her lame attempt at a jest. "Nothing could be further from the truth. I wish there was something I could say that would help you, but honestly, there was nothing in Tommy's demeanor that day that leads me to suspect foul play. Tell you what. Why don't you let me do a bit of digging around? I'll see if I can't scare some information out of old Rex, the shyster."

Jessie grinned. Jordan had never made any bones about the fact that Tommy was his preferred accountant in the firm.

"Would you? Really?"

"I'm not sure what help I can be, but if it will put a smile back on that pretty face of yours, I'm willing to try."

"Oh, thank you, Jordan, you've already been more help than you know. If you remember anything else about that day, will you call me?"

"Of course, my dear. You will be the first person I call."

She said her goodbyes and walked to her car feeling lighter than she had since Tommy's death. She still hadn't discovered any answers, but Jordan genuinely seemed to believe her and wanted to help. For the first time in a long time, she didn't feel as if she was wandering around in a dark room with no doors. Jordan had just offered her a flashlight and, God willing, a way out—back into the sunshine that had eluded her for months.

Maybe she wasn't so crazy after all.

CHAPTER 2

ne month later

"I can't believe I let you talk me into this," Jessie said as she walked up to the front porch of the huge ranch house. The party she'd been reluctantly dragged to was already in full swing if the blaring music and loud voices coming from inside were any indication.

"You need to get out, Jess. You can't hide out in that tiny apartment of yours forever. You need to live a little," Todd said, wrapping his arm around her shoulder and dragging her forward.

"I'm not ready for this. I told you that," she said, repeating the argument that had begun several days ago when Todd, her best friend since childhood, had told her he was taking her out to a party.

"No," Stephen said, walking on her other side. "I believe what you said was you weren't ready to go out and meet other men. That's not going to be a problem here."

"Because?" she asked, waiting for Stephen to elaborate. He

and Todd had been very closemouthed about where they were going.

Stephen laughed. "Our friend Jacob James lives here and throws this party every year. It's an annual event he likes to call Gay Fest."

Jessie rolled her eyes at Stephen's joke. He and Todd had been a couple for nearly a decade and she adored them both. They'd rallied around her after her husband's death. Although she lived over three hours away, in the city, they'd made the trek to Denver to spend many weekends with her in an attempt to help her through her grief. She was an only child, estranged from her mother and stepfather, and in her mind, Todd and Stephen were her family now.

"Very funny, Stephen. Really. Hysterical." She replied deadpan as Todd laughed.

"It's just a party, Jess. You used to love to go out. We'll down a few shots, dance around Jake's backyard, you can throw your bra on the bonfire, we'll all sing karaoke and—"

"Oh Jesus, you never said *anything* about karaoke." She groaned, stopping mid-step.

Stephen gripped her arm and started moving her toward the door. "Just ABBA songs," he said.

"Shit," she muttered. They made their way up the front porch and into the house. The place was packed with people and Jessie found herself instantly besieged by Todd and Stephen's friends. Jacob was the first to greet them and Jessie instantly liked the man.

"Well, it's about time you got the girl over here for me to meet," he said, playfully chastising Todd. "I mean, you do live a *whole* mile away. I've heard all about you, Miss Jessie, and I've decided I'm going to steal you away from Todd and *we're* going to be best friends." As he spoke, he linked arms with her.

Todd grabbed her free hand and pulled back. "Get your own damn best friend. Jessie is mine," he teased.

Jessie laughed and shoved them away. "I'll be friends with both of you if you get me something to drink. I have a feeling I'm going to have to be very drunk to tolerate spending time with either of you tonight."

"Way ahead of you," Stephen said, fighting his way back through the crowd. He handed her and Todd each a cold bottle of beer. "Good turnout, Jake."

"Tell me about it. My brothers are gonna go through the roof when they see how many people have shown up. Attendance seems to double every year. Going to have to start renting a banquet hall at this rate."

Stephen laughed. "Well at least it's not raining. I noticed you've got a good crowd hanging around out back."

"Doc's out there right now, working to start the bonfire, and we've cleared off the patio for dancing. My brother Matt's band is setting up to play later."

"You're lucky to have such cool brothers," Todd said, and Jacob nodded.

"Tell me about it. They're the best. Even Mark helped me set up a bunch of tents in the backyard and cleared away some of the living room furniture so people can crash on the floor or outside if they want. Of course, after that, he hit the road. He's still not comfortable around this many gay men," Jacob joked. "I told him I had lots of guys I'd like to set him up with. Man, you should have seen him spin tires in the driveway to escape."

"You shouldn't tease the poor guy," Todd said. "At least your brothers tolerate the fact you're gay. My parents are still convinced therapy and drugs can cure my homosexual affliction."

"Hey, Jake. Where are the chips?" someone yelled from the kitchen.

"Ah, the duties of hosting never end. Why don't you all head out to the backyard? Once everyone's well on their way to wasted, we'll start the ABBA singing contest."

"Oh crap," Jessie muttered so only Todd and Stephen could hear her. "I thought you were joking about that."

The guys laughed and they walked through the house to the back door. There were even more people gathered on the lawn. Most were men, but Jessie spied a few women scattered amongst the partiers.

"Who are all these people?" she asked.

"Jacob's got lots and lots of friends. We don't exactly live in the most liberal-minded of communities, so a few years ago—after he came out—he decided to start holding a Gay Fest. Started out with just a dozen or so friends who shared the lifestyle. Word seems to have spread though, and now folks have started driving from as far as two hundred miles away to attend. It's just a fun night where we can let down our guard and party it up," Todd answered.

Jessie nodded. "That's cool."

She tagged along behind her friends as they reconnected with acquaintances from previous parties. They always introduced her and she tried to join in the conversations, but her heart just wasn't in a festive mood. Before her husband's death, she'd loved a good time as much as the next person, but lately it seemed to take too much energy—something she was definitely lacking. The memory of Tommy floated through her mind. She was certain Todd had suggested this quick vacation hoping that the break would clear her thoughts and encourage her to stop pursuing shadows that weren't there.

Shadows that called her every night.

For the past month, she'd been plagued by midnight phone calls. She'd tried to have them traced, but the number belonged to one of those pay-as-you-go cell phones. The police and Todd had chalked them up to a prank caller, and Jessie wished she felt as certain the calls were harmless. There was something very frightening about the silence that always greeted her at the other end of the line.

"You're drifting," Todd said, leaning down to talk loudly into her ear. They were standing far too close to the speakers for her sanity. She spotted a bar set up at the end of the patio with a few empty stools.

"Drifting? I can't even hear myself think. I'm going to go drum up another beer. You guys want anything?" she asked.

"Naw, I'm good," Todd said as Stephen shook his head. She waved and walked away. Climbing up onto one of the tall barstools, she sighed heavily, looking back at the crowd. It really was a terrific get-together. Jacob definitely knew how to throw a hell of a party.

"That's not a fun face," a voice said from behind the bar.

Jessie turned to find a handsome man smiling at her. *Holy wow*, she thought as she looked into the man's deep green eyes. His dirty blond hair was neatly trimmed, and he had honest-to-God dimples. Inwardly she groaned. Just my luck, she thought. First spark of attraction she'd felt since her husband died and, of course, it was toward a gay man.

"Oh, I'm having fun," she assured him. "Just a bit tired and not in much of a party mood."

"How about a liquid pep-me-up? I'm mixing drinks tonight because I'm not in a party mood myself. Seemed easier to volunteer for this job rather than to fight my way through the revelers and try to participate in small talk," the man answered. "I'm Caleb, by the way."

"Jessie," she replied, reaching out to shake Caleb's outstretched hand. "Jessie Warner."

"I don't think I recognize you, Jessie Warner. Are you from around here?"

"No, I'm here on vacation. I've been visiting with Todd and Stephen for the past couple of weeks. They live about a mile down the road."

"I know those guys pretty well. I forgot Todd mentioned he had company. Best friend from kindergarten, I think he said."

Jessie rolled her eyes and laughed. "Yep, that's me. Todd loves to tell everyone exactly how long we've known each other."

"Got to admit, I figured Jessie, the lifelong friend, was a man," Caleb said. As he spoke he mixed several liquors with orange juice before handing it to the man sitting next to her.

"Thanks, Caleb," the man said, walking back to his friends.

"Everyone thinks that. Curse of my name," she said.

"What are you drinking?" Caleb asked.

"Oh, just beer. I'm heading back home tomorrow and wouldn't want to do it with a headache."

"Smart woman," he said, uncapping a bottle of ice-cold beer and handing it to her. "Where's home?"

"Right now, it's Denver."

"Right now?" he asked.

"Todd and Stephen are trying to talk me into moving here. I'm a website designer and I basically work out of my house. My friends think I need to move out of the big, bad city." Her words were a joke, but she had been giving their request some serious consideration.

She would never have dreamed of leaving Denver before Tommy's death, but over the past eight months, she'd had more than her fair share of bad karma. She'd been mugged a few weeks earlier and although she hadn't been seriously hurt, it had triggered a fear in her that hadn't been there before. Between that, the prank calls, the feeling of constantly being watched, and her unfounded suspicions about Tommy's death, she was one giant mass of nerves.

Since coming to stay with her friends, the paranoia had gone away. No more late night calls, no eyes watching her every move. Todd and Stephen lived on a nice-sized ranch just outside Saratoga, Wyoming and the peacefulness of the area, the beauty of the landscape was certainly calling to her. She'd only been here two weeks, but she was already starting to feel like her old self. She was tired of being frightened—jumping at every sound, flinching at every sudden movement.

"Well, I may not be impartial, but I don't think you could pick a better spot on earth to settle down than right here," Caleb said.

"Oh, so you're a local? Not one of the masses who drive hours to attend Gay Fest?"

Caleb laughed long and loud at her question, and she wondered what he found so funny. "No," he finally answered. "I didn't drive at all. I live here with the host. Jacob's my insane-but-loveable kid brother. And, sweetheart, I ain't gay."

Jessie giggled at his response until she felt a hand on her shoulder.

"Well, doesn't this just figure." She turned to see Jacob and Todd standing next to her. Jacob was shaking his head in mock disgust. "Only two straight people at the whole damn party and they find each other. It's like they've got radar or something," Jacob said to Todd, who laughed.

Jessie shook her head, grinning at Jacob's joke and feeling slightly surprised at how pleased she was to discover Caleb wasn't gay. She didn't even want to consider why that should matter to her. She was nowhere near ready to start thinking about dating someone else. The pain of losing Tommy was still too fresh, too intense.

"I was hoping we might borrow you for a second, Jess," Todd said.

"Borrow me for what?"

"We want you to kick off the karaoke contest," Jacob answered. "Todd says you two used to tear up the elementary school circuit with your song and dance routines."

"Forget it," she said firmly. "I'm too damn old and too damn sober for that."

She felt a nudge at her elbow and looked down to find Caleb pushing a shot glass at her. "As luck would have it, Jessie, I'm a doctor and I'm fairly certain I can take care of that sober problem of yours. Take this shot. It'll make you feel better. Then get up on that stage and sing. It's a party and it looks like it might do you some good to let your hair down."

"Now that's what I'm talking about," Todd chimed in. "Set us all up with a round of those, Doc."

Caleb poured the tequila, and she was secretly appeased when she watched him include himself in the group. On the count of three, all four of them downed the drinks.

Jessie winced as the hot alcohol burned her throat, but after feeling cold for months, she welcomed the sudden warmth. Maybe Caleb and Todd were right. She needed to cut loose, laugh, give herself one night to let go and forget.

"What song are we singing?" she asked as Jacob cheered.

"'Super Trouper'," Todd answered. "Jake and I are gonna be your backup."

She heard Caleb laugh behind her and turned quickly, narrowing her eyes. "You owe me for this," she teased.

"Sweetheart, I look forward to paying up."

"*O*h hell, what time is it?" Jessie asked, leaning her head against his shoulder as they rested against one of the large logs circling the bonfire.

Caleb felt like a damn teenager on his first date with this lovely woman. He'd seen her the second she'd arrived in the backyard and he hadn't been able to take his eyes off of her. Her long, light brown hair shimmered with auburn highlights accentuated by the firelight. Her chocolate-colored eyes were sweet and had been just a little sad when she'd first sat down at the bar. He wondered about that sadness, but as the night progressed, it had gradually disappeared until all he could see now was a woman genuinely enjoying herself...with him.

As an ER doctor, he didn't have a lot of time for dating, and he struggled to remember the last time he'd spent an entire evening with a woman, talking and dancing and laughing. His brothers constantly chastised him for his workaholic tendencies, but he didn't think there was anything wrong with being committed to his career. Sure, he worked long hours and he was *on* call more than he was off, but that was all a part of the job. Lately, Jacob had begun suggesting that Caleb open up his own practice here in town and start dating, an idea he'd previously rejected outright.

However, after spending the evening with Jessie, he realized something he had never noticed before. He was lonely. He'd assumed his patients and his brothers were enough for him, but now he couldn't help but wonder if something vital was missing from his life.

Jessie was a fun companion, and he was more than a little bit sorry about the fact she was leaving in the morning. Although Denver wasn't terribly far away, something about her demeanor told him that tonight was likely all he would get.

"It's after one."

"Ugh," Jessie said, straightening up. "I think my morning departure is suddenly looking like an afternoon one."

He grinned. "Probably not a bad idea. You've had quite a bit to drink."

"That's sort of the pot calling the kettle black, isn't it?" she joked.

He shrugged. "I don't have a three-hour drive tomorrow and I've got plenty of time to sleep this off. I don't have to be back at work until Monday morning."

"I think my chances of dragging Todd and Stephen away are next to nil," she said, her voice betraying her tiredness.

He looked across the yard and spotted her friends in the middle of a huge mass of swaying bodies on the patio. His brother's band was playing and they showed no sign of stopping anytime soon.

"I'll walk you back if you're ready to leave," he offered.

"Oh, that's okay," she said. "I can wait around."

He thought for a moment he saw a flash of fear in her eyes, but she quickly shuttered it away. "Seriously, Jess. It's only about a mile. I don't mind walking you."

She glanced toward the path and again he sensed her reticence.

"I'll have you know I was a Boy Scout. You have my solemn pledge that I will get you home safely." He rose before reaching down and helping her to her feet.

She grinned guiltily as she swayed a bit, betraying her tipsiness. "All right then. I mean if you can't trust a Boy Scout, who can you trust? Let me go tell the guys I'm leaving."

He nodded. "I'll let Jacob know where I'm going and meet you at the bar in five."

Caleb watched her pick her way through the couples who were making out by the giant bonfire, and he smiled at her drunken clumsiness. She apologized to a man whose drink she knocked over before dancing her way across the patio to her friends. He looked around and spotted his brother entertaining a large crowd by the bar.

"Hey, Jake," he called out. "I'm going to walk Jessie back to Todd's guesthouse."

Jacob's eyebrows wiggled suggestively, obviously reading far too much into his actions.

Caleb shook his head. "She's gotta drive back to Denver tomorrow and her friends aren't ready to leave. I'll only be gone a little while. You got things under control here?"

Jacob pulled him aside with a mischievous grin. "Everything here is fine and I think Jessie is a great girl. Take your time." Then he adopted a stern face and for a minute, Caleb was struck by how much Jacob looked like their father. "However, I feel I should remind you to practice safe sex," he said in a deep voice, mimicking dear old Dad perfectly. Jacob reached into his pocket and pulled out a condom. "Here, take this just in case."

"Jake, you're drunk and a dumbass so I'm not going to embarrass you in front of your friends by kicking your ass and making you cry like a big baby," he teased. "I'm just escorting her home," he repeated, despite the small hope he harbored that maybe tonight could include something a bit more. There was a special quality about the woman he couldn't quite put his finger on. He put his hand up to refuse the silver foil packet.

"There you are. You ready?" Jessie asked from behind him. Caleb hastily grabbed the condom Jacob was swinging around and thrust it in the front pocket of his jeans to hide it before Jessie could see. God only knew how she would interpret that move, and he fought the impulse to punch his brother for nearly ruining the whole night with his damn foolishness.

Turning, he wrapped an arm around her shoulders and directed her toward the dirt path that connected to the James Ranch.

"Ready," he said as they set off, away from the loud music and into the quiet night together.

CHAPTER 3

*J*essie unlocked the door to the guesthouse as Caleb stood beside her on the porch. She shook herself for her damned reservations in walking home alone with him. It was obvious Caleb was a kind man. Tonight had been one of the nicest nights she'd had in a very long time, thanks to him. He was fun and funny and her damned anxiety was clearly getting the best of her. She never used to be such a nervous Nelly, suspicious of everyone she met.

She was grateful to Todd for his offer of a place to stay, a retreat of sorts these past two weeks. It was hard to admit it, but she felt better simply getting out of the apartment she'd shared with Tommy, surrounded by memories at every turn.

"I have a feeling you're going to have quite a long wait until you can hit your bed. Wanna come in for a cup of coffee?" she offered, sorry to see her night with Caleb end so soon. He was an easy man to talk to.

"I'd love coffee," he said. "Now that I'm away from the madness, I'm not looking forward to plunging back into it right away."

Jessie grinned and led him through the small house.

"Todd and Stephen have done a hell of a lot of work on the ranch. It needed a major facelift and some big time renovations when they moved in. Looks great now," Caleb said. Stephen had inherited the ranch from his parents after their tragic deaths in a car accident two years earlier. Before that, he and Todd had resided in Denver and the two of them had been her constant companions along with Tommy since they'd all lived in the same apartment complex. She and Tommy had missed them when they moved away, but they'd understood their friends' desire to find an easier pace of life and their dream of setting up a bed and breakfast at the house. She knew Stephen, born and bred on this ranch, had never truly been happy with life in the big city and his high-stress job at an investment firm.

"Yeah, I came up with my husband right after they left Denver. I honestly can't believe all the improvements they've made. They'll be ready for business soon."

Jessie had been making the coffee as she spoke, but even with her back turned she sensed Caleb's sudden tension. She turned to see his eyebrows lowered, his face serious and upset.

"Is something wrong?" she asked, wondering what she could have said to have produced such a rapid change in his disposition.

"Husband?" he asked and she saw his eyes dart to her ring finger. She given up wearing her diamond engagement ring, but she couldn't seem to part from the actual white gold wedding band.

She sucked in a breath at his question. She'd carefully avoided talking about Tommy all night. She'd wanted a night to forget, a night to pretend that her life was normal and happy and that she hadn't had her heart ripped out of her chest eight months earlier.

"I'm a widow," she said, and the sound of that simple word

released the flow of ice-cold water throughout her body once again. For a few hours, she'd been warm. Hell, between Caleb and the alcohol, she spent more than a few moments on fire and it had felt so damn good.

"I'm sorry," he said, rising and crossing the room to take her icy hands in his. She didn't realize until his touch that she was shaking. In just one evening, he'd diminished the shadow of fear that constantly hovered over her. He'd rejuvenated her, made her feel alive.

She shook her head, desperately willing away the chill, the sadness. Dammit, she didn't want to be cold anymore. She was tired of being afraid. "It's been eight months and I'm afraid I sometimes tend to talk about Tommy in the present tense, like he's still here."

"Had he been ill?" he asked and she smiled sadly. He sounded very much like a doctor.

"Freak accident. He slipped on a patch of ice and hit his head on a car door. It was late and brutally cold and he was the last person leaving work that night. It was several hours before I found him and by then—"

"You found him?" he asked, pulling her gently to a chair in the kitchen. He pushed her down before sitting next to her. He never released his grip on her hands, and she knew he felt the coldness in them as he began to rub them with his own as if to warm them.

"I was concerned when he didn't come home and didn't answer his cell. He was an accountant and it was audit season, so he worked late occasionally, but it wasn't like him not to call and check in. Finally, I worried myself into a frenzy and decided to drive by his office, fully prepared to give him holy hell for scaring me so."

He nodded. "I'm sorry it was you who found him."

She shrugged and closed her eyes. She was a master at

controlling her tears, yet here with Caleb it seemed harder to do. She'd managed to push her pain deep inside her, and she even found it easier of late to discuss Tommy's death. Tonight, whether it was the alcohol or her tiredness or Caleb's compassion, the emotions were threatening to bubble over and she refused to let that happen.

"Well, I suppose I managed to bring tonight's fun level down. That's me—the official ruination of all parties," she tried to joke. She pulled her hands out of his comforting grip and went back to the counter. "Do you like cream and sugar in your coffee?"

"No, I drink it black, and, Jessie, you didn't ruin anything. You're going through a damn hard time right now, dealing with something no one should ever have to deal with. Don't be so hard on yourself. I wish I could give you an easy fix, but I'm afraid nothing except time will cure this."

She grinned over her shoulder, determined to return to the easy banter they'd enjoyed all night. "That's quite a bedside manner you have, Dr. Caleb." The flirtatious line felt rusty and foreign as it fell from her lips, but Caleb didn't seem to notice.

He gave a short, brief laugh. "Oh yeah, I'm a master at bedside—" He paused mid-sentence and she was surprised when he walked over to her and placed his hands on her cheeks. "Christ, Jess. I want to kiss you so badly it hurts."

"So kiss me," she whispered, uncertain where the words had come from, his and hers. From the second he touched her face, she wanted him with a passion she'd thought long gone.

He leaned down and took her lips gently, sweetly, but she refused to be patronized, treated with kid gloves. She was a living, breathing woman and she wanted him. Wanted him beyond reason, beyond care.

She reached up, gripping his hair in her fingers roughly, pulling his face more firmly to her. She opened her mouth and welcomed his tongue, before pushing it out of her way to explore his lips, his teeth with her own.

He moved his hands down to her waist, his grip stronger, more certain, more controlling. She was giving him everything her broken shell of a body had left to give, and she sensed he was more than ready to take her up on the offer.

His lips slid from hers, gliding along her cheek to her earlobe, down her neck. The whole time he worshipped her with his mouth, his hands roamed, finding their way beneath her T-shirt to her breasts. She groaned at the hot touch of his hands against her taut nipples, and he ground his hard erection into her pussy.

"God," she gasped, his touches, his lips, his body pushing hers rapidly into overdrive. "More," she demanded. "Please, Caleb. More."

He continued his sensual assault and she fought to keep up. She shoved his hands off her body for a moment so that she could pull his T-shirt over his head. The image of his bare, sculpted chest was a visual treat, but she couldn't make herself take the time to enjoy it. She was on fire, and her body was demanding that she take everything he had to give immediately. She leaned down, nipping at his small, hard nipples and he hissed with delight. His hands began working at the button and zipper of her jean shorts, shoving them and her panties over her hips, leaving her bare from the waist down.

Somewhere in the recesses of her mind, she wondered what the hell she was doing, but that thought was quickly squelched by a single touch of his fingers against her clit.

"Yes," she whispered hoarsely. His hand delved farther and soon she found herself roughly pushing her hips toward him, forcing the two fingers he plunged inside her deeper, harder, faster. She was cresting on the edge of an orgasm within moments, but she refused to come alone. Caleb had given her so much tonight. Without realizing it, he'd offered her an escape, a refuge from the mourning, and she wanted to give him back some small part of the incredible pleasure he was building inside her.

"You," she demanded. "I want you." She struggled to free his cock from his pants, her hands clumsily attempting to find his zipper. He helped her, and as soon as his erection was free, she gripped him, stroking the rock-hard, yet velvety skin.

He moaned against her mouth, taking her lips in a volatile kiss that blew every thought, every emotion out of her mind. Nothing, nothing on earth mattered at this moment, but this man, this feeling.

She vaguely heard the tearing of foil and glanced down in time to watch him rolling on a condom.

"Hurry," she cried. She had only a second to react as he lifted her onto the counter and stepped between her outstretched legs. He paused as the head of his cock entered her. Looking into her face, his gaze locked onto hers, leaving her with the impression that he could see straight into her soul. No doubt he was giving her a chance to refuse.

"Hurry," she whispered again and he smiled. A smile so sweet and kind, she felt tears prick at her eyes. Then he was inside her, hard and full and wonderful.

Together, they thrust against each other in a familiar rhythm that felt completely unique and new, and she was lost in the sensations, the wonder of the act.

She came far too quickly and was pleasantly surprised when he refused to give way to her climax.

"Not enough," he spoke through gritted teeth and she knew he was right. This magic was too special to waste on a quick ending.

Harder and faster he moved, his hips pumping into her with a ferocity that should have hurt, but instead felt too astonishingly perfect to dispute. She welcomed each of his blows and when her orgasm came again, she screamed with the power, the force of the impulse.

She heard Caleb's cries mingle with hers as hot jets of semen caressed her womb. He rested his head against her shoulder as she clung to him, too overwhelmed by the emotions inundating her to let him go.

After a few minutes, he slowly extricated himself from her tight clasp, and she felt him slide out of her. She missed his body the instant he left her.

"Oh hell," he muttered. "Oh, baby." He looked up at her with regret, and she sensed the word *sorry* on his lips.

"Caleb?" she asked, confused by his apologetic response to such a powerful act.

"The condom broke," he said.

The second the words passed his lips, she recalled the feeling of his seed filling her.

"It's okay," she reassured him.

He seemed to ponder her words before grinning guiltily. "It is?"

She nodded and he leaned forward, kissing her so long and lustfully, she suspected they could spend a lifetime in the kitchen without ever taking a sip of their now-cold coffee.

"I'm clean, Jess. I swear it," he muttered against her lips.

"Me too," she answered. "I've only ever been with Tommy."

He kissed her harder, and she couldn't decide if he was trying to comfort her or to erase her dead husband's name from her lips.

"Stay with me," she whispered and again she was shocked by her words. She'd spent eight months' worth of lonely nights in a cold, hard bed and just for tonight, she wanted to feel Caleb's arms wrapped around her as she slept.

He nodded his assent before helping her off the counter and wrapping her securely in a bear hug. She wasn't a short woman, but Caleb's height, his broad shoulders dwarfed her in comparison and made her feel safe, protected.

Arm in arm, they walked to the bedroom. They helped each other finish undressing and crawled under the cool sheets together. She curled into his outstretched arms and immediately fell into the deepest sleep she'd had in months.

*C*aleb felt a slight movement on the bed next to him and for a moment, he tried to figure out where the hell he was. Straining to make out the room in the darkness, he remembered Jessie and the kitchen. The bed moved again, and he glanced over to the naked woman lying next to him. She had her back to him, but he could see her shoulders shaking. He heard her soft, strangled gasp for breath, and his heart broke at the sound of her silent crying.

"Oh, Jess," he whispered. "Please don't cry, baby."

He heard her sniffle, but she didn't roll over to face him. "I'm not crying," she said.

He turned and wrapped his arm around her waist. She stiffened for just a moment before relaxing in his grip, letting him drag her to him spoon fashion. "You regret this," he said, shame suffusing him. They'd both been more than a little drunk, and he'd been an ass and a fool to take her so roughly. Christ, he took her on the damn kitchen counter.

"Oh no," she said, looking over her shoulder at him. His eyes had adjusted to the dark, and he could see the wet tears clinging to her eyelashes. "I don't regret this, really I don't."

"Then why are you crying?" he asked.

"I don't know why," she confessed. "God, Caleb. I'm such a mess. I can't seem to make anything in my life work lately. My head is fuzzy, my heart feels like a two-ton rock and I honestly don't know if I'm coming or going most days."

"You're grieving, Jess. All of that is natural, normal."

"It doesn't feel normal," she spat out angrily. "It feels like shit."

He leaned down to press a soft kiss on her bare shoulder and heard her sigh. "You've never been with another man. Don't you think that may be why you're upset?"

"I never thought I'd *ever* be with any man but Tommy," she said quietly. "We started dating in high school and stayed together all through college. It wasn't supposed to be like this."

He tightened his grip on her waist, wishing he could take some of her pain away, wishing he could erase every sad, scared, uncertain thought in her head. "It was obviously too soon for you. I'm so sorry, Jessie. I don't have any excuse other than to say I had a bit too much to drink tonight. I rushed you when I should have made sure you were ready for this. I've behaved like an ass."

She turned in his arms and pulled his face toward hers with her hands. "Don't say that," she insisted. "Hell, don't even think that. Tonight was wonderful, Caleb. You were wonderful and absolutely everything that I needed you to be. This sounds corny and is probably the world's biggest cliché, but it's me, not you. This last year has been twenty kinds of miserable. On top of Tommy's death, I've been getting these stupid phone calls—"

"What phone calls?"

"Just a prank caller, and then some asshole mugged me a few weeks ago and I—"

"You were mugged?" he asked, tightening his grip on her. It was no wonder the woman was falling apart. Hell, he couldn't figure out what was holding her together.

She grinned ruefully. "I'm starting to sound like a walking train wreck."

He frowned, a growing feeling of concern tugging at his gut. "You need to be more careful, Jessie. Denver is a big city and I'm not so sure I like the idea of you staying there alone considering all that's happened lately."

"You're starting to sound like Todd."

"Well, then Todd is apparently speaking common sense."

She leaned forward and kissed him lightly. "You've been so kind and patient. I can't imagine too many men who would stick around when they wake up to hear the crazy woman they just had sex with crying over her dead husband."

As she said the last words, her voice broke. He moved toward her and kissed her gently. "Shhh. Don't be silly. You aren't crazy. You just need more time."

"Time," she said with disgust. "If I hear that word again, I swear I really will go insane. Everyone says I need time, but time moves too damn slow and nothing ever changes."

He chuckled at the ferocity of her words. He imagined that once Jessie's mourning passed, she would be a force to be reckoned with. There was a powerful soul in her tiny frame. "I wouldn't say that. You went out tonight and let yourself have a good time."

"Yeah, but I had to think about having fun every minute," she added.

"And you'll probably have to think about it the next time too, but eventually, you'll remember how to have fun without having to make the conscious effort."

"Caleb, tonight with you, the party, the kitchen, it's all been amazing, but—" She hesitated and he knew what she was struggling to say.

"But it's not time for this yet," he finished for her.

"I can't do this. I can't give you what you deserve. I'm only a tenth of the person I was a year ago and until I track down the rest of myself, I—" She stopped again.

He smiled sadly, aware that she was truly a one-in-a-million woman. She'd been warning him all night in little ways that tonight was all they would have. He respected her honesty and her courage.

"I understand," he whispered, kissing her again, desperate to have one last taste of her before she disappeared from his life completely. They broke apart and he lay back, pulling her to his chest, relishing the sound, the heat of her soft, deep breaths as she fell back to sleep.

Jessie opened her eyes, squinting against the harsh sunlight and her throbbing head. "Shit," she muttered. She glanced around the empty room, surprised to find she was alone.

Rising, she threw on her robe and walked out to the kitchen. At the table, she found a note from Caleb.

Jess,

Got an early call from hospital. ATV accident—bad one. I'm sorry I wasn't here when you woke up. Call me when you're ready.

Caleb

At the bottom of the paper, he had scrawled his cell phone number. She folded the paper and considered picking up the phone right away. She missed him, but calling him now wouldn't change anything. She'd merely drag him down with her into this murk and mire she called a life. That depressing thought was just taking root when a knock at the door distracted her.

"Come in," she called out.

Todd staggered in, bleary-eyed and definitely the worse for wear. She tried to hold back her amusement and failed, giving in to her laughter.

"Oh yeah," he said, his voice uncharacteristically rough, "laugh it up. This isn't funny. This is agony. Why didn't you stop me?"

She shrugged. "You were having fun."

"Christ, I don't think there's enough fun in the world to justify this hangover."

"Why are you out of bed so early then? Go sleep it off."

"It's your fault I'm not in my bed. I crashed on Jacob's couch last night. I was staggering back about an hour ago when I passed Caleb on the path. I actually crawled into bed and tried to sleep, but you know me. Curiosity won out. What the hell happened between you two?"

She sat down in the kitchen chair and gestured for him to join her. Once he settled, she leaned her head back, closed her eyes and sighed.

"I slept with Caleb."

She expected an outburst, a loud exclamation, something noisy and dramatic, which was why she was so surprised by the silence that greeted her. She slowly dragged her eyes open, even more shocked to see Todd smiling at her.

"Did you hear what I said?" she asked.

"I heard you," he answered.

"And?" she said, frustrated by his unusual reticence in expressing his opinion.

"And I think that's great."

"Great?" Her voice sounded too loud in the tiny kitchen. Then she felt her shoulders droop and her fears came falling out in a rush of words. "You don't think I betrayed Tommy, that I was wrong to hop into bed with another man so soon? Tommy's only been gone eight months. What the hell was I thinking? I barely know Caleb. Does this mean I'm a slut? Don't you think—?"

"Now wait right there," he interrupted her. "You are not

and never have been a slut. Hell, Tommy was your first and only lover before last night. And no, I don't think you were wrong to invite Caleb to your bed. I've watched you drift away from me, from life these past few months, and I was so afraid I'd never be able to get you back. Last night, you laughed, you danced, you sang and you opened your heart enough to let a kind man love you."

She winced at his use of the word *love*, but he waved her off. "I don't mean you're in love with Caleb and I'm not saying he's in love with you, but I know you, Jess. You're not the type of woman who hops into any man's bed. You and Caleb talked last night for hours at the party and I watched you let go of some of that damn armor you've wrapped yourself in these past few months. I've known Caleb for years. He's a nice, honest, decent guy and there's no way I would have let him walk you home if I hadn't known he'd take care of you."

"I didn't bring him back here with the intention of having sex with him."

"I'm sure you didn't, but the fact of the matter is you needed last night, kiddo. I have a feeling you've turned a corner and whether you see Caleb again or not isn't really the point. You're letting yourself live again. You didn't die eight months ago. Tommy did."

"I know that," she whispered.

"No, Jess, I'm not sure you do. At least, you didn't seem to before last night."

She considered his words. Had she checked out the night she found Tommy's body? Had she been hiding, playing dead, wallowing in Tommy's death rather than moving on? She'd blamed the mugging, the phone calls, the irritating feeling she had of being watched for her escape from society. In her mind, she had a mystery to solve and that thought had consumed more and more of her time. But had she been using that as an excuse? A reason to stop moving forward with her own life?

Last night with Caleb, she'd felt as if she were coming to life again, or at least, out of hibernation. It had been wonderful, freeing, and she found it difficult—no, she found it impossible—to face the idea of returning to the coldness, the loneliness that had plagued her for months.

"So what's the plan?" he asked.

"I'm moving here," she said, the words flying from her lips without thought, and she realized that was another decision she'd unconsciously made during the previous evening.

"For Caleb?"

She shook her head. "No, for me."

"And this investigation into Tommy's death?"

She considered Todd's question. She knew he thought she was grasping at straws, trying to make something out of nothing. For months, she'd been so sure, but now? What if his death had been an accident? What if the mugging and the prank calls were nothing more than that? What if in her grief she had created this idea of a crime, just as everyone suspected?

"Maybe it's time to accept that I may never learn the truth of his death." Even as she spoke the words, she fought to believe the wisdom of them. Common sense said it was time to move on, to start living again, but her sense of conviction, the tiny voice in the back of her brain that wouldn't let her rest disagreed.

He grinned. "I would like to go on the record as saying if you'd given me the news that you were moving here any other day, I would be screaming my head off and dancing you around this kitchen. However, as my head is about two minutes away from exploding, you're just going to have to take my word for the fact that I'm happy as hell."

She laughed. "Yeah, well, I'll trust you and you're forgiven for not dancing. Seems to me you did enough of that last night."

"Don't remind me. I have a feeling the only reason I'm not crying in agony over the pain in my legs is because my head hurts worse."

She stood up and pressed a soft kiss to his brow. "You have been an amazing friend to me these past few months. I don't think I would have survived without you."

Todd shrugged and offered her a sad smile. "Tommy wouldn't have wanted you to be so miserable, and he wouldn't have wanted you to spend the rest of your life alone and in mourning."

He'd spoken the same words to her before, but for the first time, she could see, could feel the truth behind them.

Her friend was right, Tommy would hate to see her so consumed by grief and loneliness. However, her heart also knew that were the situation reversed, there was no force on earth that would stop her husband from seeing justice served. Didn't she owe the same to him?

CHAPTER 4

Jess was halfway between Saratoga and Denver when her cell phone rang. The return trip home was slowly erasing the positive effects of her vacation. The tension she'd managed to shake loose was returning to her shoulders. She dreaded the return to her cold, lonely apartment, facing long nights waiting for her faceless caller to begin tormenting her again.

She snatched the phone up from beside her on the car seat. "Hello?"

"Jessie?"

"Yes," she answered.

"Hi, this is Dawnette." Jessie was surprised to hear Tommy's secretary on the other end of the line. She hadn't spoken to the woman since Tommy's death. There had been several times when she'd wanted to call to talk to Dawnette about her suspicions, but the secretary had taken his death hard, blaming herself for not staying late to work with him, and Jessie hadn't wanted to add to the poor woman's pain.

"Hey, Dawnette. How are you?" She'd always liked her husband's assistant.

"I'm doing fine. I hope I'm not calling at a bad time."

"Actually I'm on my way home from Saratoga. I've been visiting a friend."

"Oh, that's nice." Dawnette's voice seemed distant, distracted. "Listen, I'm actually calling because, well, because there's been a bit of a problem at the accounting firm."

"A problem?" she asked.

"More than a problem. An arsonist burned the whole place down."

"What?" Jessie asked.

"Two nights ago. The fire marshal found some sort of incendiary device and he's sure it was foul play."

"Oh, how awful. Was anyone in the building?"

"No, the cleaning crew had just left, so no one was hurt at least. Thing is, they think the fire started in Tommy's old office."

Jessie considered her words. "Dawnette, the day Tommy died, he called me and mentioned finding something interesting in an audit he was doing. Do you have any idea what he meant?"

"Interesting?" Dawnette asked. "I remember he was stressed out for a couple of days prior to his, um, accident. You know how he was, always so calm, cool and collected. It was weird to see him so uptight."

"Do you know what account he was working on? What could have possibly upset him?"

"He was a brilliant accountant. He always had five or six accounts on his desk at one time. It's hard to say for sure, but I've been a secretary in accounting firms for years, and nothing short of an IRS audit or embezzlement gets an accountant as worked up as Tommy was."

Embezzlement? The word resounded in Jessie's mind and she tried to recall whether or not she'd noticed his anxiety at home. They'd both been bogged down with work. Perhaps the signs that something was bothering him had been there all along and she hadn't been paying attention.

The image of Tommy as he lay dying alone, outside in the cold, came into her mind, only this time the picture changed and Jessie imagined someone was with him, standing over him. What if someone knew Tommy was getting close to uncovering evidence that would expose his crime and the villain had decided to silence him forever?

"I'm sorry to bother you at all," Dawnette continued, "but something told me you would want to know about the fire." The soft, urgent tone of the secretary's voice clued her in that Dawnette had heard about Jessie's visit to the firm and about the nature of the questions she'd been asking. She was grateful to the woman not only for her information, but also for her call. Clearly Dawnette was one of the minority who didn't think Jessie's concerns were unfounded.

"I can't tell you how glad I am that you did."

"Well, goodbye, Jessie."

"Bye, Dawnette." She hung up and tried to focus her attention on the road. She considered the woman's comments about the fire starting in Tommy's office. She had gone over the day of her husband's death so many times she thought she'd lose her mind. Since then, she had been mugged and plagued by phone calls.

Her immediate suspicions fell to Tommy's partner, Rex, but why would he torment her and why would he burn down the firm? If he'd been part of an embezzlement scheme, he had access to all of Tommy's records. He could have destroyed or hidden all the evidence long ago. There was no logical explanation for him to burn down his own building. However, given the fact she was questioning him about who Tommy had met with, the man knew she was suspicious.

Dawnette's comments also suggested that the villain could be someone who worked for the targeted company, and once again, she felt frustrated by Rex's silence in telling her the names of the clients Tommy had met with that last day. Was Rex protecting someone? Jordan said he'd met with Tommy that morning and her husband had been acting normally. Who had Tommy seen after that? And why would the embezzler turn his attention toward her after Tommy's death? She didn't know his identity. She had no proof against him. Or did she?

She sighed and signaled as she approached the exit that would put her on the highway that would take her back to Denver. Her head ached and the familiar coldness that had permeated every part of her body returned with a vengeance.

"So much for that vacation," she muttered as she felt all traces of the optimism and happiness she felt in Saratoga drift away.

"Why are you there, Jessie?"

She shrugged, then grinned as she became aware of the fact that Jordan couldn't see the gesture through the cell phone. "I don't know. Maybe I'm simply a glutton for punishment."

"You've just returned from a lovely vacation, young lady. You should be wading through a sea of mail and laundry. Instead you're sitting outside a burned-out building. Why?"

"Hell if I know," she admitted wearily. She'd been unable to sleep more than a few hours last night as she'd tossed and turned, thinking of all Dawnette had said about the fire and the possibility of embezzlement. "The answer to Tommy's death may have been in there."

"Well, if it was, it's been reduced to rubble and ash. This isn't healthy for you, Jessie. I wish you'd take a few steps back from this investigation and take care of yourself. I thought that trip to Saratoga might help you see that continuing down this path will only lead to exhaustion and pain."

"I thought you understood," she said sadly. Jordan had been her only confidant, her staunchest supporter as she attempted to puzzle out the mystery surrounding Tommy's death. The idea of continuing the search alone again depressed her.

"I do understand and you must know I'll help you in any way I can, but I care about you and I have to admit to being more than a little worried about you. You've become the daughter I never had, dear Jess, and I would give anything to see you happy again."

She smiled at his kind sentiment. "Just help me see this through to the end, Jordan. Your friendship, your belief in me has meant more than I can say."

"Then that is precisely what you'll continue to have. So how long are you going to sit there?"

She laughed lightly. "Not long. I've got too many errands to run downtown today to dawdle for long."

"Well then. I'll leave you to your ruminations, Sherlock Holmes. I have a board meeting to attend. Goodbye, Jessie."

"Goodbye." She clicked off her cell and looked at the burnt-out shell of her husband's office building. She recalled the day he and Rex had decided to open the firm together and smiled as she remembered Tommy's excitement as he led her through the building the afternoon they'd signed the contract to buy it. She was glad he wasn't here to see his dreams, his future plans reduced to a pile of charred planks and dirty ashes.

She was surprised when a car pulled up beside her. Glancing over into the driver's seat, she found Rex looking at her. Obviously, he wasn't happy to find her here. She forced a faint smile and opened her car door as he opened his.

"Hey, Rex."

He looked tired, sad. "What are you doing here, Jessie?"

"I guess the same thing as you," she replied. "Remembering."

He crossed to the front of his vehicle and leaned against the hood. She joined him.

For a moment, she felt sorry for him.

At least, she did until he spoke. "Still trying to build conspiracy theories out of thin air?"

She fought back her anger at his hostile tone. The man had suffered a second major blow to his career in less than a year, so she struggled to make her reply kind, non-threatening. He and Tommy, while not bosom buddies, had worked together in relative peace and harmony for many years. Losing his partner and now his office had to be taking a toll on him.

"I'm just trying to make sense of all of this, Rex."

"Dammit, Jess. Sometimes life kicks you in the teeth just for the fucking hell of it. Why does it have to mean something?"

Her temper rose at his casual dismissal of what he had to see as further proof that her suspicions weren't unfounded. "What is wrong with you? Are you so apathetic, so cowardly, that you prefer to close your eyes to everything that's going on around you rather than confront it head on?"

"What am I facing? Tommy fell and hit his head. It was an accident. An arsonist threw a Molotov cocktail in the window of my office building. In case you failed to notice, we live in a relatively large city where crime is on the rise. Jesus, you were just mugged. Surely, you aren't pretending that crime doesn't exist in Denver?"

"How did you know about the mugging?" she asked, shocked to discover he knew about it.

"Jordan mentioned it the last time he was in."

She nodded and considered his answer. Jordan, true to his word, had been trying to discover more information regarding Tommy's clients, and she suspected her dear friend had been harassing Rex relentlessly. The thought offered her a bit of petty pleasure. Rex had always been the weaker of the two accountants, perfectly content to ride Tommy's coattails as her husband landed account after account, building their firm into one of the most prosperous in the city.

A new thought occurred to her. How was Rex doing now that he was the driving force of the firm? What if he'd burned down the building himself in an attempt to hide the fact he was failing on his own?

She mentally shrugged. Rex's lack of business savvy certainly didn't explain Tommy's death, the mugging or the damned phone calls.

"What accounts was Tommy working on?" she asked when Rex turned back toward the destroyed building and sighed heavily. She hoped his obvious exhaustion would weaken his defenses.

"You're relentless," he said, turning toward her, anger written on every line on his face. Stress had taken its toll on the man as she noticed how much he'd aged in the last year. Tommy had always called him his pretty boy partner, teasing Rex relentlessly for his vanity and playboy lifestyle. His typically clean-cut face was shadowed with a couple days worth of growth. He had dark circles under his eyes and his mouth was drawn tight, his ever-present cocky grin missing.

"I prefer the word determined," she said.

"You're a fool." He raised his hand quickly and she fought to hide a flinch. He shook his finger in her face angrily and by his loud, harsh words, she knew she'd pushed him too far. "And an annoyance. I'm going to tell you one more time, Jessie.

Tommy's death was an accident and this was a random act of arson. Now I want you to get off this property before I call the police and have you charged with trespassing. I don't want to see you here again."

She started to argue, but whatever restraint he'd held on his fury slipped completely. "Get the *fuck* out of here!" he yelled.

She sucked in a breath at his livid tone and cold face. She'd never been afraid of Rex, but at that moment, with his narrowed eyes and clenched fists, she sensed a cold-blooded hostility she'd never seen before.

She climbed into her car and pulled out of the parking lot, fighting to still her trembling hands. Glancing in the rearview mirror, she could see his heated gaze following her as she drove away. Apparently she'd lied to Todd. Her move to Saratoga would have to wait.

*C*aleb dragged himself into the ranch house after pulling a double shift. He was pleasantly surprised when he opened the front door to find the place back in order and all the guests finally gone.

"Hey, Doc," Jacob called, coming down the stairs with a full garbage bag. "Everything okay at the hospital?"

"Yeah, the flu seems to be making its rounds though. Left us short one doctor and two nurses."

"You got home late from the party," Jacob said, placing the heavy bag down. "Or should I say early?"

Caleb rolled his eyes. No doubt his brother was hoping for some juicy details. "I'm tired, Jake. I'm going to bed."

"Too tired to talk, huh? I wonder what on earth could have made you so tired."

He shook his head and grinned. "Not going to let me rest, are you?"

"Nope, so you might as well spill it all," Jacob replied. Caleb resigned himself to telling Jacob about his night. He had always been closest to his baby brother, despite the wide gap in their ages and the fact they shared few common interests.

Jacob was a reader, a writer, an artist, while Caleb lived his life firmly ensconced in the sciences. Jacob liked loud rock music, while he preferred a slow country melody. Caleb was a red-blooded heterosexual male, while Jacob...well, Jacob was not.

It had taken him some time to come to grips with the idea that his youngest brother was gay, but seeing the transformation in his brother, who'd always been too quiet, too insecure while growing up, was worth the effort. Jacob had grown into a confident, outgoing young man and Caleb was extraordinarily proud of him.

"Jessie is an amazing woman," he said.

"So I hear. Todd is crazy about her," his brother said, "and worried about her."

He nodded. "Her husband died about eight months ago, some sort of accident."

"Yeah, I remember Todd telling me about it at the time. Said Jessie shut herself up. Never went out, didn't cry, talk, smile."

"She loved her husband," he said, the image of Jessie crying softly in bed returning to him. "We made love," he added quietly.

"Made love or had sex?" Jacob asked. "There's a difference, you know."

"I know," he confessed. "And I said it right the first time."

"Shit, one night and you're falling for her."

He shrugged and turned away from his brother. "If I am, it doesn't matter. Jessie's not ready for a relationship."

Jacob placed a comforting hand on his shoulder. "She may

not be ready now, Doc. That doesn't mean she'll never be ready. I'm just happy that you're finally putting yourself out there. At last. Started to think you were going to milk this damned bachelor lifestyle until the grave."

"Kind of jumping the gun, aren't you? I spent one night with a woman who isn't ready for a relationship. Let's face it, Jake, it's probably a little too late for me to be considering the dating scene. I'm too old and set in my ways."

"You're not old at all. The only thing wrong with you is that you've spent your whole life giving to others and now you've forgotten how to take something for yourself."

"What's that supposed to mean?" Caleb asked, confused by his brother's comment.

"You give one hundred and twenty percent of your attention and time to that hospital, to your patients, to us, but, Doc, when's the last time you took something because you needed it? Hell, when's the last time you took something just because you wanted it?"

When he'd graduated from medical school, all he'd wanted was to help people, to be a success. As the eldest brother, he'd taken on the responsibility of caring for his brothers after their parents passed away. He'd never been involved in a serious relationship because he'd never had the time. His one night with Jessie supported the truth of his brother's observations. He was lonely, and the lovely widow had uncovered some latent yearnings he'd never realized were there.

"You know, for someone who thinks he's so smart, you would think that talent would carry over to buying decent condoms. Where in the hell did you get that one you gave me that night?"

"You gave it to me," Jacob said.

"When?"

"When I was heading out to junior prom." His brother adopted the same deep voice he'd used last night, this time, no doubt trying to sound like a pompous, younger version of him. "You said, 'Jake, I know how boys are and prom is a big night. Make sure you practice safe sex'."

"I thought you were mimicking Dad last night with that line."

"Shit, when would Dad have ever given us condoms and said the word *sex* to us? You were the one who explained the birds and bees to me."

"Looks like I did a hell of a job," he joked and Jacob laughed.

"You did fine, dumbass. Holy hell, you didn't try to use that thing, did you? It's ancient."

Caleb bit his tongue, unwilling to confess his idiocy. "Why are you still carrying the damn thing?"

"Sentimental value. I like to think of it as my lucky charm. Actually, if you don't mind I'd like it back."

He felt his face flush a bit at Jacob's request.

"Crap, you did use it."

"You didn't mention wanting it back," he said.

"Yeah, well. I didn't actually think you and Jessie would hook up and then I figured you were smart enough to realize I was imitating you and that you'd see how fucking old the thing was."

"It was dark and I was more than halfway to drunk, Jake."

His brother laughed. "Just tell me it didn't break."

"It broke," he said.

Jacob's jaw dropped and Caleb watched the color slowly seep out of his brother's face.

"It's okay. Jessie assured me it was fine. She must be on the Pill or taking those birth control shots. I'm clean and she's only ever been with her husband, so it's not like STDs are an issue either."

"Phew, that's a relief. I almost made myself an uncle. Who'd have thought it? And at Gay Fest too."

Caleb laughed and picked up the bag of garbage. "Shut up, you idiot. What's left to clean up around here?"

CHAPTER 5

"Thank you, Officer," Jessie said, closing the door behind the policeman and quickly throwing the deadbolt in place as well as sliding the chain into its notch. She turned and looked at the mess that was her apartment.

She'd driven to the grocery store after her conversation with Rex, then headed to the post office to pick up the mail that had accumulated while she was on vacation. She'd even treated herself to lunch at a new tapas bar, hoping that by forcing herself into normal activities, she could stop feeling so out of control, so helpless.

She didn't realize as she left the restaurant that she was driving back to hell. Someone had broken into her apartment while she was out and the culprit had certainly done a number on the place. Nothing had been left untouched or undisturbed. It didn't appear that anything had been stolen. Her television, stereo, even her big bowl of loose change were still in place.

On the plus side, the police were now admitting that she seemed to have attracted the unsavory attention of some criminal. They still didn't think this break-in had anything to do with

Tommy's death, but at least they didn't think she was blowing things out of proportion anymore when she mentioned the feeling of being watched.

Some consolation.

According to the police officer, either the person was a vandal trying to wreak havoc and scare her or he was someone looking for something. Regardless of the asshole's intentions, she was immediately besieged with the same uneasy, fearful feelings she'd just spent the last two weeks on vacation trying to cure herself of.

Reaching for her cell, she started to dial Todd's number. She'd only punched in a few digits when she stopped and considered calling Caleb. She felt certain he would know what to say, know how to help her. She wished she had extended her trip, stuck around a few more days. She felt a bit like a coward for leaving town without even saying goodbye to him.

"Shit," she muttered to herself.

One night.

She'd spent one night talking to the man. They'd had sex once. It was over. The last thing she needed right now was to start thinking of Caleb as anything more than a one-night stand.

She finished dialing the phone.

"Hey, Jess," Todd answered on the third ring. "What's up?"

"Someone broke into my apartment. Trashed the place," she said, her annoyance overshadowing her initial fear.

"Are you kidding me?" he asked.

"Am I laughing?" she answered.

"Shit, Stephen and I will pack up and head out this evening to—"

"No," she said, interrupting him. "You aren't driving all the way down here. Nothing was stolen. The police have come and gone and all I have to do now is clean up. I can do that on my own."

"What do you need me to do?"

"I've got three more months on this lease and then I'm getting the hell out."

"Screw the lease and come to Saratoga now," Todd interjected.

She took a deep breath and bit her tongue. She was too damn tired to argue with her best friend, and if she told him of her plans to stay close to Denver to continue her investigation into Tommy's death, the battle was likely to be epic. Evasion was her best bet. "No. I'm going to finish out the lease. I thought I'd use the time to do some major cleaning out. Do you mind if I send a few boxes your way to keep in your attic until I find a new place?"

"Of course I don't mind. I've already got that box from Tommy's office up there. You know there's plenty of room. Send them on."

"I'd forgotten about that box," she said quietly, remembering the night her husband had died.

"Christ, I'm glad you're moving here. Clearly Denver has gone mad if a woman gets mugged walking out of Starbucks and has her apartment trashed while she's out."

"Todd..." She paused, almost ready to dump all her concerns, her fears on him. She shook her head. She didn't want to worry him. Whatever was going on, she would get to the bottom of it alone. "I'll be fine. Goodbye."

"Bye, kiddo."

She hung up and crossed the room. Grabbing a cushion from the floor, she replaced it on the couch and dropped down heavily.

Her mind began to drift back to things she had purposely

pushed away for months. Now as she looked around her destroyed living room, everything came back to her in a rush.

The last time she had spoken to Tommy had been lunchtime on the day he died. He'd called to tell her he'd be a bit later than usual getting home and that she shouldn't wait for him to have dinner. She could tell by his voice he was anxious, upset. When she'd asked him about it, he merely said he'd found something interesting in his latest audit and that he was handling it. She remembered making some joke about an interesting audit being an oxymoron and Tommy laughing.

She'd spent the evening designing a web banner and had lost track of time. Coming up for air, she'd been surprised to discover it was after ten o'clock and Tommy still hadn't come home...

After repeated calls to his office phone and cell phone, she given in to her anxiety and driven to his office. It was just before midnight and his car was the only one in the parking lot as she pulled in. She knew immediately that something was wrong because the light was on inside the car and although she was facing the passenger side, she could see the driver's side door was open.

She saw Tommy lying on the pavement beside the car as she drove closer. She threw her car into park and rushed to him, slipping on the black ice at her feet and falling to her knees next to him. The instant she touched his face, she knew he was dead. Pulling his stiff, cold body to hers, she rocked him gently, calling his name, begging him to come back to her.

The rest of the night seemed a blur. She dialed 911. She followed the ambulance to the hospital and listened as the doctor told her he was dead. Head trauma—an accidental death. She answered a thousand questions for the police officer so he could type up his report. She called Todd in Saratoga and then drove straight back to Tommy's office.

She wasn't sure why she'd come to the office rather than returning home. It was nearly dawn and she had never felt so numb. A train could have run over her at that point and she was certain she wouldn't have felt a drop of pain.

Todd found her there. "Oh, thank God, Jess," he said from the doorway.

She glanced up, surprised to see him.

"Stephen and I have been all over the place looking for you. He's back at your place right now, calling all your friends. What are you doing here?"

"Packing things up." She needed to clean out Tommy's office. He was dead. He wouldn't be back, and someone new would be moving in.

"Christ, Jessie. Why are you doing that now? Have you even been home? Have you slept at all?"

She shrugged and continued throwing items from Tommy's desk into the box she had found earlier in the filing room. "I need to get this stuff out of here, Todd. They need this space." Her voice was shrill, distant and for a moment, she was struck by the fact that it sounded like someone else was speaking with her mouth.

"Oh, kiddo, please stop. Don't do that anymore. This can wait until later." Todd came over to her and gripped her hands in his, trying to halt her actions, but she pulled them back, overwhelmed with irrational anger.

"I have to do this now," she said sharply.

She felt Todd studying her face for a long time, but she ignored him and continued throwing things in the box. A Rolodex, computer disks, a thumb drive, Tommy's diplomas, the paperweight he'd received from Jordan when they'd signed him on as a client, the fancy pen set she had given him for Christmas. Her hand paused when she picked up the frame that held their wedding picture.

"Shit," she whispered. Then louder, she repeated the word several more times. "Shit!" she screamed, throwing the frame across the room, against the wall where it shattered.

Todd reached for her as she crumpled, and together they huddled on the floor behind Tommy's desk while her sobs erupted and the tears flowed.

It was at that point that time betrayed her, began its cursed slowness, taunting her with minutes that seemed to last for days. As the memory of that night faded again, Jessie remembered Todd picking her up, walking her to his car, and putting the box in his trunk.

Sighing, she looked around at the mess and stood up. This wasn't a random act of destruction. She shivered as the sense of being watched returned.

"Damn you," she whispered to the empty apartment. "What do you want from me?"

J essie tried to concentrate on the movie, but her heart wasn't into the story. In the past, the romantic comedy had never failed to lighten her heart, but tonight, her gloominess, her misery was just too heavy to penetrate. The phone rang beside her and for a moment her heart raced in fear. A quick glance at the clock showed her it was only nine-thirty and she shook herself for her irrational fear. Checking the number, her heart began to race again, but this time for an entirely different reason.

"Hello?"

"Jessie?"

"Yes."

"Hey, Jess, this is Caleb James."

"Caleb, hi," she said, grinning widely at the sound of his friendly voice. She'd plugged his number into her cell the day after their one-night stand. It had taunted her for the past week as she considered calling him about a thousand times a day. She'd thought of her night with the sexy doctor more than she cared to admit.

"I'm not interrupting anything, am I?" he asked.

"Oh no, I'm just sitting here watching a movie."

"Do you want me to let you go? I can call back later."

Jessie laughed. "Don't you dare hang up. Some brilliant person invented this marvelous thing. It's called the pause button. Besides, I'm watching my favorite movie and I've seen it about a thousand times."

"Favorite movie? What are you watching?" he asked.

"*Overboard.*"

She giggled at the long pause on the other end of the line as she mentioned the title of the ultimate chick flick.

"*Overboard?* Isn't that the one with Goldie Hawn and Kurt Russell?" he asked. She could almost picture the look of male distaste on his handsome face.

"Yep."

"And this is your favorite movie?"

"Of all time," she answered, laughing at his disbelief.

"Oh, Jess, I gotta tell you. That really isn't a very good movie."

"Are you kidding me? It's awesome. Romance, comedy, a sexy hero. What more could you want?"

"A car chase, a few explosions, some aliens, maybe a shark," he joked.

She shook her head. "Uh oh. So let me guess, your favorite movie has to be *Die Hard, Alien* or *Jaws?*"

"Or all of the above, plus the Terminator movies," he added.

Jessie groaned and they laughed together.

"I hope you don't mind me calling you out of the blue like this."

"I don't mind at all. Todd mentioned that you'd asked for my number. I was kind of wondering if you'd call."

"Yeah, well. I should have called earlier. I've been worried about you and I wanted to make sure that, I wanted to see if—" He stumbled, but she knew what he was asking.

"I'm fine, Caleb."

"No regrets?"

"Not a single one," she assured him.

"Good."

"How about you?" she asked. She'd relived their night together so many times in her head, she'd cemented every minute of the evening in her brain in perfect clarity. She worried that perhaps she'd built the moment up to mean a hell of a lot more than it had. No doubt a handsome, successful doctor like Caleb had women throwing themselves at him on a daily basis. She'd be a fool to think that night had been as special for him as it had been for her.

"Not a single regret," he said. "Well, except..." He paused again and her heart started to pound again.

"Except?" she prodded.

"Except that you seem to have ruined me for other women. I haven't had as much fun on a date since the night you and I spent together."

Jessie laughed and shook her head. "Oh yeah, right."

"I'm serious. You would not believe what passes for conversation with a couple of the women I've taken out lately," he said.

She winced at the image of Caleb out on a date with another woman, and then shook herself for her foolish jealousy.

"You make it sound like dating is a new concept to you," she said, pulling the blanket more firmly around her and settling down in her comfortable couch. It felt so good to have a real conversation with a nice man. For the first time since her return home, she felt her entire body relax.

"Well, I have to confess, it sort of is."

"What do you mean?"

"I'm a doctor. I don't have a lot of time for dating. Or I should say I never made a lot of time for dating."

"And you are now?"

"Jacob pointed out to me the day after his party that I have a tendency to let work dictate my life. I had such a good time with you that I thought I'd try to cut back on my hours at the hospital and start going out more."

"And it's not going well?" She tried to brush away the slight tinge of irrational jealousy that surfaced when she pictured him going out to dinner and the movies with another woman.

"That would be an understatement." For several moments, Caleb related his two dating horror stories while she laughed. She was sure he didn't realize it, but she had to admit that ironically he was just what the doctor ordered. She'd been feeling unusually tired lately as her investigation into Tommy's death seemed to occupy all of her spare time.

"Clearly you aren't asking out the right sort of women," she added.

Caleb sighed on the other end of the line. "Tell Jacob. He's the one who made the list."

"List?" she asked.

"When I admitted that I might be interested in dating, Jake pulled out a list of available women he thought I should ask out."

Jessie laughed long and loud, tears streaming down her face at Caleb's admission. "Jacob made a list? For you? Oh, Caleb, no wonder it's not going well."

"Don't get me wrong. The women are straight. Well, I mean, I think most of them are."

They both dissolved into laughter together. "Do me a favor, Doc," she said, adopting the nickname she'd heard his brother use the night of the party. "Make your own list. You might have better luck."

"Yeah, I guess you're right. Todd says you're looking to move here in a couple of months."

Her heart missed a beat at his segue, and she silently chastised herself for foolishly hoping he'd asked the question because he wanted to see her again. Then she dismissed the thought. She wasn't in any better shape now than she'd been a week ago and unbeknownst to Todd, she wasn't so sure a move to Saratoga was in her immediate plans any longer. Her thoughts were still consumed by the past and Tommy's death. Until she settled that, she couldn't even consider planning for the future.

"I have a few more months on my lease, but yeah, I hope to eventually move to Saratoga."

"Good," he said softly. "You sure you're doing okay? You sound tired."

She closed her eyes and felt the words she'd intended to hold back falling from her lips. "The phone calls haven't stopped."

She thought for a moment he'd actually growled. "Have you called the police?"

"Oh, the police and I have gotten quite chummy. Someone broke into my apartment last week." While her words were light, her tone betrayed her anxiety.

"Shit. To hell with the lease, Jess. Pack your stuff and move up here now."

She smiled, touched by his concern. "You sound like Todd

again. Unfortunately, I have some unfinished business I need to take care of first."

"What sort of business?" he asked, and she took a deep breath, wondering what he would say about her suspicions concerning Tommy's death.

"I think these phone calls, the mugging and the break-in are all connected to my husband's death."

"I thought his death was an accident."

"The police ruled it as one," she said. Her breathing accelerated as she feared his response to her words. She'd been scoffed at, laughed at, her feelings dismissed by strangers for months, but the idea of receiving the same treatment from Caleb terrified her. She desperately wanted him to believe her.

"But you don't think it was?"

"No," she admitted. "At first it started as a feeling. Tommy was acting strangely when he called me the afternoon he died. Then all these strange things started happening. I guess I really became convinced when an arsonist burned down the accounting firm where Tommy worked."

"Someone set fire to his office?" he asked.

"They don't know who did it, but I'm starting to think that Tommy stumbled onto some shady dealings, perhaps an embezzler."

"What is this unfinished business you have in Denver?" His voice throughout her recitation of events had been monotone, devoid of emotion. With this question, she heard his concern, perhaps even a bit of anger.

"I want to find out the truth," she said defensively.

"Let me see if I've got this right. You believe your husband uncovered some sort of embezzlement scheme and was murdered for it. Since his death you've been mugged, robbed, tormented by phone calls and his office has been burned down."

"That's right," she said.

"And now you're determined to find this person, this killer on your own?"

She pulled the phone away from her ear as his question was delivered with a yell. The old saying *be careful what you wish for* drifted through her mind. She'd definitely gotten what she wanted. Caleb believed her and now he was furious with her for pursuing the mystery.

"Caleb—"

"Jess. I want you to stop this now. You're in danger."

"I'll be fine. I'm simply doing a bit of digging around."

"And it seems clear to me that whoever this asshole is, he knows what you're doing."

"I need to do this. I can't stop yet," she insisted.

She heard him sigh on the other end of the line and for several moments, there was an uncomfortable silence. "Regardless of what I say, you're going to continue, right?"

She stared across the room, her eyes landing on a picture of Tommy at the bottom of the ski slope, grinning from ear to ear and wearing the goofy ski cap she'd knitted for him. "I have to continue," she replied.

"Will you at least promise me that you'll be careful?"

"That I can definitely promise. Thanks for calling, Caleb."

"Would you mind if I called again? Just to check on you and maybe for dating advice and such?"

She grinned, pleased at his attempt to lighten the moment once again. "I'd love for you to call again."

"Good night, Jess."

"Night, Doc."

Jessie hung up the phone and considered continuing the movie. Caleb always seemed to bring out a feeling of security in her. Even through a phone line, three hours away, he created in her a sense of peace that didn't exist any other time.

She sighed and pushed the power button to turn the whole thing off. She was worn out. Rising, she went to check that the front door was locked when she noticed an envelope had been shoved under the door.

Her heart raced as she bent down to pick it up. She knew who it was from. The person who'd been tormenting her had been right outside her front door, just through this wall as she'd talked to Caleb. While laughing with her handsome doctor, she'd felt safe—even if only for a moment—but clearly that safety had been an illusion. She tore the seal open, and her hands shook as she pulled out the only item inside. A single sheet of paper.

As she looked at the paper, she felt herself leave her body.

An escape mechanism?

A way to escape the agonizing pain tearing through her physical form?

She felt like a spirit, like she was floating above herself, watching the scene unfold. A part of it, yet apart. She could see the woman below—her—as she screamed in horror and crumpled to the floor. She watched her body shake as the tears came out in giant, breath-gasping, rib-cracking sobs.

"Tommy," she heard herself whisper. "Tommy."

The paper contained only two words, written in bright red marker.

You're next.

Glued to the page was Tommy's obituary cut from the newspaper. She flew back down into her own body, the pain ripping through her, shredding her like a thousand knives. How long she lay crying and broken on the floor she couldn't say.

When she was finally able to rise, she noticed the dark of night had given way to the gray of pre-dawn. She walked over to the phone. Pulling out the card of the police officer who'd investigated the break-in, she dialed the number.

Her mind continued to whirl with the same words, floating through her brain over and over.

I was right.

I was right.

Tommy had been murdered and now his murderer had set his sights on her.

CHAPTER 6

$\mathcal{J}$essie dragged in a deep breath and tried to still the queasiness that never seemed to leave her these days. The virus had hit her like a ton of bricks the morning after she'd received the frightening message under the door and, in the past three months, it had never gone away. She'd blamed the lingering illness and the unending nausea on her depression.

She'd finally gone to the doctor this morning, after weeks of nagging from Todd, and she was hoping the damn man would call her back soon with the test results. Todd had a fit when she'd told him how long the virus had been hanging on, but she absolutely hated going to the doctor, which was kind of ironic considering how much she'd loved talking to Dr. Caleb James on the phone these past few months.

The phone rang and she grinned. Speak of the devil.

"Hey, Caleb," she said.

"Hey, yourself. You okay, Jess? Your voice sounds funny."

"Actually, I'm just waking up from a nap. I ate something that disagreed with me at breakfast." She wasn't sure why she lied to Caleb about her health. He was a doctor, for God's sake, and probably could have offered her some medical advice. For some reason, she didn't want him to know how weak, how vulnerable she was feeling. Their phone conversations had become her lifeline, her brief touch with sanity while everything else around her seemed to be falling apart. When she was talking to Caleb, she felt like the same old Jessie, the one she'd been before death and terror had taken over her life.

"It's not food poisoning, is it? You shouldn't mess around with that. Why don't you go to the—"

"I'm fine," she interrupted. "Honest. Actually, whatever it was has passed and I was just getting up to do some more packing. How was your date last weekend?"

"Hell." He replied so seriously and succinctly that she giggled.

"It couldn't have been that bad," she said, secretly pleased that Caleb hadn't had any more success with his own list than he'd had with Jacob's.

"I don't think there are words to describe the eternity that passed during that two-hour dinner. All she wanted to talk about was her work."

"What does she do for a living?" she asked.

"Real estate law," he replied with a groan.

Jessie smiled. "Oh my, that was probably a stimulating conversation."

"Very funny. When are you getting here? If I don't have a meal with a nice, normal woman soon, I'm likely to die of indigestion."

She'd been burning the candle at both ends lately and had decided it was time to hit Saratoga for a brief vacation. She was looking forward to relaxing and hanging out with her friends. "I'm coming next week. Hey, are you asking me out?" she joked.

"Yeah," he said. "I guess I am. Is that okay?"

She paused to consider his question. Was she ready to go out on a date? "Yeah, I think that's more than okay," she said, her answer surprising her as much as him.

"Good," he said. "Listen, I actually called for another reason. I ran into Todd last night and we had a long talk. He agrees with me that you need to stop this insanity."

"By insanity, I assume you are referring to the fact that I am pursuing Tommy's killer?" she asked, her voice seizing up with the sudden tightness claiming her chest. She silently cursed her best friend and his big mouth, praying that he hadn't told Caleb about the death threat. "Glad the two of you had such a nice chat about me behind my back."

"We're worried about you, Jess."

She hadn't told Caleb about the terrifying note she'd received. She hated keeping it a secret but given the fact that he didn't like the idea of her investigating her husband's murder, she was fairly certain he'd go ballistic if he learned that the killer had threatened her as well.

"I don't like the idea of you staying in Denver alone," he said.

"I'll be there very soon."

"Just for a visit. I don't like the idea of you—" She heard another voice in the background before Caleb came back on the line. "Looks like my break is over. Rescue squad just pulled in and I've got to get back to work. You're sure you're okay?"

"I'm fine, Caleb. Really."

"Call me as soon as you get into town."

"Okay. Bye, Doc."

"Bye, Jess."

Damn. She had hoped to keep her past problems separate from her future. And the fact was she was kind of looking forward to exploring a possible future with Dr. James. She'd given up feeling guilty about her fascination for the man weeks ago. It looked like Todd had been right the morning after her one-night stand with Caleb. She had turned a corner. She stood up and glanced at the pile of boxes surrounding her.

Her lease had expired and she was going to stay in Saratoga for a couple weeks until she figured out what the hell she was going to do with her life. Despite the fact she seemed to be living in utter limbo, she refused to stay in this apartment any longer. There were too many memories—good and bad—and she was anxious to make a fresh start elsewhere. Problem was her heart longed to live in Saratoga while her conscience screamed for her to remain in Denver until justice was served. Tommy deserved that.

She'd gone through the apartment with a fine-tooth comb as she'd packed, looking through every disk of Tommy's she could find, spending countless hours on the computer, searching through old files. She'd found nothing strange.

Despite her lingering sickness, she actually felt better mentally than she had in months. She felt happy, and there was this amazing optimism bubbling inside her that wouldn't be contained. She'd been right to decide to move out and as soon as she'd settled her mind to the idea, it had become paramount to her happiness.

The phone rang as she was reaching for another box and she silently hoped it was the doctor. At this point, she was ready to admit defeat and take whatever drugs he was willing to offer.

"Ms. Warner?"

"Yes, Dr. Griffin. Thanks so much for getting back to me. It's the flu, isn't it?"

"Actually, no. I ran a series of tests and I have to say I was so surprised by the results, I had them run the test again."

Jessie's heart beat a little harder at the doctor's words. She didn't think she could stand any more bad news. She'd had enough of that to last a lifetime. "What is it?"

"It would appear that you're pregnant."

Jessie's legs gave out at his words. Fortunately, the couch was behind her and she dropped down to the cushions. "That's impossible," she whispered.

"Is it?" the doctor asked. He had been her doctor for years. He knew she was a widow and he knew the trouble she and Tommy'd had trying to conceive.

"No," she confessed. "Not entirely impossible." She'd had sex. The condom had broken, but she had thought—

"Jessie, I was surprised too, but we hadn't actually started the fertility tests before Tommy—"

The doctor's words faded as did most peoples' when faced with saying any variation of the word *death* to her.

"We tried for five years, Dr. Griffin. My periods have never been regular and I always thought it was me. I mean never, not once, were we able to—"

"We never determined for sure if the difficulty lay with you or with Tommy. I know you've suffered from irregular periods your whole life, but I guess now, well, I guess now we know."

"Now we know," she repeated, awestruck by his news.

"Do you know exactly when you conceived?"

Jessie thought back to the last night of her vacation and Caleb. "August thirtieth."

She thought she heard the doctor chuckle. Obviously he wasn't expecting such a quick, specific answer. "Well, as this is now the end of November, we can safely say you are three months along. That also means you will probably begin to see an end to your morning sickness."

"I wasn't just sick in the morning."

"That is sometimes the case, which no doubt led to your confusion about the cause of your illness. I wish you'd come to see me sooner, Jessie. You're almost through the first trimester. I'm going to have my secretary call you tomorrow morning once you've had time to let this sink in. She'll make an appointment for you early next week."

"I'm moving," she said. "I was planning to pack up my car and a friend's truck to leave this weekend for a brief vacation." Jordan had offered to help her move her belongings to Todd's guesthouse for the time being.

The doctor was silent for a moment. "If I might suggest, have your friends load the vehicles or pay a moving company. Are you moving away from Denver?"

She thought about his question for only a moment. "Yes, I'm going to live in Saratoga."

"Ah, well, I will miss you as my patient, Jessie. Call the office as soon as you get settled and find a new doctor. Don't wait too long. We'll have your medical records transferred."

"Thank you, Dr. Griffin."

"Good luck, Jessie."

She hung up the phone and sat staring for several moments at her newly bared walls. Pregnant? Ever since their first year of marriage, she and Tommy had tried to conceive, desperate to have a child. Shortly before his death, they'd scheduled an appointment to talk to a fertility specialist. She'd truly believed she couldn't have children. Her hands went instinctively to her stomach. A baby. She was going to have a baby.

She smiled. Then she laughed, long and loud and until tears streamed down her face. She was going to have a baby. She wasn't going to be alone anymore. She would have a child to take care of, to love.

She calmed down as she thought of Caleb. Christ, one lousy night with her and the poor man had dealt with her tears, her insane life, and now she was dropping this bomb on him.

She leaned back and considered her options. She was having the baby. Of that there was no doubt. But what about Caleb?

Keeping the truth from him wasn't an option she wanted to consider. It wasn't as if she was asking him to marry her, but she couldn't live with herself if she didn't at least give him the choice to decide what role he would play in their child's life. She would simply leave the decision to him. If he wanted to wash his hands of her and the baby, so be it. However, if he wanted to know his child, help her raise it, then that was fine too. With her living in the same town, it would be easy to include him in the baby's life...and hers.

The idea of seeing Caleb again started her heart doing flip-flops. She reached over to her purse and dragged out her phone. Caleb's number taunted her. As she looked at the cell phone, she tried to imagine what the hell she would say.

Hi there, Caleb. This is Jessie. Remember when we had sex on a kitchen counter a few months ago and the condom broke? Well, guess what? I'm pregnant.

Yeah, that would be a hell of an awkward conversation. No phone call, she decided. She was leaving this weekend for Saratoga, her planned visit now a permanent stay. She would call Caleb once she was settled in at the guesthouse as they'd planned. She'd invite him over for dinner and tell him in person.

There was no question of where she would live now. A small pang pierced her heart. She'd been determined to discover the truth of Tommy's death, but there was no way she would jeopardize the life of her baby. Moving away from Denver and the ominous threat that hovered over her here was now a necessity.

Mind made up, she picked up her cell phone. Todd was waiting to hear about the results of her doctor's appointment. He'd threatened bodily harm if she didn't call him back. Shit, what would he think of this? She'd convinced him she had the flu.

She chuckled as she considered the fact that for once in her life she stood a good chance of leaving her outspoken best friend speechless.

" hanks again, Jordan. Are you sure you don't want to stay for some hot tea before you go?" Jessie offered.

Jordan had followed her all the way from Denver with a bunch of boxes in the back of his brand new black F-150 pickup truck. They'd finished moving them all into the guest-house, and Jessie sighed at the thought of unpacking all the things she'd just packed up.

"No, I'm afraid I need to head back for the city. I have a meeting with Rex in the morning. Hope it won't hurt your feel-ings if I say the man was clearly pleased to learn you were moving to Saratoga."

Jessie laughed. "I'm sure he was. I think poor old Rex has come to view me as his arch enemy."

"Ah yes, I can see it now. You are Lex Luthor to his Superman."

"The Joker to his Batman," she added with a grin. "Oh, Jordan. How can I thank you for all your help?"

"No thanks necessary. I wanted to check out this new town

you've chosen to make your home and to make sure you arrived here safe and sound." Jordan turned to Todd. "See that you take care of our young lady here."

"No worries there, Mr. Scott. I'll look after her."

"Well, I'm pleased to see that you're staying somewhere nice. Saratoga is truly lovely. So picturesque and quiet compared to the crowds and noise of Denver. Take care, Jessie, and stay in touch."

"I will, Jordan. And thanks again for helping me move."

She hugged him fondly as she and Todd walked the older gentleman back to his truck and waved as he pulled out of the driveway.

She'd taken the doctor's advice, hiring a moving van to bring the bulk of her heavy furniture later in the week, and the move had been relatively easy as a result. She had already packed up a bunch of the smaller bits over the past three months and sent them to Todd to store in his attic. Until she found a place to live, everything else she owned in the world other than her clothing was going into a storage unit.

"A baby," Todd exclaimed as they walked back to the front porch of the guesthouse. He was the only person with whom she'd shared her unexpected news, and she grinned at her friend's unabashed enthusiasm.

"I know," she gushed. "I can't quite believe it myself."

"When are you going to tell Caleb?"

"Soon," she answered. "I was going to get settled and then call him to come over for dinner one night. You think he'll be okay with this, right?" Since her decision to tell Caleb about the baby in person, she'd worried incessantly over his response.

"He'll be fine with this, Jess, and if he's not, then screw him. You know Stephen and I will help you raise the baby. A baby," he repeated in awe.

"I know," she agreed.

"No more prank phone calls?"

She had called Todd the morning after she'd received the death threat. He'd come to Denver and spent a week with her, trying to convince her to move to Saratoga immediately. She'd been tempted, but at the time, she'd been determined to find Tommy's murderer and she knew Todd would try to stop her.

"No," she said. "Fact of the matter is I've hit a roadblock. I've gone over every scrap of evidence I could find in the apartment. I've questioned every person I can think of who may know something about this possible embezzler and I've found absolutely nothing."

Her friend looked at her and nodded. "Jess, I understand your need to find this guy. I really do. If the roles were reversed, I'd want Stephen's killer brought to justice. But now there's this baby and I don't think—"

"I'm finished, Todd." As she spoke the words, she realized they were the truth. For the first time in nearly a year, she felt an overwhelming need to plan for the future. The past had consumed too much of her present and now there was too much to lose.

"In the past eleven months, I've been mugged, tormented by phone calls, received a death threat, and had my apartment trashed. Tommy's office building has been burned to the ground and I—"

"Christ, do you have to spell it out in black and white like that?" Todd asked, interrupting her. "You're scaring the shit out of me." She could see the genuine fear in his eyes.

"This baby is all that matters to me now. I loved Tommy more than anything on earth, but he wouldn't want me to jeopardize this child's life, even if it brought his murderer to justice." The truth of her words resonated in her heart.

"That's a nice idea, Jess, but aren't you forgetting something?"

"What?"

"What makes you think the bad guy is going to give up on you?"

"He's been quiet since the death threat. Maybe he merely wanted to scare me away and he'll see this move as a sign of his success. He didn't follow me here last time. I spent two weeks here with you last summer and there were no phone calls and I didn't feel like he was watching me."

"I'm ashamed to admit that when you first mentioned the feeling that you were being watched, I thought it was just that overactive imagination of yours."

"Things are going to be better now. I'm sure of it. It's a fresh start."

"Jessie wills it and so it will be," he joked. "We're having Thanksgiving dinner early tonight."

"I wish you hadn't gone to so much fuss. I swear, Todd, with the way my stomach has been acting lately, I didn't really miss the holiday."

He had declared he and Stephen would throw her a late Thanksgiving, since she'd elected to stay in Denver over the holiday rather than spend the actual day with them. She'd been bogged down with work, packing and dealing with her morning sickness. Plus she'd been afraid to risk the long drive with her nausea.

"Stephen and I have to pack up for our convention after dinner. I'm sorry we're leaving the day after your arrival."

"Don't be silly. I'm here to stay so we'll have plenty of time to spend together. Besides my only plans for the next few days are to go house-hunting and relax. Go to the convention and start drumming up some business for this bed-and-breakfast of yours. You've worked hard and the place looks magnificent. I have no doubt it will be the toast of Wyoming soon."

Todd laughed. "I'd just settle for being the toast of Saratoga."

"I thought you said there weren't many bed-and-breakfast inns in Saratoga."

"So it's an achievable goal," he joked. "I can already smell success."

"All I smell is that yummy turkey," she teased, laughing. She pushed her friend back toward the main house. "Go away, you idiot. I need to unpack."

As her friend stepped away, Jessie glanced around at the surrounding woods. She hadn't felt her tormentor's eyes on her during her last visit, but the sensation was definitely here now.

She was tired of playing mouse to this villain's cat and she prayed her intuition was wrong. There was too much to live for now. Her hands instinctively went to her stomach. She wasn't showing yet, but it wouldn't be long.

Please leave me alone.

The future was quickly approaching and she felt the powerful need to escape the past before it arrived.

*J*essie bid farewell to the real estate agent and climbed into her car. She was disappointed in the houses the realtor had shown her, but the woman assured her there were many more choices. She wanted to buy a house with a backyard big enough for a swing set and room for a child to run around, to grow up.

Discouraged, she tried not to lose heart. There was always tomorrow. Suddenly that idea didn't seem to bother her as much as it used to.

She'd said goodbye to Todd and Stephen early this morning as they'd left for Denver for an innkeeper's convention. They hoped to learn more about the bed-and-breakfast trade as well as drum up some business and make contacts in the field. She was pleased for her friends. They truly seemed to have found their niche in life and she hoped they would find success.

Driving down the country road toward their ranch, her thoughts drifted to Caleb and the baby. She'd intended to call him this morning, but chickened out at the last minute.

As soon as I get home, she thought. *I'll call him the second I get home.*

She was anxious to share what she prayed he would think was good news. The problem was she didn't really know Caleb James that well. They'd spent one fun, drunken night together and had spoken on the phone no more than a dozen times. Sometimes Jessie worried that she had built the man up in her mind, made too much of his kindness. He had come to her at a time when she'd been terribly lonely and grief-stricken. He'd made her laugh, made her feel like a desirable woman. Hell, he'd made her feel alive.

She slowed down at a particularly nasty curve in the road, squinting against the brutally bright afternoon sun. She reached up to put down her sun visor when another car came into view. For a split second, she considered the fact that this was the first vehicle she'd seen on the road since leaving the town limits, then she realized the car was on her side of the road and close. Too damn close. She swerved to the right sharply, attempting to avoid hitting the other vehicle. Her actions took her off the road, and she had only a second to panic as she saw the tree directly in her path.

Her scream was cut short when her car crashed roughly into the large tree. She felt a sharp, hard blow to her head and her surroundings became fuzzy. Her car horn blared nonstop intensifying her pain, and she blinked against the grayness at the edge of her vision.

"It'll be okay, Jessie" a man said from beside her. She tried to turn her head, but the action hurt too badly and she gasped at the cruel, throbbing ache.

"Help me," she whispered, fighting not to lose consciousness.

"I'm sorry. I..." the man murmured. His calm tone penetrated her panicked mind as his words drifted away from her. Relief suffused her. Someone was with her. He would help her. She gave up her fight and succumbed to the darkness.

CHAPTER 8

"Dr. James, the rescue squad just called ahead. They're five minutes away with a car accident victim. Woman, late twenties, early thirties. She's sustained head injuries and is complaining of pains in her stomach," the nurse said as Caleb emerged from the break room. He'd been just about to leave for the day when the call came through. Trauma was his specialty.

"They're here," an orderly shouted from the ambulance entrance.

The EMT pushed the stretcher in and Caleb could hear the woman's anguished cries as she got closer.

"Dr. James," the EMT said as he approached them.

Looking down, he was shaken to the core to see Jessie, bleeding and in pain on the stretcher. "Jessie? Jesus, baby."

"Caleb? Oh God, please help me. It's hurts."

He struggled to catch his breath. He was an ER doctor and no damn stranger to blood or pain, but seeing Jessie, crying in agony, he had to fight against the overwhelming feeling of nausea and fear. She'd obviously suffered a nasty cut somewhere on her head. There was an uncomfortable amount of blood on her face and in her hair. The EMT had a bloody pad pressed against her brow line.

"It'll be okay, Jess. I'm here. I'm going to take care of you."

"It hurts," she gasped, clutching her stomach, and Caleb realized she'd obviously sustained more serious injuries.

"Where, Jessie? Where does it hurt?"

"Ow," she said, attempting to bend forward, fighting off the EMT who was holding her still.

"Try not to move, sweetheart." He walked beside her as they rolled the stretcher into the first available examining room.

"No," she sobbed. "The baby. My baby."

Caleb froze in horror at her words. Baby? He pulled off the sheet covering her and felt his body turn to stone at the sight of the blood pooling around her hips. Taking a deep breath, he forced himself to shut down the emotions whirling inside him.

He glanced at the nurse by his side. "Mollie, prepare for a possible D&C and I'm going to need blood typing." Looking at the EMT, he gestured for the man to remove the bandage he was using to apply pressure to Jessie's scalp.

"I don't think it's that bad," the man said.

Although it had bled a lot, the bleeding seemed to have slowed down. "She'll need stitches," he said. "And possibly a tetanus. Keep pressure on that. It can wait for now."

Jessie seemed to calm at his words. He bent forward, gently wiping away a tear that had fallen down her cheek. "Where does it hurt, Jess?"

"Stomach, cramps," she said hoarsely. "Head."

"Anywhere else?"

"No," she whispered.

"How about here?" He slowly and methodically checked her ribs, arms, and legs for other injuries.

"The baby?" she asked.

Caleb stopped his ministrations and looked at her. He knew the baby had been lost, but his courage deserted him. "I'll do what I can," he said. "I'm going to give you something for the pain now. It may make you a bit drowsy."

He gave Jessie a shot and once again had to fight back his frustration, his fears, his anger at the situation. She winced when he pressed the needle in, but didn't complain. Within moments, her eyes drifted shut, and he managed to take his first real breath since she'd been rolled into the emergency room. The idea of her suffering any amount of pain was like a dagger in his chest.

"A miscarriage?" Mollie asked softly.

He nodded sadly. "I'm afraid so."

"Poor thing," his nurse muttered. "You know her?"

Caleb nodded, his words trapped by the lump in his throat. "Let's see about getting her cleaned up. She's going to need stitches to close that gash. Start an IV."

* * *

Jessie squinted against the brightness of the room blinding her and sending an unbearable shooting pain through her head.

"Ow," she said, lifting her hand to her head. She was surprised to feel a bandage covering her hair, just above her forehead. Dizzy and disoriented, her eyes flew open wide when she realized where she was. Hospital.

"Easy," a deep voice said beside her.

"Tommy," she whispered, her head pounding, the drummer beating out a furious rhythm against her brain.

"No."

Caleb's face as he leaned over her after they pulled her out of the ambulance flashed through her foggy mind.

"Caleb." She tried to focus on his face despite the pain created by the light.

"I'm right here, Jess." He reached out to take her hand, and she was amazed by the comfort that surrounded her whenever he was around.

"What happened?" she asked, her thoughts seemed hazy and distant, a jumbled-up mess in her mind.

"Car accident," he replied. "Do you remember anything?"

She closed her eyes and tried to recall. She was driving back to the guesthouse after a trip to town. The sun was in her eyes, another car. Then nothing. "Sort of," she said after a few moments.

"You cut your head open. I had to put in about two dozen stitches."

Her hand automatically returned to her bandaged head. "My hair?"

Caleb grinned at her and she found herself returning the smile. "The first thing women always want to know about. I didn't let them shave your hair. It made the stitches tricky to put in, but I didn't think you'd want a big bald patch on the top of your head."

She smiled until another memory came crashing over her. Her hands flew to her stomach. She looked at Caleb, but her question wouldn't come. It didn't need to be asked. She knew. She knew by the empty feeling inside her and the sadness in Caleb's eyes that she'd lost her baby.

"No," she whispered, tears springing to her eyes. She squinted against them, but nothing would stem the flow. The pain in her head was forgotten as her heart cracked painfully in two. "No."

"I'm so sorry, Jessie. There was nothing I could do. I think you miscarried during the trip to the hospital in the ambulance."

She nodded once, turning her face from his kindness, his compassion. She'd lost their baby. The baby she'd failed to tell him existed. Closing her eyes, she gave in to the loss, the agony, and for several minutes, she let the tears fall. She hadn't realized until that moment how much the little being living inside her had come to mean to her. All her hopes for a happier future had been wrapped up in the tiny baby who would never know life.

She was surprised when she felt a weight pressing down on the bed beside her. Glancing to her left, she saw Caleb climbing on to the hospital bed, lying next to her and reaching over to embrace her. She turned to him, wincing slightly at the pressure the position put on her stitches.

"Shhh," he soothed, carefully wrapping his arms around her as she felt the dam break completely. She sobbed her heart out against his chest, clinging to him and silently wishing he would never let her go. She was so tired of being alone. For the briefest of times, she'd had the baby—his baby—with her. Now she was on her own again, besieged with a grief that seemed to know no end. She hadn't cried like this since the night she discovered Tommy had been murdered, but then she'd needed to remain strong, lest she fall apart irrevocably. There had been no one to share her pain with on a daily basis. Now with Caleb to watch over her, to help her carry the load, she let it all out.

She wasn't sure how long she lay with him. His right hand rubbed gentle circles on her back, while his left hand cradled her arm, careful not to disturb the IV. He whispered soft, comforting words in her ears. She thought she might have drifted to sleep for a little while because when she opened her eyes, the light in the room seemed dimmer, less harsh.

She pushed up on to her elbow to look at him.

"Lie down," he said, his voice lined with the slightest bit of command.

"I'm sorry," she said. "I'm keeping you from your work." She suddenly felt awkward in his presence, uncomfortable, guilty.

"My shift is over," he said, gently pulling her head back down to his shoulder. "Was it our baby?" he asked.

Her heart constricted painfully at his question, and she fought against the fresh onslaught of tears. She wasn't the only person in the room who'd lost something today.

"Yes," she whispered.

He lay so still, she fought against the desire, the need to lift her head, to see his face. What was he feeling? Anger, sadness, relief?

"I was going to tell you," she said at last. She wanted him to know the truth. She'd never meant to hide her pregnancy from him. Never intended that he wouldn't know of the child they'd created. "I only just found out myself. I was going to come see you, talk to you." She pushed up again, desperate for him to see the sincerity of her words in her face. "I would never have kept you from your child if you'd wanted to be a part of his or her life. I swear it, Caleb."

"I believe you," he said and she could see in his face that he did. "And I'm sorrier than you could know. You would have been a wonderful mother." His kind words undid her and she closed her eyes, fought against the tears. She refused to cry anymore tonight. "You really should try to get more rest. I'm afraid the police have been here a couple of times, wanting to talk to you about the accident. I have a feeling they're still hanging around. I've also managed to track down Todd."

"He and Stephen are out of town, for business."

"No," he said. "They're on their way back here. I asked Jacob to call them, to let them know about the accident."

"I wish you hadn't done that," she said as Caleb started to rise. He helped her lay back and checked the IV in her hand. "I always seem to be interfering with their life." She winced when he touched the needle. "Can you take that out?"

"No," he said. "You've lost quite a bit of blood. You need the fluids."

"Please," she repeated. "I really hate needles. Take it out."

He shook his head. "Maybe tomorrow. If you're a good girl tonight." His words were teasing, but the mirth didn't reach his eyes.

"Knock, knock."

She looked up to see Todd standing at the doorway and the tears she thought she'd battled away returned full-force.

"Dammit, you shouldn't have come," she choked out as her best friend came into the room. Caleb stepped away and Todd reached down and grasped her face in his hands.

"I can't leave you alone for one second," he teased, and she laughed through her tears. "What do you mean I shouldn't have come? Of course, I need to be here."

"You're supposed to be at your convention. This was your chance to advertise for the bed-and-breakfast. I'm always screwing everything up for you."

"Hush," he whispered as her words grew more slurred with the sobs that were wracking her body. "Are you okay?"

"The b-baby," she whispered, unable to say more.

Todd glanced over his shoulder at Caleb and then back at her.

"He knows," she said, in answer to his unspoken question.

"I'm sorry, Jess. Jesus, I'm sorry." Todd placed his forehead against hers, and she honestly felt as if her friend was attempting to will some of his strength into her. She took several long, deep breaths and tried to smile, although she felt certain she fell far from the mark.

"Go back to Denver," she whispered. "Go to your convention. I'll be fine here."

"Are you crazy? There's no way I'd leave you here alone."

"Um, excuse me," came a deep voice from the doorway. Jessie looked up to find a police officer standing there. "Now that you're awake, Ms. Warner, I was hoping I could ask you a few questions about the accident."

She nodded her assent and the policeman walked in. Todd claimed the chair to her left, never letting go of her hand and she was grateful for his support. She winced slightly as a fresh wave of cramps hit her. Caleb must have noticed her pained look as he walked around her bed and adjusted something on her IV.

"You'll suffer with the cramping for a few days, I'm afraid," he muttered, low enough she was certain she was the only one who heard.

She nodded stiffly, refusing to think about the return of her period and what that meant.

"Ms. Warner. I've been to the accident site and I have to say you were lucky you were wearing your seatbelt. You hit that tree pretty hard. Can you tell me why you ran off the road?"

"It was the other car," she said. "The afternoon sun was shining in my eyes, so I didn't see the other vehicle right away. When I did see it, I realized it was in my lane and that the only way to avoid it was to swerve. Unfortunately, the tree was there."

"What other car?" the police officer asked.

She was taken aback by his question. "I-I don't know exactly what it looked like. As I said, the sun was rather blinding. The man stopped to help me. He's the one who called 911."

The officer shook his head. "There was no one else at the accident scene and the 911 call came in from an elderly woman who happened along later, coming from the same direction as you. She saw you in your car and called dispatch."

"But the man spoke to me. He knew my name. Said he was sorry," she said. Her thoughts had been confused upon waking up, but now that she recalled the scene, it was becoming much clearer.

"He knew your name? You knew him?" the officer asked.

"No," she replied. "I mean I don't know who—"

Todd cleared his throat and her eyes flew to him.

"The embezzler," she whispered as Todd nodded slightly.

She closed her eyes, a wave of exhaustion threatening to take hold. She was so fucking tired of this, of everything. Maybe if she could just sleep for a few years, she would wake up to find life much easier.

"Tell him all of it, Jess," Todd said, and she opened her eyes in time to see Caleb's head jerk up at his comment.

"Tell him all of what?" Caleb asked.

The policeman leaned forward. "Do you think someone purposely ran you off the road?"

She shrugged. "Possibly." She glanced up at Todd's scowl. "Probably. But I have no idea who."

Together, she and Todd explained to the police officer and Caleb about her mugging, the apartment break-in, and the fire at the accounting office. She mentioned her feeling of being watched all the time and her belief that Tommy's death wasn't an accident, but was instead murder. She mentioned all the things that she'd done over the past year to investigate his death. She could feel Caleb's disapproving looks, and once she heard him mutter something about putting herself in danger.

Then she told them about the death threat. She kept her gaze glued on the police officer as she spoke of the letter that had been slid under the door and what it said. She was too afraid to see Caleb's face, too afraid to see his anger, his disappointment in her for hiding such a dangerous secret.

The policeman took down her information and promised to

call the Denver precinct to get copies of her police reports regarding the other incidents. He gave her his card and said he would be in touch.

Through it all, Jessie fought to remain awake. Her body and mind were weary beyond belief and she felt as if she could sleep for a year.

"You need to rest," Caleb said, and he started to tinker with her IV again. No doubt to increase the pain medication that would help her sleep.

"Wait," she said, glancing over at Todd. "I'll only be able to rest peacefully if you promise to go back to your convention."

"No way," Todd said.

"Please," she said. "I've monopolized your life this past year. This is your chance to get a jump start on your dream. Go back. I'll be fine here. I swear. I'm stuck in this joint until at least tomorrow." She looked at Caleb for confirmation.

"You'll be released tomorrow or the day after," he said.

She nodded, continuing her argument with her friend. "I'll get a ride back to the guesthouse and lock myself in, I promise. I'll stay in bed and I won't move until you and Stephen get back."

"Jess, we wouldn't be back for four days. There's no way—"

"You're not going back to the guesthouse," Caleb interjected.

"Fine, then I'll stay in the big house. You've just installed that alarm system," she said, looking at Todd, who was still shaking his head no.

"You aren't going there either," Caleb said.

Jessie looked over at him, confused by his firm refusal. "You just said I could leave here—"

"You're coming home with me. You're staying at the James Ranch."

"No," she whispered, but Caleb ignored her and leaned

down, his face so close to hers she could feel his warm breath against her cheeks.

"You are coming home with me until you are one hundred percent well and this bastard who's tormenting you is caught. This is *not* negotiable." Caleb stood up and adjusted her IV. "Promise you'll come with me," he said gruffly. She didn't answer, her eyes fighting to remain open and he tapped her cheek gently. "Promise, Jess. Say it."

"I promise," she whispered, willing to give, do or say anything for just a few minutes of sleep.

"Good," she heard him say before the night went black.

"Caleb," Todd began, standing.

"No use arguing, Todd. I meant what I said. She's staying with me, regardless of whether you go back to your convention or not."

"Why?" Todd asked.

He considered the man's question and decided Jessie's best friend wouldn't accept less from him than the absolute truth. "She lost her baby. We both did. I want us to be together to deal with that. She's been through hell this last year and I want a chance to help close up some of those wounds."

"You love her," Todd said softly.

Caleb shrugged. "I don't know her well enough for that. But I do know I want the chance to fall in love with her. She's beautiful, strong, courageous, and I'm fucking tired of seeing her with tears in her eyes."

Todd smiled and nodded. "Tell her I'll see her in four days. But be forewarned. I'm calling your ass for progress reports every hour until I get back."

Caleb grinned and shook the man's hand. "Fair enough."

CHAPTER 9

"$\mathcal{I}$ don't need a wheelchair, Caleb. I'm perfectly capable of walking out of this damn hospital on my own." Jessie pouted.

"You're going to be a difficult patient, aren't you?" he teased, helping her stand and pushing her gently into the chair. "I told you, the wheelchair is hospital policy."

"Stupid policy. If I've been deemed well enough to leave this place, I should be allowed to do it on my own two feet."

"Stop grumbling and enjoy the ride." He pushed her through the hallway with a grin on his face, happy to see her energy had returned enough that she was fighting with him. He'd kept her in the hospital an extra day because he'd never seen anyone quite so drained or exhausted. Her head injury and miscarriage alone weren't grounds to keep her another night, but he wondered how much she'd slept in the past few months. In addition to her fatigue, she was too thin. She was underweight for a woman her height and he intended to see that fact change as well. It was clear to him that Jessie had not been looking after herself since her husband's death.

"You know, I really think it would be best if you just dropped me off at Todd's guesthouse. I feel much better."

"Nope, you promised to stay with me at the ranch and that's where we're going."

"Yeah, but you drugged me to get that promise."

Caleb chuckled at her words, aware they were probably true. "Sweetheart, I'll be the first to admit I'm not above using any means at my disposal to get what I want."

"I just don't understand why you'd want me around. I'm not gonna be very good company for a while."

He pushed the wheelchair up the passenger side of his pickup truck and helped her climb in. She swatted his hands away when he attempted to buckle her in. "I can do it," she said.

Her hormones were going to be out of control for a while due to the miscarriage and he knew her irritability was just a part of that. He watched as she hooked the seatbelt in place before looking back at him.

"What are you staring at?" she asked belligerently.

"I've got a beautiful woman in my truck. Let me savor the moment."

She smiled guiltily at him. "I'm being a bitch, aren't I?"

He shook his head. "Not that I've noticed."

"I'm tired of being in the way, of being a pest and a bother to everyone I know."

"Who are you bothering, Jess?"

She shrugged sadly. "Since Tommy's death, I can't seem to do anything on my own with any degree of success. I've always been independent, but now every time I turn around, Todd and Stephen or you have to rush to my rescue. It's a pain in the ass."

He laughed, understanding how much it would frustrate her to think she was putting others out with her problems.

"You are never a pain in the ass. If anything, I'm the one

being selfish in this instance. I'm looking forward to talking to you again, getting to know you. One night and a few lousy phone calls weren't enough for me."

She seemed taken aback by his words, and he smiled as a light blush colored her pale cheeks. "They weren't enough for me either. I've thought about you a lot since August."

Her admission pleased him, and he was secretly relieved that his obsession with her wasn't one-sided. "I think it would be good for both of us to be together right now. Especially right now," he added.

She nodded and offered him a sad smile. "Maybe you're right."

"Shall we go?" he asked.

"Ready or not," she added with a feigned shudder and he laughed. He pushed the wheelchair back to the hospital before climbing into the truck, pulling out of the parking lot and onto the highway.

"Don't look so grim. I'm not taking you over to the dark side."

"Four brothers, living alone together. I'm reserving judgment on that dark side comment until I see for myself."

*W*hen they pulled up to the ranch, she was surprised to see the other three James brothers waiting for her on the front porch.

"No one works?" she asked.

He shook his head. "Not out of the house. Mark and Matt, the twins, keep this place a working ranch. We've got quite a bit of cattle, and business has been good enough lately that they're looking to expand and hire on a couple of ranch hands."

"Yee haw," she cheered, and he laughed. "What about Jacob?" she asked.

"Right now he's working on his master's degree online and he's been doing some freelance writing for a couple of magazines. I keep telling him he's going to have to buckle down at some point, grow up and get a real job like an adult. Not sure he listens though."

He got out of the truck and crossed around to her side of the vehicle before she'd managed to unhook the seatbelt.

"Who are you, the Flash?" she teased, startled by his super quick appearance.

He reached in when she started to climb down and lifted her into his arms. "I can walk," she said, squirming to be put down. Having Caleb's strong arms around her after so long brought back a rush of memories of their single night together. This man surrounded her, filled her with such a feeling of safety and comfort, it made her giddy, light-headed. He was the only person who'd managed to wiggle his way under her guard since her husband's death. While her mind screamed it was too quick, too rushed, her traitorous heart insisted it was right and good.

"Yeah, well, humor me." He carried her up the front porch, and she smiled at Jacob as he held the door open for them. Caleb didn't stop for introductions with the twins, but instead carried her through the house to a back bedroom. He crossed the room and gently placed her on the big bed. It took Jessie only a moment to take in her surroundings.

"This doesn't look like the guest room," she said as she glanced at the dresser covered with a variety of bits and bobs, all rather masculine looking. Her gaze traveled to the open closet, full of clothing.

"It's not," he said. "It's my room."

She shook her head and started to climb out of the bed, but he halted her with a firm hand on her shoulder, holding her down. "Oh no. I'm not stealing your room from you. I'll be perfectly comfortable in the guest room."

A disturbing thought crossed her mind. "Oh crap, you do have a guest room, don't you? Please tell me you're not trying to be a gentleman because all that's left is some lumpy couch."

He laughed. "We've got a guest room, but you aren't using it. Lean back against those pillows."

She complied, but only because the room was beginning to spin a bit. Damn, she hated feeling so weak. "Caleb, it's sweet of you to offer me your room, but there's no reason why you should be inconvenienced—"

"Not going to be an inconvenience at all. I'm not staying in the guest room either."

Jessie's heart began to race at what he was insinuating. Surely he didn't mean—

"I'm going to be staying in this room with you," he added, confirming her fears.

"Oh no, you're not." Her heart's race ended as quickly as it began, and she wondered if it had exploded with the thought of what he was proposing. Share a room with Caleb?

He grinned at her words, but didn't try to refute them. Mainly because she was certain he was ignoring her.

"I mean it, Caleb. There is no way you and I are going to sleep in here together. We barely know each other."

Her comment seemed to give him pause and he stopped to look at her. She returned his stare and for a moment it felt as if they were communicating not with words, but by looks. The second she'd mentioned their relatively short acquaintance, she'd known she was wrong. Maybe they hadn't spent a great deal of time together, but somehow, perhaps instinctually, she felt like she did know this man—very, very well. She bit her lip, uncomfortable with his close scrutiny and watched him nod slowly. He felt it too.

Leaving her in his bed, he crossed the room and picked up a suitcase she hadn't noticed before and opened it. "Jacob went by the guesthouse and packed up some of your clothing. He couldn't get it all in one trip, so he said he'd go back later for the rest."

"I don't need all my clothes. I won't be here that long. My head's only sore, and after a couple more days of sleep—in the guest room—I'll be back in tip-top shape."

"Jess, you promised to stay here until you were well *and* until the man who's been tormenting you is caught. He's been after you for the better part of a year if I understand the situation correctly. You could actually be here for quite a while."

She sighed and tried to make sense of what the hell was happening. As she watched, he began shuffling his clothing around in the dresser to make room for her things. He looked entirely too pleased with the idea that he'd managed to maneuver her not only into his house, but into his bedroom.

She fought desperately to restrain the small part of her that was thrilled to see her clothing next to his. What he was suggesting didn't seem like such a bad thing. She was tired, lonely and scared. Maybe for just a little while, Caleb could keep those emotions at bay for her. A few nights of good, solid, peaceful rest and she'd be back on top of her game, ready to face the world.

No, she dismissed the thought as soon as it came to her. Regardless of what she might need, might want, this was wrong.

It's too soon, she thought tiredly.

"You might as well stop wasting your time," she said, gesturing to him as he walked to the closet and began hanging up her shirts. "I'm not staying here beyond the end of this week and I most definitely *am not* staying in this room with you."

He continued unpacking and she fought back her growing annoyance at the fact he was ignoring her.

"Do you hear me, Caleb?" she shouted, her anger breaking out.

"I hear you, sweetheart, but there seem to be a few things you don't quite understand."

"Such as?" she asked.

"I'm your doctor and I fully intend to keep my eye on you twenty-four seven until I'm convinced that you're well. You've suffered a nasty knock on the head and that's not something to take lightly. There is also some danger of infection with—" he paused, but she was grateful when he finished his sentence, "— a miscarriage."

She'd spent a year around well-meaning people who censored their words carefully in regards to death. She appreciated that Caleb didn't attempt to pretend the truth didn't exist.

"You can keep an eye on me in the guest room."

He grinned. "I'm not finished yet. There are dark circles *under* the dark circles beneath your eyes and —"

"Gee thanks," she said. "Look that good, do I?"

"You look good enough to eat, but damn tired, Jess. There's some asshole tormenting you and until he's caught, I don't anticipate getting much sleep. I can see in your face you're afraid, that you haven't been sleeping well. I'll rest a whole hell of lot easier if I've got you within reaching distance and maybe you will too."

She was floored by his concern, touched by it.

"And the last reason is a purely selfish one," he continued, "but it's probably the main one."

"What reason is that?"

"I want your clothes in my closet and I want *you* in my bed."

"That doesn't make sense," she said. "I mean, we barely

know each other." She repeated the words weakly, but he merely dismissed them for the lie they were.

He shrugged, his smile the perfect blend of mischievous boy and confused male. "Didn't say it made sense. Just telling you why you're staying in this room. Besides, if none of those reasons work for you, there's always the fact that I'm bigger than you and I can make you stay."

She laughed at his threat and rolled her eyes. "Ah, the macho male shit has emerged. Terrific," she added. "You know after a few days in my presence, I have a feeling all of those reasons of yours are going to seem like pretty cold comfort and you'll beg me to move back to the guesthouse. I'm not a woman who is easily commanded."

He laughed. "I never thought you were." He rubbed his hands together as if in anticipation. "This is gonna be fun."

She grinned. Fun. Yeah, it was.

*J*essie pushed her chair back and stared at the computer screen. Her mind raced in a thousand different directions and no matter what she did, she couldn't seem to calm it down. She'd hoped starting back to work would help and she'd tried to concentrate on the web design before her until the pictures and words began to blur together.

She closed her eyes and rubbed her forehead, trying to head off the headache building in her temple. Guilt assuaged her as she thought about her actions this past week.

There was no other way to say it. She'd become an utterly horrible person since moving into the James Ranch. Her emotions were riding on some sort of never-ending, hellacious roller coaster and she was aggravated by her complete lack of control. She'd always prided herself on being level-headed, easygoing. This week, she'd fluctuated between acting like a screaming banshee and producing enough tears to flood a town, and she couldn't believe the James brothers hadn't tossed her out on her ear.

A loud sigh escaped as her frustration bubbled to the forefront.

"Trouble?" Caleb asked. He was lounging on a couch in the corner of the office reading a medical journal, and she bit back her annoyance at his overprotective, hovering tendencies. He had become her personal shadow.

At first, she'd been touched by his concern, but lately irritation had taken over. Every time she raised her voice to him, he responded with a serenity that made her want to shake the living shit out of him. She was an emotional wreck since losing the baby—their baby—and it infuriated her to see him walking around like Dr. Calm, Cool and Collected.

To make matters worse, every time she tried to call the police to see if any progress had been made, he distracted her, telling her to give them some space and more time. She was beginning to suspect he was trying to curb her attempts at finding Tommy's killer, their baby's killer. Prior to the car accident, she'd planned to stop looking for the villain. Now, in light of yet another loss at the hands of the same asshole, she was out for blood. She wouldn't rest until she uncovered the man's crimes and saw him locked in a jail cell for the next three eternities.

"Jess, is something wrong?" he repeated when she failed to answer.

"No," she said sharply, hoping her short, terse answer would deter him and he'd leave her alone. She desperately wanted to call the police officer from the hospital again. Surely they had some idea what sort of car had run her off the road.

No such luck. Caleb continued speaking to her.

"Maybe it's too soon for you to try to jump back into your work," he suggested. He'd made the same comment several times in the last few days.

"Gee, Caleb, you think?" she said, her tone bitchy and piercing.

As always, he let her angry comment pass without response and she squeezed her eyes shut against the uncontainable fury brewing in her chest. She'd bitten his head off no less than twenty times since breakfast and every time he met her insults with infuriating silence.

"I just don't want to see you push yourself too hard too soon, Jess. Give yourself some time to—"

She cut him off with a sharp hiss. "Shut up!" she yelled.

She rose from her chair so quickly it fell backwards, crashing against the floor, but she ignored it, crossing the room to stand in front of him. "Shut up."

He rose slowly from the couch and for the briefest moment, she saw a flicker of anger in his eyes before he shuttered the emotion away.

"Jess," he began calmly, but she was too far gone to appreciate any of his conciliatory attempts. She was itching for a fight. Itching to tell the heartless bastard what she thought of him.

"Don't," she said, pushing her finger into his chest. "Don't tell me to calm down, don't tell me what I can and can't do, and don't be so fucking nice to me." Her voice was loud, piercing and for a moment she wondered what the hell she was saying. Her breathing was labored, hard, but she couldn't contain the hateful harpy she'd unleashed within herself.

She watched his eyes go hard with fury and felt an irrational relief at the heated look.

So Mr. Detached from the World could have a human moment.

"Fine," he yelled back. "Fine, Jess. I'll stop being nice. Stop trying to help you."

"Help me? Since when is hovering over me like a goddamn cloud helpful?"

He erupted in response. "You know what? To hell with this. To hell with this and to hell with you! You walk around with your fucking anger and sadness hanging out all over the place and nothing I do or say helps."

"If you want to help me, call the cops, ask some questions. Let's find this guy."

"Find him? Christ, Jess. Are you seriously still going to pursue this man? After everything he's done?"

"Yes, of course, I am. I would think you would want to find him now too."

Caleb's eyes narrowed and she could see his attempt to control his temper wavering. "I'm trying to be patient, trying to be understanding—"

"Understanding? Is that what you call this stone façade of yours?"

"You want me to behave like you? Chasing every shadow and biting off everyone's head every minute of the day?" he roared.

"I'd rather be emotional than emotionless," she taunted. "I'm so sorry if my pain annoys you. All the more reason I would think you'd want to get the hell away from me. Go ahead, Caleb, go ahead and tuck your head back in that hard shell of yours and pretend nothing's wrong."

"I'm trying to be here for you. I don't want to leave you alone."

"Why the hell not? It's clear I'm an annoyance to you. Why don't you just escape my miserable presence rather than maintain this irritating stoic hovering of yours?"

"What the fuck is that supposed to mean?" he yelled.

"It means you're like a goddamn robot. Doesn't anything ever bother you? Hurt you? We lost a baby, Caleb. We, not just me."

He sucked in a sharp breath at her words, and she watched with agony as his angry eyes flooded with pain. "You think I don't feel that loss? You think it's not ripping me to shreds knowing that our baby, that we—"

His voice broke and Jessie's heart shattered. What the hell had she done? She'd felt so alone in her grief over the miscarriage—she'd mistaken Caleb's calmness for coldness. She'd lost control of herself again—fallen once more into the bottomless pit of grief and anger. Only this time, she'd taken Caleb down with her.

"Caleb," she whispered when a single tear escaped his eye. "I'm so sorry. I didn't think you—"

"Cared?" he finished for her when her voice seized up. "I fucking care, Jess. I just didn't want to dump my pain on your shoulders. You were having a hard enough time with your own grief."

"Dammit," she cried, her anger flaring up briefly. "I'm not fragile. I'm not weak."

"I never thought you were," he said.

"Why do we have to grieve separately? Why does it have to be my pain and your pain? Maybe we could just share—" Her voice broke, but Caleb didn't seem to need to hear the rest. He engulfed her in his embrace, clutching her so tightly she struggled to breathe.

"I'm so sorry," he murmured against the top of her head.

"I thought you didn't care," she mumbled against his chest and he hugged her tighter.

"Jessie. When I saw you on that stretcher, when I realized you'd lost our baby and I was helpless to save it, I died a million deaths. I thought I'd failed you. I'm a doctor. I'm supposed to be able to save people, but I couldn't—"

"Oh God, Caleb. Don't say that. Don't even think that. You took care of me. You couldn't have done anything."

"You've been so angry and I've felt like I deserved your scorn, your hate because I couldn't save our baby."

"Hate? I don't hate you. It's just, nothing seems to bother you and I felt like I was the only one who felt the loss."

Caleb placed his hands on her cheeks drawing her face up to look at him. His thumbs gently wiped away the tears falling from her eyes. He grinned, but she could still detect the slightest trace of pain in his eyes. "Seems we've both been misreading each other."

She nodded. "I'm sorry. Sorry for yelling at you and sorry for thinking you didn't care. I'm not sure how I could have believed such a thing."

He kissed her forehead before resting his brow against hers. "I should have told you how I felt. I don't think you're weak, Jess. Christ, just the opposite. You're the strongest, most amazing woman I know."

She tilted her head up and placed a light kiss on his lips. "No more hiding our feelings. If you're hurting and need a shoulder, come find me. I can take it, I swear."

"And if I'm annoying you, tell me to get the hell away from you," he said and she laughed.

He reached around her shoulders and pulled her close again as she rested her cheek on his chest. "I'm glad you're here," he murmured. "I don't think I could stand to go through this without you."

She smiled as she listened to his strong heartbeat. For nearly a year, she'd lived alone with her grief. Having Caleb with her as she struggled to overcome another devastating loss helped more than she could have imagined. Made her pain more bearable. However, as he held her, she realized that she was still alone. She would continue to live with Caleb, but her search for the killer would be a solitary one.

"Feel better?" he murmured against the top of her head.

She nodded and pulled back to look at him. "Thank you," she whispered.

"For what?"

"For being here. For sharing some of the load."

He looked at her closely and she suspected he wasn't completely satisfied with the way they'd resolved things. He sighed, clearly dismissing his thoughts, his concerns for the time being and kissed her forehead.

"I'll always be here. And, Jess," he paused, "I'd like to share all of the load."

CHAPTER 10

Jessie slowly rocked on the front porch swing, overwhelmed by a feeling of contentment, peace. She'd been living at the James Ranch for over a month. During the first two weeks after the miscarriage, she'd fluctuated between extreme grief and anger as her hormones triggered excessive emotions that seemed destined to battle for dominance forever, and Caleb's assurances that her behavior was normal didn't make her feel any less out of control.

The sound of Matt and Mark fighting about some video game drifted out to her and she grinned. The James brothers were a loud, raucous, fun bunch of guys, and she spent most nights in the family room, watching movies or playing board games with them, laughing until her sides hurt. Her life had fallen into an easy routine, and she was surprised by the overwhelmingly welcoming reception of Caleb's brothers. Jacob made room for her in the family office, and the two of them spent most afternoons side by side working on their laptops, her on web designs, while Jacob tapped away on class assignments or magazine articles. Mark and Matt welcomed her into the kitchen, and as a trio they made all the meals, often challenging each other to ridiculous cooking competitions.

The holiday season she'd dreaded had come and gone. She'd approached her first Christmas without Tommy with trepidation. However, the abundance of new males in her life—the James brothers as well as Todd and Stephen—had kept her so entertained, so surrounded and outnumbered, she'd never had a single moment alone to be sad. As they'd celebrated the New Year, Jessie realized she wasn't viewing the coming months with fear or uncertainty, but rather with excitement and anticipation.

She called the Denver and Saratoga police departments weekly—much to Caleb's dismay, but the detectives at both precincts seemed to have hit a wall in the investigation, and she was beginning to suspect the officers were viewing her continual calls as a nuisance.

Nothing new there.

Jordan kept her abreast of happenings in Denver and he'd informed her that Rex had fallen on hard times. The accounting firm was struggling without Tommy's business savvy and Rex's attempts at finding a capable partner had failed. According to Jordan, the man's lack of management skills, combined with the mess of reestablishing the data lost in the fire, had destroyed any credibility the firm had once claimed.

Jordan had been a blessing, checking in weekly, helping her to rehash all the details until she thought she'd go mad. Jordan had befriended Dawnette, recruiting the secretary for her help, but she was unable to shed much light on which of Tommy's clients could have been up to any shady activities. She'd offered a few names, all of whom Jordan had done background checks on. Jessie spent night after night pouring over the information her friend supplied, frustrated by her lack of success. There was clearly a vital piece of the puzzle missing, but despite her tireless efforts, she simply couldn't find it.

Since his botched attempt to take her life, the embezzler had been quiet. No more phone calls, no more death threats, but she knew better than to become complacent. The man was nothing if not patient. For weeks, she'd run through the accident in her mind, the man's voice eerily familiar and yet she still couldn't put a face to it.

She continued to look for a house to buy, often scanning the classified ads in the newspaper, despite Caleb's insistence that she wasn't going anywhere until she was safe from her unknown assailant. Jessie was beginning to believe he would be happy to keep her at the ranch permanently. Unfortunately her feelings about such an occurrence ran the gamut from utter joy to sheer panic.

Caleb had filled his brothers in on her stalker prior to bringing her home from the hospital and although, she couldn't actually prove it, she suspected they'd worked out a schedule ensuring that she was never at the ranch alone. She'd shared some of Jordan's findings with Caleb but she sensed his interest was based more on his need to assure her safety than in actually catching the killer.

She sighed as she thought of Caleb. When they'd first met, she'd felt like half a person, and as the weeks passed, she realized he had helped her find the part that was missing. For the first time since Tommy's death, she felt like Jessie again.

After dinner, Caleb had gone back to the bedroom to change into comfortable clothing and she'd come outside to think. He spent most days and more than a few nights at the hospital and she was struck by his devotion to his work, his dedication to his patients. They continued to share his bedroom—platonically—often talking into the wee hours of night. He was an amazing man, a dedicated doctor and the better she got to know him, the more she genuinely liked him as a person.

"There you are," Caleb said from the front door. "I've been looking for you. What are you doing out here? It's chilly."

"It's not cold," she said, shaking her head at his endless pampering. It was actually a rather balmy night for early January in Wyoming. "It's a nice evening and I thought I'd enjoy the fresh air. Come sit with me." She patted the cushion next to her.

As he approached, she found herself fighting back the undeniable sexual attraction she felt that constantly over-whelmed her senses whenever he was near. While he'd never broached the subject of sex or alluded to the desire to extend their relationship beyond the bonds of friendship, she sensed that his brothers and her friends viewed them as a couple and she struggled with that idea. She embraced their newfound closeness and enjoyed his companionship. The problem was she had enough friends and she wasn't entirely sure that was all she wanted from her handsome doctor.

There was a large part of her that longed for Caleb to touch her, to make love to her. Her body ached for much more than his casual touches. Every night, he offered her a sweet, rather brotherly goodnight kiss on her brow, and he'd never done more than hold her hand while they watched television.

However, there was another part of her that balked at her growing feelings for him, a small bitter piece of her heart that chastised her for her unfaithfulness to Tommy. There was also the undeniable fear firmly planted inside her that insisted love hurt. By falling for Caleb, she felt certain she was setting herself up for more heartache and pain.

His touches, though sweet and friendly, had started to grate on her nerves, and lately she'd begun to wonder if he would ever kiss her again. Despite all the fears and worries tugging at her mind, the truth was she desperately wanted him to kiss her.

He joined her on the swing and wrapped his arm around her shoulders pulling her close.

"How old are you, Jess?" he asked after a few quiet contented moments had passed.

She smiled at his question. After hours and hours of conversation, she just realized she'd never asked his age either. "Twenty-eight," she said. "I'll be twenty-nine on February twenty-first. How about you?"

"Thirty-four. You're awfully young to be a widow," he added.

She shrugged, surprised by his words. He hadn't mentioned Tommy in quite a long time.

"I suppose so," she said, wondering at his strange mood tonight. He'd been unusually quiet throughout dinner, but she'd merely thought he was tired from work.

He looked down at her and she glanced up at his face, hoping to be able to read something about what he was thinking. She was shocked to see undisguised lust and desire in his eyes.

"Caleb," she whispered.

He leaned down and brushed the rest of her words away with his lips. The kiss was soft, yet she didn't mistake the intensity of the feelings behind it for a minute. He still wanted her. She felt like singing.

After several moments, he pulled away, resting his forehead against hers. "If you aren't ready for this, Jess, tell me now."

She closed her eyes and considered his words. Back in August, her grief over Tommy, her guilt of betraying his memory had had too strong a grip on her heart. Now, her heart felt freer, more open. It felt like it was hers again.

"I'm ready," she whispered against his lips. He took her cheeks in his hands and pulled back, forced her to meet his gaze.

"I don't just mean for tonight."

"I know," she said. She reached up to run her fingers through his thick, dark blond hair and smiled.

He returned her grin and pulled her closer, this time kissing her with all the power she felt tugging at her body as well. Like two people who'd been trapped in the desert for months, they were suddenly at a pool of cool water and neither of them was able to restrain themselves from diving in.

"Bedroom," he murmured against her lips and she giggled. They stood up together and he grasped her hand in his. She shook off his grip at the front door.

"Race ya," she called as she ran down the hallway to his room. She saw Jacob grinning at them from the kitchen door, shaking his head, but she didn't have time to acknowledge him. She hit the bedroom and sprinted for the bed, jumping onto it a split second before she heard the door close behind her, the lock being turned.

Rolling onto her back, she fought not to groan as she watched Caleb pull off his shirt. Though they had shared a bed for over a month, they'd both worn T-shirts and soft lounge pants each night and Caleb did all of his dressing for work in the adjoining bathroom. She hadn't seen his bare chest in months, and the image of him walking toward her, unzipping his jeans threw her libido into overdrive.

She sat up as he reached the side of the bed, pulling her sweater over her head. He stilled her hands when she started to peel off her pants as well.

"Slow down, Jess," he said, dragging his hand through her hair. "We've got all night."

She fought back a groan of frustration. "I don't wanna go slow," she said, fully aware of the fact she sounded like a six-year-old complaining about eating broccoli. He laughed and she narrowed her eyes.

"Tough," he said.

"Caleb, please," she said, reaching up, anxious to have his hot, hard body against hers.

He bent at the waist and kissed her, gently at first, but it quickly built in intensity and pressure until they had to break away to catch their breath.

He reached around and unhooked her bra, pulling the lacy material away from her overheated flesh. With a firm hand on her shoulder, he pushed her onto her back, kneeling over her.

"You've gained some weight," he said, taking her full breasts into his hands. "I'm glad. You were too damn thin." He toyed with her nipples as he spoke and she tried to decide whether or not to take offense at his words.

"I think I've finally discovered why you never married," she teased, wondering if he realized how touchy women were about their weight.

"Why's that?" he asked as he bent down to suck her taut nipple into his mouth. She gasped at the sensitivity, the pressure his suckling sent through her body, centering on her pussy.

"Never mind," she breathed, and he chuckled before turning his attention to her other breast. She knew from the leisurely way he nibbled, licked and kissed he would not be rushed tonight despite the fact her body was screaming for more. She ran her fingers through his hair, pulling him closer, holding him to her. She wanted this man more than she thought possible.

For a moment, she thought of Tommy and she stiffened. Caleb must have sensed the shift in her body.

"Jess?"

She shook her head and relaxed in his grip. Tommy's beloved face flashed in her mind, grinning at her, nodding, and she was overcome with the sudden feeling of rightness. She smiled to herself. If her late husband could have picked any man on earth for her, she knew beyond a shadow of a doubt he would have selected Caleb.

"That's a mysterious smile," he said, lifting up and moving her to the center of the bed.

"No," she said, "it's a happy smile."

He grinned at her and she saw a look of pleasure suffuse his face. He reached down and unbuttoned her jeans. He kissed her lips, her cheeks, her forehead as he released the zipper. She lifted her hips as he tugged the denim down over her legs, dumping her jeans and panties on the floor by the bed. When he had her completely naked, he knelt before her and simply looked. She thought she should be embarrassed by his intense scrutiny, but his face was too awed, too appreciative, and she suddenly felt like the most beautiful woman on earth.

"I didn't get to see you properly the first time," he murmured. "Thank God I didn't." She jerked back a bit, confused, until he finished speaking. "I would have been tormented mercilessly by the memory of this body. Wouldn't have been able to sleep a wink for wanting you."

"I want to see you," she said, propping up on her elbows and gesturing at his pants. "Please."

He rose from the bed and as she watched, he finished taking off the rest of his clothing. She sucked in a breath at the size of his erection and the undeniable proof that this man truly did want her. Rolling to her side, she stopped him from returning to the bed with a quick touch to his stomach. Moving closer, she dragged the tip of one finger down the length of his cock and fought back a giggle at his anguished "Dear God".

Leaning down, she breathed in the essence of him as her mouth watered for one little taste. She placed her lips over the head of his cock and swirled her tongue over his sensitive, hard flesh. She was inundated with the smells and flavor that were so distinctly Caleb. The drop of fluid she captured at the tip was salty, while she could detect the slight scent of his soap still lingering from the shower he must have taken before coming to find her on the front porch.

His hands moved to her head as she took more of him into her mouth, and she began a back and forth motion with Caleb's fingers guiding her, holding her. The words that fell from his lips seemed to be the mindless chatter of a man in the throes of something too powerful to fight, but she found comfort in his praise, his directions.

"You're killing me, Jess," he said breathlessly when she swallowed him to the back of her throat. His hands tightened almost painfully in her hair for a moment, proving his words true. She knew he was struggling to hold back, knew he would never intentionally hurt her, but she didn't want his restraint, his calmness. She wanted him to be as wild as he'd made her feel that first night at the guesthouse. She wanted to bring him to his knees with delight and desire. She dragged her hand along the inside of his thigh and cupped his balls. He hissed, while pushing his cock more firmly inside her mouth.

She squeezed gently and felt a sense of incredible victory. She felt her Caleb, her gentle, peaceful friend disappear, as Caleb, the hot, insatiable lover she'd only met once reappeared.

He used his hands to move her head against his cock and she followed gladly. She massaged his balls, teased him with her tongue and teeth, groaned against his rigid flesh, all while fighting back her own growing desire, pressing her legs together to fight the incredible pressure building there.

"Dammit," he said, pushing her away before his imminent eruption. He'd been so close, too close and she growled with frustration.

"Caleb," she started to argue, but he cut her off with a hard, demanding kiss that seemed to last an eternity.

She was vaguely aware of him reaching over to the dresser and donning the condom, but she was too lost in the touch of his lips on hers, the feeling of his hard body as he pushed her back on the bed.

When he finally gave her a reprieve, separated for a moment so that she might gasp for air, he spread her legs and moved between them.

She glanced down, felt his fingers touching her swollen clit, rubbing it firmly, once, twice, and she shattered. Struck down by an orgasm she never saw coming. He continued to touch her as she shook, crying out with the intensity of it. His fingers prodded into her, driving her up the cliff again. Not content with her first climax, he worked her tender flesh until she felt as if she'd sell her soul to the devil for one more, just one more.

"So wet," he murmured, but she was too mindless to hear, to comprehend.

He moved his cock to her opening and slowly pushed his way in. She wanted to scream, to demand he fuck her, thrust in hard, but he wouldn't be moved from his present torturous path.

"Please," she cried when at last he'd seated himself fully.

"Together this time," he whispered into her ear as his hot breath singed her cheek. Her whole body felt like a live wire, ready to spark. Her skin was sensitive to every touch, every breath.

He moved out with the same cursed slowness, and she pushed against his chest in frustration.

"Hard," she gasped, desperate and begging. "Fast," she hissed. "Now."

He stopped moving completely on his retreat, only the head of his cock still within her. She squirmed beneath him, shook her head, but he never moved, never gave into her body's anxious demands.

"Look at me," he said, and she fought back a snarl. It was all she could do to keep her eyes from rolling into the back of her head. He didn't understand. She'd never needed with this intensity, never wanted with this much passion.

"Look at me," he repeated, and she forced her gaze to his, awestruck to see he did understand.

"Don't take your eyes off of me," he commanded. She only had time to nod once before he shoved back inside her with all the power, all the might she wanted. She fought to close her eyes against the tremors building in her body, but she felt captured by his gaze. She watched as he made love to her, felt as well as saw each powerful thrust.

Caleb.

Their eyes never faltered and when they came together, though her vision clouded with glorious, white hot stars, she never lost sight of him.

Caleb.

He held himself over her, adoring her, loving her, caressing her with his gaze, and she gave him back the same affectionate look.

He dropped down on his elbows to kiss her cheek and as he did so, he breathed the words she never thought she'd hear again against her skin.

"I love you," he whispered.

He did. She'd seen it in his eyes. It was that look that had held her, restrained her during their lovemaking, binding her to him, but she could see now she hadn't been captured at all. She'd been freed.

Caleb.

His name pounded in her brain and tattooed itself on her heart, the image of his face slowly seeping into the wounded organ, breathing life back into the bits of it that had died with Tommy.

"I love you too," she said.

CHAPTER 11

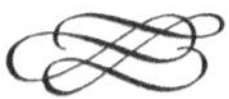

"Move in here," Caleb said the moment she opened her eyes. She was lost in the mesmerizing memories of their night together and struggled with his abrupt, unexpected choice for a morning conversation. She had hoped they could pick up where they'd left off the night before.

"In case you haven't noticed," she teased, "I've been living here for over a month."

"Move in with me, Jessie. Get your stuff out of storage, move those boxes out of Todd's attic and stop looking at those damn real estate ads in the paper."

She stared at him, uncertain how to answer. He was usually easygoing, fun, but his seriousness, the relentless determination she sensed in his face, took her unaware. "I'm not sure what to say."

"Then say you will." His words, though seemingly light, sounded strained, tense.

"No. It's not as easy as that. This is all too fast. None of this is happening the way it should be."

"The way it should be?"

She could see she'd angered him with her quick refusal, but she couldn't shake the idea that they'd approached their entire relationship starting with the middle first. "I don't mean I'm not happy here with you, but good Lord, look at us. We had sex the first night we met and made a baby. Three months later, we meet again and within two days, I'm living in your house, in your bed. This is nuts. This isn't how normal people date. Hell, we haven't even been on a date."

He laughed at her words and shrugged. "So we'll go on a date. I'll take you out to dinner and then we'll swing by that storage unit you're renting and empty it. Sounds like a pretty romantic evening to me."

"Will you be serious?"

"I am being serious. I don't want to follow this so-called accepted path of yours or to color within the lines. I'm not a young man with his first crush. I'm thirty-four fucking years old and more than old enough to know what I want without following some preconceived idea of how people are supposed to meet and fall in love."

"It's too soon," she repeated. She couldn't even begin to ponder what he was suggesting. She couldn't, in good faith, plan a future with Caleb until she'd laid the past to rest. Until Tommy's killer was caught, her life wasn't truly her own.

"To hell with that," he yelled, and she winced at his sudden anger, feeling her own rise in response. "I know you're hurting, Jess. I know you've suffered for your love and I'm sorry about that. And maybe I haven't felt that pain personally. For years, I've let my job rule my life, but that's changed since you. I love you."

"You don't understand," she said. He couldn't know the agonizing price they would pay if all of this suddenly ended one day.

"You're wrong. I'm surrounded by death and dying every-day. I've watched people with broken bodies overcome amazing odds, fighting for life. Your heart's been broken, Jess, but you aren't letting it heal. You're picking at the wound, keeping it open, fresh, painful."

"So I'm just supposed to forget about Tommy? Pretend he never existed? Let his murderer get away?"

"Christ. Of course not. But Tommy died, Jess. Not you. Stop curling up in a ball and throwing your life away on some wild goose chase."

"Wild goose chase?"

"I don't want to lose you, Jess."

His words beat a painful tattoo on her heart, and she realized her reasons for rejecting him weren't solely based on her search for a killer. "I could lose you," she whispered, the true root of her fears flying out. "You could die on me."

"Do you want me to promise I'll never die, Jess?" he asked.

"I don't need you to promise to live forever. I just need you to outlive me." She tried to force a grin to her lips, a lightness to her voice that would contradict the truth of her request. It was an irrational, impossible demand, but she still wanted his reassurances.

"You know I can't promise that. Love is all about risks."

She shook her head slowly, terrified by the truth of his words.

"Then your decision is made," he said.

She rose from the bed. Dammit, why did it feel like every step forward was followed by ten steps back? She felt like she needed to justify her concerns, her fears. "I *am* fighting for my life, fighting to move on, but it's not that easy, Caleb."

"I never said it was." His voice was quieter, but no less angry, no less frustrated.

She reached down and picked up her sweater, uncomfortable with her nudity in the face of their argument. Rather than put it back on, she held it in front of her like a shield.

He stood as well and paced to the window of the bedroom, fury evident in every step he took.

"I'm sorry," he said with a sigh after a few tense, silent moments. "My words were uncalled for, but I feel like I'm fighting a fucking ghost." He turned and she could see the pain brimming in his eyes. "It's a fight I can't win, Jessie. I need you to stop taunting his killer, daring the man to come after you. I want you to look forward, not back. Are you turning down my offer to live here permanently because you don't want to be with me or because of some misguided loyalty to Tommy's memory?"

She stared at him as her hands begin to shake. Her insides felt cold, the feeling reminding her of the months she'd spent alone and grieving for her lost husband.

Why was she refusing Caleb? She loved him, she knew that with all her heart. She knew he loved her, she could see it in his face as he stared at her now, his heart firmly held in her trembling hands. He'd handed it to her and now he was waiting for her next move. She could crush it, destroy it and him or she could accept his gift of unconditional, unreserved love.

She fought to say the words she knew he needed to hear, but her voice deserted her, the same old fears and anxieties creeping in and striking her mute. She shook her head, unable to utter a single sound. She knew he could see her panic and she saw the exact moment when his patience ran out.

"That's it," he yelled, coming toward her so quickly she didn't have time to move despite the fact that the look in his eyes warned her she shouldn't simply move, she should run.

"I'm the man who's here now," he said, roughly pulling the sweater from her hands and throwing it to the floor. "I'm the man who loves you, who wants you, who's tired of playing second fiddle to a dead man. You want to hang on to your ghost, your past? Fine, try it. I dare you. I dare you to think of another man right now."

As he spoke, he turned her abruptly, pushing her down on the bed, covering her body with his, taking her lips roughly. She didn't have time to consider his words or the meaning behind them as he took absolute possession of her. His hands, his tongue, his lips caressed her body, touched her everywhere, kissed and tasted every square of skin as she squirmed beneath him, silently begging him for more. While he staked his claim on her body with his hands, his words infiltrated her mind, stealing every fear, every worry away, scattering them like dust in the wind. He never stopped speaking. Words like *mine, love, need* and *forever* drifted through all the cold, dark places in her mind, erasing the lingering thoughts that told her being with this man was wrong.

Her legs parted as his covered cock pounded inside her quivering, needy body and she welcomed him gladly, taking each hard thrust he gave, guilt suffusing her as she felt him working to drive out all the demons for her. He was offering her a second chance at happiness. With every touch, kiss and word, he forced himself not only into her body and mind, but her heart. As they came with hoarse cries, she knew there was nothing on earth more precious than this moment, this man.

The image of Tommy as he lay cold on the ground outside his office flashed through her mind. He was dead and his killer still walked around free. She'd loved Tommy too. Didn't he deserve closure, justice?

Caleb lay on top of her for several moments before pushing himself to her side, gathering her in his arms. She turned to look at him, ashamed at herself for causing the undeniable pain that laced his gaze.

"I do love you, Caleb," she said.

"But?" he said and she knew he'd heard the hesitance in her voice.

"But I can't stop looking for Tommy's killer. I can't believe you'd ask me to. This man killed our baby too."

He shook his head sadly. He was silent for so long, she wondered if he would ever speak. When he finally did, his voice was cold, emotionless. "There's more to living than avenging the dead, Jess. In fact, what you've been doing this past year can't even be considered a life—you're merely existing."

Tears stung her eyes at his cruel words, and she felt an invisible wall spring up between them as he moved away from her and rose from the bed.

"You think I don't know that?" she asked, her voice thick with the anguish lodged in her throat.

"Do you?" he said bleakly. "Because from where I'm standing, you seem to be reveling in your grief, in your anger. It's feeding you. It may be keeping you alive, but that's all it's doing."

She swallowed heavily. "I'm sorry I hurt you. I didn't realize that I'd dragged you so deeply into my own pain. It's just I can't stop. Please don't ask me to."

"If you continue, he'll kill you. He *will* kill you and I can't accept that. I'm not about to sign on for a lifetime of looking over my shoulder wondering when the villain is going to strike you down."

"Don't do this, Caleb," she said, her voice loud, panicked. "Don't force me to make this decision."

"What decision?" he yelled. "Jesus, Jess. I'm asking you to move in, to embrace a future with me. I love you, goddammit. What's on the other side of that? What's keeping you from saying yes?"

"This man," she said. She was finding it difficult to catch

her breath in light of the fears crushing her chest. "He killed Tommy. He killed our baby. You should want him to pay for that."

"At the risk of losing you?"

She was struck mute by his anguished question. "You won't lose me," she whispered.

"No," he said, his voice eerily devoid of emotion. "You're right, I won't. Apparently I never had you to begin with. I'm sorry. I won't bother you with my silly plans for the future again. It's clear that's not what you're looking for."

He started to move toward the door, but before he left, he bent down to kiss her lips softly, briefly. The light touch was clearly one of farewell. "Don't make plans to leave the ranch," he warned. "I meant what I said in the hospital. You will remain here until I'm satisfied you're safe. I'll be in the guest room if you need me."

"Hey, Todd. What brings you over here?" Jessie said, stepping out onto the front porch to greet her friend. It had been a week since Caleb moved into the guest room, and the silence that had reigned in the house since then had taken its toll on her.

"You look like shit," Todd muttered.

"Gee thanks."

"Dammit, Jess, how long is this going to go on?"

She shrugged. "I have no idea what you're talking about."

"Liar. Jake said you and Caleb had a fight. It's clear you're both hurting, so go make up, have some sweaty sex and move on."

"It's not that easy," she said. She hadn't told Todd any of the specifics about her fight with Caleb. The words simply wouldn't work their way around the miserable lump clogging her throat.

"It can be as easy or hard as you make it. Wanna talk about it?" he asked. He'd offered his shoulder more than a few times this week and for the first time in her life, she'd refused it. She couldn't cry anymore. There weren't any more tears left in her body.

She shook her head. "What's all that in your car?" she asked, determined to change the subject.

"I figured you could use a distraction," Todd said, putting his arm around her shoulder. "If you don't want to talk about your troubles, then I'm going to make you forget about them."

"How?"

"I'm gonna load you up with work."

"Work?" she asked.

"Yep. Stephen and I want you to do a proper webpage for us. I know you helped us with that mock-up, and at the beginning it was good enough, but business is booming and we want to make a lasting first impression."

"Um, okay. Sure," she said. In the past, she'd loved the idea of creating a new webpage, designing a site that was unique and inviting, but the prospect of starting this project held little excitement for her.

"Try to contain the enthusiasm there, Jess," Todd teased and he opened the car door.

"What is all this stuff?" she asked.

"Boxes. Some of your stuff from the attic. I figured if I was going to put you to work, the least I could do is give you back some of the tools of your trade. I dragged down these two that were labeled *office*. I also brought by some pictures Stephen took that we'd like to incorporate on the webpage as well."

Jessie picked up one box while Todd grabbed the other, and she secretly wished she was moving the boxes into the ranch for good. The moment the thought passed through her mind, she dismissed it. She refused to think about anything that touched on her argument with Caleb. Her heart had been cut open by his injured look, and the wound seemed to have become infected by the silence permeating the house.

Caleb had reverted back to form, working double shifts at the hospital. Jacob and the twins had pulled out all the stops over the past week in an attempt to cajole Caleb out of his bad humor, but they were wasting their time. Until she moved out, she knew Caleb wouldn't do more than sleep in the house, but the damn man and his misguided principles refused to allow her to leave. She'd actually packed up, prepared to move back to the guesthouse two days ago only to be met at the door by the twins. No amount of begging or badgering would budge them, and she'd eventually given in angrily and returned to Caleb's bedroom—alone.

"Well, come on then," she said as they climbed the stairs and entered the house. "Here's hoping your plan works because I have to admit, I'm tired of thinking."

Todd laughed. "Damn, Jess. Those aren't real comforting words considering the fact that I'm asking you to create a webpage that will help boost business."

She smiled at his jest, then laughed. She would push her worries aside for an afternoon. Shut out the damned world and escape into her computer for a while. Who knew? Maybe when she came back, her life wouldn't seem so bleak.

*S*everal hours later, Jessie stood up and stretched. They'd planned the basic format for Todd's webpage before he'd returned home and excited by the prospect of a distraction and a new project, she'd thrown herself into the design. Mark and Matt had driven to Laramie for the weekend and Jacob was puttering around in the kitchen, baking a cake for a friend's birthday.

Jordan had called to check in earlier, but she'd been too tired to rehash the same old, pointless information. She'd said goodbye, claiming she needed to work on Todd's website and unpack some office boxes her friend had retrieved from his attic. Shortly after she hung up the phone with Jordan, Caleb called Jacob to say he would be working late. *Big surprise.*

She walked around the room, trying to work out the kinks in her neck and back from sitting in front of the computer for so long. As she paced, she studied the room and imagined some of the improvements she would make to it if she lived here. The walls were screaming for a fresh coat of paint and given the stack of books and files on the floor, it wouldn't hurt to invest in another bookshelf and perhaps a file cabinet. She quickly stopped her plans as the pain in her heart that she'd pushed away for a few hours returned with a vengeance at the thought of a future that wouldn't be.

She turned and her gaze landed on the two boxes Todd had brought by. Kneeling down, she opened the first, somewhat relieved to find it filled with the things from her home office in Denver. She'd been worried she would have to dig through mountains of stuff in the storage unit to find her reference books if they hadn't been in one of these boxes. Pushing the box aside, she opened the second one.

Her heart stopped as she saw the broken glass of the frame holding her wedding picture to Tommy. She fought for a breath as she realized this was the box she'd packed the night her husband died. She pulled out the broken picture, running her finger over Tommy's face.

"I miss you so much," she whispered to his smiling image. Reaching back in, she pulled out the pens, the paperweight. She lifted up the Rolodex and spun it as a multitude of names flew by, some she recognized, others she didn't. Could one of these names be the name of the man who killed Tommy?

At the bottom of the box, she found a handful of disks and the relatively new thumb drive she'd put in Tommy's stocking the previous Christmas. It had been a silly, last minute gift, but the man was forever digging through disks for things and she'd insisted the flash drive would help him be more organized. She doubted if he'd even used it. While technology was her love, numbers had been his, and she'd had to drag him kicking and screaming through it every time the firm introduced some new software.

Was the evidence that would put the murderer away on one of these disks? It certainly hadn't been on any of the disks in their Denver apartment. She felt a slight shiver of excitement at the thought that perhaps at last, she would uncover the embezzler's identity. Rising, she carried the disks and thumb drive over to the computer and sat back down despite her body's protesting muscles. Caleb wouldn't be home for hours and she didn't like sleeping in the bed without him. She'd been spoiled by his presence and after nearly a year of sleeping alone, she found herself reluctant to return to a cold, lonely bed.

One by one, she systematically worked her way through the disks. She'd done much the same thing when she was packing up her apartment in Denver. Although she was no accountant, she had a basic working knowledge of spreadsheets and ledgers. She clicked in and out of files, aware Rex would have a fit if he knew she had such information. Once she finished looking at them, she would destroy them.

She'd finished looking at the last disk and reached over to pick up the thumb drive when she was struck by the silence in the house. As she worked, she'd heard Jacob humming in the kitchen, the clattering of dishes, but now there was nothing.

She knew Caleb's brother well enough to know he wouldn't go to bed without saying goodnight. The hair on the back of her neck stood up, and she felt a familiar prickling as the same nagging sense that she was being watched returned.

"Jacob," she called out, standing and walking to the office door. She felt foolish for the fear that was suddenly coursing through her. For a moment, she was paralyzed, waiting, praying for Jacob's reply. When it didn't return, she repeated his name, this time her voice breathless, shaking. "Jacob."

"I'm afraid your friend has been detained."

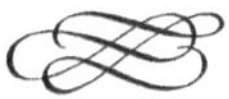

CHAPTER 12

"Jordan?"

The man drifted out of the shadows in the hallway and walked toward her slowly. As he came into plain view, she was assaulted by several things at once. His kind face suddenly looked menacing, he was pointing a gun directly at her and it was his voice she'd heard after her car accident.

"It was you," she whispered, besieged with an uncanny awareness that all her fears, all her questions and concerns were about to be answered. She was also overwhelmed by the conviction that before the night was over, there was a very good chance she would be dead.

"Of course it was."

She fought her growing panic, trying to figure out a way to escape. Unfortunately, one horrifying thought interfered with her ability to plot, to plan.

Jacob.

She was overcome with terror for her dear friend. Surely he was alive. Surely she would have heard a gunshot.

"Where's Jacob?" she asked, surprised by the sudden strength in her voice that belied her total, utter horror.

"He's not dead," Jordan replied, gesturing with the gun for her to step into the office. She backed away, continuing until he harshly commanded her to stop. "Don't move any farther," he said. "Your friend won't die as long as you give me what I want."

She shook her head, inundated with confusion, panic. "I don't know what you want."

He seemed taken aback by her words and she watched a strange, dark smile cross his face. "You really don't, do you? Ah, Jessie. All of this unpleasantness could have been so easily avoided if you'd only behaved as a normal, grieving widow. I should have known the night of Tommy's death that it wouldn't be so easy."

"Tommy's death?" she repeated. "Don't you mean Tommy's murder?"

Jordan shook his sadly and for a moment she almost believed the crocodile tears forming in his eyes. He'd fooled her once with his false pretenses, but now, with his mask off, she saw him for the heartless killer he was.

"It was inevitable, Jess," he said.

For the first moment since she saw him, her fear gave way to anger at his use of her nickname. Only her friends called her Jess and hearing it fall so casually from this bastard's lips infuriated her. "That's Ms. Warner to you," she replied hotly.

He laughed at her words, shaking his head. "Such spirit—even in the face of death. God, you are magnificent. You truly don't realize what you have, do you?"

She knew what she had. Knew that she'd only just found the proof tonight. "I have the evidence that proves you're an embezzler. I have the means to put you behind bars for a very, very long time."

"Very good, Jessie, very good. For nearly a year, you've held my downfall in your hands. This all could have been avoided. All of this could have ended the night of Tommy's accident, if you'd only accepted the police report, only accepted the truth of Tommy's death."

Jessie felt a streak of red-hot anger flood her system. "The police report was wrong. His death was no accident. You killed him, you fucking murderer," she screamed, as all regard for her own safety vanished in the fury she felt toward this man.

"I'm sorry to disillusion you, my dear. I know you did so like the idea of a murder, but the sad fact is Tommy's death was an accident. I only meant to frighten him, threaten him. I held a gun on him in the parking lot and demanded that he give me the evidence he'd accumulated against me or you would pay the price with your life. The foolish boy refused to listen and actually tried to unarm me."

She smiled at the image. Tommy had never fit her mold of what an accountant should act or look like and she imagined he'd been quite amazing, threatening to expose Jordan to the authorities.

He continued speaking. "I managed to shove him off, but he fell on the slick surface and hit his head. I watched him die, Jess. Watched as the life left his eyes, but I can assure you, it was not my intention to kill him. I had hoped that—with the proper motivation—he would come to work for me."

Jessie felt her blood turn to ice as this man she'd considered a friend described her husband's last precious minutes of life as if he were recounting the plot of a movie or a book.

"I can't tell you how much his passing has haunted me," Jordan added.

Several months after Tommy's death, she had researched brain trauma. She knew that in addition to the hypothermia he'd suffered, his brain had swollen, the flow of blood disrupted. Perhaps if he had been found sooner he could have been saved. That thought had caused her weeks' worth of sleepless nights as she berated herself for not going out to look for him earlier. To learn that Jordan had stood over Tommy's injured body and watched him die brought all her anger to a full-blown boil.

"You fucking, nasty, repulsive bastard." Her hands instinctively clenched into fists, but Jordan waved the gun, reminding her of her helplessness without words. "You won't get away with this," she whispered. "You may kill me, but the police will find you, they'll lock you up."

"Tommy made the same threat. And yet, here I stand, the one with all the power once again."

"A gun isn't power. It's a coward's weapon. Besides, you haven't won yet. You still don't have your evidence," she replied.

"Oh, but I do. It resides on that thumb drive lying on the desk behind you. Tommy was so proud of that new bit of technology when you gave it to him. Bragged about how much easier his life would be without having to shuffle through stacks and stacks of CDs. Hand it to me, Jessie."

"No."

He shocked her by slapping her. She hadn't expected such violence from him. Though she was terrified, there was a small part of her that had believed he wouldn't hurt her. The needles coursing through her cheek from his hard blow dispelled that tiny hope.

"So Tommy figured out what you'd done. Why not be a man and own up to your crime? You were his friend. *You were his friend.*" She battled desperately against the tears in her eyes as she struggled to keep her voice from breaking. She refused to let him see her pain, her fear.

Her face was on fire from where he'd struck her, and the

realization that he intended to kill her suddenly inundated her. Her heart raced as her breathing became shallow, labored. Her hands shook uncontrollably and she clasped them tightly behind her back to hide the evidence of her terror. He'd killed Tommy. He would kill her. Caleb's prediction had come true.

Caleb.

The thought of everything she'd left unsaid to him flooded her body, drowning her heart in a sea of regret. She'd given up the last year of her life, trying to uncover the truth of Tommy's death and now that she'd found the truth, she realized how precious little it mattered. She'd squandered her one real chance at happiness, at a lifetime with Caleb. Oh how she wished she could turn back the clock.

What have I done?

Jordan pulled her from her thoughts. "Tommy really was a bright young accountant. So much smarter than that idiot partner of his. I must admit it gave me no pleasure to silence such an amazing mind. Oh, what I would have given to have him join my team. But he threatened to expose me, Jessie. Threatened to tell the world about my crime. I couldn't allow that to happen. I simply couldn't."

"So it all comes down to money," she said with disgust, wondering if she could stall long enough for help to arrive.

Help? What help?

Caleb was working late and the twins were out of town. God only knew what Jordan had done to Jacob.

"Money does make the world go round, my dear," he said, and she felt a twinge of pity for the man in front of her.

"No, Jordan, it doesn't. Love does. But you'll never know that. Never understand what that means. I could almost feel sorry for you if I didn't hate you so."

"Love," he scoffed. "And what pray tell will that buy me?

What has love gotten you? Nothing but heartache and despair as far as I can tell."

Her face flushed with anger. "Love hasn't caused me pain. You're the one doling that out. It's love that's saved me." As she spoke the words, she realized the truth. Caleb had offered her love, security, a bright future. And like a fool, she'd thrown it all away on vengeance and a misguided desire for a justice that wouldn't make one damn bit of difference. Regardless of whether or not Jordan paid for his crimes, Tommy would still be dead.

"Why did you come after me? I didn't know what Tommy had discovered." She desperately tried to come up with some plan for escape. She had to get away from here and find Jacob. She could run to Todd's house, call the police and Caleb, warn him to stay away. She shuddered to think what lengths her brave doctor would go to, to save her from this man.

He smiled at her sadly. "You were perfectly safe in the beginning. Think about it. Your problems didn't begin until you began asking questions about things that were better left alone."

The prank calls, the mugging, the break-in. All of those events began after she'd seen Jordan at the accounting firm.

"You simply couldn't leave well enough alone."

"I had the thumb drive," she interrupted.

"A surprise turn of events, I will admit. What wife cleans out her husband's office the night he dies? I searched Tommy's office the day after he died, pretending to have left my glove there the day before. His stupid secretary was too preoccupied with his death to care about me—a trusted client—going in to retrieve a lost belonging. I managed to wipe his computer clean with a clever virus in under five minutes."

"So that should have been it."

"Oh no, my dear, I can assure you I leave nothing to

chance. Tommy and I had a meeting shortly after Christmas and I watched him store all of the audit information on the flash drive."

"How did you know I had it?" she asked.

"I overheard Dawnette talking to one of the other secretaries about you coming in and clearing out your husband's office during the night."

Jessie sucked in a pained breath. She'd inadvertently thwarted Jordan's attempt to retrieve the evidence against him.

"I expected you to mourn normally, but again, my dear, you surprised me. Finding you at the accounting office months later and hearing your suspicions, well, I knew I had to act. The problem was you rarely left that stupid apartment for more than an hour at a time and I needed lots of time to search it thoroughly. I stole your purse, hoping perhaps you carried the thumb drive with you, but you didn't."

"Quite a resume you've built for yourself, Jordan. Embezzler, mugger, murderer."

Jordan laughed, though she could detect no pleasure in the sound of it.

"I've become a great many things this past year. I even broke into your apartment to search for the disk."

"You burned down the accounting firm."

"Yes."

"Why?"

"Insurance. When I failed to retrieve the thumb drive from your apartment, I decided to hedge my bets in case I'd missed it in the office. I have to admit that until tonight, I didn't realize there was the possibility that the evidence was in Todd's attic."

"You ran me off the road."

"Yes," he confessed.

"You hoped the car accident would kill me."

Jordan smiled sadly. "I must confess the idea of killing

doesn't sit well with me, but you were becoming a liability I could no longer afford. A car accident seemed preferable to—"

"Shooting me?" she asked as she looked at the gun in his hands. She noticed they weren't as steady as she thought. Jordan wasn't lying. He took no joy in the idea of killing her.

"But alas, my dear, as I said earlier, I've become a great many things this year, not the least of which, is—as you so eloquently put it—a murderer. All I have to do is pull this little trigger and all my troubles go away."

She shivered with the realization that he seemed perfectly prepared to do just that.

"Another dead body isn't going to help you."

"Perhaps not, but this gun doesn't belong to me."

She frowned, confused, until he answered, "It belongs to Rex. Your husband's former partner has fallen on some rough times. Your death, along with some information I planted in the man's home, should make for a rather smooth getaway. The police are about to discover that your husband uncovered his partner laundering money. The two argued and Rex killed him. When you discovered his perfidy, he killed you as well. You said it yourself, my dear. Rex considers you his arch enemy."

"I don't understand why you didn't just take the money and run. You were safe. Regardless of my suspicions, no one believed me. You'd killed Tommy. You'd gotten away with it."

"Had I? What were you doing tonight?"

She'd been moments away from finding the evidence. He grimaced as her face must have confirmed the truth. She'd been on the verge of uncovering his crime.

She tried to look covertly around the room, desperate to spy anything that could be used as a weapon. Her back was up against the desk, the only thing on the surface, her laptop. It wasn't much, but perhaps she could use it to knock the gun out of his hand, to give her the precious few seconds she needed to run.

"You won't win," she said.

He laughed coldly. "But, Jess, don't you see? I already have."

This man had killed her husband and unborn child, tormented her for nearly a year. Her anger welled up and, strange though it seemed, she felt a certain level of relief, of peace at being able to confront him finally. All thoughts of self-preservation vanished in the face of finally being able to tell this asshole what she thought of him. An image of Caleb flashed through her mind. She'd asked him to promise to outlive her and he'd refused. Seemed she didn't need the promise after all.

"You're a murderer and coward. Believe me, whether you kill me or not, you're still the loser in this room because you will never be anything more than those two things."

"Now, now, Jessie, there's no reason why we can't be civil. Give me the evidence and maybe I'll decide to be generous and let your lover and his fag of a brother live."

His threat terrified her. Did he intend to wait here until Caleb returned? Would he kill Caleb and Jacob? She couldn't let him hurt another person she loved.

"Oh, I'll be civil. I'll be civil as hell when they flip the switch on you in the electric chair."

"Give me the thumb drive, Jessie," he demanded.

She turned slowly toward the desk. This was it, she thought. The moment of truth. She reached for the small thumb drive, picked it up, then quickly grabbed the laptop as well, turning at the same time and swinging hard. She had one shot. One chance or she was a dead woman.

. . .

"Caleb?"

"Jake? What's wrong? I can barely hear you."

"Someone is here. A man." Caleb struggled to make out his brother's words, at first thinking the connection bad, then realizing Jacob was gasping in pain.

"Are you hurt? Jesus, where's Jessie?" he asked as his fears came crashing down on him. He'd pulled a double shift at the hospital hoping to avoid the pain that awaited him at home. Suddenly pure terror had adrenalin coursing through his body.

"I don't know. She was working in the office. There was a tapping on the back kitchen door. I thought it was that mutt that's been coming around. Someone hit me on the head, hard. I just woke up a few minutes ago and I think I'm locked in the shed out back. I can't see anything. Luckily whoever took me down didn't think to look in my front pants pocket for my cell."

"I'm on my way home. I'm almost there. Sit tight, Jake."

"Caleb," his brother said and he could hear the pain in Jacob's voice. "Don't come alone. Call the cops. Go get Todd and Stephen. They have hunting rifles. You need help if you're going to save Jessie. If you get killed, she'll never survive."

His brother's words resonated in his mind. *She'll never survive.* Dear God, she had to survive. She had to live because the fact of the matter was he'd never survive without her.

"Don't move, Jacob. I'll be there soon...with help."

He disconnected, then called 911. He reported a break-in and requested an ambulance as well as the police, but they lived too far out to expect assistance soon. He called Todd and Stephen who assured him they'd have weapons ready. Thank God, he'd already been nearly home. If he'd received Jacob's call while still at the hospital, he'd have gone insane trying to cover the distance.

Within five minutes, he pulled up in front of Todd's house.

True to their word, both men were waiting for him on the front porch, weapons in hand.

"We've discussed it," Stephen said. "If the man who knocked Jacob out has Jessie, then the best way to approach the house is by foot."

Caleb wanted to argue the point, but he could see the value in their plan. By driving up to the house, they might force the hand of the villain by announcing their presence.

"I'm running the whole way," he said quickly, turning toward the dirt path that connected their houses.

"Lead on," Todd said. "We'll be right behind you."

They arrived at the ranch after a few minutes. Todd and Caleb crept to the back porch door, while Stephen went to the shed to free Jacob and make sure he was okay. If the man had surprised her in the office, there was a good chance they were still there. They entered the kitchen carefully. Each step a painfully slow process in their attempts to remain undiscovered, silent.

As they approached the hallway, Caleb could make out voices speaking in the office, one speaker clearly female. After two more steps, he could distinctly hear Jessie's voice. His heart rejoiced with the knowledge that she was alive, unharmed. He wasn't too late.

His relief only lasted a second as he heard the report of a gun.

"No," he cried, racing for the office door, noise be damned. He skidded to a stop at the doorway, taking in the scene before him. Jessie was on top of an older man, pounding away at him with both fists flailing, pummeling the bastard as he struggled for freedom. There was a pool of blood on the floor beneath them and Caleb's heart stopped at the sight. Who was bleeding? Jessie or the man?

He and Todd stepped into the room with their weapons

aimed at the stranger, who stopped fighting when he saw them. Jessie, however, continued to attack the man, seemingly unaware of their presence.

Caleb saw Todd's eyebrows fly up to his brow line at the vulgar, angry words that flew from Jessie's lips. "You won't hurt them. I won't let you, you fucking asshole. I'll never let you hurt Caleb."

"Jordan," Caleb heard Todd whisper.

In her furor, she hadn't seen them come into the room. Caleb carefully laid his weapon on the desk, while Todd kept his gun trained on the man. He walked over to her and attempted to pull her away from the stranger, but Jessie kept swinging, kept cussing. She fought him as he tried to drag her away and her anger turned toward him.

"Let me go," she screamed. "He was supposed to be our friend. He's a murderer. A murderer!"

"We've got him, Jess. Todd's got the gun on him. He won't get away. The police will be here soon." He continued talking, trying to make his words penetrate her incensed, persistent attack. She knew this man?

"He said he'd hurt you, hurt Jacob. He killed Tommy," she choked out as Jacob and Stephen came rushing into the room. Jacob was unsteady on his feet, a goose-egg sized lump on his forehead. Caleb only spared them a glance as he felt his heart break at her anguished words. This man had been a friend and he had killed her husband.

"Then he'll go to jail," he whispered softly, engulfing her arms in a tight embrace from behind, more for comfort than restraint. The fight drained out of her slowly as he rocked her, soothed her with a quiet *shhh*.

"He killed our baby," she whispered.

For a moment, he fought back his own overwhelming rage at the stranger on the floor, this man who had caused so much pain, so much suffering over the past year. Suddenly jail seemed too good for the bastard, and Caleb's grip on her slackened.

Jacob stepped forward and he wondered if his brother had read the murder in his gaze. "He'll go to jail, Caleb," he said, repeating the words he'd just uttered to Jessie.

A siren blasted in the distance and he fought down his anger. Justice would be served tonight. Murder would be avenged.

"The blood," he said, looking at the pool of it on the floor.

"I knocked the gun out of his hand. It discharged when it hit the wall and the bullet went into his leg."

He tightened his grip on her at the thought of how closely she'd come to taking that bullet. As her anger gave way to agony, she collapsed in his arms, the pain of the past year escaping in a barrage of sobs that seemed to see no end.

"I'm so sorry," she cried. "So sorry. I love you. I love you, Caleb."

"It's okay, Jess. It's over now," he whispered repeatedly. "It's all over. You're safe now. I won't let you go."

*J*essie curled up on the couch in the living room and read the article about Jordan Scott's arrest in *The Denver Post*. Information regarding the millions of dollars he'd embezzled over the course of twenty years made national news, and the image of the man handcuffed to the stretcher as he was rolled into the hospital brought her only a small measure of comfort. Tommy was recognized for uncovering the man's costly crime. Jordan had been her husband's friend and he'd killed him. The idea of the man paying for his crimes, however, didn't make her as happy as she'd thought it would.

Today was the one-year anniversary of her husband's death. She hadn't mentioned that fact to Caleb although she suspected he knew. He'd inexplicably been missed in the ER rotation today. He told her it had been a scheduling error on the hospital's part, but she knew he had taken the day off to be with her.

The night before, Caleb had crawled into bed with her and held her as she cried herself to sleep. This morning when she awoke, he'd been gone. She'd made a mistake. She'd chosen revenge over love and happiness, and she wondered if she'd ever be able to make amends, to make things right again. She loved Caleb, wanted to be with him, to spend a lifetime with him. But how could she convince him to take a chance on her after she'd rejected him, hurt him?

She picked up her old wedding photo from the end table beside her and looked at Tommy's smiling face. "We got him," she whispered. She smiled as she recalled her happiness on her wedding day. The lead singer of the band had shown up drunk and the table holding the wedding cake had actually collapsed, but through it all she and Tommy had laughed and danced and loved. She thought she'd never feel such happiness, such love again.

She was wrong.

Caleb had found her, pulled her out of her misery. Helped her recover her lost soul, breathed life into her empty shell of a body and slowly, methodically put all the pieces of her shattered heart back together.

She laid down the picture and looked at her left hand. She pulled off her wedding band and placed it on top of the photo. "I'll always love you," she said to Tommy's image. "But I have a new life now and a chance at happiness."

She sensed Caleb's presence before she saw him. How long

he'd been at the doorway she couldn't say. She smiled tremulously when she glanced at him.

"Are you sure?" he asked, gesturing at her wedding band.

She nodded. "You never asked me to take it off," she said, the statement belying the question behind it.

He shrugged and remained silent for so long, she wondered if he'd dismissed the conversation. "I don't want to erase Tommy from your life, Jess, and I'm not trying to fill in as a replacement."

"I've never considered you a replacement. God, never."

He smiled as he sat down beside her, pulling her into his arms. "Good. He was an important part of your life. All I've ever wanted is to be the same thing."

"You are the *most* important part of my life," she said, placing a soft kiss on his cheek. "Caleb, if the invitation to move in is still open, I really want to make a future with you. If you'll have me."

"If I'll have you?" he asked, taking her face in his hands. "How can you ask that? You are the only woman I've ever wanted in my life. I love you, Jess."

"No more living in the past, I promise. You're my future and I love you."

CHAPTER 13

"Where are we going?" Caleb asked as Jessie took him by the hand and led him down the front porch steps of Todd and Stephen's house. Nearly a month had passed since Jordan's arrest, and Todd had decided to throw a Valentine's Day party for the guests at the inn and friends. After a marvelous dinner, everyone had moved into the large living room for a game of charades and the game had become quite heated as the men competed against the women. Mark and Matt had made some sort of secret side bet with a guest of the B&B, a beautiful young woman named Bridget, and it seemed both sides were determined to win at any cost. They'd begun to argue over one of the clues and Jessie used the distraction to pull Caleb away.

"I thought we could take a walk," she said, leading him across the yard.

"A walk? No offense, Jess, but it's cold as shit out here."

"We won't be outside for long." She reached into her jeans pocket and pulled out the key to the guesthouse.

"What's that for?" Caleb asked, pressing himself against

her back and placing a quick kiss at the nape of her neck as she unlocked the door.

"I was wondering if you wanted to come in for coffee," she said, repeating the question she'd asked him in August. "Looks like that game is going to go on for some time."

"I'd love coffee," he murmured in her ear as she opened the door. They stepped into the dark house together and Jessie giggled as memories of their first night together surrounded her. She walked into the kitchen, but rather than start the coffeepot, she leaned against the counter and smiled at him seductively.

"You keep looking at me like that and you're going to find your pants around your ankles," he teased.

"That doesn't sound so bad."

His gorgeous green eyes narrowed and he stepped closer to her. "I want to kiss you so badly it hurts," he said, and she was assaulted by the glorious memory of their single night in this tiny house and the heated, sexy tone of his voice.

"So kiss me," she whispered.

He wrapped her up in his embrace and his lips took everything she had to offer. Not satisfied with just her lips, he forced her mouth open with his tongue, claiming every gasping breath she struggled to take. Their tongues tangled together, playful one moment, hard and desperate the next. She had never been kissed so thoroughly or gloriously in her life.

She felt his hands drift to her waist and in seconds, Caleb's promise of shedding her pants came true as she felt the stiff denim material fall to her feet. She toed off her sneakers, then kicked off her jeans and panties. His strong hands lifted her to the counter and she welcomed him between her legs, pulling him closer. His hands brushed her clit as he struggled to unzip his jeans and she gasped at his accidental touch.

"Christ, Jess. I can't wait to be inside you," he said between kisses. She looked down to see him pull a condom out of the back pocket of his jeans before pushing them down his hips to his knees. If she hadn't been so hot, so needy, she would have giggled at his haste, his undeniable desire. He moved to open the foil packet, but she stopped him with her hands.

"No," she said.

"Jess?" He paused, looking at her.

"Don't put it on," she added.

He stared at her for several silent moments, but she refused to back down, refused to be denied. She knew what she wanted, knew where she was meant to be. "Please," she whispered.

"If we do this," he said, his voice thick with the same emotions that clogged her throat, "you marry me. I won't, I can't accept less than that."

"I'll marry you," she said softly.

He smiled at her, his beloved face so sincere, so wonderful, she fought back tears. She loved this man with a passion she'd never experienced, with a heart she'd thought dead to the emotion. He'd given her so much in such a short time, and she didn't know how she'd survived a single second of her life without him.

He threw the condom on the counter and stepped closer, pushed inside her while taking her to paradise.

Over and over, he pounded inside her body as she struggled to bring him into her. She needed him so badly, she was shocked when he retreated from her entirely. "Turn around," he said, lifting her down. She turned to face the counter as he bent over her back, entering her from behind. This position fit her needs perfectly as she pushed against him, each thrust touching her womb and her heart.

She fought back a scream as her orgasm coincided with his climax, his hot sperm filling her. She smiled to herself, so sure that this night was giving her more than just love recovered. For several moments, they clung together and she soaked up the pleasure, the joy of being in his arms.

The sound of his chuckle caught her attention and she pushed up, turned to face him. "What's so funny?" she asked.

"Your name will be Jessie James after we marry."

"Oh shit," she muttered, shaking her head. "That's not good."

"It's actually quite appropriate," he said, bending down to place a quick kiss on her lips.

"Why's that?" she asked suspiciously.

"Because you stole my heart the first night we met."

She laughed, thrilled by his sweet words. "I love you so much, Doc."

"And I love you, Jessie James."

BECAUSE YOU LOVE ME

This book is dedicated to Jonathan—for all the ebook-related did you know this? information. And to Helen—for reading my stories and making me cool author stuff. Marriage made us family, but life made us friends.
Special thanks also go out to Karmella, Zina and Kim for their "ranch life" expertise. I couldn't have written this book without your insights and cool, real-life experiences!

Bridget Wilder ducked behind the boxes and wondered how the hell she got here. Slowly, she peered around the shipping crate that was currently hiding her. She was armed with nothing more than a minirecorder, her car keys, cell phone and a tube of cherry ChapStick. If things went down badly, she was screwed.

One of these days she was going to take lessons at the shooting range and get a permit to carry a concealed weapon. Sometimes she thought she was the only journalist in New York City who wasn't packing heat. Not that her job as the *What to Do in the City This Weekend* girl was all that hazardous to her health. Worst on-job injury she'd ever received was food poisoning from a hot dog at a street fair.

Now, that was all about to change. Her mind whirled over the information she hoped to receive tonight. The Honorable Judge Lucian Thompson was on the take. He was as crooked as they came and she was about to get rock-solid proof. She imagined the implications her front-page story would have for the city's court system. How many guilty criminals had Thompson sent back out on the streets simply to fill his own pocket?

The editor in chief of her newspaper was going to freak out when she presented him with this article. She grinned in excited anticipation. This was the kind of story—the kind of break—every struggling reporter hoped to receive in her life. She pictured herself as a young Woodward or Bernstein— except, of course, she had a rocking manicure and hot pink Converse tennis shoes. Her picture would be splashed on every TV station and in every newspaper as the reporter who set New York City on its ear with her groundbreaking investigative report.

She checked the time on her cell phone. Her informant, a friend from college, was late. Lyle had lived in the same apartment complex during their senior year. He'd asked her out a few times early on. She'd genuinely liked Lyle, but they had absolutely nothing in common—he was into mysteries and sudoku, while she was a romantic comedies and shopping kind of girl. One night after drinking too much red wine, Lyle had tried to kiss her. More than a little bit tipsy, she let him. It had lasted less than fifteen painful seconds. Then they'd pulled apart and started laughing hysterically. It had been obvious to both of them there was no sexual attraction. With the pressure of a relationship gone, the friendship had blossomed and grown.

After graduation, she'd landed a job at *The New York Reporter,* a small newspaper in the city, while Lyle had been hired as a network specialist for the city court system. She'd teased him after he landed the job that she was glad he'd learned to use his computer skills for good rather than evil. She had no doubt Lyle could hack his way into any computer system if he put his mind to it. Bridget considered that now and worried about the means he'd used to discover the information he was about to share with her.

A door opened at the far end of the abandoned warehouse. She'd laughed when Lyle had given her directions to the place for "the drop", as he called it. Her friend was far too fond of Tom Clancy novels, and she knew he had every episode of *Criminal Minds* saved on his DVR. She started to rise, but recalled Lyle's warning. *Count to one hundred before you expose yourself. I want to make sure no one's followed me.*

She'd rolled her eyes when he issued that directive, but given the creepy surroundings and the nervous butterflies in her stomach, it suddenly didn't seem like such a bad idea. Crouching lower, she slowly began to count in her head. She hadn't made it to thirty when the doors of the warehouse opened again. Peering from behind the crate, she watched as two men came into the large room. Lyle, who'd been standing in the middle of the room, whirled to face them.

Bridget's heart raced faster as pure, sheer terror coursed through her veins. Lyle had said he would come alone and he'd insisted she do the same. Given her friend's nervous stance, she knew these men hadn't been invited to the party.

"Well, well, well. What a surprise. You're out late, Lyle."

Fuck. Her breathing picked up when she recognized Judge Thompson's voice. This was bad. Very, very bad. She sank lower, her back pressed against the rough crate. She forced herself to think. There had to be something she could do to protect her friend.

"Judge Thompson." Lyle's voice was steady. Bridget's respect for her geeky friend went up several notches. "Didn't expect to run into you here."

"Didn't you?" The judge's question was laced with malice. "Surely you didn't think your computer tampering would go unnoticed."

"Tampering?"

Bridget's breathing accelerated and her hands shook as she reached into her pocket. Pulling out her cell phone and her minirecorder, she struggled to hit the red dot. Perhaps she could capture the judge saying something incriminating she could use to barter for their freedom. Unfortunately, she wasn't holding her breath the device would pick up much. She was too far away.

Quietly placing the recorder on the ground, she turned her attention to her phone, dialing 911. The operator's voice sounded unbearably loud in the warehouse and Bridget froze. There was no way she could talk to the person on the other end without being discovered.

Lyle and the judge continued to speak, but Bridget found it difficult to make out their words as blood coursed through her body, pounding in her ears like a bass drum. The operator spoke again. Bridget was paralyzed with fear. She had to do something, say something, but she was too terrified to speak, even in a whisper.

As she peered around the crate, Bridget's stomach plummeted to her feet. The judge had pulled out a gun. The men were still speaking and by their comfortable stance, she knew her presence was unknown. The judge and his accomplice were completely focused on Lyle.

"Who are you meeting here?" the judge asked.

Lyle put his hands out nonchalantly. "I'm not meeting anyone. Just taking a little nightly stroll."

The judge's henchman threw a punch at Lyle's face. Bridget heard the cracking of bones and suspected he'd broken Lyle's nose. Lyle made no move to defend himself or to fight back. He simply raised his hands to his nose, trying to stem the flow of blood.

"Don't be a smart-ass." Judge Thompson sneered at Lyle.

Bridget was distracted when the 911 operator spoke once more. She needed to act, needed to do something before Lyle was hurt even worse. Keeping her eyes on the men in the center of the room, she lightly whispered the address to the warehouse. The operator attempted to ask more questions, but Bridget had already spoken more than she dared. None of the men had heard her whispers, and it gave her foolish hope. Perhaps the police would arrive in time. Perhaps the cops would burst in with guns drawn to capture the villains and save them.

"Give me the flash drive." The judge held an outstretched palm toward Lyle, the other hand still holding the all-too-threatening gun.

"Flash drive?"

"Don't be any more stupid than you already have been. I know what you have in your possession. You can give it to me now and try to beg for your pathetic, meaningless life, or I can take it off your dead body. Either way works for me."

"Either way sounds like a death sentence for me."

If Bridget hadn't felt like beating the shit out of Lyle for his cavalier attitude, she would have cheered on his bravery. He wasn't cowering or pleading. He was incredible.

As the seconds passed, Bridget prayed the night's silence would be broken by approaching sirens. None came.

"Give it to me," the judge demanded.

Lyle shook his head. "You didn't think I'd actually bring it here, did you?"

Bridget prayed that was true. If Lyle didn't have what Judge Thompson wanted, surely that bought him more time.

The judge looked at his accomplice, jerking his head toward Lyle. "Check his pockets."

Lyle didn't put up a fight as the bruiser began searching his pockets. Bridget closed her eyes and released a silent curse when the man pulled a flash drive out of Lyle's right pocket.

"You don't think that's the only copy I've made, do you?" Lyle's voice rang out across the vast space, his words clear and welcome.

Yes, Bridget mouthed. Keep them guessing...and talking. Where the fuck were the police?

The judge shrugged as if unconcerned. A malicious smile covered his face and Bridget knew things were about to go as bad as they possibly could. The scene began to unfold in slow motion as the judge lifted his hand and fired one shot directly into the center of Lyle's chest. There was no warning, no time for Lyle to run or dodge. One minute he was standing there, the next he was lying on the floor.

Bridget sat stunned, motionless. It was as if time simply stood still. She didn't breathe. Her heart didn't beat. Ice-cold numbness consumed her.

The judge's voice broke the spell. "Search the rest of the warehouse. Make sure no one else is here."

She was dead. Glancing around, she realized she'd placed herself in the worst possible position for escape. She was hiding along a far wall, and the only way to the lone door at the front of the building was by crossing the vast space where the judge stood, where Lyle lay inert on the floor.

Distant sirens pierced the night and all three living occupants jerked. The judge's henchman gave up his search and the two of them hastily escaped. The sound of a car's doors slamming, an engine starting, and peeling tires on the pavement told her they'd be long gone before the cavalry arrived.

Bridget picked up her minirecorder and phone, then rose from her hiding spot. She forced her legs to support her. As if treading through waist-deep mud, she fought her way to the center of the floor. She knew what she'd find there, knew what she'd see. Lyle had been dead the second the judge pulled the trigger, his life extinguished in the blink of an eye.

When she reached her friend, she dropped to her knees by his side. His lifeless eyes were still open, a slight look of surprise covering his frozen features. She studied his face, memorizing it, imprinting it in her mind and on her heart. She'd let him down. He'd trusted her with the information he'd uncovered. Only her. And she'd failed him.

Picking up his hand, she held it gently in hers.

"I'm sorry, Lyle," she whispered. "So sorry."

The sirens grew louder, cars pulling up outside the warehouse. She didn't rise to meet the police. Instead, she remained with Lyle and let them come to her. They entered with their weapons drawn and approached cautiously. Once they determined she wasn't a threat, they took stock of the scene and called for a coroner.

Calmly, she answered all of their four thousand, two hundred and twenty-two questions. She saw the look of surprise on all the cops' faces when she named Judge Thompson as the murderer. Finally, a million years later, they let her leave—with a police escort.

Climbing the stairs to her apartment with the rookie cop shadowing her ascent, Bridget made a silent vow to her friend. The judge would pay for tonight's crime as well as all the others. She wouldn't rest until justice had been served...for Lyle.

CHAPTER ONE

*S*ix *months later…*

Bridget stared at the piece of paper in her hands, her eyes no longer focusing on the words she'd committed to memory months ago. Sighing heavily, she glanced out the window at the picturesque, snow-capped mountains in the distance. Sometimes she still found it hard to believe how much her life had changed in such a short span of time. This time a year ago, she was typing up local interest pieces in a four-by-four cubicle at the *Reporter*'s offices. Her only view back then was of a computer screen. To add some life to the dull cubicle, she had a calendar thumbtacked to the wall with scenes similar to the real-life one she was staring at now. In New York, she pretended like the calendar was her window with a view.

With one pull of a trigger, her life had altered overnight.

"The words in that letter aren't going to change no matter how many times you read them."

She grinned, glancing over her shoulder at Rodney. "You say that every time I pull it out."

"Maybe that's because you're looking at it every five

minutes like you're going to see something different. Not sure what you're hoping to find." Rodney claimed the comfy armchair opposite hers, stretching his feet out and crossing them at the ankles.

Rodney Jackson had been assigned to protect her after the arrest of Judge Thompson. The murderer hadn't spent a single night in jail for his crime, making bail almost immediately. Apparently judges—crooked or clean—looked out for each other.

"There has to be something we're missing."

Rodney looked around at the small sitting room of the bed and breakfast where they were currently hiding out. "You can say that again. Seems to me we've hit a dead end."

She shook her head. She wouldn't—couldn't—accept that. "No, Lyle's put all the pieces here. We just have to figure them out."

Apparently Lyle had stopped by her apartment prior to his appearance at the warehouse. He'd slid a coded letter under her door that she'd discovered when she returned home that night.

At first, she hadn't had time to acknowledge or even attempt to crack the code contained in the message. She'd been instructed to quickly pack a suitcase, and then she'd been placed in the very capable hands of Rodney, who had become her protector, guardian angel and best friend.

Rodney rested his head against the cushioned back of the chair and sighed loudly. "I don't know, Bridge. It's not looking good."

Guilt pricked at the edges of her conscience. The dear cop had put his life and career on the line for her. She hated feeling like she'd failed yet another friend.

"We're in the right place, Rodney. I know it. We just have to figure out the rest of the puzzle, and we'll have all the evidence we need to take down a hell of a lot more criminals than just Judge Thompson." Lyle had given up his life to see not only the judge brought to justice, but the judge's entire network as well.

She sighed. He had also died for her. He'd brought the evidence to her instead of a more seasoned reporter because he wanted to help her get a promotion, a break in her career. Bridget intended to see that his sacrifice wasn't wasted. She'd find the evidence, see the bad guys put behind bars, and then she'd take New York by storm. She'd become the greatest reporter ever and write a front-page article telling the world what Lyle had done.

She looked at the letter again. The paper had lost its crispness due to her constant handling. It was now soft as thin cotton and just as flimsy. Lyle's damn love of mysteries and puzzles was currently driving her insane. He'd clearly coded his message in a way—he'd thought—only she would be able to solve. Unfortunately, he'd been too clever for her.

He'd penned the letter as a memory—one they didn't share. To anyone reading the message, they'd think it a short, funny story about a drunken night in college. Bridget knew better. Lyle had mentioned there were copies of the flash drive the judge had taken from him. Copies that held the information he'd uncovered regarding the judge's illegal affairs. When she thought back to the night he was killed, she was certain Lyle had said that one statement louder than everything else. Actually, she had proof that was true, because it was one of the few things her minirecorder had picked up in the warehouse. She knew to the very depths of her soul that Lyle's letter would lead her to those copied files.

After several months of traveling from safe house to safe house—and she used that term lightly—she'd managed to convince Rodney they should pursue the clues left in the letter rather than sit idly by, awaiting the beginning of the trial.

When it became apparent someone inside the New York police department was selling out their whereabouts to the judge and his accomplice, they'd decided to go it alone. Rodney had taken to calling her kitten, claiming she had the nine lives of a cat. Bridget was pretty sure she'd already used up at least eight of them. There was no way she could face the open end of a gun again and survive.

"I must've lost my mind, letting you talk me into coming here."

She leaned forward, resting her elbows on her knees. "Don't talk like that. We're so close. We have to be."

"Christ, Bridget. We're no closer to finding those files now than we were when we were still in Oklahoma."

"The code indicated Saratoga. You discovered that piece of the puzzle yourself." She held out the paper and pointed to the first line in the letter. It simply said,

Bridget,
Remember in college when Sara got totally trashed at the toga party?

It was Rodney who had shared the fact that some codes were based on numbers. By counting every sixth word, they came up with Saratoga. Bridget recalled Lyle saying one time that he was born in Wyoming. When Rodney had said the word Saratoga, something clicked with her. Unfortunately, his every sixth word theory had run dry after that sentence. The code of six didn't appear to work for the rest of the missive.

"And here we sit in the middle of Bumfuck, Wyoming, with a crooked judge's hit man hot on our heels with no backup and no disk or flash drive or whatever the fuck it is we're supposed to be looking for."

"The copy the judge took off Lyle the night he was killed was a flash drive. I bet that's what we're looking for."

Rodney shook his head. "Regardless of what the information is stored on, we still don't know where it is. I need to call in, tell my chief where we are. As it is, I'm pretty sure he's ready to fire my ass the minute I show myself."

Twice, a hit man had shown up at the safe house where they were hidden, and twice, Rodney had managed to smuggle her to safety. Following the last failed attempt on her life, they'd holed up in an abandoned apartment building outside Oklahoma City for three days while trying to figure out their next move. When Bridget had shown him Lyle's letter and laid out her reasons for wanting to break the code and find the information, Rodney agreed to help her. They'd gone rogue, unable to trust anyone in Rodney's department.

"Rodney, the damage is done. We can't undo the fact that we've cut ties from them. You knew when we took this route your job was in danger. Don't cave now. Not when we're so close. I guarantee if you go back to New York with the information to bring down so many criminals, there's no way your chief will fire you. Hell, you'll probably be hailed as a hero and given the key to the whole freaking city. They might even throw you a parade."

Rodney chuckled. "Christ. You could talk a billionaire into giving up all his money. Never met such a persuasive woman."

She grinned. "Not persuasive. That makes me sound like some crooked politician. I prefer the word *determined*. What we're doing is right, Rodney. You know it is or you never would have gone along with this plan in the first place. It's too late for cold feet."

"And what happens if the hit man shows up here? This isn't like the last two places. They were secluded with preplanned escape routes. We're sitting ducks here. And the worst part is I can't ensure the safety of the other guests in this bed and breakfast. The owners are nice guys. I'd hate to put them in danger."

Rodney had a very good point. They'd come to Saratoga with no plan other than to find the flash drive. Rodney had been in a hurry to get them off the road and to find them a place to stay, so he'd opted for this secluded B&B away from the town rather than the hotel on the main thoroughfare. Even though it was peaceful and off the beaten track, they'd been on their own for too many months, and it was hard not to feel exposed in the relatively full B&B. Just their luck, they'd chosen Valentine's weekend to go it alone. They were surrounded by lovers on romantic getaways.

"We'll just have to be on our guard."

Rodney raised an eyebrow. "And how will that be different from any other day these past six months?"

She laughed. "Why don't you see if the owners will let you use their computer? Maybe you can find a secluded cabin somewhere around here that we can rent for cheap."

"Cheap being the operative term."

They'd cleaned out both of their bank accounts just before hopping on a bus from Oklahoma to Wyoming. Without the protection of the police department, money was going to be tight. Neither of them dared to use their credit cards.

Rodney rose. "I'd rather walk the perimeter of the property again. Try to map out some sort of plan in case the bad guys show up. Why don't you do the cabin research?"

"You mean I can leave the room?" She'd expected Rodney

to keep her under lock and key in the tiny room, and while she wouldn't complain, she didn't relish the boredom that would ensue.

"Well..." he hedged.

She stood quickly before he could change his mind. "This sounds like a good plan. It will be too suspicious if I stay in this room. Better if we act normal." She gave Rodney a quick kiss on his cheek. With his short black hair and light brown skin, he was the poster child for biracial beauty. Handsome as sin with a body to die for, he was also completely, one hundred percent out of the closet.

Another loss for our side, Bridget thought when Rodney added a strong hug to her kiss. Rodney had confided one evening several months ago that his sexual preferences had come to light shortly before her unfortunate evening in the warehouse. Some of the fellow officers in Rodney's precinct had revealed their true colors as homophobes and roughed him up one night after his shift ended. The asshole officers had been suspended, but the chief had thought it best to put some time and distance between all parties. As a result, Rodney had been assigned "babysitting duty", as he called it. Their first few weeks together had been strained to say the least as Rodney harbored some serious anger over the assignment and Bridget wallowed in grief and guilt over her part in Lyle's death.

The night after the first attempt on her life, they'd started talking rather than avoiding each other. Eventually Bridget's grief lessened and Rodney's anger abated. Since then, there wasn't a thought either of them had that wasn't shared.

"Just don't leave the house, kitten," he cautioned.

"I won't."

"And try not to engage in conversation with anyone. Don't establish eye contact or let anyone see you."

She barely caught herself before she rolled her eyes. "That might be tough when I ask to use a computer."

Rodney shook his head. "This is a mistake. Maybe it would be best if you didn't leave this room."

She grinned at his overprotective nature. "I won't go farther than the sitting room downstairs. I'm researching cabins, remember? Finding us somewhere else to stay. I'll be in and out so quickly no one will remember I was even there."

He sighed. "Don't go on any personal accounts. No checking email or IMs or—"

She held up a hand to silence him. "Preaching to the choir, Officer. Believe me, I know the drill by now."

He reached up and ruffled her hair before turning and heading out the door. Before he crossed the threshold, he issued the same warning he'd been giving her for months. "Be careful, Bridge."

Walking to the dresser, she straightened the hair Rodney had mussed up. Studying her reflection, she realized that, for the first time in a long time, she looked more like her true self. She wondered at the transformation.

For months following Lyle's murder, she'd worn dark circles and a haunted expression. She'd been a stranger even to herself, jumping at every sound, trembling every time the lights went out. Her mother used to despair about her habit of rushing into danger headfirst without a care to the consequences. In the course of ten minutes, that rashness, that faux bravery had been wiped out. It had taken her a long time to get used to the new, far-too-cautious woman she'd become.

The self-assured gleam in her dark brown eyes was gone, replaced instead by wariness. That look no longer seemed strange.

This is the new normal.

Picking up a hair band, she pulled her dark blonde hair into a ponytail. It had grown quite long since she'd left New York.

"That's what happens when you lead a life on the run. No time for the hairdresser," she murmured. Maybe she'd look up hair salons in town while she was searching for a secluded cabin to rent.

That thought was dismissed almost immediately. Money was too tight. She and Rodney had spent nearly two hours last night trying to figure out how long they could exist on their own before they ran out of funds. There were three weeks left before the judge's trial began. They had enough money for perhaps two, if they were thrifty.

Bridget released a long breath and dismissed that worry from her mind. She and Rodney had adopted the "one day at a time" motto the second they left Oklahoma. For today, she had a roof over her head and enough money in her pocket for food. She also felt safe for the first time in months. After the attack on their first safe house, Bridget hadn't had a peaceful moment, constantly looking over her shoulder. She wasn't sure what was so different now, but she knew—to the depth of her soul—that she and Rodney were in a good place. No one in the world knew where they were or how to find them. It felt as if the weight of the world had been lifted from her shoulders for a little while. She intended to enjoy the respite.

Walking into the hallway, she locked the door to her room and descended the wide staircase. Glancing in several of the B&B's common rooms for Todd or Steven, the hotel proprietors, Bridget took a few minutes to study the beautifully restored old home. When they'd arrived yesterday afternoon, Rodney had hustled her to their room immediately, sequestering her there while he checked out the property and secured food for their dinner. It felt good to be free.

She was about to cross the foyer to check the other side of

the house when the front door opened. Her new habit of hide first, ask questions later emerged and she panicked, trying to dodge back the way she'd come. In her haste to escape, her foot caught on the edge of the Oriental rug, and she took a hard tumble.

Four boot-covered feet appeared before her. She felt strong hands on either side reaching down to help her up.

"Sorry," she said, keeping her head down. It was foolish to think anyone in this small, middle-of-nowhere town would know who she was, but Rodney had taught her well in the art of making herself as invisible as possible. She fought to suppress her trembling hands. Her heart was racing a mile a minute. God, why did she have to be frightened of her own shadow? She hated living like this, feeling this way.

"You okay, miss?"

All of Rodney's tutoring went out the window as her nipples pebbled and a slight shiver of arousal wove its way through her body. She lifted her face to see the owner of that deep, sexy-as-hell voice. Identical faces etched with concern greeted her.

She opened her mouth to speak, but no sound emerged. Standing before her were twin Greek gods, kings of the western frontier, complete with rugged, dimpled cheeks, blue eyes that —honest to God—twinkled, and shaggy, made-for-running-her-fingers-through dark brown hair only partially concealed by cowboy hats.

If she'd lived a hundred years ago, she would have felt compelled to fucking swoon. Instead, her twenty-first-century sensibilities took over and she simply muttered, "Holy double wow."

Both men grinned widely at her ridiculous comment. "I take it that means you're not hurt, darlin'."

Her pussy clenched at his term of endearment. Could there

be anything hotter than a gorgeous cowboy calling her *darlin'* with that slight country twang? Briefly she imagined him—hell, who was she fooling, them—whispering it to her while they lay together naked in bed.

She cleared her throat and forced herself to stop staring—and drooling—like a love-struck teenage girl. "I'm fine. Clumsy and embarrassed, but otherwise unscathed."

The hot cowboy on her left chuckled. "Unscathed, huh? Pretty talk. Where are you from?"

"New York," she confided before her brain engaged to scream a warning. Jesus. Rodney should have locked her in the room. She was going to blow their cover in under thirty seconds, and all because of a couple good-looking men. Stupidity due to horniness was not something her cop friend would forgive easily.

"City girl," the other cowboy said, though his tone indicated interest more than disdain.

She nodded, determined to keep her mouth shut before any more little tidbits—like the fact she was hiding out from a corrupt judge—fell from her desperate-to-taste-the-cowboys lips.

"I take it you're one of the guests staying here?" her hot cowboy number one asked.

She paused, decided the question was harmless and nodded once more.

"So what brings a city girl to our neck of the woods?" This question was posed by hot cowboy number two.

She and Rodney had sketched out a rough explanation for their visit with the intention of refining it this morning. Now, it appeared she would have to fly by the seat of her pants. "I'm here with my half-brother." Shit, five words in and she was already straying from the script. She and Rodney had agreed to pose as a couple, but for some reason, she didn't want these two men to think she was in a relationship.

That thought led to a major internal eye-roll.

Right, Bridget, like you have so much time to try to hook up with a cowboy—or two.

"Vacation or business?"

"Vacation," she said. "I've always wanted to try my hand at being a cowgirl." Where the fuck had that come from? She'd never considered such a thing in her life until laying eyes on these two Wonders of the Western World.

"Well, now. If you need some help with that, Matt and I are pretty good teachers."

Matt. Cowboy number one had a name.

"You teach a lot of cowgirls the ropes, do you?" she asked with a lilt in her voice. Christ, could her flirting be any more obvious? Why not post a sign on her forehead that said, *Hasn't been laid in a year.*

Matt's smile grew, his dimples deepening. A girl could fall into those bottomless caverns on his chiseled face and never be found again. She could think of worse places to get lost. "My brothers and I own the ranch next door. We train horses, give riding lessons. Stuff like that. We'd be more than happy to help you give that cowgirl lifestyle a whirl if you're interested. We'll even supply the rope if that's what you fancy."

Her brain went straight to the gutter and she had trouble focusing after *riding lessons.*

She recalled a song she and Rodney had heard on the radio while holed up in Oklahoma. The chorus of the song told listeners to save a horse and ride a cowboy. They'd laughed their asses off as Rodney had twirled her around the small kitchen in a ridiculous city-folk attempt at Texas two-stepping.

"Hey, there you guys are." Todd, one of the owners of the

B&B, appeared from a back hallway. Bridget had only seen him briefly the night before. "I was starting to worry."

"We got sidetracked by a pretty lady," Matt said, winking at her.

She wasn't sure how that simple gesture, which would have seemed somewhat creepy in the city, could be so charming here. Her core temperature rose another notch.

Todd joined their small group and held out his hand to her. "I'm afraid I didn't get to introduce myself to you properly last night." He turned to the cowboys to explain. "Bridget and her companion appeared in the midst of the kitchen fire."

She hated to say how much that fire ordeal had thrilled Rodney to no end. He'd considered their less-than-noteworthy arrival the first bit of good fortune after several months of shitty luck and declared no one would even remember they were there. She was quickly destroying that luck. She was supposed to be invisible, not engaging in a conversation with three men, two of whom hadn't taken their eyes off her since entering the house. She struggled to regret that, but it was turning her on too much. It was a bit disconcerting to discover her libido outranked her sense of self-preservation.

"Bridget Carson," she said, quickly recalling the fake name Rodney had used last night when they checked in.

"I'm Todd Branner, Steven's other half. He was the tall, terribly handsome fellow who checked you in last night."

Bridget nodded, smiling at Todd's description of his boyfriend.

"I'm sorry I couldn't greet you, but our ancient stove finally gave up the ghost in grand style. Nothing like going out in a blaze of glory."

"So I heard. I'm relieved no one was hurt and there was no serious damage," she said.

Todd shrugged. "Only damage was to my Baked Alaska,

which was a crime of epic proportion. Besides, I always keep a fire extinguisher in the kitchen for Steven's night to cook."

"I heard that," Steven said, rounding the corner.

"Busted," Todd joked.

They all laughed. Bridget felt the tension that hadn't left her body in months begin to loosen. It felt good to be back in the land of the living, among people whose biggest concerns were issues at work and burned dinners.

The front door opened and her fears reappeared in an instant. It took all the strength in her body not to move behind the two large cowboys. They could shield her from the newest arrival easily with plenty of bulky muscles to spare.

Rodney entered and took in the scene in silence. She saw surprise, annoyance and anger cross his features in the span of a single second.

"There's my baby brother," she said with forced cheerfulness, praying Rodney would pick up her cues and roll with them. She'd shot their cover story to hell.

"Hey, sis." Rodney appeared lighthearted, but his eyes were piercing hers. He wasn't happy to find her out in the open with half the neighborhood in attendance. "I thought you had a headache."

He was giving her a quick out. She needed it. "Just looking for some aspirin."

"Oh," Todd piped up. "You should have said something. Didn't mean to keep you standing around. I have a big bottle in the kitchen. Let me go grab it."

Matt turned to Rodney, reaching out for a handshake. "I'm Matt James and this is my brother, Mark. We live next door."

At last, a name for cowboy number two. Matt and Mark James.

Bridget moved toward Rodney, who gave her a questioning look, uncertain what to say to these strangers. Filling in the blanks for him, she took over the introductions. "This is my half-brother, Rodney Carson. And I'm Bridget, which you already know."

"You're both from New York City?" Mark asked.

Rodney's piercing gaze shot daggers in her direction, but she pointedly ignored him. "Yep. We're both city slickers."

Matt glanced her way once more. "If you're serious about the cowgirl lessons, Bridget, you're welcome to come over to the James Ranch. We'll have you roping and riding in no time."

She nodded noncommittally. "Thanks. That's a nice offer."

"Here we are." Todd handed her two aspirin and a glass of water.

Rodney placed a firm hand on her lower back. For a minute, she expected him to pinch her in true sibling style. She could tell he was mad enough to. "I think maybe you should go back upstairs, Bridget, so you can lie down."

"Okay." Great, she wasn't looking forward to the coming eruption. She'd never seen Rodney lose his temper, but she could tell he was on the verge of it at the moment.

Matt glanced at the kitchen door. "Guess we've put off the backbreaking reason we're here long enough."

"Backbreaking?" she asked.

"Matt and Mark came over to help us drag out the oven from hell. The replacement will be delivered this afternoon and I wanted a chance to clean up the mess. Little washing and touch-up painting and we should be right as rain. Dinner may be a bit late though, and I'm afraid lunch is just going to be cold-cut sandwiches."

"No problem," Rodney said smoothly. "Need a hand with the stove?"

Matt slapped Rodney on the back in a friendly manner. "Hell yeah. That fucker is ancient. Probably weighs a ton."

Rodney turned to her. "Go on up, Bridge. I'll be there in a little while. Once we've sorted stuff out in the kitchen."

No doubt her protector intended to minimize the damage she'd done in terms of compromising their cover story. Climbing the stairs, she tried to summon a bit of guilt for messing things up. For some reason, she couldn't do it. Foolish or not, she felt safe here. Her gut told her she could trust these people. It had been a long time since she'd experienced that. It gave her hope for the future. Maybe she wouldn't always be frightened. Maybe the old Bridget was still inside, lurking, waiting for the right time to reemerge.

Please let that be true.

She had reached the door to her room when she recalled Matt's tempting offer. She smiled and let herself pretend she really was on vacation. She may be a city girl, but she had no doubt she was more than ready to saddle up and ride with those cowboys. She could just imagine all the juicy daydreams she could conjure up in regards to the James brothers.

Maybe her time spent in this room wouldn't be so boring after all.

For the first time in a long time, the downhill spiral of her life appeared to be changing direction. Yee haw.

CHAPTER TWO

The next morning, Bridget sat down for breakfast in the B&B's dining room. As she'd expected, Rodney had given her an ass-chewing of epic proportions the previous afternoon. It was well deserved, but she was still smarting a bit from it.

The only reason she had been allowed to come back out in public was because Rodney had determined Todd, Steven and the hunky twin cowboys were decent guys who didn't have a clue who she and Rodney really were. Besides, as he'd said, the damage was done. There were now witnesses who could identify them to anyone who came looking. The four men would become suspicious if she suddenly took to hiding in the room. He'd decided it would be better if they went about their business as if everything were normal. However, he stressed she wasn't allowed to set one foot outside the inn.

So much for her riding lessons dream.

Because of the mess she'd made, Rodney's new goal was to find a secluded cabin to rent in the woods near Saratoga while they tried to piece out the clues in the remainder of the letter.

Much to her chagrin, they would have to leave the B&B immediately. Bridget was loath to return to the solitary existence that had become her normal life the past few months. While Rodney was nice company, she hadn't realized how much she'd missed people until yesterday's flirtatious conversation with Matt and Mark. She was tired of being alone and lonely.

Guilt pierced her heart with that thought. Lyle's face as he lay dead on the cold warehouse floor flashed before her eyes. She was doing this for him. She'd made him a promise that night. Three more weeks. Twenty-one days until she could see justice served. She owed that to Lyle. Until then, it was too selfish to wish for anything else.

Once she'd repaid that debt, she'd figure out a way to return to her own life. She just prayed she could find it again.

"That's not a very happy face."

Bridget jumped, nearly spilling the glass of water Todd had put in front of her only a few minutes earlier. "Oh God!"

"Damn. Sorry. Didn't mean to scare you." Quick hands reached out to catch the water.

Speak of the devils. Bridget glanced up to find Matt and Mark looking down at her.

"Hey," she said, the racing of her heart no longer based on fear. The sight of the cowboys sent her body into overdrive. "What are you guys doing here?"

Mark removed his hat, running his hand through his hair. "Todd offered us a big breakfast as a thank you for moving the oven. We don't turn down one of his western omelets."

"They're that good?"

Matt followed his brother's lead, removing his hat as well. "Best in the state. Sorry about scaring you. Thought you saw us walk in."

She shrugged off her unwanted fears, forcing a lie from her lips. "I was daydreaming."

"Must have been some dream to take you so far away. Didn't look like a particularly nice one either," Mark said.

She used to believe nightmares were only for sleeping. However, after spending the past six months wide awake in the midst of a horrible dream, she now knew better.

She forced the unpleasant thought from her mind and painted on a smile. For now, she was exactly where she wanted to be—surrounded by nice people in a place that felt safe and homey. She'd focus on that instead. She gestured at the empty seats across from her. "Would you like to join me?"

Mark grinned. "Thought you'd never ask."

She rubbed her hands on her lap as they each claimed a chair at the table. Sweaty palms? Was it due to anxiety from her earlier concerns or girlish nervousness over being so close to the James twins? Rodney would kill her for pushing her luck, but she was running perilously low on common sense or care these days.

The months since Lyle's shooting had passed in one long blur of constant pain, limitless fatigue and never-ending motion. She was tired of being suspicious of everyone.

Prior to Lyle's murder, she'd never known a stranger. She'd won *friendliest* in her high school yearbook's Who's Who, and she missed talking to people, hanging out with friends, dating. Most of all, she really missed sex. Not that she was promiscuous, but criminy, it had been nearly a year since she'd even kissed a member of the opposite sex. She wasn't cut out for a chaste lifestyle.

On top of the everlasting horniness, it was exhausting to look at everyone as the enemy. She hated walking into a room and wondering if someone there was plotting her death. There was something comfortable about the handsome twins that told her she could trust them.

Matt leaned back in his seat, stretching his long legs out beneath the table. His foot accidentally rubbed against hers. She had to fight to keep her libido at bay. "How's your headache?"

She frowned for a moment, wondering what he was talking about. Then she recalled Rodney's lie. "Oh, it's fine. All better."

Todd came out of the kitchen and made a beeline for their table. "I was starting to wonder if you guys were going to take me up on my omelet offer."

"We had a bit of trouble with one of the horses this morning. One of the Appaloosas threw a shoe. It set us back a bit of time," Mark replied.

"Well, it's no problem. I've still got my new stove fired up and hot. I know what you guys want. What about you, Bridget?"

"I'll just have a bowl of cereal." She wasn't a hundred percent sure breakfast was included in the price of the stay.

Matt shook his head. "Cereal? No wonder you're so skinny. She'll have an omelet too. On us."

"Oh, you don't have to—"

Mark reached across the table and patted her hand. "We're not letting you leave Wyoming without trying this omelet."

She laughed. "Well, in that case, I suppose I'd better relent."

Todd poured each of them a cup of coffee before heading back to the kitchen. She'd postponed coming down for breakfast, thinking she could avoid the rush. She thought her plan had worked as she'd had the whole place to herself for a few minutes. Funny, how the space had seemed large and cold when she'd been alone with only her sad memories. Now, with the James twins flanking her, the room seemed pleasantly crowded and decidedly warmer. For the first time in a very long time, fate was smiling on her.

Mark leaned over and put his cowboy hat on the vacant table next to them. "Did you give any thought to our offer for riding lessons?"

She tried to find a way to put them off without seeming rude. There was simply no way she could afford to pay for lessons even if Rodney agreed to it, which he wouldn't. He'd gone off early this morning to find them somewhere else to stay, and he'd been very firm in his instructions that she "lay low". There was a good chance he'd succeed in securing them a new hiding spot, and by afternoon, they'd be crawling into some other lonely hole.

"I have a confession," she said. Both men were looking at her intently. She was entranced by their similarities. They were mirror images of each other. It was almost unnerving.

Matt grinned. She'd noticed yesterday that Matt had a slight cleft in his chin his brother didn't share. It was her only clue in telling them apart. "They say confession is good for the soul."

"There's a difference between wanting something and doing something." She almost winced as she said the words. She wanted something—two somethings—but there was no way she could do anything about that desire. Mainly because she was running for her life, and secondly, who wanted two men... at the same time? It was ludicrous. "While the idea of being a cowgirl sounds like fun, I'm deathly afraid of horses."

The words weren't exactly a lie. She'd nearly been run down by a horse-drawn carriage in Central Park as a child. The experience had stuck with her, and since then she'd given those carts, as well as police horses, a very wide berth.

Mark shook his head in disbelief. "What? How can you be

afraid of horses? They're the most loving, gentle creatures on earth."

She shrugged. "They're huge, attract flies, and their eyes are on the sides of their heads. I find that very unnerving."

Matt burst into laughter. "I'm not sure I've ever heard that excuse for a fear of horses, but you've got a point."

Mark gave his brother a warning glance that was more amused than annoyed. "Don't encourage her. She shouldn't be afraid of horses."

Bridget leaned closer. "I'm not sure it's fear as much as I'm simply not familiar with them. The only horses I've ever seen were city creatures—police horses or ones hooked to carriages. The whole concept of getting up on one of those things isn't a comfortable concept to me. I mean, if you want to know how to get from midtown to Canal Street on the subway, I'm your girl. You want to know the quickest route from point A to point B so the taxi driver doesn't rip you off, ask me. Put me on a horse and I wouldn't even know how to make the thing go. It's not like you can put money in the slot and have it take off."

Matt chuckled. "Girl, you haven't lived until you've ridden a horse."

"I'm fine with the subway and taxis, thank you very much. I prefer my modes of transportation to have wheels, not legs."

Todd emerged from the kitchen carrying three large platters. Bridget's eyes widened at the sheer volume of food on her plate. "You expect me to eat all of that?" There were two pieces of thick toast slathered in butter, an omelet the size of her pillow, and at least five pounds of potatoes, whipped up hash brown style with green peppers and onions.

Since going rogue with Rodney, they'd existed on peanut butter sandwiches and cereal. Her mouth watered and her stomach growled.

"Don't worry, sweetheart," Matt said, snatching a slice of

toast of her plate. "We'll help you finish whatever you can't eat."

She reached over and grabbed a piece of his toast to replace hers. "Don't worry about me. We city girls know how to eat."

Mark picked up his fork and lifted an eyebrow. "I find that hard to believe. You're too skinny to be that good an eater."

"You know, that's the second time you boys have called me skinny. I'm starting to feel like that's an insult."

Matt's gaze drifted down her body, away from her face. "Believe me, there's no insult intended." His eyes lifted and met hers once more. "You're damn easy on the eyes."

She blushed at his compliment. There was something so open, so honest about both men that she found it hard to resist them. She tried to dismiss the thought from her mind because she certainly wasn't going to have a chance to get to know either of them better.

Conversation slowed as the three of them dug in to their enormous breakfasts. She had to hand it to the twins. It was, by far, the best omelet she'd ever had, and for the first time in a long time, she let herself enjoy a meal. Lately, eating had become something she had to do to survive. Back in New York, she'd loved going to different restaurants, trying different things. She missed the salad at Carmine's and the little Thai place in Hell's Kitchen.

"Damn, Mark, doesn't look like we're going to get to help her clean her plate after all," Matt joked.

Glancing down, Bridget realized she'd polished off all of the eggs and was almost finished with the hash browns. "I can't believe I ate all that, or how good it was."

Mark wiped his mouth with his napkin and put it back in his lap. "You looked like you hadn't eaten in a year. I'm glad you enjoyed it."

"I did. I can see why you'd ask for that as payment for work. Todd's an amazing cook."

Matt put his fork down and leaned back in his chair, looking relaxed and well fed. "We come over here quite a bit for breakfast and lunch. Used to be four bachelors living in our house. Cooking wasn't something we had a lot of time for."

Bridget leaned forward and rested her arms on the table. She was genuinely curious to learn more about them. "Four bachelors?"

Mark joined in the conversation. "Matt and I live with our older brother, Caleb, and our kid brother, Jacob. Caleb's a doctor at the local hospital, so he works some screwed-up hours. Jacob does a lot of the cooking, but he's what you might call a free spirit, so counting on him for vittles is risky. Whenever he gets involved in a project—whether it's an article he's writing or something for his college class—it can be days before he looks up."

Bridget's ears perked up. "Article?" She missed her writing more than she could say.

Matt nodded. "Yep. Kid loves to write. He freelances for a couple of magazines and newspapers. Mainly stories about gay rights, living life outside the closet, stuff like that."

"Your brother is gay?"

Mark stiffened up slightly and she backtracked quickly, afraid she'd offended him. "I wasn't asking to pry or to insinuate anything is wrong with that. Fact is, Rodney is gay too. I was thinking maybe we should introduce them."

Matt laughed. "You want to hook our brothers up?"

Bridget grinned. "No...well, maybe."

If Rodney was feeling as lonely and horny as she was these days, maybe a hot hookup with a cowboy would take the edge off. Lately, Rodney had been wound up tighter than a spring. Not that she blamed him. In all likelihood, he'd lost his job at the police station the day he'd stepped off the radar with her. His future was as uncertain as hers at the moment. "Is your younger brother as hot as you two?"

Bridget wasn't sure where the words had come from, but the deadly dimples reappeared on both of the men's faces as their smiles grew.

Mark leaned toward her, taking her hand in his. She hoped he couldn't feel the sudden trembling there. "You think we're hot?"

Both of them had moved closer, and she had to press her legs together to still the sudden twinge in her pussy.

Matt grasped her other hand. "Who's hotter—me or Mark?"

She burst into laughter as she studied their mirrored images. Mark rolled his eyes at his brother's inane comment. Then she realized there were other definite differences besides the cleft chin. As she learned more about them, they suddenly didn't seem so similar.

Matt was clearly the fun-loving one with a great sense of humor. There was a wicked twinkle in his eyes that guaranteed he was always up for a good time. In contrast, Mark seemed the epitome of a country gentleman: kind, more serious. She had no doubt he was the type of guy who opened doors for women and insisted on picking up the tab.

"I plead the Fifth on that question. So what did you mean when you said it *used* to be four bachelors? Did someone move out?"

Mark shook his head. "Nope, someone moved in."

Bridget's heart skipped a beat. Did one of them have a girlfriend? She'd never considered they may already have significant others. "Oh?"

Matt offered the explanation. "Caleb got himself a girlfriend, Jessie. We're expecting him to pop the question any day now."

She smiled, foolishly relieved. "Nice. You like her?"

"Jessie?" Mark asked. "Oh, heck yeah. She's a helluva lady. Been through a rough patch this past year. She and Caleb deserve a little happiness."

Bridget could relate to tough years. "So she'll live at the ranch with all of you?"

Matt shook his head. "Nah. I figure they'll want to start a family pretty soon. Since Mark and I run the ranch, it's hard for us to move out. We need to be close to the stables. Caleb mentioned building his own house closer to the main road to make it easier for him during the winter when he's on call. We have a fairly long driveway, and after it snows, it takes some effort to plow it so he can get out."

She was used to snowy winters in New York. It was one of the things she'd missed this year. She and Rodney had spent a great deal of the last few months hopping from safe house to safe house in the south. They'd celebrated Christmas in Phoenix and the temperature had been in the eighties that day. At the time, she'd considered the lack of snow a blessing. With the heat and unfamiliar surroundings, she could pretend it wasn't Christmas, and it kept her homesickness at bay.

"Sounds like you own quite a bit of property."

Mark nodded. "We do okay. Our family's lived in this area for several generations. It's home."

"It must be nice to have such solid roots. I grew up in the city, but my parents were originally from Jersey."

"You have any other brothers or sisters besides Rodney?" Matt asked.

Bridget sucked in a sharp gasp of air. It had been on the tip of her tongue to say she was an only child. She knew she was treading on thin ice, tempting fate by talking to them, but Matt and Mark were so easy to be with, they made her forget what a fucking mess her life was at the present. "No. It's just him and me."

Mark frowned. "No parents?"

She shook her head because it was easier than making up another long story she'd likely screw up later. She hated lying to them. Her folks were alive and well and retired in Hoboken. She was also certain her mother hadn't slept a wink since Bridget had gone into protective custody. Another pound of guilt she'd had to carry around. Her heart ached at the thought, and for one very foolish moment, she wanted to confess the truth to Matt and Mark, to tell them about Lyle, the judge, the murder. She had nearly convinced herself it was a good idea to unload all her burdens on their very capable, strapping shoulders and had even opened her mouth to speak the words when fate stepped in.

"Hey, Bridget. I wondered where you were."

Rodney walked up to the table. He didn't seem as annoyed to find her out and about today as he was yesterday. She suspected that was because he'd spent some time getting to know the James brothers. He'd confided last night this seemed like a safe place and the people were genuinely nice.

Maybe she'd talk Rodney into telling Matt and Mark about their plight. They seemed like the kind of men who'd be willing to help.

She smiled and held out her hands. "Looks like you found me. Matt and Mark treated me to the best omelet in, hmmm, I'm trying to remember." She looked at Matt. "Did you say in the state or in the world?"

"Universe," Matt replied, adding to her joke.

"Gotcha, the best omelet in the universe," she finished. When Rodney looked at her empty plate with an expression of hunger and jealousy, she felt a pang of guilt for not saving him half. "I should have saved some for you."

He shrugged good-naturedly. "That's okay. I'll grab something later."

"Actually," Todd said, coming out of the kitchen with a full plate, "I've kept this warm in the oven, hoping you'd come back soon." He placed the dish at an empty spot at the table and gestured for Rodney to sit down. "This is on the house, to say thank you for helping us move the dinosaur stove out of the kitchen yesterday."

Rodney quickly claimed the chair, not remembering to speak until he'd shoveled in two enormous mouthfuls. "Thanks."

Matt laughed. "I can tell you two are related. Never seen two people go after a plate of food with the same level of enthusiasm."

Mark turned to Rodney. "We were just trying to convince your sister to come over to the James Ranch for riding lessons."

Rodney swallowed quickly. "Riding lessons? I don't think we'll have time for that. We're leaving soon."

"Oh, darn," Todd said. "I thought Steven said you'd be here through the week."

"That was the original plan," Rodney said, "but now I'm not sure we're going to be able to stay that long."

Bridget tried to ignore the sudden ache she felt at the idea of picking up and moving on yet again. Hanging out with the twins had been a nice change after months of monotony. It had been so long since she'd allowed herself to let herself feel pure, simple attraction. Lyle's murder had skewed her ability to judge people and their motives and while she longed to accept Matt and Mark's offer of friendship, fear held her back.

"Well, you have to stay through tonight at least. I'm making a Valentine's Day feast. We thought we'd follow that up with dessert and games," Todd offered.

Bridget glanced Rodney's way, trying to determine exactly how fast he wanted to move. She couldn't tell from his facial expression if he'd even found them somewhere new to hide.

Rodney nodded. "That sounds great. We wouldn't leave until tomorrow or the day after at the earliest."

Bridget released a slow breath. One more night. She looked at the twins. "Will you two be here?"

Matt gave her a wickedly sexy grin. "You looking for a Valentine, Bridget? Because if so, I'm your man."

Mark rolled his eyes. "Did you ever consider that she might be interested in a real man, rather than a guy who acts as old as his shoe size? What size are your feet again? Eleven?"

Matt scooted his chair closer and grasped her hand. "I doubt she's looking for some boring stick in the mud. Be my Valentine, Bridget, and I'll show you a good time."

Her face flushed as she envisioned how good that time could really be. She needed to get a grip. "You two are incorrigible. I'm not really in the market for a Valentine, so how about if I just promise to keep you in mind if that changes?"

"You got a boyfriend?" Mark asked.

She shook her head. "No, that's not it."

Matt squeezed her hand. "Then I've still got a chance."

She laughed. "Maybe you didn't hear my brother, Rodney. We're leaving soon."

Mark shrugged as if unconcerned. "Maybe we can convince you to stay longer."

It would take very little for either man to convince her to stay. They looked at her with an unnerving hunger in their gazes. Her body was responding to it—hook, line and sinker.

She considered herself passably pretty, though certainly not what anyone would call a raving beauty. She didn't wear makeup and usually wore her long hair pulled back. In New York, she dressed in more conservative, professional attire at work. However, since arriving in Wyoming, she hadn't been out of blue jeans.

She'd had her fair share of dates and even lovers, but none of them had ever looked at her like Matt and Mark were looking her at that moment. Worst of all was the fact she was attracted to *both* of them. What the hell was she supposed to do with that unnatural feeling? If they stuck around and she indulged in a little play, she'd have to choose. For the life of her, she couldn't decide which James brother appealed to her more.

Rodney saved her from having to respond. "You're welcome to try to convince her, but it won't work. We really do need to leave."

Todd began clearing away the dirty dishes. "I hope nothing bad has come up to disrupt your vacation."

Rodney shook his head. "No. Just some things we need to take care of at home."

All of them rose from the table. The James twins picked up their hats and put them back on. She had never realized how sexy the cowboy look truly was until she'd met these two men who wore it so damn well.

"Well, I guess Matt and I should head back to the ranch. We'll be back later for dinner. Save me a seat next to you, Bridget."

Matt wrapped his arms around her shoulders and leaned down to whisper in her ear. "Save the other side for me."

She wasn't sure if she'd truly heard the sexy innuendo in his tone or if it was wishful thinking on her part.

Her power of speech temporarily left her, so she merely nodded.

"See you later, Bridget," Matt added, placing a friendly kiss on her cheek.

Mark shook Rodney's hand and the two of them left as Todd returned to the kitchen.

Rodney glanced around the room to make sure they were alone. "Damn. Looks like you've made quite an impression on those guys. Might be better if we left now. They're both eyeballing you like you're the prime rib at a banquet."

She grinned at his analogy, but didn't bother to deny the truth of it. She didn't even want to deny it. It felt too good. Two of the hottest men she'd ever laid eyes on were attracted to her. She was going to hold on to this high for as long as it lasted. Given her current position, it didn't appear she'd manage to maintain it for longer than a day.

"Did you find somewhere for us to stay?" she asked.

Rodney shook his head. "I found a couple possibilities—cabins in pretty secluded areas, but the issue is going to be money. I asked Steven if I could borrow his truck to do a little exploring. I'm just about to head out to take a look at them."

"Why bother if money is going to be an issue?" Bridget wanted to stay at the B&B. A city girl at heart, she took comfort in having more people around. Hiding out in quiet cabins unnerved her. She'd had no idea how loud nature was, how much squirrels scampering in leaves could sound like a villain with a gun sneaking up behind her.

"You're not going to like this, but I'm checking to see if we could hole up in one without going through the realtor. I got the impression from the rental website that neither of these places gets used much in the winter. Weather tends to be an issue."

She looked at Rodney with amazement. He was the most honest, law-abiding person she'd ever met. "You're going to break in?"

"Bridget. We're low on money and running out of options. The trial starts in three weeks. We just have to hang in there that long. I'll call my partner a couple days before we need to return, explain why we took off and ask him to secure us transportation back to the city."

"We came here to try to find the information Lyle had on the judge. We can't exactly do that if we're stuck on some mountainside, squatting in someone else's house."

"Yeah, about that." Rodney took Lyle's letter from his pocket. "I was playing around with this earlier and I want to show you something."

They reclaimed their seats at the table. Bridget could hear Todd cleaning up in the kitchen, singing along loudly with the radio. She grinned at his off-key accompaniment to Lady Gaga's "Born This Way". She wasn't sure where the rest of the guests had gone, but aside from his performance, the house was relatively quiet.

Rodney pointed out the part of the code they'd already broken. "So if the first sentence is every sixth word, then we're left with Sara and toga. *Bridget, remember in college when Sara got totally trashed at the toga party.* If you count six more words after toga, it takes us five words into the next sentence."

Bridget nodded. "We've done that. *Silly girl swore to God and then on her mother's grave she would give up alcohol.* The next word after toga is God, but counting out six more words leaves us grave. God's grave."

She'd repeated that phrase a million times in her head. They'd searched the only churchyard cemetery within the city limits the moment they set foot off the bus. They'd been so certain they would find a clue. Instead, they'd come up with nothing.

"What if it's not every sixth word? What if in the second sentence it's every fifth?" Rodney asked.

She glanced at the paper and re-counted. "Godmother's? Oh my God. What if it is?"

"Do you know if Lyle had a godmother? Who she was?"

Bridget closed her eyes, forcing her memories of Lyle to the foreground. She should have been a better friend. She didn't have a clue. She racked her brain trying to remember, but nothing came to her.

"Fuck," she finally admitted. "I have no idea."

Rodney only looked slightly disappointed. "So go five more words over and you get the word *up*. I have no idea what that means, but count five to the next sentence and I think Lyle gave us a clue about that the godmother."

Bridget looked at the third sentence. "Ellen."

Rodney nodded. "Ring any bells?"

She shook her head. "No, but I suppose we could ask around. What do you think the chances are his godmother has his last name—Turner?"

"Slim to none," Rodney replied. "And the rest of that sentence doesn't seem to offer up a surname. I tried highlighting every fourth word, thinking maybe it was a countdown code, but that doesn't seem to work either."

Bridget continued reading silently. *And then Ellen told her that the key was "drink in moderation first."* "Every fourth word leaves us with *the* and *in*. Those are pointless."

"Yeah. I know. And then the last line is still hanging out there."

She reread the final sentence of the missive. *Always loved that wealth of unhelpful, impractical information. Call me later, Lyle.* "What if we just pull out words that look important?" she suggested.

Rodney sighed. "We've tried that, remember? Too many words. Too many variables. Plus we still have that damn *up* hanging out there unexplained, which could mean my godmother Ellen theory is shot to hell."

"We're closer now."

Rodney leaned back in his seat. "Yeah. I guess. But I have to tell you, if Lyle weren't already dead, I'd probably kill him for leaving us such shitty clues."

Bridget laughed. "You'd have to get in line. Why he thought I could figure this out is beyond me. He must've tried to explain how to work sudoku puzzles to me a thousand times, but I never got it."

"We still have some time. There's three weeks until the trial. We'll just keep plugging along until then. At that point, we're going back to New York—with or without the flash drive. I'm going to grab the keys to Steven's truck and go check out the cabins."

"You know, if the cabins don't work out, we could always just stay here. We have enough money to cover us for most of the three weeks if we're careful. It feels safe here."

Rodney gave her a knowing grin. "You can't kid a kidder, Bridge. Safety has nothing to do with it. There are two fucking gorgeous cowboys here, and you're hot to get into their sexy-as-shit, too-tight jeans."

She narrowed her eyes. Apparently, she hadn't been the only one checking out the James brothers' Levis. "Yeah, well, just remember they're my cowboys, hot stuff. You can look, but no touching."

"Believe me, those two don't play for my team."

She laughed. It had become a pass-the-time game on the bus trip from Oklahoma to Saratoga for her and Rodney to decide whose sexual-orientation team their fellow travelers played for. "Maybe not, but their brother does."

Rodney closed his eyes and rubbed his temple. "Christ, kitten. We're running for our lives here. We don't have time to get laid."

She stuck out her lower lip in playful pout. "All I'm asking for is a few more days. If we really are looking for a woman named Ellen, we'd have a better chance finding her if we're closer to town. Besides, imagine if their younger brother is as hot as them. You've gotta be feeling the effects of this forced abstinence as much as me."

"Here comes the persuasion again," Rodney muttered. "Fine, Bridget. I'll admit it. I'm horny as shit and tired of sharing a room with you. It's not like I can take care of my own needs with you snoring across the bedroom."

"I don't snore."

"But I'm not about to jeopardize your life or mine for a quick screw with a cowboy I'll likely never see again after we leave here. We're so close to end, Bridget. Let's don't fuck it up now."

He was one hundred and twenty percent right. Damn him. "And you say I'm the persuasive one. Fine. I'm focused again. Promise."

He reached out and patted her on the shoulder. The gesture was meant to comfort her. She wanted to shrug it off, rail at him, but she couldn't. He understood her frustrations because he shared them. It wasn't fair for her to blame him for something that was ultimately her fault. Would Lyle still be alive today if she hadn't suggested he share the information he'd uncovered with her? If she hadn't planted the seed that they break the news by splashing it all across the front page of the newspaper? If she'd insisted that they call the cops first?

Rodney refolded Lyle's letter and put it back in his pocket as he stood. "Why don't you expand on your friendship with Todd? See if you can't find a way to figure out who this Ellen might be."

She forced her concern aside at Rodney's worried glance. She gave him a jaunty salute. "Aye aye, Captain."

He laughed, fooled by her feigned attempt at lightheartedness. "I won't be gone long. Don't get in to any trouble."

"I won't."

She watched him leave but made no move to rise. She was suddenly feeling very tired.

Three more weeks and the running would stop.

Three more weeks and she could return to her normal life. That thought didn't bring her as much comfort as it used to. She wasn't the same woman who'd escaped New York in the middle of the night. That woman was driven, obsessed with climbing the ladder of success. That woman let her best friend sacrifice his life simply to provide her with information for a lousy newspaper article.

That woman didn't exist anymore. Her life had been snuffed out the instant the judge's bullet pierced Lyle's flesh.

Three weeks.

Then what?

Bridget waved her hands madly, trying not to let her frustration with her charades partners show. She'd always been far too competitive for her own good, never quite mastering the idea of losing with grace. As Rodney, Todd and Stephen continued to yell out inane, stupid, *wrong* answers, she could see the James brothers grinning gleefully as the clock continued to tick.

"Disco!" Todd yelled and Bridget rolled her eyes. Losing at charades was not going to make for a fun night.

She looked at Rodney in desperation, but he only gave her a quick, sympathetic grin and shrugged, clueless to even venture a guess at her gestures. She couldn't be mad at him for sucking at charades. Even though, they were only posing at siblings, she couldn't love him more even if he were her true brother. He'd saved her life countless times, while consoling her through the guilt and anguish associated with Lyle's death. He got a bye. Her other two partners, however, did not.

"*Saturday Night Fever!*" Stephen added. "John Travolta."

"Jesus," she muttered.

"No talking," Matt chastised as Mark called, "Time."

"Tidal wave," she said, gesturing that she clearly thought her actions had made that clear.

"Tidal wave?" Todd asked. "How the hell was all this—" he starting waving his hands around, and she narrowed her eyes at his imitation, "—supposed to be a tidal wave?"

"I guess I could sort of see it," Stephen conceded. "Now that you say it."

Bridget collapsed into the nearest chair, throwing her hands up in exasperation, while everyone laughed.

She'd met the youngest James brother, Jacob, at dinner, and Bridget suspected Rodney was now regretting his assertion that they put a leash on their libidos. There was clearly some chemistry between the two men.

Jacob grinned. "Well, that was the tiebreaker, and the James boys have successfully trumped you guys again. That's three games to your two."

They'd begun the evening playing a guys-versus-girls match with other guests in the inn, but as more and more people headed up to bed, the teams had shifted.

Bridget grimaced when Mark and Matt rose from the couch in unison.

Before the last match, some competitive trash-talking had started up and she'd foolishly made a side wager with the brothers. Her father had always tried to impart the concept of playing games for sheer enjoyment, but she'd never been able to resist the almighty bet. She rarely played Monopoly, Truth or Dare, or basketball without some sort of extra incentive—typically monetary—to make things interesting. Dad always told her that her "betting ways would bite her in the ass". Though she hadn't always come out on top, she could admit with not a small amount of pride that she won far more often than she lost. Problem with this wager was she didn't regret losing to the James twins at all.

"Well," Matt said, reaching forward to help her rise from her seat. He pulled her toward him—too close for comfort. He whispered in her ear in a voice only she could hear. "Shall we settle up the terms of our wager?"

Mark slapped Todd on the shoulder in a friendly gesture. "Great game. Enjoyed trouncing you again."

"Again?" Bridget asked, taking a step away from the incredible heat of Matt's body. She was used to being the tallest woman in most rooms and often used her height to her advantage in situations where she wanted to intimidate. Matt and Mark eclipsed her five foot eleven frame by almost half a foot. She suddenly found herself in the overshadowed position.

"How many times have we played charades with you guys?" Matt asked as Todd shrugged.

"I don't know," Steven replied. "Maybe ten, twelve times."

"And how many times have we won?"

Todd groaned. "Every time."

"Every time?" Bridget asked. Matt shamelessly winked at her and she knew she'd been bamboozled.

"Who wants coffee?" Stephen asked, clearly unaware of the undercurrents flowing between her and the twins she had every intention of kneeing in the balls the second the opportunity presented itself.

"I'll have some." Jacob stood up. "In fact, I'll make it if you copy down the recipe for that stew you made tonight. Jessie loved it, and I was thinking I could make it for her birthday."

Stephen looked around the room. "Where is Jessie?"

Todd wiggled his eyebrows. "She asked for the key to the guest house. She and Caleb snuck out about forty minutes ago."

Jacob shook his head. "Jeez. I swear, sometimes I think I'm

gonna have to turn the hose on those two before they burn the house down with all those heated looks."

Mark laughed. "I keep waiting for some of that passion to burn out, but it hasn't yet."

"It's getting worse. Who knows? Maybe tonight will be the night he finally pops the question." Matt placed a friendly arm around Bridget's shoulder when she took a step toward the stairs and her room. She'd promised Rodney she'd behave, but that vow was getting pretty damn hard to keep.

She thought she could escape while the men were preoccupied with talk of Jessie and Caleb. She'd met the couple tonight at dinner. Their undeniable love for each other nearly took her breath away. She wasn't sure she'd ever seen such a bond between two people. She had no doubt her parents loved each other, but by the time she was old enough to recognize that emotion, theirs had cooled to the lukewarm companionship evident in most long marriages.

"Goin' somewhere, darlin'?" Mark drawled.

She was well and truly stuck. "Doesn't look like it."

"That's right," Matt agreed. "You made a bet, so it looks like you'll just have to stick around a couple more days to make good on it."

"I wasn't aware that I was working with a handicap taking on Todd and Steven as my partners. You cheated."

Mark chuckled. "Didn't peg you as the type to renege on a bet."

"I'm not going back on my word. I'm simply saying you knew the cards were stacked against me and you still pressed for the wager."

Rodney turned to look at her. "Wager?"

Mark saved her from answering. "Deal was if we won, she'd let us teach her how to ride a horse."

Matt pulled her closer. "We'll start first thing in the morning. Takes a while to get the hang of it though, so y'all might have to put off leaving for a couple days."

She expected Rodney to lose his temper over her foolishness. What she did not expect was for him to shrug as if he didn't have a care in the world. "That's fine. No rush." He glanced at Jacob. "Want some help making that coffee?"

She grinned at her friend's transparent new attitude, especially when he checked out Jacob's ass as they followed Steven and Todd to the kitchen.

She turned around to gloat about the hookup, but Mark held up his hand. "Don't even say it. You were right. A man would have to be blind to miss the sparks flying between those two."

"And you guys are okay with that?" She was surprised to discover two hardcore alpha cowboys living in the heart of the West who weren't squicked out about their brother's homosexuality.

Matt shook his head. "We've known about our brother's sexual preference for a very long time. Had plenty of time to get used to the idea. It's not a life I'd choose for myself—I like boobies too much—but if he's happy, I'm happy."

Bridget laughed. "You like boobies, huh?"

He nodded. "I like your boobies."

She swatted playfully at Matt's arm. "You need to keep your eyes pointed at regions directly north of my boobies." She indicated her face. "There's nothing down here for you," she teased as she pointed at her chest.

Matt let his gaze linger on her chest. "That's where you're wrong, sweetheart. There's plenty down there for me."

Mark rolled his eyes. Taking Bridget's arm, he led her to the sofa, where they sat down together. "Ignore my brother. He's missing a filter or two and usually says completely inappropriate things as a result."

She moved closer to Mark on the sofa, enjoying the jealous glare from his twin. "So I wouldn't have to worry about that with you?"

Mark hopped on board the flirting train, putting his arm along the top of the cushion at her back, gathering her closer. "Absolutely not. I can assure you I'm a complete gentleman."

Matt plopped down on the couch on her other side, grasping her hand. She was ultrasensitive to every touch, every glance from these men. She wasn't sure she'd ever been so hot for a man. Unfortunately, this wasn't one man, but two.

"Get away from my girl."

"Your girl?" Mark asked.

Though she could tell they were teasing, Bridget decided she'd be wise not to let the game go too far. "Oh no, you don't. I'm not getting in the middle of a pissing contest. Something tells me the two of you take too much pleasure in it."

Matt shrugged. "We're brothers. It's in the sibling rivalry codebook."

She laughed. "Find something else to fight over. I'm only here for a few days more and I'd like to spend them in relative peace and quiet. I've had enough violence to last me a—"

She froze as both men's faces turned from smiling to scowling in an instant.

Shit. Way to go, big mouth.

"Violence?" Mark asked.

She struggled to find a way out of the mess she'd just made. "I just meant fighting amongst siblings."

Matt looked toward the kitchen. "Siblings? Do you and Rodney fight? Does he hit you?"

"Dear God, no. He's the mildest, kindest, most compassionate man on the planet. How could you ask such a thing?"

Mark turned her face toward his with gentle fingers on her chin. "Violence is sort of strong word for simple arguments between a brother and a sister. You know you could tell us if something's wrong, Bridget. We'd keep you safe."

She'd never received a more welcome invitation. For the second time in one day, her heart ached to share her painful secret. Common sense reared its ugly head. "Help me? You don't even know me."

"We know enough to see you're in some sort of trouble," Matt said. "Rodney's constantly running odd errands around town without you, while you're supposedly on vacation. You've yet to leave this inn and, well, you're a tad bit jumpy. What's up with you two?"

How could anyone be that observant? Maybe Rodney had been right about them hiding somewhere more secluded. They obviously had shitty poker faces. "Nothing's up with us. Everything is as we said. We're just here on vacation."

Matt looked like he wanted to press the subject further, but Mark's heavy sigh cut him off. "Okay. We'll go with that. For now. If you change your mind and want to talk, the door's open."

She forced a lighthearted grin to her face. "Nothing to talk about. I'm downright dull."

Mark shook his head. "I seriously doubt that. So, about these riding lessons—"

While Rodney had given her the go-ahead, it didn't change one very simple truth. "I was stupid to make that bet. I wasn't kidding when I said I'm afraid of horses."

Matt squeezed the hand she'd forgotten he was holding. "We'll take it nice and slow, sweetheart."

"In other words, you're not letting me out of the bet."

Matt grinned at her. "Not on your life. You're going to spend the next three days—"

"You said it would take two days."

The mischievous rogue winked at her. "You said you

wanted to learn to be a cowgirl. That takes time. Trust me, at the end of four days, you'll be—"

"Four days?" As much as Bridget hated to make the break, she forced herself to stand and walk away from the incredible heat of their strapping bodies. Facing them where they still sat, she put her hands on her hips. "You are a shyster and a con man. I agreed to riding lessons. I'm fairly certain that can be achieved in one day."

Mark stood slowly. "Three days."

"Two," she countered.

Matt jumped up and shook her hand as if sealing the deal. "Two days plus one date."

"Date?"

Matt retained the hand he held, using it to pull her closer. "You just shook on it. We teach you how to ride, and you let me take you out dancing one night."

"You get to take her dancing?" Mark interjected. "I don't think so. The whole idea behind this wager was mine to begin with. If anyone's taking Bridget out on a date, it's me."

Bridget threw her hands up. "Enough. I'll agree to three days of riding lessons if you two agree that we're just going to remain friends. No more fighting."

Matt looked like he wanted to argue about the friends idea, and Bridget tried to suppress the part of her that hoped he'd press the issue.

"Fine," Mark said, though his tone indicated he wasn't happy about her demands.

She grinned. "It's better this way. Trust me."

Matt shrugged. "Maybe. Maybe not."

"I'm going to head into the kitchen for some dessert. Do you guys want some?"

Mark shook his head. "No. I think I'd better head back. One of the horses was acting strangely this morning and I'm worried she's getting sick. I want to check on her before I go to bed."

"I'll walk back with you," Matt said. They'd told Bridget earlier in the evening there was a small path toward the rear of the house that led straight to the James Ranch. "Jacob can ride back in the truck with Caleb and Jessie or on his own if the two love birds don't make it back from your guest house. You mind letting them know we left?"

Bridget shook her head. "No, not at all."

Mark tapped her nose playfully. "We'll expect to see you at the ranch bright and early tomorrow morning."

She narrowed her eyes. "What's bright and early? Nine? Ten?"

Matt laughed. "I was going to say six. Maybe another compromise? How's seven thirty sound?"

"Painful," she groaned. "But I'll be there."

Mark reached for her hand and lifted it to his lips. She suppressed a slight shiver when he pressed a quick, hot kiss on her palm.

Never one to be outdone by his brother, Matt upped the ante, placing a friendly kiss on her cheek. "Night, sweetheart," he drawled, his hot breath tickling her sensitive skin.

It was a clear moonlit evening. There was enough light from the night sky that Mark and Matt could make their way across the yard without using the flashlights they'd grabbed from the truck before embarking on their return trip home.

Mark managed to hold his tongue all the way to the head of the path, a feat Matt didn't think his brother capable of. Once they reached the edge of the woods, he let loose, saying everything Matt was thinking.

"What the fuck is going on here?"

Matt pretended to be oblivious. "What do you mean?"

"Don't play dumb with me. We're both attracted to the same woman."

Matt thought attraction seemed a mild word to describe what happened to him whenever he was in the same room as Bridget. Miffed at his brother for presenting a very big roadblock between him and his desires, he decided to make Mark work for it. "So?"

Mark stopped walking and gripped Matt's arm, forcing him to halt as well. "So? So we don't fight over women. We never have. Not once."

"I don't see us fighting over Bridget."

Mark threw back his head in annoyance and glanced skyward. Matt waited him out. Matt knew his twin, knew Mark didn't like confrontations. While Matt tended to throw fists first and ask questions later, his brother's temperament was the polar opposite. Sometimes that was irritating, but most times it saved them from bruised knuckles and fat lips.

When Mark looked at him once more, Matt could see he was calmer. "I'd really like to go out with Bridget. On a date."

Matt lifted one shoulder. "I'm not holding you back. She is. In case you forgot, she's here on vacation. Seems sort of silly for us to get so worked up over something that can't be more than a short-term fling at best."

Mark stared at him for a long time. Matt was grateful for the shadows of the woods. His brother knew him too well. If they'd been standing in broad daylight, he'd have seen the fact Matt was lying written all over his face. "If that's really how you feel, then do you mind if I ask her out for dinner tomorrow night?"

"Hell yes, I mind." The words flew from Matt's lips quickly and loudly.

Mark chuckled. "Yeah. That's what I thought. Shit."

"We're both being stupid, you know that?"

Mark nodded, repeating his words back to him. "Everything you said is right. She's here on vacation. She lives in New York City, for God's sake."

"She's also beautiful, funny and hiding something," Matt added to the list.

"Yeah, I've noticed that last thing too. I'm worried about her. You think that's the attraction? We're curious?"

Matt shook his head. "Hell no. Curiosity's got nothing to do with it. For a few minutes, I thought it was your white hat, defender of the downtrodden bullshit coming out, but I don't think that's it. You don't think Rodney is hurting her?"

"No. I don't. You heard the way she jumped to his defense tonight. None of that was pretense. She's not afraid of him at all. Besides I've seen the way he looks at her. He's definitely protecting her from something."

"Yeah, well. I'm glad she has him. I just wish she'd tell us what's bothering her. She was running from us yesterday when she took that tumble in the foyer. I saw her face when we walked in. It was pure fear."

Mark turned and started walking along the path toward their ranch, running his hand over his face. "I'm not sure I've ever felt so many feelings all at once. It's like I want to protect her and kiss her and, Christ, fuck her."

"Keep her."

Mark glanced at him, but he didn't stop walking. "That's on the top of the list. Couldn't make myself say it. That's wrong. I know that. I mean, hell, we just met her yesterday."

Matt bent forward and picked up a large stick lying in the middle of the path, tossing it to one side. "Caleb said he fell for Jessie the first night they met. Said he knew after one conversation she was special. That she was the one. Hell, Dad popped the question to Mom on their second date. Said he wanted to ask her to marry him on the first one, but didn't want to appear forward!"

Mark chuckled. "So what you're saying is this is a James flaw?"

Matt stuck his hands in his pockets. "What I'm saying is Mom said yes and Jessie's still with Caleb. Maybe we James men just know when we've met our soul mate."

Mark stumbled for a step, but kept walking. "Soul mate? You know, there's a problem with that theory if you're right."

Matt knew. It was a big fucking problem too. "Yeah. I know. All those things you want to do for Bridget, I want to do too. So what's the answer? You want to arm wrestle for her?"

Mark chuckled. "I think Bridget gave us the answer. We ignore what we want, we offer her friendship for as long as she stays, and in a few days, she goes to New York and life goes back to normal around here."

Matt knew his brother's words made sense, but for the first time in his life, normal didn't seem like enough. "Yeah. Normal. You realize that's not going to work for me, right?"

He'd expected his brother to laugh at his joke, but it was met with only silence. They'd reached the edge of their property when Mark stopped walking once more. "Normal sucks. I think maybe it would be better if we took turns on the lessons. Since I usually work with the beginners, I'll take tomorrow with her. You can take over the next day."

Although Mark's comment seemed innocuous, Matt suspected there was more behind the words than appeared. He could see the sense of his brother's suggestion. There was no way the two of them could be alone with Bridget and not start up the rivalry for her attentions again. They'd always been too competitive for their own good. By dividing the time, they'd kill two birds with one stone. They'd prevent World War III from erupting between them, while they each would have a few precious hours alone with Miss Carson to press their suits. "What about the third day?"

Mark shrugged. "I guess we let her choose her teacher for that day."

"To the victor goes the spoils?"

"Something like that. Listen, Matt. Regardless of who she chooses, we have to agree not to let it come between us. I know we're brothers, but we're best friends too. I don't want to lose you over a woman, no matter how great she is. Deal?"

Matt accepted his brother's outstretched hand and shook it, adding just a touch of force to the squeeze. "Deal. May the best man win."

Mark returned the pressure, adding to it. "Don't worry. I will."

Matt tightened his grip even more, before releasing his brother's hand. "Going to be fun watching you fall on your ass."

"Cocky 'til the end. Just remember I warned you. Race you to the barn?"

Matt had already set off at a run when he yelled the word "Go!"

Of course, Mark was too wise to him, and he'd taken off at exactly the same time. They both slapped their hands on the barn wall at the same second.

A tie. Matt couldn't help but wonder who would come out ahead in their next race. It struck him that he liked the feel of the tie, of no one coming out ahead, of sharing the win with his brother.

Maybe a draw wasn't such a bad thing.

Crap. What the fuck did that mean?

CHAPTER FOUR

Bridget had been surprised when Matt and Mark informed her they were taking turns with her riding lessons on her first day at the ranch. She'd been disappointed by the prospect of not getting to spend time with both of them, but she could hardly argue with their logic. Regardless of the wager, someone still had to run the ranch.

During her first day of riding lessons, she and Mark had begun a battle of cultures that carried over to her second day spent with Matt. While Bridget insisted there was nothing like a big city existence, Matt and Mark claimed the best way of life was found in the country. They continued to press their case with lots of little examples and, though it hurt her to admit, she could definitely see the appeal of their lifestyle. The first two days had flown by in a flurry of fun and laughter.

However, this morning, she'd woken up with a sinking feeling in the pit of her stomach. It was her last day of lessons. Her excuse to see the twins would end this afternoon. She hadn't expected that knowledge to depress her so much. The past few days had felt like a welcome respite from the endless, horrifying months since Lyle's murder. She'd been able to close her eyes to the ugly terror that surrounded her at every turn and wallow in the warmth, humor and beauty of James Ranch. She wasn't sure she'd ever been anywhere nicer in her life. It was going to be much harder to leave than she'd realized.

Unfortunately, time was not her friend and she had to go. She and Rodney hadn't had much luck in tracking down the godmother Ellen, though if she was being truthful, Bridget could admit neither of them was trying very hard.

Rodney accompanied her to the ranch each day for her lessons, but once she was in the care of either Matt or Mark, he'd disappear into the house to visit with Jacob. She knew he was still watching over her, still anxious about her safety, but she suspected this break from reality was a welcome retreat for him as well. It was as if they'd stepped out of hell and straight into Eden. Neither of them was in a hurry to return to the cold, hard truths of their real lives.

She walked into the barn with Mark and Matt, wondering who would take over her lessons today and greedily hoping they'd both stay with her. She'd lost a tiny piece of her heart to each of them over the past few days...and for completely different reasons.

Mark had a slow, easy country charm she was hard-pressed to resist. He'd taken charge of her lessons the first day, introducing her to the horses and leading her step by step through the process of riding. He was a patient teacher. He'd never rushed her or become frustrated with her reticence around the animals.

Several times throughout that first day, she'd gotten off Jewel, swearing she was never getting back on. She hadn't realized when she'd agreed to the lessons how high off the ground she'd be or how out of control she'd feel. Neither sensation set well with her. Mark had gotten her through her initial qualms by telling her funny stories about his childhood spent on the ranch with his brothers and the horses. Somehow he always managed to calm her misgivings simply by sharing some embarrassing mishap he'd endured. By making light of his own fears and failures, he'd alleviated hers, giving her the courage to try again. His genuine love of the four-legged creatures had rubbed off on her, and she couldn't remember why she'd ever been afraid of horses to begin with. The horses on the ranch were as tranquil and gentle as their owner, Mark.

She'd also spent most of that day in a constant state of arousal. She wasn't sure if Mark's touches—boosts into the saddle, hugs when she did well, shoulder rubs to relax her— were intentionally meant to seduce her or just small kindnesses on his part, but she'd had to take a very cold shower upon returning to the inn. In the end, she'd spent most of that night dreaming of the handsome cowboy making love to her under the stars. She'd woken up more sexually frustrated than she'd been when she lay down.

Jewel snorted as she approached and batted her large nose at Bridget.

"You're spoiling my damn horse," Mark teased. "She used to be an amiable animal. Three days with you and she's making demands."

Bridget grinned and pulled the sugar cube she'd lifted from the inn's kitchen out of her pocket. "I won't apologize for that. We girls have to stick together."

"So it's a battle of the sexes, is it?" Matt asked.

She grinned at the fun-loving cowboy. She'd laughed more yesterday than she had in the entire previous year. Matt was a natural-born comedian as well as a talented musician. She'd learned he was part of a band and after much cajoling on her part, he'd cut their lesson short yesterday afternoon to play a few songs for her on the guitar. He was an incredible singer.

Watching him strum his acoustic guitar had sent her body into overdrive. When his deep, rich voice started singing a country love song, she feared she'd orgasm on the spot. Last night, she'd tossed and turned again, but instead of her gentleman cowboy, Mark, it had been Matt spicing up her dreams with visions of rough, hungry sex against the barn wall.

She'd woken up today weighted down by the realization she was falling...for both of them. She wasn't sure whether to rail at the world or thank her lucky stars that her time in Wyoming was destined to be short. There was no way she could choose between the two men, but the thought of leaving and never seeing them again was too painful to contemplate.

"I don't know if it's a battle of the sexes or self-preservation. If we waited for men to give us our pleasures, we'd wait forever. Better we girls learn how to take care of ourselves."

Matt stepped up behind her, wrapping his arms loosely around her waist. "I'd be more than happy to take care of some of those pleasures for you, Bridge. All you have to do is say the word."

His close proximity didn't feel strange or surprising. Probably because he'd touched her almost constantly the day before. Unlike his brother, she'd had no question about Matt's seductive games. More than once, he'd wrapped his arm around her shoulder, pulling her close to his side to press a friendly kiss to her head. He'd held her hand most of the day. Once he'd bent over and picked her up, tossing her playfully into a pile of hay before kneeling down and tickling her until she begged for mercy.

She glanced over her shoulder, enjoying Matt's closeness. He smelled nice—cologne and horse and hot-blooded man scents mingled to drive her mad. Her hormones flared to life, kicking to the curb the common sense she'd battled to maintain. To hell with bad timing and bad judgment. She was hot and horny, tired and hungry. She offered Matt a sexy smile. "Oh yeah? And what exactly would that all-powerful word be?"

Matt's grip tightened and he slowly pressed his chest to her back. The sudden nearness drew her attention to the hard cock he was sporting in his jeans. She joined the intimate tango, pushing her ass more firmly against his erection and wiggling slightly.

Matt groaned softly. "Damn, sweetheart. Any word would work right about now. Please, fuck, yes, banana. I'd accept any of those."

"Banana, huh?" She reached back and let her fingers lightly graze the thick banana currently residing in his denim.

"Jesus," Matt moaned.

Mark cleared his throat. "Y'all realize I'm still here, right?"

Bridget licked her lips, her gaze landing on Mark's firm, full mouth as she imagined the slow, deep, thorough kisses he would offer. "I know you're here."

Mark studied her now-moist lips and she knew they were on the same wavelength. It would have been impossible for either man to miss the longing, the need lacing her tone.

What the hell was she inviting? She'd decided days ago she wouldn't come between the brothers. God knew she couldn't choose between them. She shook herself for her thoughtless behavior. She wasn't being fair to them.

Turning, she pulled away from Matt's embrace, putting some distance between her and the cowboys.

"So," she coughed, attempting to dislodge the lump in her throat, "who's my teacher for today?"

Neither man answered. She wondered if she'd pushed them away with her thoughtless, teasing games.

Great, Bridge. Way to go too far. There was a name for women who acted like she had and it wasn't a nice one. The words *cock tease* taunted her.

Panicking, she changed the offer. "Actually, I feel a bit guilty pulling you away from your chores. What if we skipped the riding lessons today and I helped you do whatever it is you usually do?"

Matt laughed. "You want to play rancher for a day?"

"It's my last day. I'd sort of like to spend it with both of you. I know there are a lot of daily chores you need to get done around here, so put me to work."

Mark looked at his brother. She noticed the silent communication in the glance. She'd never met two men who were so different and yet so close.

In the past two days, she'd learned a great deal about them. Typically the information had come from the other twin. Mark had spent ages telling her about Matt's crazy exploits in high school—always with pride in his voice. He confessed to being envious that he'd never felt so free to go wild.

Yesterday, Matt admitted he didn't take things seriously enough and he sometimes wished he were more responsible like his twin. There were times when she actually got a sense they were each trying to hook her up with the other brother, while flirting with her at the same time. It was confusing, heady, and wonderful to be the center of such flattering attention.

"Well?" she prompted.

Matt took his hat off and plopped it on her head. "You're on. But be warned, we're not going to take it easy on you."

A dare. Oh my. He sure did know the way to her heart. "Bring it on, cowboy."

The day passed in a blur of activity and hard work. It was an eye-opening experience for a city girl whose idea of working with her hands prior to meeting the James twins had basically meant sitting at a computer and typing eighty words a minute. They'd begun the day by feeding all the horses. Matt and Mark had nearly twenty-five different types of horses at the ranch—Appaloosas, paints, thoroughbreds, even one that was part Arabian. Some they owned, others they simply boarded and trained. She toted two tons of water and feed. When she groaned, Mark told to count her blessings that the temperature wasn't below freezing, or they'd be chopping ice instead as their water heater was on the fritz. After the horses were supplied with food and water, they cleaned out stalls.

Matt and Mark teased her when she sat down on a bale of hay, thinking they were finished.

"Wow. I think I have hay in every crevice in my body. It's even in my ass. How the hell could I get it there?"

Matt laughed as he plopped down beside her. "Well, you are sitting on a hay bale."

"Smart-ass. It was there before I sat down."

Matt reached over and picked a strand of the prickly stuff out of her hair. "You wield a mean pitchfork. You had that shit flying everywhere. Literally."

She narrowed her gaze. "Very funny. I have blisters and I itch."

"Ready to cry uncle, city girl?" Matt asked.

She looked at him with disbelief. "We aren't finished?"

Mark chuckled and offered her a hand, helping her stand. "We haven't even started. That was just the preliminary stuff."

Matt rose as well and dusted off the back of his jeans. "Don't worry, Bridget. We won't think less of you if you go inside and warm up with Jacob and Rodney. Ranching life isn't for everyone."

Why didn't he just double-dog dare her to keep working?

"What's next?" she asked, ignoring her sore fingers, the

twinge in her back and the three dozen itches begging to be scratched. Fucking hay.

Mark grasped her hand and led her to a stall. "Now we do the fun work."

For the next few hours, they worked the horses, taking the animals through their paces. Matt explained the learned routine to her, educating her on training techniques and reining patterns. Bridget was put in charge of walking the horses during their cooldowns, then brushing them before they were put back in their stalls. She spent most of the afternoon in quiet contemplation, simply enjoying the company of the horses and the view of Matt and Mark as they worked. She was surprised to discover how late it had gotten when Mark declared they were finished for the day. Her days of work at the newspaper never flew by so quickly.

Mark wrapped a friendly arm around her shoulder. "Damn. Sure was nice having some help. We finished up almost an hour earlier than usual thanks to you."

She glanced at her watch. It was nearly five p.m. and they'd told her that they typically started at five a.m. "Really? Wow. That's a damn long day for you guys. You do that every day?"

Mark nodded as they walked toward the house. "We do an abbreviated routine on Sundays. Day of rest and all that."

They walked into the house together.

"Hey, Bridge," Rodney said as they entered the living room. He and Jacob were watching TV. Bridget noticed Rodney was sitting in his usual chair by the front window—the one that gave him a bird's-eye view of her and the stable. "I was starting to worry these guys were going to keep you out there all night."

She grinned. Her whole body ached, but it was a good pain. For the first time in a long time, she felt like she'd actually accomplished something with her day. "Ranching work is tough."

"Why don't you two stay for dinner?" Matt asked.

Jacob pulled his feet off the coffee table in front of him and sat up. "Actually, I've been trying to convince Rodney to go bowling with me tonight."

"I told you," Rodney said, "I suck at bowling."

Bridget knew the words for a lie, not because she'd ever been bowling with Rodney before, but because she could tell when he wasn't telling the truth. There was a definite gleam of longing in his eyes. She wished they were here for a different reason. Wished both of them could take a chance on what they desired.

Matt tossed his hat on a table by the wall and ran his fingers through his hair. "It's not the bowling you need to go for. It's the root beer floats. Ellie Parker makes the best floats..." He paused and glanced at Bridget.

"In the universe?" she supplied.

He nodded. "Yep. Universe."

She laughed, then noticed a strange look on Rodney's face.

"Ellie Parker?" he asked, cueing her in to the vital comment she'd missed. Ellie? Ellen?

"You should go," she said quickly. "You've been sitting around here for three days while I was having all the fun. Why not take some time for yourself?" She tried to act light and casual, but this was their first break on the Ellen clue. She knew Rodney would never take her into town, never expose her to so many people. It wouldn't be a big deal, however, for him. He'd gone to town several times already.

"Well," Rodney hedged. She could see he was torn between his duty to protect her and his desire to find the flash drive.

"If the guys don't mind, I'll just hang out here with them until you and Jacob return." She knew Rodney would feel safer if she was in the care of the twins. Over the past few days,

Rodney admitted he'd loosened his guard a bit because of how closely Matt and Mark watched her—even without knowing the danger she was in.

"We can all eat dinner together. Then you guys can hit the bowling alley and we'll hang around here and watch a movie until you get back," Matt offered. "Got a couple new ones from Netflix. If we're lucky, they won't be any of the crap ones Jake picks."

Jake threw a punch at his older brother's arm. "I guarantee you Bridget would rather watch a movie I picked than one of your stupid horror flicks."

"Horror?" Bridget asked. Back in New York, horror had been her favorite genre. However, since Lyle's death, she's lost her enthusiasm for it. She had enough fodder for her nightmares without adding someone else's fictional fears to the pile.

Mark grinned. "Don't worry. I think we got the new *True Grit* in this pile. That was my pick. Nothing like a good old-fashioned western."

She laughed. "Great. More examples of why the country beats the city. Can't wait." She looked at Rodney, hoping she'd convinced him to go. "Sounds like a fun night. What do you say, Rodney?"

He was quiet for a moment, then he sighed. "I say what's for dinner? I'm going to need some nourishment before I make an ass of myself at the lanes."

Jacob laughed. "I took out some chicken. Thought I'd make curry."

"Damn," Rodney said, rubbing his stomach. "That sounds good."

Jacob looked at his brothers. "Why don't the three of you clean up while Rodney and I get supper going? Bridget, you can use the bathroom in the guest bedroom if you want. I bet you're itchy after spending all that time in the barn."

He wrinkled his nose as he said the word barn. Bridget laughed. "The ranching gene sure missed you, didn't it?"

Jacob didn't take offense. "I figure it hit two of the four of us. Caleb's no fonder of the ranch than I am. Fifty-fifty's not so bad, although my dad might have disagreed."

Jacob's comment about his father sent a string of questions running through her mind. There was so much she didn't know about Matt and Mark that she was curious about. Hell, she sighed. She wanted to know everything about them—their histories, their dreams, their desires, their bodies.

She pushed the image of her two cowboys away. It was an illogical, impractical dream. She couldn't have both of them and she couldn't choose. Better to keep things light and easy. "I'd love a shower."

Jacob started down the hallway, leading her to the guest room. "I'll grab a pair of sweats and T-shirt from Jessie's dresser. She won't mind you wearing them. It'll save you having to put your dirty clothes back on."

After popping the question the night of their Valentine's Day feast at the inn, Caleb had whisked Jessie off to Colorado for an impromptu vacation to celebrate. According to Jacob, they weren't due back to the ranch for three more days.

"Thanks, Jacob."

"Sure thing. Hey, is your brother seeing anyone in New York?"

She grinned. "Wow. That was pretty direct."

"I learned a long time ago that the best way to get an answer is to ask the question."

"Spoken like a true journalism major." She'd had to stop herself several times from talking shop with Jacob whenever he mentioned some article he was writing or something one of his online professors had said. She missed her writing terribly. Watching Jacob tap away at the keys on his laptop had left her more homesick than anything else these past few weeks.

"I'm not going to lie, Bridget. I like Rodney. A lot. But I get the sense there's something holding him back. Keeping him from taking a chance with me. I figure there must be someone else."

There was someone else, she wanted to say. Her. He was holding true to his promise to protect her, to keep her safe. "There's no one else, Jacob."

Jacob looked relieved and confused by her response. Then she watched both reactions replaced by sadness. "Oh, well, I guess maybe it's just me he's not interested in."

"No," she said hastily. "That's not it at all. Rodney really likes you. I can tell. It's just we're on vacation. I'm sure he's hesitant to start something because of the distance. I mean, what if you guys hooked up and it was truly wonderful? It would make leaving that much harder." Her words were spoken on her behalf as much as Rodney's. She could easily let herself fall into Mark or Matt's arms, but where would that leave her when the time came to return to New York?

Jacob shrugged. "Seems like a poor excuse."

"What?"

"We only get one shot at this life, Bridget. I'm definitely not letting geography dictate where I'm allowed to find my happiness. Might have to explain that concept to your brother tonight over root beer floats."

"Love at the bowling alley?" she teased.

"Nothing classier. I'll go grab you those clothes."

Jacob left her alone. Rodney wasn't the only one depriving himself a shot at true happiness. If there was one lesson she should have learned in the past year, it was that life is precious. Fate was handing her a chance for something better, something richer, and she was throwing it away by blaming timing and distance and a crooked judge for her loneliness. There was only one person holding her back and that was herself.

Walking to the guest bath, she started tugging off her shirt. What if her destiny, her happiness was here, on this ranch in the middle of Nowhere, Wyoming? Her problems were still going to be here in the morning, but what happened in a month —after she'd testified?

Where would she be then?

She turned on the water, letting it heat up. Stepping beneath the steaming jets, she let the water soothe her sore muscles.

She was too tired to think anymore. Tonight, she just wanted to be. To feel.

Tonight, she wanted to take a chance.

The only question was...with who?

$\mathcal{M}$ark stretched out, leaning back on the couch. Bridget was nestled between him and Matt. They'd eaten far too much at dinner, in addition to polishing off an entire bottle of wine and most of another. He was completely relaxed and thoroughly happy.

They'd opted to watch *True Grit*—a movie he'd wanted to see for months. For some reason, it couldn't hold his attention. It wasn't a bad movie. The problem was every fiber of his being was focused on the slim, tall beauty lounging by his side.

So much for their grand seduction schemes. He and Matt had thought they'd plead their own cases, make their own moves and then let her choose. Instead, she'd blown their plan out of the water, asking to spend the day with both of them. Ridiculous as it seemed, her choice pleased him. He'd enjoyed today much more than his day alone with Bridget—which had been great. For some weird reason, it seemed more natural when they were all together. Crap. He needed to lay off the wine.

Bridget sighed and rested her head on his shoulder. Mark

savored her closeness and decided to expand on it. He lifted his right arm and wrapped it around her shoulder. He glanced over at his brother. He expected to receive a dirty look. Instead, Matt gave him a friendly grin, before his brother reached down to lift Bridget's feet on to his lap. She didn't resist, turning to her side slightly and moving into the new position with ease. Mark shifted sideways as well, opening his legs so that Bridget could settle between them, reclining against his chest. He watched his brother pull off the clean socks Matt had loaned her when she complained that her feet were cold. Matt began rubbing her feet and Bridget released a pleased groan.

"That feels so good," she whispered.

Mark took advantage of her complacency, wrapping both arms around her waist, loving the feel of her weight against him. He and Matt were tall men. It was unusual to find a woman who fit them so well. Bridget's height was perfect—the top of her head coming to his chin. He wouldn't have to bend over far to find her sweet lips.

The moment the thought crossed his mind, Mark wanted to act on it. Instead, he simply cuddled her, soaking in the soft scent of shampoo in her hair. None of them even pretended to watch the movie. The dim lighting, the comfortable couch, the wine—all of it worked together to wrap them up in a cocoon of warmth. Time passed slowly as Matt continued his gentle rubbing of Bridget's feet.

She sighed blissfully, playing absentmindedly with Mark's hands where they lay on her stomach. Slowly, Matt moved his massage upward, his hands creeping along her shins and then higher, to her thighs.

Bridget's breathing grew shallower, more labored. Mark could feel the desire growing in her body as she began to gyrate slowly, her hips tantalizing the now-apparent erection in his pants. There was no way she could mistake what she was rubbing against with her slight movements.

Unwilling to remain a casual observer, Mark began his own gentle caresses. Lifting the edge of Bridget's T-shirt, he dragged his fingers over the soft skin of her stomach and waist. Bridget sucked in a deep breath, but didn't reject either of their stroking explorations. After a moment, she sighed, laying her head on his shoulder and releasing a soft moan.

Mark was more turned on then he'd ever been in his life. He wondered what his brother was thinking of this. He watched Matt's hands as they traveled closer to the juncture of Bridget's thighs. Christ. This was quickly reaching a point of no return.

He looked up at Matt's face, captured his glance. Mark tried to convey his concerns. They were traveling down an uncharted path.

Matt gave him an easygoing grin that in most circumstances would have annoyed the shit out of Mark. Tonight, right now, the smile felt right, comforting, encouraging.

Even so, there was a small part of him that couldn't let things go any further without asking permission. He knew Bridget wasn't drunk, but she'd definitely had enough wine to take the edge off.

"Bridget," he whispered in her ear.

"Hmmm." She was completely relaxed. He'd never seen her so peaceful or at ease. While the past three days had cemented in his mind that something was definitely wrong in Bridget's world—she still jumped at shadows and she'd visibly begun to shake after their old ranch truck backfired—she'd yet to confide in them.

"Are you okay with this, darlin'?"

She turned her head to the side, glancing at him over her shoulder. She nodded once. "Yeah, I am. Are you?"

Leave it to Bridget to worry about his response to the unconventional dilemma they were currently in. "Yeah. I'm good. How about you, Matt?" he asked, looking up at his brother.

Matt leaned forward, shrinking the distance until all three of them breathed the same air. Mark had shared a room with this man for his most of his younger life, the two of them only opting for separate bedrooms a few years earlier. There were no secrets between them, but this....

This moment was changing something, altering some solidly accepted norms in Mark's life.

Matt kept moving until his lips were a fraction of an inch away from Bridget's. "I'm good," his brother whispered. "But I'm not finished. I want more."

Mark wasn't sure if his brother's words were meant as a warning or if he was simply stating the facts.

"I want more too," Bridget confessed. "But this is, I've never, I don't know how—"

Mark chuckled. "It's new to us too, Bridge. We'll find our way together."

Matt placed a quick, soft kiss on her lips. Then he moved away once more. As he drifted back to his spot on the couch, Matt grasped the waistband of Bridget's sweatpants, pulling them and her panties off in one fell swoop. Bridget stiffened slightly as Matt lifted one of her legs, pulling it to the opposite side of his waist. Then, she opened them even further, throwing her other leg over Mark's. It gave Matt enough room to kneel between her open thighs.

Mark lifted his hands, rubbing her tense shoulders to relax her. "You're beautiful," he murmured in her ear.

The words and caresses seemed to soothe her. Her body went soft once more.

Matt's hands stroked the inside of her thighs and Bridget

shivered. Her body was heating up and she was definitely becoming more aroused with each pass of Matt's hands on her skin.

Bridget and Mark both stilled as Matt's fingers advanced on her pussy. They barely took a breath when Matt ran a single finger along the slit between her legs. Then Bridget gasped, her hips thrusting slightly, seeking more.

Matt looked at their girl and winked. "She's soaking wet, Mark."

Mark chuckled. "I trust you know what you're doing down there."

His brother's gaze drifted to Mark's face rather than Bridget's. Mark had never seen such pure, genuine happiness there. Then he realized he felt the same way.

"Tell you what, bro. You let me worry about the *below the waist* regions. By the way, are you going to sit there all night or were you planning on hopping in?"

Bridget giggled at Matt's joke. "I love being with you two. I'm sure there's something wrong with that, but I'll be damned if I can make myself care."

Matt winked at her. "There's nothing wrong with this."

Matt touched her once more, his finger stroking her clit until Bridget was writhing uncontrollably in Mark's lap. Her ass continued to brush against his cock until Mark thought he'd lose it right then and there.

"Please," she pleaded.

"Please what?" Matt asked. "Please this?" He thrust two fingers into Bridget's pussy. Her head reared back roughly against Mark's shoulder.

Unable to watch and not be a part any longer, Mark shifted slightly to one side. Twisting Bridget's face just enough that Matt could continue his ministrations, Mark gripped her hair and claimed her lips. She didn't resist, didn't try to pull away.

Her breathing was heavy as Matt continued to fuck her with his fingers.

Mark thrust his tongue into her mouth, relishing the spicy combination of curry and red wine on her lips. She was delicious.

Retaining his grip on her hair with one hand, his other drifted down to explore the one place neither he nor Matt had reached yet. He cupped one of her firm, full breasts. Bridget gasped and tried to break the kiss, searching for air. Mark couldn't let her go. He pulled her lips back to his, pushing his tongue into the wet, warm cavern.

Bridget responded instantly, returning his kiss. Her trembling body and soft groans told him she was enjoying the interlude. Twice, she gasped. Mark was tempted to peek at what his brother was doing that she liked so much, but he couldn't force himself to release her lips to do so.

After several moments of touching, kissing and groaning, Bridget pulled away.

"God," she cried. "I can't take much more. I think, I can't, I'm going to—"

Each unfinished thought was interrupted by a gasp or a shiver. Neither Mark nor Matt needed to be told what was going on.

Matt continued to thrust his fingers inside her. "I want to see you come, Bridget. I want to feel it on my fingers."

Bridget reached down, her fingers digging into Mark's thighs. "I think that's inevitable."

Mark shifted, so she was completely reclined against his chest once more. He gathered her close, taking her breasts in both hands, cupping them, squeezing and teasing her tight nipples.

Matt pulled his fingers out for a moment. "Think you can

take three?" He didn't wait for an answer; rather, he upped the ante and resumed the play.

Bridget bucked hard and Mark tightened his grip. She was likely to squirm herself right off the couch.

"Oh my God," she said loudly. Mark grinned. The three of them were wearing more clothes than they'd shed and it was still the hottest sexual encounter of his life.

"Can't. Stop." Bridget's hips moved faster, trying to claim more of Matt's fingers. His brother increased the pace, the power.

"So. Good." The words seemed pulled from her chest and then she went stiff, her body reverberating as if struck. Her fingers tightened against his thighs and Mark knew he'd wear her bruises there tomorrow.

Matt slowed his motions as Bridget's orgasm hovered. Time seemed to stand still for a split second—all of them frozen in this amazing place. It was just long enough for Mark to understand the importance of what was happening. He'd turned a corner, found a new path, and there was no way in hell he was going back now.

Then all the air seeped out of Bridget's body. She was replete, spent, sated.

Matt pulled his fingers away as Bridget lay lifeless against Mark.

"I think she fell asleep," Matt whispered.

Mark twisted his head enough that he could see Bridget's face. Sure enough, her eyes were closed.

"Guess we wore her out."

Matt chuckled. "Yeah. Can't imagine how though. I mean all she did was a hard day of work on the ranch, eat a big dinner, drink a couple glasses of wine and indulge in a little foreplay with two horny cowboys."

Mark tried not to laugh, afraid he'd wake her up. "Help me get up. I don't want to disturb her."

Matt rose and lightly lifted Bridget off Mark's chest. Once he'd managed to untangle himself from her boneless limbs, they lay her back on the couch. She rolled over onto her side, but didn't stir. Instead, she seemed to fall into a deeper sleep.

"I suppose you're gonna want to talk about this." Matt's tone proved he was uncomfortable with the prospect of getting into a conversation.

"Actually I'm not sure what to say." It was the truth. The whole experience had caught Mark off guard. He wanted to suggest they sleep on it, but he knew he'd want the same thing in the morning that he wanted right now. He wanted Bridget. And he wanted to share her with his brother.

Matt was visibly shocked by his response. "You're not freaking out?"

Mark shook his head.

"You're not going to analyze the shit out of this and give me a million reasons why it's wrong?"

Again, Mark shook his head no.

Matt's shoulders fell, and for the first time in his life, Mark realized he'd done something that shocked his brother. He'd spent a lifetime being the reliable one, predictable and boring to the end, while Matt was the loose cannon.

"I'm not sorry about what happened tonight, Mark."

Mark turned to face his brother. Clearly Matt still expected him to balk. "I'm not either."

Unsatisfied, Matt pressed the issue. "I'm not stopping here. I want Bridget in my bed." Matt paused, then added the words they both needed to hear, out loud. "In our bed."

Mark chuckled. "We don't normally share a bed, Matt, or a room, for that matter." They'd each taken their own rooms after their father's death.

"You know what I mean."

Mark was amused by the evening's odd turn of events. Matt, always the clown, was suddenly too serious, while Mark couldn't suppress his happiness long enough to curb the jokes. "I know what you mean. I think the term you're looking for is ménage a trois. Or maybe you prefer threesome?"

Matt scowled. "What the fuck is wrong with you? I'm trying to be serious here."

Mark sobered up. "I know that. And I am taking this seriously. There are a million reasons why this whole thing won't work. I don't give a shit about any of them. This is right. Picking it apart and studying it piece by piece isn't going to change a damn thing. So, it looks like we just take this a day at a time, a step at a time, and hope for the best."

Matt's frown deepened. "Who are you and what have you done with my brother?"

Mark laughed, then reached up to place a friendly hand on Matt's shoulder. "I'm beat. What do you say we call it a night? It's obvious Jake has convinced Rodney to stay in town for that damn moonlight bowling thing he loves so much." It was well after midnight. The local alley held several special nights where they turned off the normal lights at midnight, casting the alley in nothing but black light. Jacob loved bowling in the glow-in-the-dark effect, laughing at how silly they all looked with their bright white shirts and gleaming teeth. Their kid brother had dragged them to the event more than a few times.

Mark reached for a blanket and covered Bridget up. "She looks so peaceful, I hate to move her."

Matt agreed. "Let her stay. That couch is more comfortable than my bed. It'll be late when Jake and Rodney get back. Jacob will probably put Rodney in the guest room when they see Bridget's asleep."

"Yeah." Mark grinned. "I like the idea of her sleeping here."

Matt put his hands in his pockets. "Be better if she was sleeping between us instead of alone out here."

"We try that tonight and she won't get much sleep. My cock is about to explode."

Matt nodded sympathetically, then he gave Mark a wicked grin. "Yeah, mine too. But she's too tired. She needs the rest. You know, it's a shame I'm going to beat you to the cold shower." As he said the last sentence, Matt took off down the hall, racing to the bathroom the two of them shared.

Mark laughed, but didn't attempt to outrun him. Matt had too much of a head start. Instead, he bent down in front of the couch and ran his hand lightly through Bridget's soft hair. God only knew what tomorrow would bring. If he was lucky—very lucky—he'd find a way to convince her to stay in Saratoga for a while.

Or forever.

Footsteps pounded behind her, coming closer in the darkness. Bridget tried to run faster, but she'd already run too far. Her chest was on fire, the pains in her side excruciating. She'd never manage to escape this time. He was too quick, too close. She'd nearly reached the main road. Hopefully she could wave down a car. Right now that was her only hope for escape. Headlights pierced the pitch black night. She was so close. If only...

Strong hands gripped her from behind. Bridget screamed, trying to break free. They tightened on her arms as she continued to struggle.

She screamed louder as the headlights of the car blinded her.

"No!" she yelled.

"Bridget. Bridget!" A deep voice called her name, but she didn't have time to respond. She needed to get away.

"Let me go!"

"Bridget. Open your eyes." Another voice. A familiar one. A friendly one.

She froze, her breathing and heart still in a race with each other, both moving too fast, too hard.

"Open your eyes, darlin'." Mark's fingers brushed her cheek and she opened her eyes. "It's just us."

Matt was sitting beside her on the couch, attempting to untangle her from a blanket.

Neither man had time to say anything else because at that moment, Rodney burst through the front door, running at full speed, gun in hand, ready to do battle.

"Wait!" Bridget cried, terrified her protector would shoot Mark or Matt. Rodney's eyes were wild with fear and concern.

"I heard you screaming," Rodney said.

She shrugged guiltily. "Nightmare." She'd suffered far too many bad dreams since the night of Lyle's murder, but none since arriving in Saratoga. She'd foolishly hoped they'd stopped coming.

Rodney slowly lowered his gun, his relieved face revealing a new problem. Before Bridget could consider a solution, Jacob —who'd run into the room right on Rodney's heels—asked the inevitable question.

"Why do you have a gun, Rodney?"

Rodney turned to face his new friend, and Bridget imagined she could see the spinning wheels in his mind searching for an answer. She wanted to tell the James brothers the truth. She knew with every fiber of her being that she could trust them. She also knew Rodney wouldn't let her.

"It's my fault," she said quickly.

Rodney glanced at her, his face issuing a warning for silence. "Bridget."

The lie came to her in an instant, falling from her lips far too easily. Six months of hiding, pretending to be someone else, had taught her well. She'd become the queen of subterfuge and half-truths. "I got mixed up with a nasty guy in New York. We dated for a while, but then things turned sort of abusive. I tried to get away from him a few times, but he kept finding me. I even got a restraining order, but that didn't help either. Rodney and I decided to get out of town, try to let things cool off. I thought we'd be safe here. I mean, Saratoga's halfway across the country, for God's sake."

Rodney nodded as she wove the tale, then added his own pile of crap to the lie. "I got a call from a friend a few days ago. She said she thought Lucian had figured out where we were. That's why we were going to cut our vacation short."

Lucian. Judge Thompson. Bridget would have laughed at Rodney's inventiveness if her heart weren't aching. Lying to these men who'd offered her nothing less than kindness, friendship and the greatest orgasm of her life didn't sit well with her.

Throughout their impromptu storytelling, Bridget kept her gaze on Rodney's face, too afraid to look at Matt and Mark. Were they buying this? What were they thinking?

Finally, she looked. She glanced at Mark, then at Matt. Both of them were wearing identical scowls.

"This is the secret you've been hiding?"

Bridget thought there was a hint of disbelief lacing Matt's tone, but she chalked it up to her own paranoia. She nodded.

"Why didn't you tell us, Bridget? We would have helped keep you safe." There was no mistaking the hurt in Mark's question.

"I was embarrassed," she said. "I felt stupid."

Matt grasped her hand, squeezing it tightly. "Don't say that. Don't even think it. You didn't do anything wrong."

She wished that were true. She sniffled slightly, surprised by the strong desire to cry. She hadn't cried once since Lyle's death. "I've done so many things wrong."

Her conscience collapsed around her. She'd been a fool to put this family in danger, selfish to consider her own desires over their safety. What if Thompson had found her? Had arrived at this house tonight?

She'd given these wonderful men no warning about the risk they were taking by just being with her. To add insult to injury, she heaped lie on top of lie and still they gathered around, willing to protect her against an unknown evil.

One man had already died for her selfishness. She wouldn't let anyone else pay that price.

"We need to get back to the inn, Rodney."

Rodney nodded. "Yeah. I think maybe that would be best. Um...maybe you should get dressed."

She blinked in surprise, then glanced down, mortified to discover her bare legs sticking out from beneath the blanket. Mercifully, Rodney couldn't see exactly how naked she was from the waist down.

"Okay."

"Wait," Matt said, putting his hand on her arm to prevent her from rising. "Why don't you two spend the night here? Now that we know what's going on, we'll be better prepared."

She shook her head, fighting back the tears at his chivalrous offer. He had no idea what kind of shit storm awaited her. Even if Thompson's henchman didn't find her, she had no choice but to return to New York City. While there, she'd continue to be sequestered during what was certain to be a highly publicized trial.

"No." She couldn't continue with the charade. Much as her

heart longed to stay here, she knew she'd only be living on borrowed time. That wasn't fair to Matt and Mark. "We really should head back."

Wrapping the blanket securely around her, she headed toward the guest room and her own clothes. She'd only made it one step in the room when she felt a tear slide down her cheek. She batted it away quickly. Matt and Mark would never let her leave if they saw her crying. She took a deep breath and dressed quickly.

All four men were standing in the living room when she returned. While Jacob looked disappointed, Matt and Mark looked downright miserable.

"I had a great time." She felt like she owed them at least a little bit of truth. The reality was tonight had been one of the best evenings of her life. She reached for Matt's hand, then took Mark's in her other. Squeezing tightly, she smiled, trying to hide the sadness behind it. "Honestly. You're both amazing men. I can't thank you enough for…" She paused, a million words flying through her mind—the riding lessons, the omelet, the friendship, the sex. Finally, she just said, "Everything."

Mark's face darkened. "You make this sound like a good-bye."

While it had to be farewell, she also realized how much harder this would be if they knew she was planning to run. "Does it? I don't mean it that way. I guess I'm just overly tired. I'll see you both tomorrow."

And that was the most painful lie of all. She swallowed, but the lump forming in her throat held tight. She was saved from having to speak again when Rodney stepped up beside her.

"You ready to go, Bridge?"

She nodded and let him lead her away from the ranch.

Away from them.

CHAPTER SIX

*B*ridget opened her eyes the next morning, then closed them again quickly to shut out the bright stream of morning sunshine.

Still here, she thought.

She and Rodney had gotten into a hushed-voices version of World War III last night after Jacob dropped them off at the B&B. It had been their first major disagreement since being thrust into each other's lives six months earlier.

When they'd tiptoed up to their room shortly before two a.m., Bridget had been ready to start packing their bags immediately, but Rodney told her she was overreacting. She'd just managed one of the most difficult tasks of her life—walking away from Matt and Mark in order to keep them safe—and he said she was overreacting?

Her head had exploded as they heatedly argued—in whispers lest they wake up the other patrons of the inn—for nearly an hour. She'd lost the fight.

Rodney informed her they had nowhere to go and no money to purchase transportation out of town. He also insisted that he was determined to crack Lyle's code and find that flash drive. According to him, he couldn't go back to New York without it and expect to keep his job. Even with it, he feared he was facing the unemployment line. Rodney intended to continue searching for Ellen, the godmother, even though Bridget was beginning to think that clue was as wrong as "God's grave" had been.

She'd told him as much and then accused him of only wanting to stick around for Jacob. Rodney got angry and said she only wanted to run because she was hot for two cowboys and too chicken to do anything about it. After that, they'd gone to bed, the silence in the room suffocating her until she finally managed to drop into a restless sleep.

"I know you're awake."

She didn't open her eyes or acknowledge Rodney's comment. She was still mad.

Her bed dipped and she felt Rodney's thigh press against hers as he sat next to her. "Bridget? I'm sorry about last night."

She opened her eyes and looked at him. She didn't like the tired look in his eyes or the sadness on his face.

"I'm sorry too." She was. She'd been overwrought. Her mother always accused her of being melodramatic. Last night had been a perfect example of that character flaw.

Rodney grinned. "Things always look better in the morning."

She considered the fact they were stuck in a strange town with no money and a hit man on their trail, and were no closer to finding the flash drive. Then she remembered Matt and Mark, the way they'd caressed and kissed her last night. She smiled too. Maybe things weren't so bad after all.

"So I take it you and Jacob had a good time last night?"

Rodney leaned closer, his face answering her question without words. He looked downright cheerful. "It was okay."

She laughed, picking up her pillow and lobbing it at his head. "You go to hell for lying."

He dodged her blow. "Hey, I'd say in comparison with your evening, my night was only okay. I just can't imagine how your pants—and panties—ended up on the floor."

Fucking observant cop. "I'm not answering that."

"Come on, kitten. We've been living celibate lives here. You gotta give me some details. Inquiring minds want to know. Which James twin were you with?"

She blushed. She thought he'd figured it out already, but apparently he hadn't. Saying it aloud was going to be tough. "I wasn't with either of them. We just sort of fooled around some."

Rodney nodded. "Okay. So you fooled around. Who with?"

She opened her mouth, determined to put him off, but then she thought better of it. She needed advice. Bad.

"Both of them."

Rodney was silent for only a moment, and when he opened his mouth, it wasn't to speak or judge or condemn her. It was worse. He laughed. Loudly.

Her temper was piqued. "This isn't funny."

Rodney continued to chuckle. "You're damn right, it's not. It's fucking hot. Holy shit, girlfriend. I knew you were pretty cool, but I had no idea—"

She smacked him on the shoulder. "I've never done anything like that before. Hell, I've never even had a one-night stand. This is just..." She threw her arms out in frustration. "I need advice here. I'm flying blind. Big time."

"And you think I can tell you how to proceed in this little threesome you're indulging in? Don't mean to disillusion you, Bridge, but I suck at dating one person at a time."

"You don't think I'm, oh, I don't know, sort of slutty for messing around with both of them?"

He shook his head. "You don't have a slutty bone in your body. Do you think this is normal for them? I mean, maybe it's a twin thing."

"No," she replied quickly. "They said last night it was new for them too. I'm not sure why I'm even letting myself get carried away with this. We have to leave soon and then—"

A knock at the door prevented her from finishing.

Rodney stood and opened the door. Matt and Mark stood in the threshold. She glanced at the clock. After their late-night argument, she and Rodney had slept in. It was nearly eleven o'clock.

"Still in bed, sleepyhead?" Matt asked.

Rodney came to her defense. "We had a bit of a rough night. Thought we'd treat ourselves to a lazy morning."

Mark walked in to the room, concern written on his face. "More bad dreams?"

She shook her head. "No. It was nothing really. Everything's better today."

"Good," Matt said, entering the room and lifting up a basket. "Because we're taking you on a picnic."

"A picnic?" She laughed. "It's February. And freezing outside."

Mark shrugged, unconcerned. "Where's your sense of adventure?"

"Inside, where it's warm," she joked.

Matt shook the basket lightly under her nose, the scent of fried chicken causing her hungry stomach to growl. "Seems a shame to waste this big lunch."

"Where are you taking her?" Rodney asked.

Mark never missed a beat. "It's a secluded place on the James Ranch, Rodney. No one will see her there. Promise."

Rodney seemed appeased by his answer. "Sounds like fun, Bridge. You should go."

"What about the ranch? The horse training. Surely you haven't finished all your chores."

Matt picked up her jeans from the floor and tossed them to her. "There's a local guy who helps out sometimes whenever one of us is sick or we need a day off. All work and no play..."

Mark headed back toward the door. "Get dressed. We'll wait for you downstairs."

"Okay." Her head chastised her heart, which was racing at the thought of spending an entire afternoon alone with the handsome twins again. She'd been so determined last night to avoid them, to keep them safe.

The door closed and she looked up, surprised to find Rodney still there.

"You okay?" he asked.

"I'm weak-willed and stupid."

He walked over and sat down beside her once more. "No, you're not. You're a beautiful woman who's falling in love."

"I don't deserve to fall in love. Not after what happened with Lyle. If I hadn't insisted that he bring me that information instead of going to the cops—"

"Stop," Rodney said firmly, his voice laced with anger. "Don't you ever say that again. You were not responsible for Lyle's death. He called you. He offered you the information."

"I should have told him no. Told him to go straight to the police. Instead, all I could think about was myself. I wanted that damn promotion so badly. God, I screwed it all up. I should have insisted we meet in public instead of that abandoned warehouse. I should have put my recorder somewhere where it would have actually picked up voices. I should have insisted we take backup."

"You can't live your life based on *should have*, Bridget. Lyle was a grown man. He knew what he had. His death was not your fault. Lucian Thompson killed him. Not you. You're a good friend. You've put your life on hold for months so that you can see that murderer brought to justice. You're risking your life to find the information that can bring down God knows how many more criminals as well."

Rodney's words were comforting, though she couldn't quite let them penetrate the part of her that would always feel responsible for Lyle's death. Still, she appreciated his effort. "Thanks."

"Go on your picnic. Have fun. Hell, one of us may as well try to get laid."

She laughed. "What will you do today?"

"Same old, same old. The Ellie Parker lead was a bust. Struck up a conversation with her while she was making my shake. Her given name is actually Ellison. She gets offended when someone calls her Ellen. Really? I'm pretty sure there's an Ellen somewhere in this damn town. I'm going to find her. Tell you what. I'll meet up with you at the James Ranch later this afternoon. For right now, it looks like we're still on the day-by-day plan. Lucky for us, there are three cowboys willing to help us wile away the hours."

*M*att leaned back on the large, plush quilt and grinned at Bridget as she dug into the chocolate mousse they'd packed with enthusiasm. For a slim woman, she sure did enjoy her food. The picnic had been Mark's idea. Matt had to admit it was inspired.

The gazebo rested in the middle of a meadow on the east end of the James Ranch. Their father had built it for their mother as a wedding gift during the first year of their marriage. It was positioned with the perfect view of the mountains on one side and the ranch—far off in the distance—on the other. The winter she'd been diagnosed with cancer, their dad had added the glass windows and the small gas heater, so Mom could rest in comfort while enjoying the view of "her" mountains, as she called them.

Neither he nor Mark came here often. They'd always considered it their mom's place, but bringing Bridget had felt right.

"I have a confession," Bridget said.

"Another one?" Mark teased.

She swatted him with her cloth napkin. "Very funny. I've never had homemade fried chicken before."

Matt sat up. "Get out of here. Really?"

She nodded. "Really. My mom didn't like to cook. My experience with fried chicken doesn't stretch much beyond a red and white tub with a picture of the Colonel on front."

Mark reached over and lightly tugged on a strand of her hair. "Damn. It's downright scary how much of life you've missed out on. You may need to make plans to stick around her a few more weeks, so we have time to catch you up."

"A few weeks," she teased. "You think that's enough time to expose me to all the wonders of good country living?"

"Better make that months," Mark added. "Or even a year, just to be sure."

Though Matt knew they were kidding around, he also knew there was a strand of seriousness behind his brother's request. Matt wanted more time with her too. More time to figure out what this feeling was and what to do with it. He'd known Bridget less than a week, but he felt certain he was falling in love with her.

"A year would be nice, but I think I'd lose my job if I stayed away that long."

Matt tilted his head. "You know, after all this time, I've never thought to ask. What do you do for a living?"

She paused, and again, Matt was struck with the uneasy

suspicion that Bridget was still holding back with them. Something about her confession the previous night had felt off. Several times today, he'd felt the same sinking awareness that something was very wrong. It was more than a nasty boyfriend looking for her. A quick glance at his brother confirmed Mark was thinking the same thing.

"I—"

Before she could finish, Matt placed his fingers against her lips. Pure instinct drove him. "Don't." He wasn't sure how he knew it, but his gut told him she was about to lie. "You don't have to tell us if you don't want to. It's not important to us what you do. We like you just fine."

She seemed taken aback and fell silent for several moments. Matt let his gaze travel to the snow-capped mountains outside. He could see the appeal of this place, could understand why his mother loved it so. When closed in the warm, cozy gazebo, the worries of the world disappeared, ceased to matter.

"I'm a reporter for a small newspaper."

Matt looked at Bridget and grinned. At last, she was beginning to trust them with a bit of the truth. "Jacob will go crazy when he finds that out. He'll pelt you with a million questions."

She laughed. "Yeah, I bet he will."

Mark moved closer to Bridget. Matt waited for some spark of jealousy, expecting the move to ignite his competitive spirit. Nothing happened. Well, not nothing. His cock moved from its semihard state to fully erect. Freud would have had a field day with this predicament, but Matt didn't care.

"We all seem to be ignoring the elephant in the room." Mark ran his hand through Bridget's hair. She'd worn it down, rather than in her usual ponytail. Matt preferred it this way.

"Elephant?" Bridget asked.

"Last night."

Mark let those two words answer her question.

"I keep thinking I should feel bad about that," she said. "But the truth is I don't. I'd sort of like to do it again."

Matt couldn't resist teasing her. "You mean orgasm and then pass out?"

She laughed. "Don't start with me, cowboy. That was your fault. I worked my ass off on *your* ranch and drank the wine *you* poured."

Mark tugged on her hair. "Spoken like a true woman. Blame the man."

"There are two of you and one of me. You better be sure I'll score my points where I can."

Matt lifted the picnic basket out of the way and scooted closer. "Fair enough. So let's explore this *do it again* comment."

She raised her hand and cupped Matt's cheek. Her soft hand felt good against his skin. "This time I'll stay awake. And this time, I don't want to be the only person removing clothes."

Her hand drifted down to his long-sleeved shirt, her fingers caressing his chest. Suddenly, he resented the cloth that restricted her touch. He took her hint and pulled his shirt off completely. Behind her, Mark did the same.

For several moments, she looked at them, her fingers touching them, learning them. "I can't believe I'm here. I can't believe you want me."

More truth. Matt sensed the walls crumbling a bit. He reached for the hem of her shirt and lifted it. She helped him remove it, remaining still, letting them look their fill.

Mark broke the silence first. "How could we not want you, Bridget? You're beautiful."

She turned and pressed her forehead against his brother's brow, then she moved closer, initiating the kiss. Matt watched the two of them, blown away by the intense beauty of their actions. They broke the kiss and Bridget turned to look at him.

Matt claimed her lips. He'd only gotten a brief taste the

night before. Today he intended to make up for that. For several moments, he lost track of everything except Bridget's lips—her taste, her smell, her soft moans. When he opened his eyes, he discovered Mark had removed her bra. Looking down, he saw his brother's hands wrapped around Bridget's middle, cupping her breasts, playing with them.

Matt moved downward as Mark lifted her breast to his mouth. Matt accepted the offering. Sucking lightly at first, Matt gradually built up the pressure until Bridget cried out in pleasure. He looked at her. "You like that?"

She nodded, her breath coming in ragged gasps. "So much."

He glanced at Mark, who nodded. They were brothers. Twins. They'd spent a lifetime communicating without words. That bond suddenly seemed stronger than ever.

Mark lifted her other breast and Matt repeated his playful game, alternating between hard sucks and light nips on her nipple. Soon, Bridget was begging for more.

Matt released her breast with a soft pop. Mark pressed her down onto the blanket. Lying on her back, she lifted her hips as Mark stripped away her jeans and panties.

Matt's heart nearly stopped beating as he got his first good glimpse of their girl in all her naked beauty. "God, sweetheart. You're gorgeous."

She smiled. And blushed. Everywhere.

Mark chuckled. "I think it's my turn to play down here."

Matt watched as Mark skipped the preliminaries and went straight for the kill. She squealed when his brother's lips grazed her clit. Mark used his tongue with skill, driving Bridget out of her mind within moments.

"No," she finally cried out. "Not again. Not just me."

She reached over and grasped the waistband of Matt's jeans. "Take them off. I want to taste you too."

A wave of lightheadedness passed over him. Matt glanced at Mark, who'd paused.

"Do it, bro." Mark's grin grew. "Do it or it's my cock she's going to taste."

Mark and Bridget laughed softly as Matt moved with haste. "No way. She asked for me."

"I want you both."

Matt wasn't sure he'd ever heard sweeter words. He stood up briefly to strip off the remainder of his clothes, then he knelt on the quilt.

Bridget reached for him the second his knees hit the floor. She wrapped her palm around his cock and lightly tugged, indicating she wanted him closer.

Moving forward, he didn't stop until he'd straddled her upper chest, the head of his cock poised a mere inch from her mouth.

Bridget hissed and Matt looked over his shoulder. Mark had resumed his actions, his tongue dipping in and out of her sheath.

Bending forward, Matt gripped his cock, dragging the head of it over her lips. "You sure?"

She smiled, then opened her mouth, welcoming him in. At first, he kept his thrusts shallow, never pressing more than the head of his cock inside, but soon she grew greedy. Gripping his ass, she pulled him closer, trying to force more and more of his girth inside.

"Easy, sweetheart," he murmured when he felt the back of her throat. She shook her head lightly and the motion felt incredible. Matt closed his eyes, fearing he'd come too fast. Watching her take him so deeply inside her mouth drove him insane.

She groaned against his flesh on the next pass and he knew

she was getting close to finding her own release. She tightened her grip on the base of his cock and sucked harder.

Stars flew behind Matt's eyes. They'd have to perfect the art of longevity later. She was too perfect, too fucking good at this. He began to move faster in and out of her mouth. Her nails pierced the skin of his bare ass, driving him on, demanding more.

She writhed beneath him, finding her own pleasure. Matt felt her body stiffen with her orgasm as the first spurt of come escaped his cock. Together the two of them shuddered. Matt wasn't sure when he'd ever come harder. Or longer.

At last, as the strength drained from him, he pulled out of her mouth, falling to her side on the quilt. He'd expected her to fall asleep as she had the night before. He was surprised when she lifted her arms to Mark instead.

Somewhere along the line, his brother had unhooked his jeans. He stroked his cock roughly.

"Come here," Bridget invited, but Mark shook his head.

"I'm too close, Bridge. I wouldn't last three seconds between those sweet lips of yours. I want to come on your stomach, your breasts."

"Yes," Bridget whispered as Mark moved closer. He leaned over her body, as he held himself a few feet above her. With his other hand, he stroked himself, quicker, harder.

Bridget lifted her hands to her breasts. Cupping them. Holding them up as she played with her nipples.

It was quite a show. Matt couldn't take his eyes off her. She was a seductress, sexy as hell.

"Goddammit, that's hot, Bridget." Mark's voice sounded rough, almost pained. "I'm going to come now. Jesus. I'm coming."

Bridget smiled as the first drops of Mark's come hit her stomach, then the tips of her breasts. His brother was decorating her delicate skin with pearls and Bridget accepted each one with genuine pleasure.

When the last of Mark's offering fell, so did he. His brother collapsed on the other side of their city angel, wrapping his arm around her and pulling her close. Mark placed several soft kisses on her cheek.

"Spend the night with us," Matt said, silently praying she would say yes. There was no way he could let her go back to New York yet. Maybe not ever. "Stay with us tonight."

She looked at him, then nodded. "I'd like that."

Matt moved closer, resting his arm along her stomach, parallel to his brother's. Together the two of them held her, sheltered her. It felt perfect. They were an ideal union of three, and it was right.

CHAPTER SEVEN

As they pulled up to the house, Bridget tried to suppress her giddy grin. She was riding in the middle of a pickup truck—a pickup, for God's sake—between the two handsome twin cowboys who'd just rocked her world. She wasn't sure how she could be so incredibly happy while living in the midst of a nightmare, but there it was. Pure happiness.

They walked into the house together. Matt held her hand as Mark lightly wrapped his arm around her waist. She wasn't sure how to explain it, but no matter what they did, they fit.

Rodney rose from the couch as they entered the living room. Bridget knew instantly he had news. From the look on his face, she suspected she wouldn't like it. Jacob walked from the kitchen with two beers in his hand.

"Hey guys. We weren't sure when you would be back. Rodney just got here and wanted to go out looking for you. I convinced him to have a cold one and hang out instead. How was the picnic?"

"Great," Matt said, lifting the empty basket. "That beer looks pretty good. You want one, Bridge?"

She nodded, though her gaze kept drifting back to Rodney. She needed to find a way to get him alone. "Do you mind if I go visit Jewel?"

"Not at all," Mark said. "I can go with you if you'd like."

"Actually, I thought maybe Rodney would want to come. I've been meaning to introduce them."

Rodney stepped forward quickly. "Yeah, I'd like that. All she talks about is this horse."

When it looked like Mark would offer to tag along, Bridget tried to cut him off at the pass. "You know, I'm kind of cold. Do you think Jessie would mind if I borrowed one of her sweatshirts?"

Mark shook his head. "I doubt it. Why don't I go get it and I'll meet you two in the stable?"

"Sounds great." Bridget hastily grabbed Rodney's hand and tugged him toward the door. As they stepped into the yard, she looked at him. "Talk fast."

"I think I found Ellen."

"Oh my God. Really? Where is she? Can we talk to her?"

Rodney reached into his pocket and pulled out a scrap of newspaper. "I tore this out of today's paper."

It was an obituary for Ellen Updyke. Bridget looked at the name for several moments.

Rodney couldn't resist pointing out the obvious. "Up. Ellen."

Bridget nodded. "That's her. I remember that name. God. I'm such an idiot. One night we were talking about our families. Lyle mentioned his godmother. I made some stupid joke about it being a rather unfortunate name. I forgot."

"Lyle must have remembered the joke."

A horrible thought crossed Bridget's mind. "Oh my God. Was she killed?"

Rodney shook his head. "No. She was old. Seventy-three. According to this, she had a heart attack."

Bridget felt a wave of relief pass through her. "Oh thank God. I mean, not that she's dead, but—"

"I know what you mean, Bridget."

"What are we going to do?"

"I was going to see how you felt about staying here at the ranch tonight."

It was what she wanted, what she was about to request, but she was surprised to hear Rodney suggest it. "Here? Why?"

"Because I think I'm finally selling the last of my soul to the devil. I'm going to break into a dead woman's house to look for a flash drive."

"I'll come with you."

Rodney quickly refused. "The hell you will. I've broken every rule beaten into my head during my police training since we left Oklahoma. Leave me some scrap of dignity. I'll feel a hell of a lot safer with you here. Besides you're about as quiet as a bass drum. I can't imagine how hard it would be try to go into someone's house undercover with you."

She narrowed her eyes, ready to protest his insult, but they didn't have time for the argument. And he was right. She was clumsy as hell, especially in the dark.

"Fine. I'll stay here. What happens if you don't find anything?"

Rodney sighed. "Then I'm afraid we may have to crash the reception after the funeral. Maybe try to question the relatives. Somehow."

She could tell from his tone Rodney didn't like that option.

"You two didn't make it very far," Mark said as he joined them.

Rodney quickly shoved the obituary back in his pocket as Mark handed Bridget a sweatshirt.

"Not sure where Jessie keeps her sweatshirts and I didn't think she'd appreciate me rifling through her drawers. Brought you one of mine. Might be a bit big."

"This is perfect. Thanks." For several minutes, she tagged along as Mark showed Rodney around the stable, introducing him to the horses. It gave her time to consider Lyle's message. They'd broken the first half of the code and it had led them to Ellen Updyke in Saratoga. Bridget silently prayed Rodney would find the flash drive tonight, so they could put the rest of infuriating puzzle away.

After dinner, Rodney claimed he had a headache and announced he was heading back to the inn for the night. Neither of the twins questioned his departure, obviously assuming she'd set it up with him because of their invitation.

Jacob declined to watch a movie with them, opting instead to head to bed with a book.

Matt grasped her hand and started to take her into the living room, but she held back.

"Where's your bedroom?" she asked. She'd spent most of dinnertime alternating between anxious butterflies in her stomach and an ache between her legs. She wanted to sleep with Matt and Mark, even if the idea of taking on two wholly masculine, very virile men at the same time made her nervous as hell.

Mark pulled her close. "Bridget, we don't have to do anything tonight if you aren't ready. There's a guest room that you're more than welcome to—"

She held up her hand. "Stop right there. The only way I'm sleeping in a guest room is if you two are with me."

Matt took the hand she'd raised in his and led her down the hallway. "Then so be it. Both of our bedrooms are upstairs, but so is Jacob's. Tonight we'll sleep in the guest room. Lucky for us, it has a nice, big bed."

She followed Matt into the room, then turned to watch Mark close the door and lock it.

He gave her a guilty grin. "Just making sure we're not disturbed. Jake is a nosy fucker. Wouldn't put it past him to come looking for us later when we don't come up."

She giggled. "Do you think he'll be scandalized when he realizes we're all in here together?"

Mark shook his head. "My kid brother? Hell no, nothing shocks that guy."

Matt turned her to face him. She sucked in a breath at the pure hunger in his gaze. Rather than speak, he simply bent forward and kissed her. His lips grazed hers softly at first before he deepened the action. She reached up to wrap her arms around his neck, letting her fingers glide through his thick, dark hair.

His hands grasped her face, gently turning her head this way and that so he could advance the kiss, keep his lips on hers. It was heady, dizzying, perfect.

She heard Mark approach, felt his hands grip her waist from behind. He didn't try to break her and Matt apart. Instead, he added his warmth to the union, pressing his lips softly against the back of her head.

After a lifetime of amazing kisses, Matt stepped back and let her turn into Mark's embrace. Mark took over, claiming her lips. She waited for Matt to touch her as well, but he didn't. Mark didn't give her a chance to wonder about Matt's absence for long.

As his lips devoured hers, he worked the button and zipper on her jeans loose, then pushed the denim over her hips.

He released her lips and she reached down to strip the jeans the rest of the way off. All of her nerves fled in an instant.

There was nowhere else on earth she'd rather be at this moment than with her two beautiful men.

Glancing over her shoulder, she giggled when she spotted Matt. While Mark had entertained her with kisses, her second lover had been busy. Not only was he naked, he'd lit several candles in the room and pulled down the sheets on the bed.

"Anxious?" she asked.

"Impatient." Matt reached for the hem of her shirt, tugging it over her head. No sooner had the material hit the floor than Mark had her bra following.

She stood, soaking in Matt's muscular physique. There was no question he was a physically strong man who worked outside for living. His skin was darkened by the sun and his muscles had muscles.

Mark's sudden movement caught her eye and she watched as he removed his clothing. The identical features didn't stop at their faces. Mark's body was as beautiful as his brother's.

"Damn," she whispered when her gaze drifted to the lower regions. Though she'd sampled a bit of both men this afternoon, she hadn't had a chance to study their physiques. Neither man was hurting in the cock department. She squeezed her legs together as her arousal built.

Mark moved closer, kissing her again. She loved the feeling of his bare skin against hers. Every inch of her was on fire, sensitive to the touch. Matt's hand brushed her ass and she jumped a bit.

Mark noticed the movement. "Okay?"

She didn't want him to misinterpret her response. "So horny."

Matt chuckled. "Well, we can take care of that. In fact, I think we better do it soon because my cock is about to explode." He took her hand and led her to the bed as she laughed.

Never in her wildest dreams could she have imagined a

night like this. She never would have thought herself bold enough, brave enough to do something society would dub so completely scandalous. And yet, here she was, embarking on one of the most exciting adventures in her life.

As she lay down on the bed, she was surprised how easily Matt and Mark followed her. It was a new experience for them as well, yet neither of them was balking or shy. Instead, they seemed completely focused on her.

Mark lifted her slightly, moving her to the middle of the mattress before covering her with his body and kissing her once more. She liked his kisses, liked the time he took exploring her mouth. She'd had lovers in the past who treated kissing as an item on the sex list—once they'd given her a few, they'd checked it off and moved on.

As Mark continued to kiss her, Matt let his fingers do the walking, caressing her breasts, stroking her stomach, rubbing her feet. There was no part of her left untouched, and after several moments, her body began to react like a live wire, sparking at every subtle brush of Mark's tongue in her mouth or Matt's fingers on her skin.

"God," she said, breaking away to suck in some much needed air. "Please. I need more. I'll die without more." She was about to spontaneously combust. She'd never thought there could be such a thing as too much foreplay, but she needed a man inside her. Now.

Matt reached beside the bed, toward the nightstand. "Well, we can't have that. We're just getting to the good part."

He grabbed two condoms, tossing one to his brother.

"Matt," his brother warned. "I thought we agreed we were going to take this slow."

"No," she said loudly. "Please, I'm begging you." She squeezed her legs together, trying to find some relief. She'd never felt so empty, so needy.

Matt grinned at his brother. "You can go slow later. I'm just going to help her take the edge off."

Before she could respond, Matt was between her legs, his cock poised at the entrance to her body. Their eyes met as he pushed inside. No more questions, no more kisses, just the two of them looking at each other as their bodies joined. It was amazing.

Once he reached the hilt, he paused for a second. He gave her a goofy, completely adorable grin. "We're doing it."

She giggled. "Yeah, we are."

He didn't say more as he started to thrust inside her. She groaned in relief and pure pleasure as he moved—his cock filled her completely, and for the tiniest second, she considered that he seemed to be made for her.

That thought was driven away when he started to move faster, deeper. She threw her head back on the pillow and cried out. They'd teased her for too long and Matt felt so damn good. She was close.

"Matt, I—"

"It's okay, Bridge. We've got all night."

Then it came. The touch.

Glancing to her right, she saw Mark lying next to them on his side with his head propped up by one hand. He was watching her face, her reactions. When she looked down, she noticed his other hand had entered the game. He wiggled his finger and applied more pressure to her clit.

She exploded. Matt groaned, his thrusts becoming erratic, slower as her pussy clenched around him.

"Jesus, sweetheart. Fuck. I wanted to go longer, but—"

Matt gave up. His climax began just as hers started to wane. Mark pressed against her clit again and she screamed. The motion triggered a second, quick orgasm. She'd never, never had a second orgasm in a single night.

"Holy shit," Matt gasped. "So fucking good. So hot. Christ, Bridge, I thought you were going to squeeze my cock off. Your pussy should be declared a lethal weapon."

She grinned, loving his dirty compliment.

Mark's finger disappeared as Matt withdrew and fell to the mattress on her opposite side.

Mark sat up. "That's quite a bedside manner you've got there, bro. Do you have to describe everything in vivid porn detail?"

Bridget could tell he was more amused than annoyed. Still, she felt she should come to Matt's defense. "I like it. Makes me hot."

Mark gave her a crooked grin. "Don't encourage him. I'm sure he'll only get worse."

Bridget lifted her arms to Mark. She should have been exhausted. She expected to feel wrung out and hung out to dry. Instead, the moment she saw Mark and his lovely erection, she got her second wind.

Mark accepted her silent invitation, covering her body with his. She was a tall woman. She'd never felt tiny in any man's presence, yet Matt and Mark left her feeling petite, almost delicate. She liked it.

Mark kissed her again, but rather than the long, deep, soul-searching kisses he'd given her early, these were shorter, quicker, but just as sexy and romantic. "You sure you're up for another round? We can wait a little while. Give you a chance to rest."

She was touched by his thoughtful gesture, then she glanced down at his painfully erect cock and shook her head. "No way. I want you now." It was the truth. Though she'd only known these men a few days, it felt like much longer to her. She wasn't sure if in the past she would have jumped so quickly, but she was different now.

Since Lyle's death, since her life had become a day-by-day attempt at surviving, she'd learned to take each moment as it came and to enjoy it. The old Bridget would never have jumped into a threesome so quickly, never would have taken this chance.

The old Bridget was a fool.

"Come inside me, Mark," she whispered.

He quickly donned his condom and then he was there. Like Matt, Mark knew how to use his equipment.

Her smile grew at the thought and she briefly considered saying it aloud. Matt would have laughed at her raunchy joke, but she knew Mark was trying to make this moment special for her. His gentle soul touched her.

His movements, unlike his brother's, were slower, more controlled, but no less potent. Mark paid attention to her body's cues, her quick intakes of breath. He read her body's language to slowly and methodically drive her to the peak once more. Unlike Matt's quick, explosive style, Mark took his time and gave her time to get there too. She wasn't sure how long they clung to each other, their bodies pulsing together, but she was brought back to earth when she heard Matt mutter the word "beautiful" beside her.

It was beautiful. Every part of it. Mark reached down and stroked her clit. He'd learned during her interlude with Matt how much that simple touch turned her on. It had the same effect again. It was the trigger to her climax, and she cried out as she came. Mark joined her. Together, they trembled and gasped as their bodies took their pleasure.

Sated, Mark pulled out of her, then bent down to kiss her. Once he moved to her right, Matt gripped her chin and pulled her face toward his, adding his kiss to the mix.

"Best night ever," he murmured when they broke off the kiss.

Mark and Matt, though identical, had offered her two very different experiences. Mark, ever the gentleman, was a romantic, thoughtful lover. When he placed his hands on her cheeks and pulled her in for a kiss, she thought she'd melt, while Matt brought out the fun parts of sex, talking dirty and making her laugh. It was the ideal combination.

She agreed with Matt's sentiment wholeheartedly. "Best night ever."

*B*ridget tiptoed down the hallway the next morning. It was well after six a.m., but neither man had stirred. She was wearing Mark's sweatshirt and Matt's boxers that she'd snatched from the floor. She grinned as she recalled the night. She should be back in bed, sleeping like the dead as well, after the workout the twins gave her. Instead, she was wide awake and giddy.

Walking into the kitchen, she opened the refrigerator, searching for ingredients. She wanted to surprise the guys with a big breakfast. Pulling out eggs and a package of bacon, she put them on the counter, then grabbed the coffeepot and headed for the sink.

She'd just started to hum, a sure sign she was out of her mind with joy, when she heard a light tap on the back door. Looking over, she saw Rodney waving to her frantically.

Her good mood vanished in an instant. His face betrayed that his news wasn't good. She opened the door and instantly shivered as a burst of cold air struck her.

"Get your clothes. We're getting out of here."

"What happened?" she asked. "Did you find something in Ellen's house? Did you get caught?"

Rodney looked around the kitchen to make sure they were alone. Her heart began to race. She'd seen him go into warrior-mode only twice before, both times when the hit man took his shots at her.

"I didn't find anything in the house, but we're going to have to give up on that, Bridget. He's here."

Her stomach twisted into knots. "He?"

Rodney tilted his head, didn't answer. He didn't have to. "I searched the house last night. Didn't find a fucking thing. That Ellen woman didn't even own a computer. Went back to the B&B and started looking at the message again. I'll be damned if I can figure out the fucking code, so I tried your suggestion. The next sentence has the word key in it. Decided maybe I was looking for the wrong damn thing."

"You think he gave Ellen a key?"

"Well, he sure as hell didn't give her a flash drive. I turned that place upside down looking. Anyway, I couldn't sleep, so I thought I'd take another swipe at the house. Look for a key."

"Did you find one?" she asked.

"Never made it back to the house. I was on the outskirts of town when I saw him walking out of one of the hotels. God knows how long he's been here. I'm trying to figure out how the hell he found us."

"I don't know. He must have tracked us from Oklahoma somehow."

Rodney nodded. "Yeah, I guess so. Bridget, we gotta move. Now."

"Where?"

"I have no fucking idea. But it's not safe here anymore. Not for you, not for our friends."

Bridget's blood ran cold at the thought of the danger she'd put the James brothers, Todd, and Steven in. Reaching down, she picked up her shoes. Fortunately, she'd pulled them off while making dinner. She lived in bare feet in her apartment. Matt and Mark had teased her about her habit of taking her shoes off the second she walked in a house. "Let's go."

"What about your clothes?"

She shook her head. "I don't want to risk waking up the guys."

"Here." Rodney took off his coat and helped her put it on. Even with the extra layer, she was going to freeze her ass off on the way back to the inn. Literally. The boxers weren't much protection. "You sure about this? You don't want to leave a note or something?"

"No. They won't let me leave easily. It's better this way."

Better, she thought, as she hastily followed Rodney along the secluded trail, her heart breaking more with every step she took.

Better, but not easier.

CHAPTER EIGHT

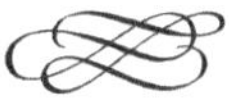

Bridget threw the rest of her clothing in a bag and glanced around the room to make sure she hadn't forgotten anything. Rodney had packed up his own things, then insisted she remain in the room while he tried to sort out their next hideout. He insisted it would be a big mistake for them to run off without any direction. It was better for her to stay out of sight. He'd borrowed Steven's truck and taken off over an hour ago. She was starting to worry Thompson's henchman had caught up with him. He'd been gone too long.

She glanced down at the floor, mildly surprised to find she hadn't paced a hole in the carpeting. She was a nervous wreck. With each moment that passed, her anxiety grew. She'd hoped to be gone well before Matt and Mark discovered her absence from their bed. What would they think when they woke and couldn't find her? Would they think she'd freaked out and run? Changed her mind?

A light knock at the door sent her jumping nearly two feet in the air. Rodney wouldn't have knocked. She froze, uncertain what to do. What if it was the hit man?

"Open the door, Bridget. We know you're in there."

Mark's voice drifted through the wall. She'd run out of time. Now she would be forced to lie again. But lie she would if it meant protecting the men she cared about from harm.

She opened the door. On the other side, she was greeted by two thoroughly annoyed lovers. They weren't happy about her disappearing act.

"Hey," she said, realizing it was an inane greeting.

"Hey yourself." Matt walked into the room and handed her a large bouquet of flowers. Her heart skipped a beat at the romantic gesture. As quickly as her joy came, it fled, an ache blooming in her chest instead. Leaving them would be one of the hardest things she'd ever done.

Mark entered the room as well, closing the door behind him.

"I have something for you too," Mark said, holding up a white envelope. His face was strangely blank, something Bridget had never seen before. He was a gentle man who'd never looked at her with anything less than kindness or humor.

"What is it?"

"We were hoping you could tell us. When we woke up in an empty bed, we were worried we'd overwhelmed you. Matt suggested we get you flowers."

She smiled and hoped they couldn't see the tears gathering in her eyes. "I like the flowers."

Mark didn't acknowledge her comment. "On the way to town, we stopped by Ellen Updyke's house this morning to offer our condolences to her niece and to see if she needed help with anything. Her aunt's funeral is today."

A ball of ice formed in her stomach. She tried to ignore it and focus on their thoughtful gesture. "That was nice of you."

He nodded, but didn't return her smile or acknowledge her

compliment. "Her niece was cleaning up the house, getting ready for the reception after the funeral."

The event she and Rodney had planned to crash. Looked like that plan was shot to hell.

Then she wondered where Mark going with this whole conversation. Clearly something had happened at Ellen's house. Had the hit man shown up there?

Her voice was weak with fear and dread. "Why are you telling me all this?"

"Gretchen, Ellen's niece, was with her aunt when she passed away. Said one of the last things her aunt did before she died was hand her this letter, telling her to guard it carefully and never show it to anyone. Said to be on the lookout for the woman whose name was written on the front."

Mark flipped the letter over and Bridget gasped. Written in Lyle's distinctive scrawl was her name, but there was no way Matt and Mark could know that. She'd introduced herself as Carson.

"Bridget Wilder?"

"You," Matt said.

She looked at her other lover. He'd been silent since handing her the flowers. It wasn't like him to be quiet. "Me?"

Matt took her continued denial like a punch in the face. She felt sick to her stomach, sorry about the lies. "I typed Bridget Wilder and New York City into my iPhone. Pulled up an article about a reporter who'd gone into protective custody after witnessing a murder. Even had a picture of you."

They knew.

"So this Gretchen, she showed the letter to you?"

She and Rodney had been right. Lyle's code had led them to Saratoga and his godmother, Ellen, but how could she explain this to the two men staring at her with suddenly angry eyes?

Mark nodded. "Unlike her aunt, Gretchen's not exactly known for her ability to keep a secret or mind her own business. She was dying to open the letter and asked my advice. When I saw the name Bridget, something clicked. I told her I knew you and that I'd deliver it for her. Needless to say, she was disappointed. I expect her to call me sometime in the next twenty-four hours to grill me about you."

Matt took a step closer to her. "You want to tell us why Ellen Updyke had a letter with your name written on it, Bridget? I get that you're in protective custody, and I think it's pretty fucking obvious that Rodney's not your brother. But none of what I read in that newspaper explains why you're here, hiding in plain sight. I thought safe houses were secluded places tucked away in the middle of nowhere."

She sighed, silently wishing Rodney was here. He'd know how to proceed. Her heart longed to tell them the whole truth, but she feared it may be too late. How would they feel once she revealed how badly she'd misled them? She'd let things go way too far with her handsome twins. The day of reckoning was at hand.

"I suspect I'll find a key in there." It wasn't the answer they were hoping for, but it was the most innocuous one she could give them. Her heart was racing a mile a minute. She'd lived every moment of the past six months jumping at shadows and running for her life, but she'd never felt true fear until this moment.

Would they forgive her for her deception? How would they feel when they learned of her role in Lyle's death? She couldn't forgive herself for letting her friend die. How could she ask them to?

"A key?" Matt asked.

She nodded and reached for the envelope. Mark handed it to her. She wanted to open it, but she hesitated.

"Go on," Matt prodded, his words almost a dare.

They were worried about her. She knew that. They'd known from almost the start that she was hiding something from them, but she'd piled lie upon lie rather than offer them the trust they'd given her so completely.

She took a deep breath and opened the envelope. A small key fell out into the palm of her hand. The letter inside simply said First Bank, 348 Main Street, Saratoga.

"That's a safe-deposit box key from the bank," Mark said. "We have one too. Got the deed to the ranch and other important documents stored there. I thought you said you'd never been to Saratoga before. Is this yours?"

She nodded. "It is now."

Matt threw up his hands in frustration. "More vague answers. What the hell is going on here, Bridget? Last night everything seemed fine. We show up today to find you packed up and ready to bail without a word."

"I wanted to leave you a note," she said, the words sounding lame even to her ears. She'd never intended to write them anything. She simply didn't have the strength to say good-bye to them—not on paper and not in person.

"You wanted to leave a note?" Mark asked. "The same way Ellen left a note for you?"

"I want to tell you, but I can't. I just can't."

"Dammit, Bridget. Why can't you get it through that thick skull of yours that we want to help? We would never—"

"What's going on here?" Rodney stood at the door looking as blindsided as she felt.

She held out the key. "Mark brought me this. It's from Ellen."

Rodney walked closer, slowly, hesitantly. He took the key and letter from her. "I see."

"Mark and Matt want to know, Rodney. Please." She

wasn't anxious to continue their earlier argument, but she was tired of secrets, of running, of hiding.

Rodney looked at her and nodded slowly. "So tell them."

She paused, her mind struggling to comprehend. Had she heard him correctly? "All of it?"

"All of it."

She smiled tremulously. "It will be okay. We can trust them. They'll help us. I know they will." *Please let that be true.*

Rodney gave her an encouraging grin, then crossed the room, claiming a chair by the window. She was used to that pose. He was looking out, keeping his eyes peeled for the villain they'd spotted earlier this morning. "Just make it quick, kitten. Time's not exactly on our side."

She sat down on the bed and gestured to the other chair in the room. Matt claimed it while Mark joined her on the edge of the mattress.

"You're worrying me, darlin'," Mark said, grasping her hand. "What's going on?"

"Honestly, it sounds like you've already figured most of it out on your own. I witnessed a murder. The killer is a very powerful, highly connected judge in the New York court system. By highly connected, I mean to politicians and the mob."

Matt nodded. "Scary shit. That doesn't explain why you're in Saratoga using Todd and Steven's inn as a safe house."

Rodney stepped forward. "This isn't a safe house. There have been two attempts made on Bridget's life in the past six months."

"Jesus," Mark muttered.

Bridget took his hand in hers and squeezed. "I'm still alive, Mark. Rodney began to suspect there was someone dirty at the police department, someone who was feeding the locations of the safe houses to the judge and his hit man."

"Hit man?" Matt shook his head. "I don't like the sound of this at all."

Bridget tried to offer a comforting smile. "Rodney and I decided to go rogue. We both cleaned out our bank accounts, and we took off for Saratoga in the dead of the night. We thought we'd be safe here because no one knew where we were."

Mark wrapped his arm around her shoulder. "Bridget, you should have told us what was going on. We would have protected you."

She was touched by the offer and overwhelmed once more by guilt. "We didn't know who we could trust. It's been just Rodney and me for so long. I guess we figured we could keep doing it on our own. I mean, I'm fine so far."

Rodney walked to the window and carefully peered out. "Yeah, well, not for long if we don't speed this up and get the hell out of here."

Matt rose quickly "Why? What's going on?"

"Bridget wasn't able to identify the man who was with the judge the night he murdered her friend. Since then, she's spotted him a couple of times—both times just before he attempted to kill her. I saw him in town this morning, coming out of the local hotel."

Mark jumped up. "We have to get you out of here."

"That's what I was trying to do," Rodney said. "I checked out the prices of bus tickets, car rentals, everything I could think of, kitten. Fact is, we don't have enough money to leave."

"So don't leave," Matt said. "Come stay at the James Ranch. You can hide there."

Rodney shook his head. "It's too close to this inn. If the hit man manages to track us to this place, you can be sure he'll be checking out the neighboring houses as well when he doesn't find us."

"The cabin," Mark said, looking at Matt. "We'll take her up to the cabin."

Matt nodded. "That could work. It's definitely secluded. We haven't been up there in a couple of years. Hell, it's so hidden that half the time I miss the turnoff to the driveway."

"Cabin?" Rodney asked. "This isn't one listed on a realtor's site for rent, is it?"

Mark shook his head. "No, those cabins are on the other side of the mountain from ours. Trust me, this is a family-owned property and I'll bet money ninety-nine percent of Saratoga doesn't even know it's there. It's perfect."

"Fine. That's where we'll go." Rodney looked at Bridget. Though his body was still tense, coiled and ready for action, she spotted the first bit of hope in his face since he'd come to find her this morning.

Despite their generous offer, Bridget felt compelled to make sure things were okay. "Are you sure you don't mind helping me? I mean, I haven't been exactly truthful."

Mark cupped her cheek with his hand. "I have a feeling we haven't scratched the surface of your secrets yet, but I figure we'll have plenty of time for you to come clean while we're hiding out at the cabin. I don't dare stay here any longer."

"Hiding out at the cabin?" Rodney asked. "I think it would be best if it was just Bridget and I staying there."

Matt shook his head. "No deal. You can stay there, but we're going to be there too."

Rodney looked like he wanted to argue the point, but Mark didn't give him the chance. He picked up Bridget's bag. "Is this all your stuff?"

She nodded. Hastily, the four of them grabbed their things and walked downstairs. Mark pulled Steven and Todd aside, quickly explaining the situation. Bridget could see from the scowl on Rodney's face he wasn't happy to have their secret identities exposed to so many people, but she could see the sense behind Mark's actions. Todd and Steven were their friends, and they needed to be protected as well.

Todd came over as Steven and Mark disappeared into the kitchen. "You poor girl. Don't you worry about a thing. Your secret is safe with us. Steven's gone to pack up some food for you to take with you. And here." Todd walked over to a locked desk. Taking out the key, he opened the top drawer and pulled out some money. "This is the money you paid for the room. It sounds to me like you need it more than we do."

Bridget shook her head, tears springing to her eyes at Todd's generosity. "No, we couldn't take that back. We put you in terrible danger by staying here." Her heart ached to realize how badly things could have—could still—turn out if the hit man showed up here.

"Hush," Todd said, shoving the money into her hands. "It's yours. I won't discuss it further."

Mark and Steven came out of the kitchen loaded down with grocery bags. Matt took Steven's load.

"Meet us out back," Mark said as they walked toward the front door. "I'll pull the truck around there, by the kitchen door."

Rodney grabbed a baseball cap from one of the tables. "Mind if we borrow this?"

Todd shook his head.

Rodney donned the cap, then unwrapped the scarf from around Bridget's neck, replacing it around her head. "We better try to hide this blonde hair of yours. Keep your face down and walk fast."

Within moments, the four of them were crammed into the front of Mark's Ford truck. After a brief trip to the James Ranch for more supplies, clothes for the twins and an explanation to Jacob, they were on their way. The trip to the cabin took over an hour on a path that was too rocky and bumpy to even be called a road.

Bridget nearly fell to her knees and kissed the solid ground when they finally arrived. She feared the ride had jarred most of her teeth as well as her brain loose.

Mark opened the door and the four of them took several trips between the truck and cabin, unloading their supplies. After several hours of unpacking and cleaning up to make the cabin habitable, they finally settled down around the table for a dinner of cold-cut sandwiches.

Matt had managed to get the generator up and running so they had power, but none of them had the energy to cook a meal.

Mark took a sip from his water bottle. "Guess we need to hear the rest of your story. Figure out a game plan from here."

Rodney put his sandwich down. "Bridget needs to be back in New York in two weeks to testify at the judge's trial. We need to lay low for about a week and a half without being spotted. Then I'm going to call my partner, tell him where we are, and ask him to secure us transportation back to the city."

"Thought you said someone was dirty in the department. How do you know you can trust your partner?"

Rodney shrugged easily. "How do you know you can trust Todd and Steven not to tell the hit man where we're hiding?"

Matt scowled. "Those guys are good friends. They would never betray us."

Rodney put his hands up in surrender. "I'm not saying they would, but I feel the same way about my partner."

"If that's true, then why didn't you just call him for help instead of taking off on your own?" Mark asked.

"My partner's as low down on the food chain at work as I am. There are channels we have to go through. He couldn't have helped us on his own without risking his job. Even though he would have done it, I wouldn't have asked. In a couple weeks, it won't matter because we're going home anyway. We're going to need protection when we get back to New York. I trust my partner to supply it."

Matt leaned back in his chair and tossed a chip in his mouth. "So we just need to hole up here for about ten days. That shouldn't be a problem."

A new concern sprang to Bridget's mind. "What about the ranch?"

Mark reached over and ran his finger along her cheek. "Jacob is calling that guy we told you about. The one who fills in sometimes. He and Jake can keep things going at the ranch while we're gone. Caleb and Jessie will be back in a couple of days and they can pitch in too. Don't worry."

Matt reached back, placing his hands behind his head and looked toward the ceiling. "There's still one thing I don't get. When you decided to strike off on your own, why come to Saratoga, and why in the hell did Ellen Updyke have that key waiting for you?"

Rodney and Bridget took turns explaining about Lyle's coded message and the flash drive. Mark and Matt asked questions and both looked at Lyle's note, impressed by the fact she and Rodney had managed to figure out so much of it.

"So you think the flash drive is in that safe-deposit box?" Matt asked.

Bridget shrugged. "I hope it is. We don't have time to try to solve any more puzzles."

Matt and Mark excused themselves after dinner, going out to check the perimeter of the property. They'd carried in several hunting rifles and a handgun earlier. Bridget had shuddered when she'd seen it, even though having all that firepower around made her feel better.

Rodney helped Bridget clear the table. She could tell something was on his mind. "What's up, Rodney?"

"I think this is a good place," he said.

"I think it is too. I feel safe here."

"Matt and Mark would never let anyone hurt you, kitten."

She smiled, his words warming her. "I know that."

"I think we should split up."

His words hit her like a glass of ice-cold water to the face. "What?"

"We're running out of time. You said yourself you hoped the flash drive is in the safe-deposit box, but what if it isn't? What if it's another fucking coded letter?"

"I don't think it is. The flash drive will be there, Rodney. I feel it."

"I'm worried about Jake."

Ah, she thought. Now they'd gotten to the heart of the matter. "Why?"

"We've covered our tracks well, but..." Rodney sighed. "Dammit, I went to the bowling alley with him. People saw us together. What if one of them mentions that to the hit man and he goes after Jake to get to me?"

Rodney had a very good point. The thought of Jacob in danger terrified her. "You want to go back to the ranch to protect Jacob."

He nodded. "I swear to you, I'd never leave if I didn't *know* you were safe here."

"I know that." She did. Rodney had been an amazing protector. "And you're right. You should go. You can protect Jacob, try to retrieve the flash drive from the bank, help out at the ranch, and keep a lookout for the hit man. You can be our eyes on the ground while we're hiding here on top of the mountain. The altitude is killing me, by the way. My ears still haven't popped." She wiggled a finger in her ear and grinned.

She knew Rodney was torn, and she didn't want him to worry.

"I'll be fine, Rodney. Go do what you need to do."

He sighed and nodded slowly. "I'll get one of the guys to drive me back down in the morning."

"Sounds like a plan."

CHAPTER NINE

Bridget stood at the kitchen window and stared out into the dark nothingness. She'd spent eight amazing days in this cabin with Matt and Mark. Every day that passed solidified her feelings for them. She was falling in love...hard.

Rodney had returned to the James Ranch the day after their arrival, leaving her and her handsome twins completely alone in their wilderness retreat. The men never let her venture out of the cabin. Instead, they spent their days playing games and talking. Most evenings they curled up on a quilt on the floor, sitting in front of the fireplace. The three of them had made love on the floor more than in the bed, none of them ever able to keep their hands off each other long enough to move to the mattress.

She listened as Mark said good-bye and clicked off his phone.

"Everything okay on that end?" she asked.

He nodded once, then shook his head.

Matt's head popped up from the book he'd been reading on

the couch. "What's up?"

Mark took a seat at the kitchen table. The cabin was one large room, each corner containing a different area. She and Mark were in the kitchen corner, while Matt was only a few feet away, lounging in the living room. Across from the living room area was the bedroom. Fortunately for them, there was a king-size bed taking up most of a side wall, plenty big enough for the three of them to play in. And play they had. The only walls in the cabin were in the fourth corner, and they contained the bathroom complete with a toilet, small sink and shower stall.

"Rodney decided to take a chance. He went to the bank today."

She could tell from the look on Mark's face the news wasn't good. "The flash drive wasn't there?"

Mark shrugged. "Rodney doesn't know. The damn bank manager claimed there was a pin number attached to this box. He didn't even get near it because he didn't know that magic number."

"Shit!" Bridget turned and banged her fist on the kitchen counter. "How the hell are we supposed to get to this damn thing?" She glanced heavenward and considered railing at her late friend. Guilt over his death aside, Lyle was really pissing her off right now.

Matt rose and came to console her. He placed a comforting arm around her waist. "No worries. We'll figure it out. Grab the note, Bridget. Let's go over it again."

"There are no numbers in that note." She had the fucking thing memorized. That much she knew.

Mark beckoned her to join him at the table. "It doesn't hurt to look."

She went to the bedside table to retrieve Lyle's message. Rodney had left it in her care when he returned to the James

Ranch. They both thought they'd cracked the thing and didn't need it anymore.

She sat down at the table, laying the piece of paper between them. "He should have gone to the bank earlier."

Since returning to the James Ranch, Rodney had curtailed his trips into town, instead remaining in seclusion on the ranch. According to Jake, Rodney had started helping out with the ranch duties and was turning out to be quite a horseman. Matt had laughed when he relayed this information. Matt thought it sounded like Jake was sort of upset that Rodney was better at riding than him after only a few days of lessons. Considering Jacob had spent a lifetime on horseback, that was saying something about Rodney's natural skill.

They'd all decided Rodney should delay his trip to the bank. First of all, they wanted to be sure the hit man didn't spot him or Bridget. And secondly, they'd genuinely thought the code was cracked. Rodney figured the flash drive was much safer in the safe deposit box, where it had been hiding for months, rather than in his possession.

After several frustrating moments of looking at the message and finding nothing even remotely like a pin number, Bridget put her head down on the table.

She was leaving the day after tomorrow. Her escape from reality was about to come crashing to a painful halt. While she'd loved every moment of her time with Matt and Mark, none of them had discussed what would happen after she boarded that plane and returned to New York. She sensed that the men, like her, were afraid to admit something they all knew.

They lived in Wyoming on the land that had belonged to their family for over a hundred years. They earned their living on that ranch. She was a city girl—born and bred. Her apartment, her job, her friends and family all resided on the east coast.

She felt a hand land on her head, lightly massaging her scalp. Mark's. She'd become accustomed to their touches, knew whose hand it was without looking. They'd played a game in bed one night where they blindfolded her, then took turns touching and kissing her. After each red-hot interaction, she had to guess which man it had been. She'd been right every single time.

Matt stood up, coming behind her to rub her shoulders. "It'll be okay, Bridge. We'll get that flash drive out of the bank. You and Rodney can take it back to New York and Rodney's job will be safe. You have to believe that. You've come too far to give up hope now."

She didn't respond. Depression was closing in fast. Leaving them was going to be the hardest thing she'd ever done. "What's going to happen to us?"

She'd resisted asking the question for days, fearing the answer, not wanting to accept the truth. She couldn't hold it in any longer.

A chair scraped along the floor and strong arms lifted her from the table. Mark. She never ceased to be amazed by his sheer strength. No one had attempted to pick her up since she was a child. He did so with ease, walking across the room and gently depositing her on the bed.

Mark lay down beside her, wrapping her up in his warm embrace. "I don't know what's going to happen, darlin'. All I know is I don't want to lose you."

Matt sat on the edge of the bed on her other side. "Me either. You kind of crash-landed into our lives, didn't you?"

She grinned. "That's one way to put it."

Matt's face sobered, more serious than usual. "We've got a lot of stuff to mark off our list before we start worrying about that. We need to get that flash drive out of the bank. We need to get you and Rodney back to New York safely and you need to testify. That's a lot of shit to deal with, and until that's off our plates, I don't think we should make any other big decisions."

He was right. She knew that. Right now, she was an emotional basket case, living in a constant state of fear, anxiety and arousal. Until she finished this latest chapter in her book, she'd be a fool to start a new one. "You're right."

"But Bridget," Mark said, turning her face toward his, "you need to know, whatever happens, we're crazy about you."

It was the closest any of them had come to admitting their feelings. If she'd felt free to speak what was written on her heart, she would have been screaming the words *I love you* to both of them. "I'm crazy about you guys too."

Mark leaned forward and kissed her. She could hear Matt taking off his clothes behind her, felt the bed dip when he joined them. Mark released her and Matt took over, offering her long, deep, tantalizing kisses as his twin got undressed. Then, together, they slowly peeled off layer after layer of her clothing, taking their time to caress each newly bared bit of skin.

By the time she was completely naked, she was flushed, hot, aching.

Every night their passion grew, every interlude more exciting, more thrilling than the one before. Bridget had become a master of multiple orgasms, something she'd never hoped to have, let alone enjoy night after night.

Mark rolled onto his back, pulling her on top of him. She loved being on top and had shared that tiny tidbit with them on their first night alone together in the cabin. She grinned at Mark's invitation as he handed her a condom. She slid it on him, then slid herself on it, both of them groaning when her ass reached his thighs. He filled her completely.

Originally she'd thought the twins were identical everywhere, but as they continued their explorations of each other's bodies, she'd learned that Mark's cock was thicker where his brother's was longer. The distinctions allowed them to stroke different pleasure points inside her. She loved the stretched sensation Mark's cock created.

She started to move, thrusting up and down along his erect flesh. She was surprised when she felt Matt's hand press on her shoulder, halting her.

She glanced back at him, confused. His face was hungry, determined. Her pussy clenched with excitement. She didn't know what he had planned, but she'd loved every erotic adventure he'd led her on. She trusted both of these men—with her body, and if she was being completely honest, with her heart.

"Bend forward." He lightly pushed on her upper back, moving her into the position he wanted. She leaned over until her breasts brushed Mark's chest. Mark wrapped his arms around her, holding her close. His cock still filled her and she shuddered, a strong wave of arousal coursing through her with this new position.

Matt stroked her ass softly and she moaned. Yesterday afternoon, she'd started a small water fight, throwing some on Mark and then Matt as a joke. They'd chased her around the cabin, threatening to spank her for being a brat. Once they caught her, they bent her over the kitchen table, pulled down her pants and put their money where their mouths were, taking turns placing erotic slaps on her ass until she was begging for them to take her. She trembled as she recalled Matt fucking her from behind as she gave Mark a blowjob.

"I haven't been bad tonight," she teased, wondering if he wanted to resume the spanking. She'd never tried such a thing before yesterday, never thought she'd enjoy it. It had been very clear to all three of them she'd loved it.

Matt ran his hand along her right ass cheek before gripping it in his large palm and squeezing. "You're right. You haven't."

She was confused by his vague answer and his hesitation. It was clear he had something on his mind, but he seemed afraid to pursue it.

Then he moved, his fingers drifting between her legs, pausing at her anus.

She stopped breathing, blinking rapidly as he pressed a single finger against the ridge there.

"Matt," she whispered.

"Say no and it stops here."

She shook her head and he paused. She hastened to explain. "I don't want to say no."

Mark's hand stroked her hair. "You understand what we're asking for?"

She grinned against his chest. Mark—ever the protector.

She lifted her head and looked him straight in the eye. "I know exactly what you're asking for."

Matt shifted on the bed. As she glanced over her shoulder, she watched him pull a tube of lubricant from the nightstand drawer.

"You keep lube in the cabin?" Her question was meant as a joke, but there was a thread of seriousness underlying it.

Matt gave her a guilty look she found completely adorable. "I packed it when we went back to our place for clothes. Along with a shitload of condoms. Call me optimistic."

She couldn't help it. She giggled. He always managed to make her laugh, even in the most serious of times.

She placed her head on Mark's chest and let the steady thumping of his heart soothe her. He ran his hand through her hair, adding to the calm that was quickly taking over. A tiny part of the old Bridget briefly woke up, telling her she should be freaking out and backtracking as fast as possible. She dismissed the thought the second it arose.

She wanted this more than she'd ever wanted anything. For

the past week, her men had been taking turns inside her body, sharing her.

Tonight, they would truly be together, a trio, the perfect blending of three.

Matt squeezed some of the cool lube on her anus, working it in slowly, first with one finger, then two, and finally three. She'd begun to squirm, anticipating his motions, as her body began to demand more. When Matt put on a condom, covering it with a generous amount of lube, she knew she was about to get her heart's desire.

He placed the head of his cock at her opening. None of them spoke as Matt slowly pushed his way in.

She felt Mark's heart begin to beat harder against her cheek. She lifted her head to look at him, but her vision was cut off when Mark gripped her face and pulled her lips to his. His kiss told her everything she needed to know. He felt it too. He knew exactly how special this night, the moment was.

They were crossing the boundary, moving into unexplored territory together. With this one act, the three of them were committing themselves and their bodies to the ménage, to each other.

Once he was seated to the hilt, Matt released a long sigh. She appreciated the care he'd taken to prepare her for this, to make sure it didn't cause her any pain. Neither of them would ever hurt her.

Mark released her lips and looked over her shoulder at his brother. No words were spoken, but she could read the silent communication between them now. She understood. They were brothers. They were in this together. It was good.

She smiled and felt a small tear trickle down her cheek.

"Bridget?" Mark asked, swiping the moisture away. "You okay?"

She nodded. "I'm great. This is perfect."

Mark grinned. "Better than perfect."

Matt reached around her chest and grasped her breasts in his hands. "Ready for the next level?"

She glanced over her shoulder, torn between laughter and happy tears. "So ready."

They took her at her word, both men beginning to move in tandem. As Matt retreated, Mark thrust in. When Matt returned, Mark moved out. The sensation of being doubly penetrated, doubly taken, was too intense, and soon Bridget felt herself spiraling out of control as orgasm after orgasm racked her body.

Mark was the first to join her in ecstasy, crying out as he came. "God, so good."

She wanted to agree, but she'd expended every ounce of breath, exhausted every scream she had.

Matt came next, squeezing her breasts as his release took over. All he said was her name over and over. "Bridget. Sweet Bridget."

None of them moved for several moments, none of them willing to break the connection. Matt was the first to retreat. Pulling out of her body slowly, he placed several light kisses on her back as he left her. Falling to her side, he threw his arms over his head.

He was a sweaty, gorgeous mess.

She laughed. "You okay?"

"Un-fucking-believable. I think that was probably the single greatest experience of my life."

Leave it to Matt to sum things up so succinctly.

It was her turn to move next. She pushed herself upright on arms that felt like Jell-O. Mark released a light groan when she lifted up and his soft cock fell out.

She looked down and repeated her question. "You okay?"

He shook his head. "I've never felt anything like that, Bridget. Never."

She agreed. She wasn't sure how she'd ever be able to go back to plain old vanilla sex with one man. Matt and Mark had ruined her.

"Ruined you?" Matt asked, laughing.

Had she spoken aloud? From the amused looks on their faces, she guessed she had. She rolled her eyes, then gave in. "For other men? Yeah. Completely."

Mark's gaze darkened. "Good. I don't want you with any other men besides us. Ever."

It was as close as any of them had come to speaking their desire for a future together.

Matt reached over and ran his hand along her arm. "Me either. Lay down, Bridget. Let us hold you."

She claimed her spot in the middle, accepting their individual cuddles as they each took turns going to the bathroom to dispose of condoms and clean up. She was touched when Mark brought back a warm washcloth and cleaned her gently.

"Sore?" he asked when he ran the soft rag between her legs.

"No."

He gave her a disbelieving look and she giggled.

"Maybe a little. But I like it."

Matt laughed. "Our little pain junkie. You need to stop teasing me like that or I'm going to start taking you seriously."

She didn't respond. Instead, she curled into Mark's embrace, wrapping her arm around his waist. Matt claimed his spot behind her, spooning her. They'd discovered early on this was their ideal sleeping position. She sighed contentedly. She had a million things to think about, to consider, but her body was simply too tired.

She gave herself up to sleep. For the first time in months, her nightmares disappeared completely, replaced by sweet dreams of her handsome cowboys.

CHAPTER TEN

The next day passed in a whirlwind of activity as they prepared for Rodney and Bridget's return trip to New York. Rodney hadn't seen the hit man since that day outside the hotel over a week earlier. They were hopeful he'd determined they weren't there and had moved on.

With the trial date quickly approaching, Rodney had returned to the cabin as they planned their departure from Saratoga. He'd secured them airline tickets under assumed names with the help of his partner on the police force. His partner had confirmed that Rodney's chief had blown a fuse after their disappearance and wouldn't be satisfied until Rodney's head was served to him on a platter.

Bridget wished the man hadn't been so forthright with the details, as Rodney had been a powder keg of nervous energy since that phone call. He was more determined than ever to retrieve the flash drive, certain it was his only ticket to salvation.

Bridget scratched her head. The black wig Rodney had procured made her head itch. She sat in the passenger's side of Mark's truck as they began their bumpy descent off the mountain. Jacob, Matt and Rodney were in Jacob's car, following behind. They'd decided to split up. While Bridget wore a disguise, Rodney didn't. His hope was if the hit man was waiting at the airport and looking for them, he'd see Rodney but not her. Rodney had booked a later flight on his own. Matt and Mark would be accompanying Bridget to New York. In the city, Rodney's partner would be waiting to usher Bridget, Mark and Matt all into protective custody until the trial began.

She'd been touched when Matt and Mark had offered to travel to New York with her. They'd already risked so much for her. While they remained with her in the city, Caleb, Jessie and Jake had assured them they would hold down the fort on the ranch. Bridget knew there simply weren't words to thank the James family for all they'd done for her.

Bridget had convinced them to make one stop on the way out of town. She was determined to make a last-ditch attempt at retrieving the flash drive. Rodney had been back to the bank twice since his initial visit, once with a list of guess pin numbers they'd created using Lyle's birthday, her birthday, and the year they graduated from college. None of them had worked. The second time, Rodney had shown the bank manager Lyle's obituary and told him he'd been left the key in the will. The manager had requested to see the will. Rodney had left in a pique of anger and frustration.

Mark pulled up in front of the bank just as it was opening. They had four hours before their flight to New York took off, but they had at least an hour's worth of driving to get to the nearest airport in Laramie.

He glanced around at the mostly deserted street. "I still think this is a mistake."

"I can't go home without trying, Mark. I know what we've spent all this time looking for is in here."

She watched Rodney get out of the car as Jacob pulled into

the bank parking lot at the side of the building. The plan was simple. Rodney would go inside to make sure the coast was clear. He'd text Mark, who would follow Bridget to the door. Then Matt and Mark would stand guard duty at the front entrance while Jacob watched the back.

Bridget's heart began to race with fear and anticipation when Mark's phone beeped. He glanced at the screen. "Looks like it's go time."

He got out of the truck, crossing to open the passenger door for her. He kept her in front of him, covering her back against most of the open street behind them as they approached the bank.

Matt met them at the door. "Ten minutes, Bridge. Then we're coming in to get you. I don't like this. I've got a real bad feeling."

She agreed, but they'd come too far to turn back now. "I'll be fast. Promise."

Walking in, she spotted Rodney standing near a side wall. He walked over to meet her. "Tell me again why we're doing this?"

Crap. Did everyone have the heebie-jeebies? "I just want to talk to the bank manager."

Rodney sighed. "I've done that. A few times. He's an asshole and he's not going to budge."

Bridget ignored his skepticism and walked to the office near the back. "Is this his office?"

He nodded.

She knocked lightly and then entered when beckoned. She had no idea what she was going to say, but she was determined she wasn't leaving this bank without looking in the safe-deposit box.

She pulled out the key and then, on a lark, she retrieved

Lyle's coded message as well. The manager smiled at her until Rodney entered the room as well. Then he frowned.

"Back again? Do you have a copy of the will?"

Rodney shot her a look that said, *This is pointless,* but he remained quiet.

She started to speak, then her gaze landed on something she hadn't noticed before written lightly across the top of the message in pencil, something that had been erased.

"Did you write this?" she asked Rodney.

He glanced where she pointed. "Yeah, I was trying to keep track of our number codes. The theory of six and then the countdown idea. I think that was what the code turned out to be, but those numbers don't make—"

He paused. There were four digits that appeared to be random. Something clicked in her mind. She pulled out her cell phone, scrolling through her contacts list. She'd never been able to bring herself to delete Lyle's name. "It's the last four digits of his phone number." She held her phone out to show Rodney the screen.

"That's pretty clever. How the hell could you not remember that?"

She scowled. "First of all, we never really wrote down the number code—I'm a visual learner. And secondly, once I plugged Lyle's number in my phone, I never looked at it again. Just hit his name on my phone list whenever I wanted to call him. It's not like I had the damn thing memorized. Hell, I don't even know my mother's number. You know, this is the problem with cell phones. No one bothers to learn phone numbers anymore."

Rodney rolled his eyes. "Whatever. I'm not about to get into a debate about the pros and cons of smartphones with you. Can we just get this show on the road? We have a flight to catch."

She wrote the numbers six, five, five, four on the piece of paper and handed it to the bank manager. He compared the numbers to his and then smiled at her.

"Very good," he said. "Follow me."

He led the two of them into a vault filled with safe-deposit boxes. Bridget used the key to open the box. Inside she found a flash drive and a letter. She grinned as she pulled them out. "Told you it would be on a flash drive."

Rodney rolled his eyes. "You always have to be right, don't you?"

"I don't have to be. I just naturally am," she teased. They'd done it. They'd broken the code and retrieved the flash drive. For the first time in months, Bridget felt like everything was going to be okay.

"God help your guys."

She knew he meant his words as a joke, but instead they sent a piercing pain straight to her heart. Okay. So maybe not everything. She'd come to think of the James twins as hers, but how much longer could that last? She was going home. There was a light at the end of her tunnel, and she couldn't see Matt and Mark in the beam.

She handed Rodney the flash drive and opened the letter. It was handwritten. Her throat closed up when she spotted Lyle's familiar messy scrawl.

Dear Bridget,

If you are reading this, two things have happened. One, you've figured out my clues—well done. And two, I'm dead. I knew the moment I uncovered what the judge was up that to my days would be numbered if I kept digging. I pursued it anyway. We all make decisions in life, Bridget. Some good, some bad. One of the best decisions I ever made was befriending you. You're honest, smart and a little bit quirky—all good characteristics in my book. I loved you despite your inexplicable fascination for Hugh Grant, scary movies and smutty pirate books.

Now it's up to you. Finish the job. Do what I couldn't. The information contained on this drive can put not only Judge Lucian Thompson away for a very long time, but also thirty-seven criminals who bribed their way to freedom rather than pay for their crimes. I leave their fate in your hands.

Your friend,

Lyle

*B*ridget swallowed hard, wiping away the tears that started to fall. She hadn't cried once for her friend. She'd been whisked out of the city under cover of darkness the night he was murdered. She hadn't been able to go to his memorial service, and as she was shuffled from safe house to safe house, she hadn't had time to grieve for him. Hearing his voice through the words of his letter opened the floodgates, and she feared there would be no stopping them now.

"Oh, damn, Bridget. I'm sorry, baby." Rodney wrapped his arms around her while she cried. "I'm so sorry."

She let her emotions go for only a few minutes. She didn't dare indulge them for longer than that. She'd already lost one friend over the contents of this drive. She couldn't allow anyone else to die. She sniffled and wiped her eyes quickly. "I know we have to go."

Rodney nodded. "I wish there was more time for you."

"No." She shook her head. "I know what I need to do. I can do it."

Rodney placed a friendly hand on her cheek. "You are one of the bravest women I've ever met. You're going to be the greatest reporter New York City has ever seen. I know that in my soul. I'm proud to know you."

She smiled, bending forward to kiss Rodney on the cheek. "And you're my hero. Thank you for everything."

Bridget tucked Lyle's letter into her pocket, while Rodney put the flash drive in his. They walked toward the entrance of the bank together. Bridget felt a strange unease when she spotted Matt and Mark's backs through the window. A wave of panic, a premonition of danger tweaked at the edge of her consciousness.

Rodney turned to her. "Stay here for a minute. Let me go first to make sure everything's clear."

"Rodney. Wait."

He winked. "No time. Don't worry, kitten. It's a piece of cake from here on out."

Her heart raced with fear as he walked out of the bank, then she took a deep breath and moved. She was about to open the door to follow when shots rang out in the street. She reacted without thought, running outside in time to see Rodney fall. She started to run for him, but she was tackled from behind. Refusing to stop, she clawed herself closer to Rodney.

"Goddammit, Bridget. No." Mark's voice sounded loud in her ear as he covered her. More shots sounded and she felt something like gravel pelt her face.

"Get her to the fucking car!" Rodney yelled, his voice laced with pain. "Bridget, take this. Get to New York." He pressed the flash drive into her hand.

She grasped his fingers. "I'm not leaving you."

An engine roared to life and a truck jumped the curb, screeching to a halt next to where she and Mark lay on the sidewalk. It provided cover from the unseen gunman. Matt flung the door open. "Jump in!"

Mark rose quickly, lifting her with him and tossing her into the cab of the truck. Matt moved over to the passenger side, his hand pressed against the back of her skull. She pulled off the stupid wig and tossed it to the floor.

"Keep your head down," Matt commanded.

More bullets hit the truck, one of them smashing the back window.

Bridget screamed. Mark climbed into the truck and floored it, spinning tires in his haste to escape.

"Rodney!" she yelled, determined they go back for him.

"Jake has him," Mark said, not hitting the brakes. "He and the security guard dragged him into the bank while we put you in the truck. They've got him inside. He's going to be fine."

Sirens sounded in the distance. The police had been alerted and God, please let there be an ambulance for Rodney.

There'd been blood. So much blood. Lyle's lifeless face formed behind her eyelids, only it wasn't Lyle anymore. It was Rodney. She choked on a sob. "He was shot. We have to go back." She tried to sit up as Mark drove past the city limits at an ungodly speed.

She'd barely lifted her head when more shots rang out, one of them striking the back of the truck.

"Fuck!" Mark looked in the rearview mirror. "The bastard is chasing us."

Matt, keeping low, peered over the seat, looking back. "Black Mercedes, tinted windows. Can't see the driver. Shit, get down! He's firing again."

Matt ducked down, covering Bridget as Mark swerved the vehicle across both lanes, trying to dodge the bullets.

Mark took a sharp turn off the main road, not bothering to brake. For a second, Bridget would have sworn they were on two wheels.

Mark slapped the steering wheel. "Mother fucker. He's still back there."

They swerved sharply again and Bridget slid into Matt's lap. Matt kept her head pressed down. She felt dizzy and sick to her stomach as the car made another hard turn, this time to the left.

Matt glanced back. "Good call taking Old Mill Road."

Mark nodded. "Figure he'll have a hard time driving. Might keep him from shooting at our asses."

They took two more turns at high speed. Bridget feared there was no way they could continue at this pace without crashing.

"Hairpin's coming up," Matt warned.

"I know." Mark jerked the wheel roughly to the right, and this time Bridget knew they were on two wheels. She felt the truck tip sideways and closed her eyes, waiting for the inevitable impact.

Instead, the truck's airborne tires hit pavement once more. Mark struggled to keep the truck on the road as the back end swerved.

A loud crash sounded from behind them. Bridget felt Mark press on the brakes.

"What are you doing? Why are you stopping?" she asked.

"Christ." Mark stopped the truck completely as he and Matt turned in their seats to look behind them. Bridget lifted her head, expecting them to push her down again. She knew when neither man took notice of her that the car chase had indeed ended with a bang.

As she peered over the back of the seat, she saw the Mercedes that had been chasing them burst into flames, the entire car engulfed in mere seconds. It had struck a tree, the car nearly sliced in half.

"The man?" she asked. "Isn't he—" She paused, unable to think of the man burning to death.

Mark shook his head. "I doubt he survived the crash, Bridget."

His words made sense. The car had been mangled beyond recognition.

For several moments, they sat spellbound in the middle of the road, watching the car burn. Shock permeated her body, accompanied by unbelievable relief. They were alive. They'd survived. Glancing down, she opened her clenched fist and looked at the flash drive Rodney had handed her. Had they all survived?

So much violence. So much death. All because of what was contained on that small piece of plastic.

Matt's cell phone rang and they jumped. Matt ran a hand over his face. "Fuck. I think I just lost twenty years off my life."

Mark's hand landed on his brother's shoulder. "At least you still have twenty to lose."

Matt nodded. "We're alive."

It was an obvious statement, and yet his tone proved he was as amazed by that fact as Bridget.

His phone continued to ring. Digging it out of his pocket, he answered. "Yeah."

He was silent as the person on the other end spoke. "We're fine, but you might want to send a police car out to Old Mill Road. There's a dead hit man on the hairpin curve."

Bridget whispered, "Rodney."

Matt nodded that he'd heard her, but continued to listen to the caller. "I'll tell her," he finally said as he hung up.

"Who was that?" Mark asked.

"Jake. He's at the hospital with Rodney. Caleb was on duty, thank God, and he's with him. The bullet lodged in his arm. He lost a lot of blood, and while the damage is pretty extensive, Caleb doesn't think it's life-threatening."

Bridget released a soft sob. Rodney wasn't going to die.

"Hey, sweetheart." Matt wrapped his arm around her shoulders, misreading her response. "Caleb knows his stuff. If he says Rodney will be okay, he will."

"I, I know," she replied through choked sobs. "I w-was j-just so scared."

Mark lifted her face, cupped her cheek and offered her a comforting smile. "It's going to be okay."

She swallowed heavily. For the first time in a long time, she believed those words. "I want to go see him."

"No." Matt looked at Mark. "Jake said Rodney was insistent we make that flight. Said under no circumstances should we bring Bridget back to Saratoga."

"What?" she said. "No, no way. I'm going back there. I want to be with him."

Matt sighed. "Bridget. We're under the gun here. The judge's trial is due to start in two days. The New York police department wants you back there and in protective custody now. Rodney said the attorneys are going to want to see that flash drive. We have to go to the airport."

She wiped away a stray tear. "I can't leave him here alone. Please don't ask me to do that."

Mark grasped her hand and squeezed it. "He won't be alone. I know my kid brother. Jake will stay by his side until Rodney's begging for privacy. That kid will stick like glue. You have my word."

Bridget smiled at the thought. She doubted Rodney would ever want Jacob to leave. She'd seen the way they looked at each other. Though Rodney insisted he and the youngest James brother were nothing more than friends, Bridget knew there was something deeper there, waiting to emerge.

Mark put the truck in drive and turned it around. "We need to get to the airport or we're never going to make our flight."

Bridget suppressed a shiver as they drove by the wrecked vehicle. "What about him?"

Matt looked out the passenger's window at the dying flames. "There's nothing we can do for him now. Jacob said he'd send the police out here. Rodney knows who he was, so he can fill in the local law authorities. Other than that, they'll just have to wait until we get back to Saratoga after the trial to answer any more questions about the details of the crash."

Bridget sat up and buckled her seat belt. She caught sight of her reflection in the rearview mirror. There were scratches on her face. She reached up to touch them.

Mark caught her motion. "Some bullets broke the bricks on the side of the bank." He held up his left arm, showing her his scratches. "I caught some of those little shattered bits too."

She shivered, partially because of the cold from the broken rear window and partially from fear.

They'd come so close to dying. So very, very close.

They sat in silence as Mark drove. There were no more words left to say.

They'd found the flash drive.

Rodney had been shot.

They'd almost been killed.

She was going home.

A million different thoughts flashed through her mind, none of them landing for long. She was tired of being scared, of being cold. If she could simply walk the last few steps—testify at the trial—her months-long nightmare would be over. It would all be over. Matt and Mark would return to Wyoming and she would be free to return to her normal life.

She was close. So very, very close.

But to what?

CHAPTER ELEVEN

*B*ridget walked out of the courtroom and pulled her winter coat around her more tightly. It was a bright, sunny day in March, but she couldn't tell it by the temperature. The weatherman had reported this morning they could expect a bone-chilling day. He'd been right. She suspected the red dial wouldn't touch the twenty-degree mark.

However, even the cold couldn't freeze the warmth radiating inside her. The jury had deliberated less than four hours. They'd found Lucian Thompson guilty of first-degree murder. The crooked judge was facing life in prison for his crime, and Lyle's murder trial was just the first of a long line of court appearances the man faced. Thanks to the information her friend had discovered, the judge was also facing multiple charges of bribery, corruption and coercion. Arrest warrants had been issued for nearly three dozen more criminals as well. Justice had at last been served.

Her solitude only lasted a moment as several people caught sight of her and swarmed. The first to reach her was the Commissioner of the New York City police force. "You and

Rodney did a big service for this city. Tell him when you talk to him, his job is waiting for him."

She nodded. While the offer was wonderful and everything Rodney had hoped for, she wished it hadn't come at so high a price. "I'll tell him."

Several reporters surrounded her, but only one familiar face stood out. Bridget's editor in chief at *The Reporter* walked up to her. "You did an amazing job with your testimony. I'm sure that's what prompted the fast decision. Listen, I was thinking, what if you wrote up a multi-article exclusive on this case from beginning to end for the paper? We'll run it on the front page over the next few weeks."

"Front-page articles?" she asked.

"Yeah, you've earned them. And Bridget, I'm promoting you from the weekend girl to the news team. You can clean out your cubicle on Monday and move your stuff upstairs to a real office. I'll even throw in a nice raise."

She was stunned. She'd landed the promotion she'd wanted for years, but strangely it didn't make her as happy as she'd expected it would. "Thank you." Clearly, she just needed time to process. Too many incredible things were coming at her too quickly.

Several other reporters from larger papers, including the *Times* and the *Post*, struggled to get closer, all of them yelling questions at her. Cameras began flashing.

"Bridget," a familiar voice shouted. Looking to her left, she spotted Matt in his cowboy hat waving at her. "Over here, sweetheart. We've got the car."

She fought her way through the pack, simply saying the words "no comment" over and over until she reached Matt. He tucked her securely by his side, using his size and strength to battle the rest of the way to the car. Mark was waiting at the curb with the engine running as Matt opened the back door, helped her in and then crawled in beside her.

As he slammed the door, more cameras flashed and more reporters descended.

"Get us the hell out of here, Mark," Matt demanded when it looked like they'd surround the vehicle.

Mark pulled out into traffic, causing a taxicab to slam on its brakes and blare the horn. "Jesus," he muttered. "The drivers in this city are fucking crazy."

He'd had the same complaint this morning. The lawyers had hoped a verdict would be reached today. They'd suggested she bring her own transportation home rather than risk being followed by the swarms of reporters onto the subway system. It had been good advice.

"Maybe you should pull over and let me take it from here," Bridget suggested when she noticed Mark's white-knuckle grip on the steering wheel. She'd learned to drive on these mean streets. She could maneuver her way through traffic like a pro.

Mark shook his head, then mumbled another curse when a large truck cut into his lane. "No. I'll get us back to your apartment."

She grinned. Her guys had been troopers, accompanying her to New York, staying in her tiny apartment under protective custody with her. They'd endured the traffic jams, crowds, and dreary weather. She'd never seen two men less attuned to life in the city, yet they'd never complained once. Never been anything less than completely supportive of her and what she needed to do.

"Who were the guys talking to you before the horde of reporters descended?" Matt asked.

"Oh. One man was the police chief. He wanted me to tell Rodney his job would be waiting for him after he recuperated."

Neither man replied to that. They all knew Rodney faced a

long road to recovery before that could happen. His arm had been badly injured by the bullet, many of the nerves destroyed. Caleb had confided last night on the phone he feared Rodney would never recover full use of the arm.

Bridget's heart ached at the thought. Rodney had risked his life and his career to keep her safe. In the end, he'd nearly died taking a bullet meant for her, and now perhaps he'd never be able to use his arm again. It wasn't fair.

Chalk up another strike against her and her damn ambition. Lyle gave his life so that she could achieve her dream job, and now there was a good chance Rodney had sacrificed his own future for her. How many lives had she wrecked in her attempts to get what she wanted?

"Who was the other fella? The one in the cheap suit?"

She laughed at Matt's description. Her editor in chief was the epitome of bad taste, complete with long sideburns and a comb-over. "My boss." She swallowed heavily, then continued, "He offered me a promotion to the news staff, my own office, even a raise."

"Hey," Mark said, glancing in the rearview mirror at her. "That's great."

"Yeah," she said. The news didn't feel any better now than it had when she'd been offered the job. In fact, it felt terribly wrong. A year ago she would have been dancing in the street after such an offer.

It was Lyle's last gift to her. She'd gotten exactly what she'd always wanted. The old saying "Be careful what you wish for..." drifted through her mind. How could she turn the job down knowing it was Lyle's greatest hope for her? That he'd given his life so that she'd have this chance?

Even Rodney had risked his own career to see her brought safely back to New York, to this future. Rodney's voice drifted through her mind. *You'll be the greatest reporter New York City has ever seen.*

They rode in silence the rest of the way to her apartment, the quietness stifling.

Matt took her hand as they walked up the stairs to her third-floor apartment. It was the first time since her return to the city there hadn't been a cop positioned outside her door.

"Free at last," she whispered.

Matt squeezed her hand.

They entered the apartment. The second the door closed behind him, Mark reached for her arm and pulled her into his embrace. He kissed her so hard her lips stung. She relished the pain, shared his need for raw, hard, no-holds-barred sex.

She gripped the hem of Mark's long-sleeved shirt and pulled it over his head. Matt was behind her in an instant, ripping first her coat, then her shirt off with haste.

"Naked," Mark demanded. None of them needed more instruction than that. She unhooked her pants, stripping them off with her panties. Matt and Mark followed suit, and within seconds they were all undressed and reaching for each other.

Mark dropped to his knees in front of her, lifting her legs over his shoulders, holding her open to his hungry mouth as Matt supported her weight with strong arms wrapped around her chest. He gripped her breasts roughly, pulling and squeezing the aching flesh as he placed a long line of hot, wet kisses along the side of her neck. She felt him suck the sensitive skin beneath her ear and knew he was marking her. She didn't care. She wanted the world to know, needed them to know, that she belonged to these two men, and that they belonged to her.

Mark's tongue drove into her dripping pussy and she cried out. He fucked her with his lips, his teeth, his tongue, driving her to the now familiar heights she'd never achieved with another man. These men were made for her.

"God," she said, gasping for breath. Matt tightened his arms, gripping her more securely. She wasn't sure how he was managing to keep hold of her. Mark was driving her insane and her body was gyrating out of control.

"Come for him, sweetheart. Let him have a taste of you. Then I'm going to put you on your hands and knees and fuck you from behind." Matt's erotic whispers combined with Mark's wicked mouth cast her into white-hot bliss. She cried out and trembled, her orgasm coming so hard and fast her bones shook.

Matt, true to his word, barely gave her time to come down from heaven before he had her on the floor in front of him. He slid into her from behind as her fingers clenched against the rug, looking for purchase. There were no preliminaries—just raw, hard, deep thrusts. She loved it.

Mark's legs appeared in front of her and she realized she needed more. She looked up, beckoned him closer with her hungry eyes. Mark knelt before her and she took his cock into her mouth.

Mark's hands flew to her head, tangling in her hair, tightening around the tresses almost painfully. The sensation drove her, encouraged her to take more. To take it all.

For several feral moments, they took their pleasures, heedless of their surroundings. The sounds of the city were overshadowed by slapping flesh and deep groans. Matt came first, his fingers gripping her hips tightly. It wouldn't be the first time he'd left finger-sized bruises on her skin. She loved them, wore them with pride, jokingly called them her war wounds.

Mark came next, the first spurt of come splashing against her throat, awakening her own building climax. She moaned when Matt touched her clit. Both men had quickly learned the secret to her release. She trembled as Mark's flesh began to deflate. She released him and then came, shuddering almost violently.

Mark backed away, his hands still supporting her head. She was sweating, panting, her skin too sensitive to the touch.

She jerked when Matt withdrew from her body and then bent over to lift her. "It's okay," he soothed.

He carried her to her bed. Both men took turns washing her as she lay on the mattress in a state of boneless, sated relief. Finally, they crawled in next to her. It was a tight fit, her double mattress a far cry from the king-size beds they'd shared in Wyoming. Her men were big; it stood to reason all their beds were big too.

She'd just about drifted off to sleep when Mark's deep voice dragged her painfully back to reality. "We're flying out in the morning."

"What?"

Mark placed a soft kiss on her head. "We have to go home, Bridget. We've been away from the ranch for too long. We didn't want to leave until we knew you were safe. With the trial over and the judge behind bars..."

She nodded, had known this moment was coming. That knowledge didn't make it any easier. "I understand."

Mark tipped her face up to his. She tried to force a smile, but failed. Her heart was breaking.

"Darlin', we were going to ask you to come home with us. We even bought you a ticket. We wanted you to move to Wyoming and start a life with us."

"Wanted? Past tense?"

She felt Matt shrug behind her, his fingers tracing light patterns on her hip. "You've been offered your dream job, Bridge. We'd never take that away from you, never ask you to give that up."

Mark looked around the room. The lights from the street cast more than a dim glow in the room. Mark had remarked on how it never truly got dark his first night in the city. She'd laughed and told him how much she'd freaked out her first night in the woods when she realized she couldn't even see her hand in front of her face.

Mark glanced toward the window, the sounds of traffic on the street below filling the room. Horns blared, large trash trucks clattered, voices carried. "Your life is so different from ours. I don't think I realized just how much until we landed in New York. We don't have a lot to offer that can compete with this. The museums, the lights, the people, the restaurants. You could spend a lifetime in this city and never get bored. There are thousand things to do here on any given night, while I can name about five outlets for entertainment back home and some of those are only once-a-year deals."

"You guys find your fun in a different way. Riding the horses, sitting in the gazebo and watching the sunset, taking long walks in the woods. That's nothing to sneeze at, you know? That stuff's really special. Nice."

Matt chuckled. "My, how the tables have turned. The country mouse is impressed with the city, while the city girl finds joy in the country. Who'da thunk it?"

They laughed softly, until silence fell between them once more.

"So you aren't going to ask me to come with you?"

Mark sighed. "Darlin', it's taking every ounce of strength in my body not to get down on my knees and beg you to come back with us. You know how we feel. The decision has to be yours. We can't live in New York City. We just can't."

Matt moved closer, his chest pressing against her back in a way she'd grown to love. She wasn't sure how she'd be able to sleep alone in her cold bed. "It's not fair of us to ask you to do anything. You'd be the one making all the sacrifices, all the changes."

"So if I stay here," she started, then her words failed her. If she stayed here, what? Her heart ached, but she forced herself to finish. "If I stay here, it's over?"

Mark cupped her cheek. "We could try the long-distance thing, but how long do you think that would last? Our days off are few and far between. These last two weeks are the longest we've ever been away from the ranch in our lives. You're starting a new position with the paper. Chances are your vacation time will be limited too."

"There's always phone sex," Matt suggested. While Mark was the voice of reason, the calm, practical one, Matt led with emotion. In this case, she felt more like Matt. She wanted to be impractical, to say they could make this relationship work despite the distance. She couldn't do it.

She shook her head. "No. Mark's right. It wouldn't work. All or nothing."

Mark kissed her forehead. "God, darlin', I'm sorry. We were stupid to live in the moment, to walk into this blindly ignoring the outcome."

"We weren't wrong. I've lived every moment of the last seven months on borrowed time, knowing I could be killed at any second. I wouldn't have missed our time together for all the money on earth. I don't regret a single thing we've done."

Matt's lips brushed a soft kiss on her shoulder. "Me either, Bridget. You're the best thing that's ever happened to me. To us."

Mark and Matt had given her far more than she could ever say. They had a quiet, confident air that was charming, irresistible, so unlike the other men she'd dated in her life. They'd opened her eyes to a world she didn't know existed—a world of horses and nature and peace. Of laughter and gazebos and off-the-charts amazing sex.

They'd offered her their friendship, their bodies, their trust and their hearts freely, and neither man had pressured her for more than she could give. She ached to explain to them why she had to stay, but the words wouldn't come. She'd never felt so torn, so shattered. She'd let so many people down in the last year—Lyle, Rodney, and now Matt and Mark. Guilt consumed her, stealing her voice, breaking her heart.

She closed her eyes and remembered the image of Lyle's lifeless body, of Rodney lying on the pavement—both men covered in blood. They'd shed that blood for her. She owed them so much. Everything.

"We better get some sleep," Mark said. "Tomorrow will be here soon enough."

*M*ark was right. The morning came too soon. Bridget sat at her kitchen table, sipping a cup of coffee, while Matt and Mark gathered their things. They'd called for a taxi, and Bridget sat waiting for the inevitable honking of its horn on the street down below.

Mark came out of her bedroom with his duffle. "Well, I guess that's about it."

She swallowed heavily, fighting to keep the tears at bay. She'd promised herself she wouldn't make this good-bye more difficult by crying. She could see the strain in Mark's face. His eyes reflected every bit of the misery she was feeling.

Matt came out of the bedroom next. His carry-on bag appeared to be stretched to the limit.

"What do you have in there?" she asked. It hadn't been that full when they left Wyoming.

Matt shrugged. "Just a few souvenirs for the folks back

home. Found a foam Statue of Liberty hat for Jessie, some golf balls with the Empire State Building on them for Caleb, and I got this really cool music box for Jake. Looks like the one in that movie he likes so much." He glanced at Mark. "Crap. Forgot the name of it. Has the dude in the mask."

"*Phantom of the Opera*," Mark replied. "Jacob thinks Gerard Butler is hot."

Bridget giggled. "Well, Jake's right. He's uber-hot." She looked at Matt. "You couldn't think of *Phantom of the Opera*."

Matt shrugged. "I don't watch that shit. Jake turns it on and starts singing along to that opera music and I head for the hills. Give me some good old-fashioned rock and roll tune or a kick-ass country song any day. Anyway, I thought he'd like the music box. Even though the sucker's bulky and weighs a fucking ton."

She stood up and crossed the room. She placed a quick kiss on Matt's cheek. "It's a very thoughtful gift. He'll love it."

A horn blared outside.

Mark walked to the window and looked down. "Our cab's here."

She'd offered to drive them to the airport, but they'd both refused, claiming they'd rather say their good-byes in private. She suspected they knew she'd fall apart the second they left. They didn't want her driving in New York traffic, sobbing her heart out.

They'd both taken her again during the night. Making love to her as if she were as fragile as glass. Her lips were slightly swollen from their never-ending, beautiful kisses. They'd left an imprint on her heart and body that she'd never be able to wash away. Hell, she'd never want to.

"Well, I guess this is good-bye," she said, the words sounding thick even to her own ears. Her throat was closing and soon she wouldn't be able to speak at all.

Mark nodded. Dropping his duffle bag, he walked over and

gathered her in his tight, all-encompassing embrace. She clung to him for several wonderful seconds before forcing herself to release him. He bent down and pressed a hard kiss to her lips.

"I love you," he whispered. "I always will."

She sucked in a breath that turned to a soft sob. She wanted to speak the words, but she couldn't make a sound. Nothing that wouldn't break the dam. Instead she nodded. Mark smiled sadly and she knew he understood.

Matt claimed her next, picking her up as he hugged her, planting lots of soft kisses against her scalp. "God, Bridge. I'm going to miss the shit out of you."

She felt the first tear fall when he stepped back. She struggled to swallow. Christ, she needed to say something, but her voice was paralyzed.

Matt ran his hand along her cheek, wiping away the tear. "You're beautiful and I love you."

His words sealed her fate. They had to leave or she'd never let them go. Images of her sobbing and clinging to their legs flashed before her. She needed to get a grip.

She held her breath instead.

They each picked up their bags and headed for the door. Before they departed, they turned and gave her one last identical, dimple-creased smile. Her beloved cowboys.

The door closed and she crumpled, releasing her pent-up breath. She held herself silent as she let the tears begin to flow. It wouldn't do for them to hear her falling apart.

Walking to the window, she watched as they appeared on the street below. They threw their bags in the trunk. Before they climbed in, both of them looked up.

She smiled through her tears and lifted her hand to wave. Matt returned the gesture as Mark tipped his hat. Then they got in the cab and they were gone.

CHAPTER TWELVE

Bridget stood at the window for nearly half an hour, watching the people on the street below without ever really seeing them. Her eyes were too full of tears to see much through the watery blur. Finally, she dragged herself to the kitchen table and slumped in the chair.

More horns blared below and she tried to block her ears. The city noise was suddenly deafening and annoying and infuriating.

She'd really let them leave. Let Matt and Mark walk out of her life without telling them what they meant to her. All her reasons for letting them go began to crash in on her until she thought she'd suffocate under the weight.

She hadn't had a choice. Had she? She thought about Lyle and what they'd shared—friendship, laughter, dreams for the future, finding true love—all those simple joys. She wiped her eyes. Lyle would never experience any of those things again.

She walked to the kitchen counter and retrieved Lyle's last letter to her. She read the words again, but this time, they took on a different meaning.

Now it's up to you. Finish the job. Do what I couldn't.

If Lyle had taught her anything—while they were together or with his untimely death—it was that life was too precious to waste. He wouldn't want her to devote herself to a job she wasn't passionate about. He wouldn't want her to give up the chance for real, true love.

Suddenly everything became so clear to her. All Lyle had ever wanted was for her to be happy. Didn't she owe it to him to live her life to the fullest, rather than wallowing in misery and guilt? She wasn't the same woman she'd been a year ago. She couldn't go back to the life she'd known when Lyle had been alive even if she tried. Life was a series of steps, of moving forward. Staying in New York would be like standing still.

She had no idea where her life was leading her, but every fiber of her being said she'd never know true happiness if she didn't take a chance at making a future with Matt and Mark. In Saratoga.

Her tears dried up and she smiled at what she was contemplating. Holy crap. Was she seriously going to move to a horse ranch all the way across the country with not one, but two cowboys? She giggled, the sound echoing in the empty room. Yep. She sure as hell was.

Her cell phone rang and she raced to retrieve it from her coat pocket, praying it was Matt or Mark. An envelope fell out and landed on the floor as she grabbed the phone.

Her heart fell when she saw her editor's number. She sighed. "Hello."

"Hey, Bridget. How's my favorite reporter? I was wondering if you'd had a chance to start working on your article about the trial. We were hoping to get it on tomorrow's front page."

The old Bridget, the one her editor knew, would have stayed up all night writing the story. Instead, she'd spent the evening wrapped up in the embraces of the two cowboys who'd changed her life. Bending down, she picked up the unfamiliar envelope.

"Um, I haven't had a chance to start on it."

There was silence on the other end for a moment. She'd shocked him.

"Oh, I see," he replied.

Opening the envelope, she spotted a plane ticket. Her ticket to Saratoga. Mark had said they'd bought one for her. Her hands began to shake as she realized what she held.

"Truth is," she began, "I think I'm going to have to pass on the article. And the promotion. And, well, my old job too. I'm quitting it all."

She wasn't sure where the words were coming from, but the moment she began speaking them, they came faster, grew stronger. She had a ticket. She was going to use it.

"I don't understand," her editor said.

"I'm quitting. I'll email you my resignation later, but for right now, I have a flight to catch."

She hung up the phone without waiting for a good-bye. Reaching for a tissue, she blew her nose and cursed herself for being all kinds of a fool. How could she have let them leave without her?

Rushing to her room, she began throwing things in a bag as she called for a taxi. She was going to be on that plane. She had to be.

*B*ridget ran through the terminal, glancing at the clock. She was an OCD flyer by nature, always at the airport hours before departure. She currently had three minutes to reach her gate or the flight was going to take off without her. If she'd had a brain in her head, she would have planned this whole thing better. Arranged for a later flight. Packed up her apartment. Given notice to her landlord. Hired a moving company. Told her parents she was moving west.

Christ. Here she was running through JFK like a lunatic, trying to catch a plane when the fact was she was just going to have to turn around and come back to New York later to clean up all the messes she'd left behind.

She grinned. She didn't give a fuck. This was fun. She was dashing headfirst into her future, leaving the old Bridget behind.

She rushed up to the desk and flashed her ticket to the airline attendant. Everyone else was already on the plane. She couldn't wait to see Matt and Mark's faces when she boarded.

She giggled as she stepped on to the plane—giddy with anticipation. The flight attendant gave her a funny look, then smiled. Apparently uncontrollable happiness was contagious.

"Welcome aboard." The attendant looked at her ticket. "Your seat is near the back. Next to that tall handsome man in the cowboy hat."

Bridget glanced toward the rear of the plane and spotted them. Her heart nearly exploded with joy.

Neither man had seen her yet. Mark had claimed the window seat and was watching the activity out on the runway. Matt was sitting next to the aisle with his head thrown back, his eyes closed. The seat between them—her seat—was empty.

She walked straight up to their row and hitched her purse higher on her arm. "Excuse me. I think that's my seat."

Both men jerked at the sound of her voice. Her smile was so huge it hurt her face, and then a sudden bolt of panic jerked her. What if their offer hadn't been sincere? What if they didn't want—

She didn't have a chance to finish her thought. Matt stood up quickly, bumping his head on the overhead compartment.

That didn't stop him from giving a loud whoop. The chatter in the airplane died at his loud exclamation and Bridget saw one of the flight attendants look their way with a worried expression.

He hugged her. A hard, full-body embrace that drove all the air from her lungs.

Mark's voice cut through the silence. "Stop hogging her."

Matt released her, helping her to her seat. Once she was in place, Mark wrapped his arm around her shoulders and pulled her as close as the armrest between them would allow. "God-damn, you're a sight for sore eyes."

She pulled back and cupped his beloved face with her hand. "Ditto. I couldn't let you guys leave without saying something."

Matt quickly claimed one of her hands, leaning closer. The airline safety video began to play, but they ignored it. "What did you forget to say, sweetheart?"

"I wanted to know if your offer still stands—"

"It stands," Mark interjected quickly. "For you. Always."

"I'd like to move to Wyoming and start a life with you guys. You saved my life, kept me safe, but more than that, you brought me *to* life. I'm not sure I knew what it meant to live until I met you."

Matt leaned over and pressed a kiss on her cheek. "You did the same for us, Bridge. Mark and I were just living, slogging our way through the daily grind without even knowing how much was missing from our lives. Then you fell down at our feet—literally—and it became obvious we had no idea what happiness was. You opened our eyes to some pretty amazing possibilities. Now I can't even imagine a life without you, without Mark. We fit together. The three of us."

Mark squeezed her hand. "You're ours, Bridget. Our city cowgirl. We'll keep you safe, always."

Matt reclaimed her attention. "And warm and happy and —" He winked at her as he added "well-fed" to his romantic list.

Bridget could see a few passengers looking in their direction, could read the confusion on their faces as they tried to figure out the relationship dynamics.

She grinned. They had a lot of things to work out, but she knew they would. "I know now that everything's going to be all right. There's nothing the three of us can't do, because you love me. And I love you."

EPILOGUE

odney sat on the front porch of the James Ranch and watched the sun set behind the mountains. An early spring was upon them and he was taking advantage of the warmer weather, needing a respite from being cooped up inside.

"I wondered where you disappeared to." Bridget came outside and joined him on the porch swing.

He could hear the television playing in the background. "You're missing the movie."

She shrugged. "I've seen it before."

The James family was watching *The Hangover*, curled up in comfort on the couches and chairs, eating popcorn, laughing at Zach Galifinakis.

"So you came back." Rodney hadn't been surprised when Bridget arrived in Saratoga two days ago, hand in hand with her handsome cowboys. Anyone could look at them and know they were meant to be together.

She looked out at the ranch. He was struck by the utter contentment on her face. After months of living together, he wasn't sure he'd ever seen the true Bridget. The one sitting beside him now. Relaxed, complacent, peaceful. It was a nice change from the constant fear and suspicion that had resided there before the trial.

"Do you think I was crazy to drop everything in New York and follow Matt and Mark back here?"

"Not crazy at all, unless you count crazy in love."

She grinned. "I don't regret the decision. Even though my mother flipped out and yelled at me for two hours on the phone for quitting my job without having another one lined up. She also wasn't too pleased to hear I'd followed a man I'd just met out west on what she views as a lark."

"A man? Not men?"

"Jesus." Bridget shuddered. "It's going to take me a while to work up to that little detail. She went seriously ballistic over me moving to Saratoga. Not sure how I'll break the threesome deal to her."

"You know, there's a newspaper in Saratoga. Maybe you can be the *What to Do This Weekend* girl here."

They both laughed and she shook her head. "That would be a damn short column."

"And the same every week," Rodney joked. "So have you given any thought to what you want to do?" He'd spent every waking moment of the last week trying to figure out his future. He glanced at his bandaged arm, and felt the now-familiar pang of fear that never completely went away grip him again. It had consumed him ever since the bullet pierced his flesh. Caleb told him he may never regain full use of the arm. He swallowed heavily. What if the hand remained paralyzed? What good was a one-armed cop? No good. In the blink of an eye, his career had been destroyed. Depression wafted through him once more. What the hell was he supposed to do now?

"Actually..." Bridget looked at him out of the corner of her eye and he braced himself. She obviously had a scheme in the works. "I was toying with the idea of trying a different kind of writing."

"Other than journalism?"

She nodded. "I talked to Matt and Mark about it and they were completely supportive."

"What kind of writing?"

"I want to write a novel—a romantic suspense."

Bridget seemed to prepare herself for his teasing, but it was perfect for her. He was amazed by her resilience and creativity. Two days out of work and she'd come up with a plan. If anyone could succeed at that career, it was Bridget. He was jealous of her confidence, her willingness to put herself out there and try something new.

"I think that sounds awesome."

"Really?" she asked, sitting up straighter. "Because I'm planning to make the first one a sort of fictionalized account of our experiences. I've already decided I'm dedicating the book to you and Lyle."

A book? Dedicated to him? "Cool."

Bridget turned on the swing, so that she was facing him. He was slightly uncomfortable under her scrutiny. "Rodney?"

"Yeah?"

"Are you okay?"

He wanted to lie. It was on the tip of his tongue to give the standard *I'm fine* response. He couldn't do it. For one thing, Bridget would see right through it, and for another, he wasn't fine. He wasn't even close to that.

He shook his head. "Not really. I'm fucked up, kitten." He swallowed heavily, a lump forming in his throat. He gestured to his injured arm. "What the hell am I supposed to do now?"

"What do you want to do?"

He was confused by her question. "What do you mean?"

"You need to go through physical therapy for your arm, right?"

He nodded.

"Are you going to do that?"

"Of course I am."

"Why?" she asked. "You sound to me like you've already written that arm off."

He scowled and started to deny her assertion. He shut his mouth instead. Hard to argue against the truth. He'd been throwing the mother of all pity parties for himself this week.

"Rodney, you're young, brave, strong and one of the most determined people I've ever met. If anyone can make a miracle, it's you."

"You're being persuasive again."

She laughed. "Nope, this is one of those times when I'm being right. You always mix those up."

He was still afraid. "I'm a cop, Bridget. That's all I know how to be. What if my arm doesn't come back? What then?"

"Well, then, you have a whole world of careers to choose from. You need to think outside the box. I can't be a reporter in Saratoga, so I'll be a writer. You can't be a cop in New York—for now," she quickly interjected. "So, you'll be..."

Lost.

It was the only word that came to his mind. Finally, he just shrugged. "I don't know."

She reached over to grasp his good hand. "You have time to figure it out. Will you stay here while you do?"

He hadn't been in any hurry to return to the city. He wished he could understand why. It just felt like there was something tying him here.

Jake's laughter drifted from the living room.

Jacob James.

If Rodney was being completely honest, he knew why he

was staying. Jake had been a godsend to him these past few weeks. Offering companionship during his recuperation. Comfort and laughter during his down times.

Rodney knew Jake hoped for—wanted—more from him, but that desire seemed pointless right now. Rodney had nothing to offer but a crippled arm, a gut full of resentment and a pile of regrets. It wasn't fair to dim Jake's bright light with the shadow currently residing over him.

"I have no idea where I belong right now."

Bridget grinned. "Well, I may not know much, Rodney, but I do know the answer to that. You belong here. With us."

Her words soothed his weary soul. "Here sounds pretty good."

"This is a good place. I knew it the first night we arrived. I don't know the answer to your problem, but I do think you'll find it here. You might even find a bit of happiness along the way."

"Happiness sounds good."

She laughed, her face painted with sheer delight. "Happiness is very good."

BECAUSE IT'S TRUE

To John and Bill. I wish your story had been longer.

PROLOGUE

Searing pain roared through Rodney's arm as black spots danced before his eyes. More gunfire pounded into the wall of the building behind him, pelting him with shards of shattered brick. He'd known something was wrong the second he walked out of the bank. Hell, he'd had a premonition all morning that something would happen, that everything was about to change. He knew better than to ignore his gut feelings.

"Rodney!"

Fuck. Bridget was out in the open. He forced himself to remain conscious despite the agonizing fire currently raging through his body. He watched Mark throw himself on top of her, shielding her from the gunfire.

"Get her to the fucking car!" Rodney yelled. Jesus. If Bridget was killed, it would be his fault. His. It was his job to protect her.

Bridget crawled closer.

He reached out with his uninjured arm. "Bridget, take this. Get to New York." He pressed the flash drive they'd spent the last month of their lives searching for into her hand. It was the key to putting the judge whose henchman was currently trying to kill them away forever.

"I'm not leaving you," Bridget insisted.

Rodney took a deep breath, praying for the strength to get her out of harm's way. Mercifully, Mark grabbed her, dragging her to the truck.

Please let her make it. He sighed with relief, the sound coming out as a harsh shudder when he watched the truck with Bridget ensconced inside pull away.

"Bridget," he whispered.

Strong hands gripped him, shocking him. What the fuck? He started to kick out, but the last of his strength slowly drained away.

"It's me, Rod."

Christ. Jake. No.

"Get down," Rodney said, the words sounding more like a bark than his normal voice. "Get inside!"

Jacob didn't reply. Instead he lifted Rodney's upper body with firm hands beneath his armpits and dragged him to the entrance of the bank. The movement was excruciating and bile rose to Rodney's throat. Waves of nausea caused by the red hot poker lodged in his arm enveloped him.

He'd been shot. It was a possibility he'd faced every day as he patrolled the streets of New York City as a cop. Who would have thought this sleepy town of Saratoga, Wyoming would be the place to bring him down?

The gunshots had ceased with Bridget's escape.

Jacob laid him gently on the floor of the bank's lobby. He saw a security guard standing next to his friend, talking on the phone. He would have grinned if he hadn't been in so much pain. If he was going to die, he couldn't think of a better last sight than Jacob's gorgeous face. Sirens sounded in the distance.

"Bridget," Rodney whispered.

Jacob knelt next to him. "Matt and Mark got her away. She'll be fine, Rod. And so will you. Just hang on, man."

She was safe. Jake was safe.

Rodney let those comforting thoughts permeate the haze of pain, though he still couldn't let go of the premonition.

Everything is changing.

His eyes drifted closed, his body shutting down.

They were safe.

But was he?

CHAPTER ONE

odney Jackson leaned against the makeshift bar, taking everything in. What a night. The backyard of the James Ranch was packed with people—gay men, lesbians, doctors from the hospital where Caleb worked, Stephen and Todd from the B&B next door, Matt's band. The list went on and on.

A year ago, he'd been a rookie cop in New York City, surrounded by crowds, tall buildings and the never-ending noise. He'd grown up in a fairly rough part of the city. Gangs, graffiti and taxicabs painted his world.

This ranch surrounded by mountains and carpeted in thick green grass was like an oasis, something he'd seen in the movies but never expected to experience in real life. It's funny how something so foreign had come to feel more like home than the place where he'd lived his entire life.

He hadn't thought of New York in months. No. The truth was he wouldn't let himself think of it. The bullet he'd taken back in March had nearly robbed him of his career, his livelihood. As a result, he'd spent months in rehab, enduring count-less hours of physical therapy to regain use of his hand.

Today, the physical therapist had released him to return to work, given him a clean bill of health. She'd basically written him a ticket back to New York and the life he'd left behind. For so long, he'd thought that was all he wanted.

Jacob James passed close by, laughing at something someone had said.

Turned out he was wrong.

He studied Jacob's face, so relaxed and happy as he chatted with an old friend. He had joked once about his and Jake's polar opposite appearances. Where Rodney was tall, lanky and biracial, Jacob was an all-American poster boy with fair skin, blue eyes and dirty blond hair. The attraction Rodney felt for Jacob had been instant and lasting.

He rubbed his arm absent-mindedly. Bridget caught his eye and walked toward him. He'd nearly lost use of his arm protecting her. He'd been assigned to guard her when she was put into protective custody. What should have been an easy—if boring—assignment went bad quickly as they were pursued by a hit man. The case had ended when the hit man died in a car chase and the bastard judge who'd been after them was sentenced to life in prison without hope of parole. Good riddance.

Despite the injury that had nearly robbed him of his career, he knew without a doubt he'd do it all again. Simply because of Bridget. She'd become more than a best friend to him. She was the sister he never had.

"Is your arm hurting?"

Rodney realized what he was doing and stopped. He'd developed the practice of rubbing the wounded area when he was trying to ease the pain. The ache had subsided weeks ago, but now he couldn't break the habit. "No. Not at all. In fact—"

he leaned closer, not wanting to be overheard, "—the PT released me today. She gave me the go-ahead to return to work."

She was the first person he'd told. He'd come home from physical therapy and searched for Jacob, anxious to share the exciting news. He found Jake helping Matt assemble the makeshift stage for Gay Fest, the annual summer party Jacob held, and the words had died on his lips. Instead of telling him about his clean bill of health, he'd lied and said the therapist had given him more exercises to do.

The lie had tasted bitter, but today belonged to Jacob. His friend looked forward to Gay Fest more than most five-year-olds did Christmas. Jacob organized the event for other homosexuals like him to come out of the closet for a night and let their hair down. Wyoming—alpha capital of the world—didn't provide a lot in the way of gay bars, so Jacob decided to amend that fact by holding his own party. Rodney didn't want to ruin the event with talk of his imminent departure.

For months, Rodney had resisted his attraction to Jacob. He'd had nothing to offer the young aspiring journalist—no job, no future plans, a crippled arm. At the beginning, he had been too blinded by self-pity to give in to Jacob's obvious interest. When he began to see improvement in his hand, Rodney's reasons for rebuffing Jacob were less about an uncertain future and more about one that couldn't be denied. He'd known the day was coming when he'd return to New York. Where would that leave him and Jacob? The answer was obvious.

On opposite ends of the country.

Bridget smiled and hugged him tightly. "I suppose I would sound selfish if I followed up my congrats by loudly yelling *Shit!*"

Rodney chuckled. "Yep. Completely selfish. But don't worry. I had the same response."

"God, Rodney. I've sort of started taking it for granted that you'd always been around. Not sure what I'll do when you're not here to listen to me bitch about my two cowboys."

"Complaining about too many orgasms doesn't really count as bitching, kitten. But I know what you mean. It's hard to spend months in someone's face and not get kind of fond of them, isn't it?" He reached up and ruffled her hair playfully.

"Hey." She batted his hand away, then grasped it to hold. "I'm more than fond of you, smartass. I love you. I'm going to miss you so much when you go back to New York."

"Yeah." He swallowed heavily. This was why he'd avoided the subject all day, hesitated to say the words. If it was this hard to tell Bridget, how much more difficult would it be to break the news to Jacob?

"What did Jake say?"

Damn. He'd tried to hide his desires for the youngest James brother, but Bridget was too savvy, knew him too well.

"I haven't told him yet."

"Why not?" she asked.

Rodney gestured around at the party in full swing. "Gay Fest is why not. This is Jake's night. I didn't want to spoil it."

Bridget nodded, giving him a sympathetic look. She'd recently faced her own life-altering decision, so he knew she understood his dilemma. However, Bridget had given up her life in New York to move to Wyoming with Matt and Mark. Rodney wasn't sure that choice would work for him. He was born to be a big-city cop, not a small-town rancher.

"I understand. He'll be super bummed when he hears you're leaving."

They fell silent for a moment, taking in the craziness of the party. Bridget laughed and pointed when she spotted Matt arm-wrestling with a guy in drag. "It's an amazing party. I mean, when Jessie described it to me, I thought she was exaggerating. Looks to me like she was holding back on some of the more insane details."

Rodney chuckled. "I'm having a blast."

"Me too. And this year, the party's even more special. It's nice to be celebrating Caleb and Jessie's upcoming wedding." Bridget's eyes widened. "Oh my God. You're not going to leave before the wedding next weekend, are you? You can't."

Jacob's oldest—and straight—brother, Caleb, had met his fiancée, Jessie, at last year's Gay Fest. They'd gotten engaged over Valentine's Day and were tying the knot in a small family ceremony.

Jessie had insisted she wanted Gay Fest to double as her bachelorette party. When Caleb reminded her he planned to be there, she told him it was going to be his bachelor party too. The mild-mannered doctor easily agreed, so in addition to the nearly fifty gay friends from all over the country whom Jacob had invited, Jessie's girlfriends from Denver and Caleb's colleagues from the hospital were also in attendance, making for an interesting night.

Rodney gave Bridget's hand a reassuring squeeze. "I wouldn't miss the wedding for the world. I only got the medical release today. It's going to take some time for me to get my ducks in a row. I mean, I'm not flying out tomorrow or anything."

Bridget blew out a relieved breath. "Good. Something tells me I'm going to need time to get used to the idea of you leaving. Shit. It's going to suck when you go."

He gave her a quick peck on the cheek. "Your folks live in Hoboken. When you come home for visits, I'm demanding equal time."

"Done," she promised.

Jacob walked up and slapped Rodney on the back. "You got a minute? I need some muscle."

"Somebody fighting?" Rodney turned, ready to roll.

Jacob laughed. "Down boy. We're not on the mean streets of NYC. A couple of the trashcans are already overflowing. I was hoping you could help me empty them."

"Sure thing." Rodney waved at Bridget and walked to the side of the house with Jacob.

When they reached the large garbage can, Jacob held onto the rim while Rodney worked to remove the overflowing bag. "Damn. Didn't take long to fill this up."

Jacob grinned, placing a new bag in the can. "Most people walk to and from the party this way. Past experience has taught me to put a couple trashcans out here or the empties end up all over the yard."

"This is quite a party."

"Why do you say that like you're surprised? I told you it was *the* event of the summer."

"Yeah, but this is one of those things you have to see to believe."

"Nope. Gay Fest isn't something to be seen." Jacob threw his arms in the air, piling on the drama. "It's meant to be experienced, enjoyed, lived."

Rodney rolled his eyes at Jacob's enthusiasm. He'd never met anyone with such a positive outlook on life. Jacob was the eternal optimist who treated every single day of his life like an adventure, a party. Rodney tried not to admit how much he envied that aspect of his friend's personality.

"Well, I think it's safe to say I'm enjoying it."

Jacob paused, giving him a friendly smile. "I'm glad. You deserve a fun night. You've been working so hard these past few months. It's about time you cut loose. In fact, I've set a goal for you tonight."

"Oh yeah. What's that?"

"Go wild."

The idea had merit. In fact, it sounded pretty damn good. "Wild, huh? I think I can handle that." Rodney put his arm around Jacob's shoulders, perfectly aware he was flirting. "How about I buy you a drink?"

Jacob laughed and followed him back to the bar they'd set up at the edge of the yard.

Caleb stepped over to them from behind the bar. "What can I get you guys? Name your poison."

"Hey," Jacob protested. "What are you doing back there? I hired a bartender so you could actually enjoy the party tonight."

Caleb placed a couple of beers on the bar. "Bartender needed a quick break, so I said I'd cover for him. What can I say? Old habits die hard."

Jacob turned to Rodney to explain. "In years past, Caleb always stood in as the official Gay Fest bartender. However—" he gave his older brother a pointed look, "—since tonight is also his *bachelor* party, I thought he should mingle rather than hide behind the counter."

Rodney gave Caleb a wink. "Can't exactly blame your straight brother for putting a bar between him and all these gay guys. This place is more crowded than most of the gay bars in the city. I've been hit on half a dozen times already and handed three phone numbers."

Jacob narrowed his eyes slightly. Rodney tried not to acknowledge how warm and fuzzy the jealous look made him feel.

"Anyone with potential?" Jacob asked.

He had to leave it to Jacob. He was a talented actor in the *play it casual* role. Rodney shook his head. "No. Not at all."

"Good," Jacob said so quietly Rodney wasn't sure he heard it at all.

Caleb wiped up the counter in front of them. "By the way,

Rodney, I ran into your PT, Joyce, this morning. Congratulations on the clean bill of health. Looks like all your hard work paid off. New York's going to be getting back one hell of a cop."

"What?" Jacob's shocked tone went through Rodney like nails.

"Jake, listen—"

"I thought you said she just gave you more exercises to do."

Caleb's softly muttered "shit" proved he knew he'd just fucked up. Rodney couldn't be angry. It was his lie that landed him in this mess, not Caleb.

"I'll leave you guys alone." Caleb walked to the opposite end of the bar and began serving up more drinks.

"Why did you lie?" Jacob asked quietly.

"Tonight was your night, Jake. I didn't want to take that away from you."

"Do you honestly think I'd begrudge you your miracle, your happiness? This is what you've worked for, Rod. I don't see how you being cleared to return to New York would take away from the party."

"Don't you?" It was a pointed question and as close as Rodney had ever come to calling Jacob on the carpet about his feelings. Rodney wasn't blind and he wasn't stupid.

Jacob cleared his throat, then looked away. He faced the makeshift dance floor, careful to avoid looking at him. "I have no hold on you."

Rodney chuckled mirthlessly. "God. I wish that was true."

Jacob's gaze flew back to his. "What's that mean?"

Rodney didn't reply. Instead, he leaned forward and placed his lips on Jacob's. They'd been together, in each other's faces for six months, and never once had Rodney given in to his desire to kiss Jacob.

The moment they touched, every suspicion he'd harbored about his feelings for Jacob crashed in on him and he knew he'd been right to fight the attraction. He also knew this kiss was fucking up all that restraint. It was too late now.

He lifted his hand to Jacob's cheek, letting it drift through Jake's soft hair. He followed suit with the other hand, cupping Jacob's face, holding the man's lips against his. Not that the grip was necessary. Jacob wasn't pulling away.

Jacob returned the kiss, his lips parting. Their tongues tangled roughly, hungrily. Months' worth of pent-up desires released themselves in their melding of mouths. There was no coming back from this.

Hours seemed to pass, yet neither of them came up for air. As for Rodney, he didn't want to break the spell. This was too fucking good.

"Get a room," one of the inebriated partygoers yelled.

Jacob backed away first, his face the perfect blend of bliss and nerves. Rodney could understand the feeling.

"Jake, I'm sorry I lied about—"

Jacob shook his head. "No. I get it now. I really do. Rodney, I'd never stand between you and what you want, you know that, right?"

Rodney nodded. Jacob had become one of the best friends he'd ever had in his life. He'd never met such a selfless, giving guy.

"You've just spent months working your ass off so you can go back to New York, back to being a cop. I want you to have that life because it's what makes you happy. It's just—"

Rodney didn't let him finish. "Your home is here."

Matt and Mark had gone to New York to be with Bridget during her trial. She'd told Rodney how caged and shell-shocked her poor cowboys looked in the big city. He feared the same would hold true for Jacob. Though his friend had no love of the ranching lifestyle, he was a country boy through and through. Jacob loved hiking, fishing, horseback riding. Hell, he'd shown Rodney the beauty of those activities as well. They'd spent every weekend of this summer camping near Little Snake River. Rodney was worried about his own culture shock when he returned home.

Jacob laughed. "I don't know about that. The biggest city I've ever been to is Denver, but I can tell you right now, I love going there, love the hustle and bustle, the nightlife."

"Visiting somewhere is different from living there."

Jacob fell silent for a few moments. Rodney suspected there was something heavy on his friend's mind.

Finally, Jacob spoke. "Is that what we're talking about? Me living there?"

Rodney swallowed heavily. Shit. They'd just shared their first kiss. Is that what he wanted? His heart screamed *Yes*.

First kiss be damned. Jacob was made for him. This wasn't a first date. He knew Jacob, knew what it was like to share a place with him, spend all-day-every-day with him. It was no damn hardship that was for sure. In fact, it was right. It worked.

They worked.

Instead, he swallowed down the reply and took the easy way out, tried to buy more time to gather his thoughts. "This is why I didn't tell you about the medical release. All of this can wait until tomorrow."

Jacob looked disappointed. "Sure. Tomorrow."

"Hey, Jake! When's the karaoke?" Jessie joined them. "You promised me a song."

Jacob's troubled look morphed into a smile that fooled his future sister-in-law. Rodney, however, could see the strain on Jacob's face. He felt guilty for dimming his friend's joy in the party.

"Song?" Rodney asked.

Jessie took a swig from her beer. "Jacob told me this afternoon he'd planned a special wedding song for Caleb and I.

Bridget and I have a bet on which ABBA number he'll be performing."

Jacob looked like singing was the last thing he wanted to do right now, but he put on a good face. "Who said anything about it being ABBA?"

Jessie laughed. "Nice try, but I know you. It'll be ABBA. Get up there. I want my song."

Jacob looked around at the crowd. "I'm not sure everyone's tipsy enough for karaoke. You know you have to time these things just right."

It was a dodge. The partygoers were well into the *making jackasses of themselves* stage of the night. Jacob's reluctance was his fault. Rodney was anxious to put the party back on track. "I don't know what number you planned to sing, but could we make it a duet?"

Jacob's heavy look slowly faded. "You'd get up on stage and sing with me?"

The idea actually made him slightly nauseous, but he owed it to Jacob. "Of course I would. How else am I supposed to go wild?"

Just like that, Jacob's smile returned. "Awesome. Come on."

He took Rodney's hand and led him to the stage. "Jessie was completely right about it being ABBA. I was going to start the night off with this song. Do you know it?"

He pointed to the list of song choices in a binder, showing Rodney his choice. Rodney closed his eyes, suppressing a groan. "Jesus. Really?"

"It's perfect and you know it."

Rodney wanted to deny it, but it was pointless. It was the perfect song for the occasion. Jacob led him to the stage and handed him a microphone. A large group began to gather around, cheering when Jacob announced the beginning of karaoke, a tradition at Gay Fest.

He pointed to Matt, who was manning the technology, to cue up the song. Matt gave his brother the thumbs up, indicating he was ready.

"This first song is dedicated to my big brother, Caleb, and to the woman who is too smart to settle for him, but is still willing to hitch her cart to his horse, Jessie."

The crowd laughed.

"And also to my best friend, Rodney, who has his own personal reason to celebrate tonight. He's going to help me sing it."

Rodney was touched by the compliment. Though they'd only known each other a short while, Jacob had become his best friend as well.

Matt pushed play on the canned music and the first strains of ABBA's "I Do I Do I Do I Do I Do" filled the backyard. Rodney's gaze never left the monitor feeding the lines to him through the first verse though he knew the song by heart. His mother had dragged him to see *Mamma Mia* the first year it released on Broadway. After that, she'd worn out her CD of the soundtrack, subjecting him to more ABBA than he'd ever hoped to hear in his lifetime.

The crowd's enthusiastic reply and Jacob's crazy dancing made him bolder and Rodney soon loosened up, throwing out a couple of Elvis's signature gyrations. Bridget stood in front of him, laughing and cheering him on. He grinned, having far too much fun until he turned to look at Jacob.

Suddenly the screaming crowd faded away as he fell into Jacob's bright blue eyes. Neither of them needed to look at the monitor, so their attention remained only on each other.

The lyrics took on a new meaning for him as they sang. The song was an outright declaration of love, but he and Jacob didn't bother to hide from that or look away. When Rodney sang the words *'Cause it's true*, he realized his feelings weren't going to go away no matter how hard he tried to ignore them. The truth was he'd fallen hopelessly and madly in love with Jacob James.

The song ended and the partiers went wild. Jessie hopped on stage and gave Jacob a kiss on the cheek, then hugged Rodney, thanking them both.

Jacob announced the next singers, handed over the microphones, then took Rodney's hand. It probably looked like an innocent gesture to the bystanders watching, but Rodney felt raw need coursing through him. He was moving in slow motion as Jacob led him farther away from the party. The noise began to fade. They were nearly to the side door that would take them into the ranch's kitchen before Rodney stopped.

"Jake, wait."

Jacob turned to face him. "I don't want to wait until tomorrow to have this talk, Rodney. I just don't."

Rodney shook his head. "You don't understand. If we go inside that house, we're not talking. We're going to your bedroom."

Jacob didn't respond, but there was no denying the longing on his face.

"Fuck it. Come on. You'll get your talk, Jacob. I can promise you that. But you're going to get a lot more than that too." Rodney tilted his head toward the backyard. "Can they do without you for a few hours?"

Jacob nodded. "My brothers will keep things rolling. Caleb just waved to me as we left the stage. He knows I'm gone. He'll take care of everything."

"Good." Rodney was finished with the discussion, the denials, the waiting. For the first time in months, his life was moving forward. He wouldn't resist. It was time he let the tide take him where it would. Better to drown in Jacob's arms than die alone on dry ground.

CHAPTER TWO

Jacob walked into his family's ranch house and tried to contain the sheer nervous excitement threatening to rattle his entire body. He'd spent months dreaming of this moment with zero expectation of ever arriving here. After living with Rodney—in separate bedrooms—and pining from afar, he'd become a natural at shielding his true feelings. From the moment he'd met Rodney, every other man had melted away.

Rodney was masculine beauty incarnate with light brown skin, dark eyes and close-cropped black hair. Rodney's mother was Italian, his father African American, the genetic combination creating the most handsome man Jacob had ever laid eyes on.

However, timing had not been on their side. When Rodney took a bullet and came very close to losing the use of his arm, the playful flirting they'd engaged in died. Rodney's demeanor changed after the shooting. Jacob tried hard to offer friendship as Rodney fluctuated between frustration, depression and anger. Jacob understood his friend was terrified of losing the only life he'd ever known. Rodney was born to be a cop.

Rodney took his physical therapy seriously, approaching the exercises with a determination that bordered on manic. The hot cop wanted nothing more than to return to his normal life. Jacob knew that. Unfortunately that didn't stop him from taking secret pleasure that Rodney was still in Wyoming, still with him after all these months. It also hadn't been enough to convince Jacob not to do the most foolish thing of all.

Fall in love.

They walked through the kitchen to the stairway that would lead them to Jacob's room in silence. At the base of the steps, Rodney placed a hand on Jacob's upper arm.

Jacob turned and smiled at the question in Rodney's eyes. "I'm not going to change my mind, if that's what you're hoping."

"Jesus," Rodney muttered. "I'd never hope for that in a million years. It's just..." He paused for a moment.

"What?" Jacob prodded.

"It's been a while for me, Jake."

Jacob closed his eyes, fighting back tears. "For me too."

After that, the words gave way to motion. Jacob took Rodney's hand and led him to the bedroom. They stopped at the threshold and kissed once more, a long, hard kiss—full of promise and hope.

Then Jacob walked in and turned on the lamp on the bedside table, while Rodney locked the door. Sounds of karaoke and loud laughter drifted to them from the backyard.

Rodney smiled as he glanced toward the window. "Great party going on down there."

Jacob shrugged. "I'd rather be here."

Rodney's gaze darkened with lust and he reached for the

hem of his T-shirt. He pulled it over his head. Jacob had seen Rodney shirtless a thousand times as the cop pitched in to help with the ranch chores. The sight never failed to leave Jacob breathless. Rodney's physical therapy hadn't just healed his arm. It kept his body hard, strong.

Unable to resist, Jacob walked toward him and ran his hand down the smooth muscular chest that had taunted him for far too long. Rodney stood still, letting Jacob touch and look his fill.

"My turn," Rodney said with a quick nod, gesturing for Jacob to take off his shirt. Unlike his cop, Jacob had opted for a dressier look and had worn a lightweight, button-up cotton shirt to the party. He was happy for his choice when Rodney's hungry gaze watched him pop each button slowly. He was only halfway down when Rodney's impatience reared its head. Reaching for him, Rodney ripped the shirt the rest of the way apart, the last three buttons flying.

Jacob's cock thickened at Rodney's roughness. His past sexual experiences had been too tentative, mere explorations and nights spent learning how to do this with equally green boys.

Rodney would be different.

Rodney stripped Jacob's shirt off, tossing it to the floor. Rather than touch the uncovered skin, Rodney pulled Jacob closer with strong hands on his waist. He pressed their bare chests together while dipping his head to Jacob's shoulder. He kissed Jacob's neck, bit his shoulder, dragged his tongue along every sensitive spot. Jacob shivered with need.

"Rodney," he whispered.

"Take off my jeans, Jake. Pull my cock out."

Jacob swallowed heavily.

"Nervous?" Rodney asked.

Jacob shook his head. "No, but I think it's going to be

obvious pretty soon that you know a lot more about sex than I do."

Rodney chuckled. "It's not about what you know, Jake. It's about who you are. Right now, I'm so fucking hot for you, it hurts." They kissed again, his words and actions setting Jacob's mind at ease.

Jacob reached for the button on Rodney's jeans. Slowly, he unfastened it and the zipper, the truth of Rodney's words becoming very apparent. Shoving at the waistband, they managed to get Rodney out of his jeans, boxers and shoes within seconds.

Jacob sucked in a deep breath when he got his first look at Rodney's cock. "Jesus," he muttered.

Rodney laughed. "Thanks. Nice compliment."

Jacob wrapped his hand around Rodney's hard cock without hesitation and Rodney gasped. "Not sure that was a compliment. Right now, I'm thinking about how much that's *not* going to fit."

Rodney closed his eyes when Jacob's hand began to stroke his thick member. Rodney released a slow groan before lifting his eyelids, his gaze capturing Jacob's. "We'll go slow. And it *will* fit."

Jacob's fear evaporated. He wanted Rodney, in his bed, his body, his life. Rodney was right. If they took this slow, everything would fit.

Problem was, slow didn't seem to be an option for them. Rodney was cleared to return to work in New York. He'd be leaving far too soon.

"Hey." Rodney cupped Jacob's cheek. "Earth to Jake. You okay?"

Jacob nodded. He was fucking this up, thinking too far ahead. Even tomorrow was too far away to worry about. He'd wanted this man forever and he wasn't going to screw it up now. He smiled at Rodney, then dropped to his knees.

Rodney jerked slightly in surprise when Jacob took his cock into his mouth.

"Christ, Jake. That feels so good." Rodney's hands gripped Jacob's head, taking control.

Jacob's cock throbbed. In the past, he'd been on even ground with his lovers as they bumbled their way through, trying to find out what they liked, what they needed. Rodney knew what he wanted and how to get there. His control of this night was weaving its way through Jacob's bloodstream like a drug. He wanted—no, he needed—Rodney's power over him. It was so fucking hot.

"Can you take me deeper?" Rodney asked as he pushed his cock closer to the back of Jake's throat.

Unable to speak, Jacob nodded once. The extra motion must've felt good because Rodney's grip on his head tightened. "Fuck yeah. Just like that. God dammit, Jake. I want to fuck your mouth so bad."

Jacob reached up and grabbed Rodney's ass. In the past, he'd given blowjobs merely as fair-trade. He'd blow his lover and his lover would return the favor. This was different. Sucking Rodney's cock wasn't a chore—it was heaven.

Rodney stroked Jacob's face, issued quietly spoken directions that were followed by praise and amazement. Rodney began thrusting harder, each pass of his cock going deeper into Jacob's mouth. Jacob had learned to open his throat and he swallowed the head of Rodney's dick.

"Fuck." Rodney acted as if he'd been burned. He reared back, pulling his cock from Jacob's mouth, retreating a couple steps.

Jacob was confused. "I'm sorry. Did I hurt you?"

Rodney dropped to his knees in front of Jacob. He cupped

Jacob's face and pulled him toward him until their foreheads touched. Both of them were panting harshly. "Hurt me? Fucking Christ. I was about to lose it, Jake. About to blow. It's going too fast. I don't want it to end so soon. I want to take your ass."

Jacob smiled. "There's not a time limit on this. Not a rule that says you can only come once tonight."

"But the party—"

Jacob wrapped his hand around Rodney's cock, using the wetness still there from his mouth to stroke the thick flesh. "We're not going back to the party, Rod. I'm not leaving this bedroom tonight until you've fucked every part of me. And vice versa."

Rodney closed his eyes and shivered. "I thought you'd want to go back eventually."

"I'm exactly where I want to be."

Rodney kissed him hard, his tongue thrusting deep, reminding Jacob they weren't finished yet.

Jacob pulled away from Rodney's lips and tugged on his cock, indicating he wanted Rodney to stand once more.

"Before we go any further, I should tell you, I'm clean."

Jacob nodded. "So am I."

Rodney rose to his feet, his hands returning to Jacob's head once more. "I'm not sure I can hold back much longer."

"All night, remember?"

Rodney directed his cock back to Jacob's mouth, driving deep on the first pass. The tenor changed and Jacob realized exactly how much Rodney had been holding back. True to his word, Rodney fucked his mouth, taking Jacob with an intensity he didn't know existed. For several moments, Jacob merely held on for the ride, loving this man's possession of him.

When he sensed Rodney was getting close, Jacob decided it

was time to take a more active role. He grasped Rodney's balls, rubbing them lightly.

"Fuck!" Rodney's motions became more erratic as his climax grew closer. "Squeeze them tighter, Jake."

Jacob obeyed. There wasn't anything he wouldn't do for Rodney. He clenched his fist tighter around Rodney's sac, then glanced up. Rodney's face contorted with what looked like pain, but couldn't be mistaken as anything less than sheer bliss. Come exploded from his cock, coating the back of Jacob's throat. It was salty, hot, addictive.

As his climax subsided, Rodney reached down and with strong hands under his arms, pulled Jacob to his feet. Rodney wrapped his arms around Jacob in the warmest, most genuine hug Jacob had ever received.

"Jake." Rodney's voice was husky, full of the same emotions that were racing through Jacob.

Jacob returned the hug, loved the feel of Rodney's arms around him. "I know, man. I know."

*R*odney clung to Jacob, uncertain he'd ever felt closer to another human being in his life. When they finally parted, he gave Jake a guilty grin. "You haven't even taken your pants off yet."

Jacob laughed, the sound flowing over Rodney like rain on a hot summer day. Jacob was so different from the other men in his past. With Jacob, there were no shields. What you saw was what you got. It was refreshing, nice.

"I suppose I should take care of that. Especially since the denim is cutting into my hard on. Starting to hurt a little."

Both of them worked together to free Jacob from his jeans. Once his new lover was naked, Rodney took a step back to enjoy the view. Jacob was perfectly formed, just Rodney's type.

Jake's pale complexion was in direct contrast to Rodney's darker coloring. He had a light smattering of hair on his chest. Rodney couldn't resist reaching out to stroke his fingers through it. Jacob was also uncircumcised, a new experience for Rodney.

Jacob's hips and shoulders were slight. While there wasn't an ounce of fat on him anywhere, his uber-trim build revealed Jacob's dislike of physical labor. Give Jake a laptop and a quiet room and his mind would run forever. The same couldn't be said of his body when faced with ranch duties. Jacob typically found a million excuses to avoid such tasks.

"Guess I should work out more," Jacob said quietly.

Rodney shook his head. "Shut up. You look great. Sexy as hell. Go lay down on the bed."

Jacob flushed slightly and his cock twitched. Rodney took delight in that response. He'd always been too domineering in the bedroom. Some lovers had balked at his commands, but that didn't hold true for Jake. If anything, Rodney's demanding nature seemed to fan the flames. Another way this night was shaping up to be the best of his life.

Jacob pulled back the sheets and crawled beneath them. Rodney joined him without hesitation. Pulling Jacob close, he kissed him, taking his time to get to know Jake's mouth, the taste and scent of him. Jacob returned the embrace with an enthusiasm that was contagious.

Rodney wasn't sure how long they explored each other's mouths, faces, ears and necks, but by the time they released each other, they were panting and Rodney's cock was hard as a rock again.

Regardless of his reviving erection, Rodney knew whose turn it was. He pushed Jacob to his back. Rising, he knelt between the sexy cowboy's legs. Wrapping his hand around Jacob's cock, he gently massaged the hard flesh while watching his lover's face. Jake's expressions told him where his hot spots were. The head of Jacob's cock was extra sensitive to Rodney's touch, so he took care to pay special attention to that area.

Bending forward, Rodney licked Jacob's cock from base to tip, enjoying Jacob's groan.

"Damn, Rod. Do that again."

Rodney grinned and repeated the action. He started to take Jacob in his mouth, but another idea came to him. Moving, he twisted until he covered Jacob's body, facing in the opposite direction.

Nothing like a little sixty-nine action.

Jacob latched on to the new position with eagerness. "Fuck yeah," he muttered.

Rodney took Jacob into his mouth, enjoying when Jacob imitated his move.

"Up for a game of Follow the Leader?" Rodney asked.

Jacob didn't reply. Instead he kept Rodney's dick in his mouth as he nodded. The wicked motion went through him like a bolt of lightning. Rodney forced himself to take a deep breath. Jacob was definitely getting the upper hand in this game.

Rodney took Jacob's cock into his mouth once more, sliding down the hard flesh until the head brushed his throat. Jacob followed suit. Rodney began thrusting—his mouth and his cock —as Jacob followed his lead.

Jacob matched his pace, his pressure. Whenever Rodney teased with his teeth or his tongue, Jacob mimicked the action. Rodney felt the pressure build in his balls, but he refused to give into it this time. This time was for Jacob. After a few more mind-blowing sucks, Rodney pulled out of Jake's mouth.

"Hey. Wait."

"No." Rodney knelt between Jacob's legs once more, engulfing his cock in his mouth without bothering to explain.

Jacob's complaints died, morphing quickly to cries of pleasure. The sexy cowboy's hands clenched in the sheets and his body began to tremble.

Rodney released his cock briefly. "Give it to me, Jake. Come in my mouth, then I'm going to flip you over and fuck your ass."

The dirty promise and Rodney gripping Jacob's cock tighter was more than enough. He'd barely gotten Jacob's cock back into his mouth before he exploded. Rodney drank down every drop of the man's come before letting Jacob's soft dick go.

Sweat rolled down the side of Rodney's face. He wiped it away. Two blowjobs in and he knew without a shadow of a doubt he'd never get enough of Jacob.

Never.

He leaned forward and kissed Jacob's stomach.

Jacob's eyes were closed and he was breathing heavily. For several moments he didn't speak at all. Then he broke the silence. "I've never come that fucking hard in my life." Jacob's voice was quiet, but sure. "I swear to God, my eyeballs rolled back in my head and I thought my heart was going to burst."

Rodney chuckled. "I understand the feeling. You did the same thing to me."

Jacob's eyes drifted open, his gaze capturing Rodney's. "I want you."

It was a simple declaration, but Rodney felt the power of it straight to his core. The words of their song drifted back to him. There *was* no denying it. Everything between them was right, *true*. Jacob had stirred emotions in him Rodney had never experienced. The sensation was overpowering, amazing, scary as shit.

The thought of leaving had been difficult to consider earlier in the evening. Now it was looking downright agonizing, impossible.

Jacob stroked his face. "Don't look so worried, Rod. It'll all work out. I've got a good feeling about this. About us."

Leave it to Jake to see a rainbow when all Rodney could spy were storm clouds. For tonight, he'd take a page from Jacob's book. Live on faith and hope.

Moving over Jacob's body, Rodney couldn't resist stealing more of Jacob's sweet kisses. Their lips met, softer this time. The hunger had abated, leaving a satisfied bliss in its wake.

Jacob stroked his back, his fingers massaging the tight muscles there. Rodney loved the firm touch of a man's hands on him and Jacob's were working magic.

Rodney ignored the demands of his cock as long as he could, unwilling to give up Jacob's embrace. Finally, he gave in to his most essential need. "Do you have lube?"

Jacob nodded. Rodney rolled to his side as Jacob leaned toward the nightstand. Grabbing the tube of lubrication, he handed it to Rodney. His face reflected pure trust and longing.

Rodney felt that look like a punch in the gut. He needed this night to be perfect for Jake...and for him. He sensed Jacob hadn't exaggerated about his lack of experience. Rodney wanted to give him a night to remember, in case memories were all they had to hold on to. Rodney shook the negative thought away.

"Roll over. Onto your stomach."

Jacob obeyed, then moved into a crouching position. Rodney knelt by Jacob's feet and stroked the smooth, bare ass in front of him. God help him. Need burned in his gut. He'd never last long.

He uncapped the tube, squeezing out a generous dollop on his finger, then on Jacob's anus. Jake shivered.

"Okay?" Rodney asked.

"So fucking horny."

Rodney laughed. "Me too." He rubbed the lubrication into

Jacob's ass as his lover groaned. One finger quickly became two. Two became three.

Jacob began thrashing, pushing against Rodney's fingers, searching for more. When he sensed Jacob was ready, he pulled his hand away. Coating his dick with lubrication, he took a deep breath and tried to calm down.

Jacob stilled, waited as Rodney placed the head of his cock in his ass. Gripping Jacob's hips, he slowly began to sheathe himself in the warmth. The tightness was almost too much. Even with the lube easing his way, it was a snug fit. Rodney was terrified of hurting Jacob, so he moved slower, giving his lover time to adjust. Sweat ran from Rodney's temple, dripping onto Jacob's back.

"Rodney," Jacob said when Rodney passed the halfway point.

"Yeah," he replied, through gritted teeth.

"Fuck me. Give up this goddamn pace and fuck me."

"It's too tight, Jake. I don't want to hurt you."

"You're killing me right now. If you don't start moving, I will."

Rodney wanted to protest, but Jacob took the decision out of his hands. With one strong backwards movement, he flung himself against Rodney.

Jacob cried out, but Rodney couldn't tell if it was in pleasure or pain. It didn't matter. He was buried to the hilt and his body was overpowering his sense of restraint. Jacob fit him like a glove.

He tightened his grip on Jacob's hips, determined to take control once more. He'd set the pace, God dammit.

Jacob's upper body collapsed against the mattress, opening his ass even farther. Rodney took advantage of the new position, retreating, then slamming in once more. He reached around Jake's waist, gripping his cock with the hand still covered in lube. He stroked him firmly, working at Jacob's dick until it was hard once more.

"Jesus, Rod. I didn't know I could, I mean, I never managed to get a hard on this way."

Rodney shook his head, amazed by the confession. Jacob had obviously been with some pretty lame lovers in the past.

"You like getting fucked hard, Jake?"

"God. Yeah. So much. No one's ever—" Jacob's words faded away. Rodney wanted to give Jacob what he wanted. Hell, he'd give him everything he had.

Jacob deserved it. He'd offered friendship regardless of Rodney's surliness after the shooting.

He'd offered a shoulder for Rodney to cry on when he'd despaired about the possible loss of his arm and his job.

He'd offered laughter when Rodney was blue, never allowing him to give into depression.

He'd taught him how to ride a horse, the beauty of midnight bowling in black lights, and how much fun karaoke can be.

More than that, he'd saved his life. Jacob had put himself in the line of fire of a hit man in order to pull Rodney to safety.

"Hold on, Jacob."

"Always."

Rodney retreated, plunging back in with all the strength and speed he could muster. He alternated his thrusts with pumps, jerking Jacob off as he fucked his ass. Jacob's loud cries urged him on, drove him to mindlessness until every conscious thought was wiped away.

Jacob's moans turned into a mantra that beat in Rodney's body like a bass drum.

"Harder. Harder," Jacob called out, gasping.

Rodney's movements matched the demand as he pounded

deeper. His balls constricted and stars flew behind his closed eyelids. "Jesus, Jake. I can't. I have to—"

"Come," Jacob demanded. "Do it. With me."

Rodney gave in, his come filling Jacob's ass in fast, furious pulses. Jacob's body went stiff as he came. Rodney tried to capture as much of the sticky fluid as he could, but it was too much. They'd have to change the sheets later or draw straws to decide who got stuck with the wet spot.

When the last drop was spilled, Rodney's strength ran out. He collapsed to Jacob's side, panting as if he'd run a marathon in record-breaking time.

"Jesus." Rodney's voice was hoarse and he realized he'd been crying out as much as Jacob. For the first time since they entered the room, he remembered the party still going strong outside. Had anyone heard?

The amps from Matt's band were cranked up loud, the sounds of "Sweet Home Alabama" rocking the house. No, Rodney thought with relief. As long as everyone was still outside, their lovemaking would have gone unheard.

"I think I'm having a heart attack." Rodney's heart was thudding so loud it was drowning out the music outside.

Jacob rolled to his side and placed his hand over Rodney's heart. "I know the feeling."

Rodney shifted, lifted Jacob a bit so he could wrap his arm around his lover's shoulder and pull him close. "I'm sticky, sweaty and I probably stink to high heaven."

Jacob grinned. "I stink too. How about a shower?"

"Together?"

"Just try to take one without me."

Rodney kissed the top of Jacob's head. "Jake. Tonight was amazing."

Jacob lifted his head. "That was going to be my line."

"So sue me." More laughter drifted from the yard. "Sorry I made you miss your party."

Jacob rolled his eyes. "Gay Fest happens every year. This. Tonight. It was special."

That was an understatement. Tonight marked a pivotal moment in his life. Rodney wasn't sure what direction he'd be heading in tomorrow, but he knew all bets were off.

His life had changed and he'd never be the same again.

CHAPTER THREE

*J*acob opened his eyes and blinked a couple times to make sure what he was seeing was real. He stretched slightly, pleasantly sore in odd places.

So it's not a dream. Rodney is in my bed.

He smiled when Rodney's eyelids drifted open.

"Morning." Rodney's voice was heavy with sleep.

Jacob grinned. He could get used to that sexy sound real quick. "Good morning."

Rodney narrowed his eyes. "That's a pretty pleased look from someone who's going to break his back today cleaning up all kinds of shit from last night's party."

Jacob shrugged. "No biggie. My brothers will help. And I'm recruiting you."

Rodney grinned wickedly. "I don't know. I'm pretty worn out. Had this hot guy making all kinds of demands on me last night. Might need a day in bed to recover."

After their lovemaking last night, they'd taken the longest hot shower in history and the heat wasn't merely provided by the water. Rodney had soaped up his hands and jerked Jacob off as he kissed him. Not to be outdone, Jacob had joined in the game. The two of them kissed for ages as they stroked each other's cocks. It was the most sensually erotic moment of his life and Jacob hoped they could do a repeat performance of it sometime soon.

"FYI, Rod. If you're in this bed, I'm in it."

Rodney rolled toward him, pushing Jacob to his back as he came over him. He placed a light kiss on Jacob's lips. "Where do you stand on morning breath?"

Jacob chuckled. "Shut up and kiss me."

Rodney sure as hell knew his way around a mouth. Jacob closed his eyes as Rodney took charge. Jacob's experiences with kissing had never progressed beyond soft, simple touches. Rodney kissed like he meant it. He cupped Jacob's cheeks, using that hold to turn his face to suit Rodney's needs. His tongue roughly tangled with Jacob's. When he broke the union, Rodney lightly nipped his lower lip.

"Hey," Jacob said, faking pain.

Rodney was unapologetic. "You taste good."

Jacob ran his arms over Rodney's muscular shoulders and back. There was something very attractive about a well-built man.

Rodney nudged Jacob's legs apart, moving until he was lying directly on top of Jacob with his weight supported on his elbows. His erection rested next to Jake's and there was no denying they'd both woken up with boners.

"Are you sore?" Rodney's voice was truly concerned. Jacob knew his lover wouldn't press for more sex if he said yes.

Jacob shook his head. "Not enough to say no to what you're offering."

Rodney grinned, then reached for the lube they'd left on the bedside table last night.

Jacob started to roll over, but Rodney stopped him. "Face to face."

Jacob felt heat rise to his cheeks. He hoped Rodney wouldn't notice, but no such luck.

"Blushing, Jake? After everything we've done together in the last twelve hours?"

Jacob rolled his eyes. "Sorry I'm not some jaded guy who's been around the block a few times. I've never done it this way, so—"

Rodney stopped him with a quick kiss. "I like showing you all this stuff, being the one to teach you a few things."

Rodney backed up his statement with action, carefully lubing Jacob's ass. Lifting Jacob's legs, he held them up as he slowly slid inside.

Jacob felt a slight pinch. It had been a long time since he'd had sex and Rodney was no small man. It felt too good to deny though. A slight tremor of fear raced through him as he considered a life without this, without Rodney. He dismissed the anxiety. They would have a serious talk about the future today. Jacob had his arguments lined up. He was ready.

"Touch your cock, Jake. I want to watch you jack yourself off while I'm inside you."

Jacob grasped his dick and rubbed it. He loved Rodney's straightforward approach to sex. If he wanted something done, he asked for it. Jacob found that personality trait a complete turn-on.

Rodney began thrusting, his gaze glued to Jacob's hand as it stroked. "Tighten your grip, Jacob. I always come too damn fast in the morning. Should have warned you. This won't take long."

Jacob didn't think that would ever be a problem. Rodney was too good at fucking him. He was already on the verge of exploding. "God, Rodney," he gasped. "So goddamn good."

"I know." Rodney was panting, his motions picking up speed. The bed was squeaking loudly. There was no way his brothers wouldn't hear it, wouldn't know what was going on. Jacob had never had sex in the ranch house. In the stable or surrounding outbuildings, sure. But never in the house or his bedroom. He'd always wanted to protect his brothers from something he thought they'd be uncomfortable with. He wasn't looking forward to facing them over breakfast.

"Stop fucking around, Jake. Squeeze that cock like I would. I want to see you come, want to see it all over your chest."

Rodney's dirty talk was a trigger and the damn cop knew it. Knew how to push Jacob's hot buttons. Jacob tightened his grip. He stroked his cock in time with Rodney's hard, deep thrusts.

"Fuck. Too late. I can't stop." Rodney's body jerked three times as he came, his face the picture of pure, unshielded bliss. It drove Jacob over the edge.

Pulse after pulse of come spurted from his dick landing on his chest and shoulders.

Rodney collapsed to his side. "Mother fucker, that's good. God, Jake." Rodney seemed to be at a loss for words, so instead he showed Jacob what he wanted to say. He pulled Jacob close and kissed him. It was passionate and beautiful and Jacob never wanted it to end.

When they separated, they lay in quiet contemplation, merely staring at each other, breathing in the same sweet air.

So this is what it feels like.

True love.

Jacob had experienced a million variations of the emotion—crushes, puppy love, unrequited love, lust mistaken for love—but he'd never felt the real deal. Until now.

Rodney rolled to his stomach, his eyes drifting closed. Jacob couldn't resist running his hand over his lover's firm ass. Soon, the casual touches turned to a massage of Rodney's tight muscles.

Rodney groaned. "That feels nice."

Jacob propped himself up on his elbow, so he could take his explorations further. He dragged his fingers along the crack of Rodney's ass, grinning when his hot cop parted his legs, giving him easier access.

Jacob decided it was time to go for broke. He had a suspicion he needed confirmed. He pushed his finger against Rodney's anus not stopping until it was buried to the first knuckle. Without lube, he didn't dream of going deeper.

Rodney's eyes opened, his gaze landing on Jacob's face.

"Is that something you want, Jake?"

Jacob wasn't sure how to reply. He'd played both roles before, been the top and the bottom. While he preferred the bottom, he'd found some pleasure in the other as well. "I don't know."

Rodney didn't move, didn't shake off his hand. "I'm not exactly wired that way."

Jacob laughed, letting his sarcasm out. "Really? Shocking."

"I'm just saying I like to be the one doing the fucking. But, Jacob, if you want—if you need that—I'd give it to you."

Jacob was touched by Rodney's offer. He took his hand away. "I don't need it. My wiring is sort of the opposite of yours. I love having my ass fucked."

Rodney grinned. "Perfect fit."

Jacob swallowed back his tears. Truer words were never spoken.

"I suppose we should get out of bed before your brothers come looking for you. Something tells me they're not going to let us get out of helping with the clean up."

Jacob nodded, then gestured to his sticky chest. "How about a quick shower first?"

Rodney gave him a wicked grin. "How about an encore from last night?"

Jacob leapt from the bed. "Race you."

Several hours later, Jacob wiped the sweat off his brow and cursed the sun. "God, it's hot."

Matt walked by him, his T-shirt wet with perspiration and clinging to him, and chuckled. "You should try getting outside every once in a while, Jake. You'd build up an immunity to heat and cold."

Jacob shook his head. "No thanks. I prefer my climate controlled by things other than Mother Nature. AC, heaters, fans—these things were invented for a very good reason."

Matt handed Jacob a load of wood from the stage they'd just dismantled. "Help me carry this to the barn."

Jacob followed Matt, well aware there was an uncomfortable conversation coming.

"You disappeared pretty early last night."

Jacob nodded. "Yeah. I'm sorry about that. Didn't mean to leave you guys running the show."

Matt led him to an empty stall near the back of the barn. "We can store the wood in here for now." They both dropped their loads.

"I'm not bothered about the party. There were plenty of us around to keep it rolling and it was fun. Listen, Caleb and Mark are worried. They wanted to talk to you, but I convinced them to let me do it."

Jake was relieved Matt had volunteered. He loved all three of his brothers dearly, but Caleb and Mark struggled with his sexuality more than Matt. It was easier to talk to Matt about this stuff because he didn't get squicked out about it.

When Jacob had been younger and needed someone to talk to about the physical aspects of gay sex, he'd turned to Dr. Caleb. In Caleb's defense, he'd done an admirable job explaining the logistics, although it was in a rather dry, medical way. By the end of the conversation, they'd both been bright red and not exactly maintaining eye contact. Since then, Jacob had avoided putting them through that again.

"I don't think it's a surprise to anybody on this ranch that you and Rodney hooked up. Hell, I can't believe it took this long."

Jacob agreed. "He was struggling with his hand. Uncertain of his future."

Matt leaned against the back wall of the stall. "Yeah. I know. Caleb says he's been cleared to return to work."

Jacob nodded. "He has."

"Sort of bad timing on starting a relationship, wouldn't you say? I mean, the guy's been here for months with no plans to leave. The day he decides to go back to New York, you hop into bed with him. Aren't you sort of leaving yourself open for some bad times when he goes?"

It was a valid question. Unfortunately the answer wasn't going to be an easy one to give. "If Rodney agrees, I'm going to New York with him."

Matt's eyes narrowed. "Oookay," he drawled. "There's something there I need explained. *If* Rodney agrees? Makes me think you all didn't discuss this or he doesn't want you to go. Truth be told, both those answers piss me off."

"We haven't talked about the future yet. I plan to bring the conversation up today. I've tried several times already, but somebody always comes around and interrupts me."

Matt grinned. "Family has gotten bigger with Jessie and Bridget and R—" He paused mid-name, but Jacob knew where he was going.

"Rodney. He's become a part of this family in the past six months. You might as well admit it. You wouldn't have hesitated to say it yesterday, so why the problem now?"

"Yesterday he wasn't fucking my little brother."

Jacob laughed. "We haven't talked about what happens next. I know what I want. I just have to hope Rodney agrees."

"New York? You want to live in the city?" Matt said *New York* the way most folks said manure. Jacob knew his country boy brother had hated every minute he'd spent there in the spring. He'd endured two weeks cooped up in Bridget's tiny New York apartment, despising the noise, the crowds and the lack of grass.

"I've never fit in here, Matt." Jacob had never admitted that to any of his brothers. He didn't want to hurt them.

"That's not true."

Jacob walked over to a bale of hay and sat down. "I've been different since the day I was born. For one thing, I don't like ranch work."

"Neither does Caleb."

Jacob appreciated Matt's support, but it wasn't enough anymore. "I'm gay, Matt. I want to live somewhere where this —" Jacob pointed to himself, "—isn't quite so odd."

Matt joined him on the hay bale. "Has it been that hard for you here, Jake?"

This was why he'd avoided this conversation. His brothers had never made him feel like an outcast, but that didn't mean he wasn't one. "No. Not at all. You guys have always had my back and, now, there's Jessie and Bridget. I've just always felt like a square peg in a round hole. I want to see what life is like somewhere else for a while."

"New York is a rough place. I'd worry about you all the way over there by yourself." Matt would always be his overprotective older brother. His concern warmed Jacob's soul.

"I'm an adult, Matt. Have been for a few years. Besides I won't be alone. I'll be with Rodney. What's safer than living with a cop?"

"Is that where this is headed? You two moving in together?"

Jacob rested his elbows on his knees and sighed. "I hope so. I'm in love with him." Jacob hadn't managed to say the words to Rodney yet. It felt like it was too soon. Problem was soon it was going to be too late.

"Yeah. That's pretty obvious. I'm glad."

Jacob looked at his brother. "Really?"

Matt nodded. "I always wondered about what it would be like when you found a guy. Worried about liking him, him fitting in with us. Shit like that. Rodney fits. It's like finding another brother. It's nice."

Jacob couldn't hold back his smile. Matt's words freed all the anxiety he'd been feeling since he'd come downstairs this morning. "You think Caleb and Mark could learn to feel that way?"

Matt gave him a funny look. "They already do, you knucklehead. First words out of Mark's mouth this morning were 'Thank God it's Rodney'."

Jacob laughed. "So I guess the only thing left to do is to convince Rodney to take me with him."

"The guy's crazy about you. He hasn't taken his eyes off you all morning. Shit, now that I think about it, he hasn't taken them off you since he arrived here in February. I got a good feeling about this. But Jake—"

"Yeah?"

"If things don't work out with Rodney or if you hate the city, you know this place is always going to be your home, right?"

Jacob nodded. "I know that."

"Hate the idea of you leaving. Gonna miss the hell out of you."

They stood. Matt reached out and grabbed him into a big bear hug.

"I'm going to miss you guys too," Jacob said, trying to hold back the tears.

"Hey, do you two need any help in here?" Rodney was halfway to them before he stopped, realizing he'd interrupted something. "Shit. Sorry."

"Nope. Nothing to apologize for," Matt said, releasing Jacob. "Jake, why don't you and Rodney finish up in here? I'll get Mark to help me take down the tents."

Jacob nodded, knowing his brother was giving him a chance to talk to Rodney. There was fuck-all left to do in the barn. "Okay."

Matt slapped Rodney on the back as he walked out of the barn.

Rodney released a long breath. "I assume this means I don't have to worry about your brothers beating the shit out of me at some point today."

Jacob shook his head. "Coast is clear."

"Well, that's a relief. I'm not going to pretend I wasn't worried about that."

Jacob resumed his seat on the hay bale and gestured to the one next to him. "Pull up a bale. Take a load off. We've been working for hours."

Rodney plopped down and rubbed his shoulder wearily. "A break sounds good."

Jacob took a deep breath, then dove in before he could talk himself out of it. "I want to go to New York with you."

Rodney glanced at him. "What?"

"You said last night we'd talk today about the future. I want to go to New York, Rod."

"How can you know you want to go to New York? You said it yourself at the party. You've never been to a truly large city. New York is as different from Saratoga as mud is from chocolate."

"Is Saratoga the mud or the chocolate?"

Rodney narrowed his eyes. "I'm being serious."

"So am I. If you want me to come with you, I will. Dammit, Rodney, I don't think you realize what it's been like for me, growing up here. Last night you mentioned gay bars. Plural. As in more than one."

Rodney nodded. "There are a lot of gay bars in the city. So what?"

"Do you know why I hold Gay Fest every summer?"

Rodney shook his head.

"So I'll have one night in the year where I don't feel like a freak. Where I'm reminded I'm not alone in my homosexuality."

"You bring the freaks here so you won't be lonely?"

He knew Rodney was joking, but the words were the truth. Jacob had never been known to have common sense when it came to avoiding difficult situations. He assumed that was sort of the curse of growing up gay in the middle of cowboy country. He figured out a long time ago he could hide in the shadows or just adopt an "I'm gay and in your face" attitude. He'd met plenty of folks who probably wished he'd cower in a corner or at least pretend to be straight, but he wasn't raised that way.

His father was probably the toughest son of bitch to ever walk a Wyoming ranch. While he struggled with his son's sexuality—dear God did he struggle—his dad had told Jacob the only life worth living was one where you could look yourself straight in the eye in the mirror and know you'd been true to yourself.

"I want a place where I'll fit in."

Rodney glanced out the window. "Todd and Stephen live right next door. They're living a gay lifestyle. It's not like you're totally alone out here."

"One gay couple within a hundred-mile radius doesn't

count. I've spent my entire life being *that* James brother. The one folks point to and whisper about. I've always wondered what it would be like to live in a place where I'm not so different."

"You know, there are still haters in the city. Hell, I got roughed up by a few guys in my department after they found out I was gay."

Jacob shrugged. "It's everywhere. I get it. I still want to go."

"What about your family? They'll go nuts when they find out you're leaving with me."

"No, they won't. I just told Matt what I'm hoping to do. He was cool with it."

Rodney tilted his head in disbelief. "Is that right?"

"Well, maybe not totally cool. He doesn't like the city much, but he understood."

"That's one brother. What about the rest of the family?"

"They'll be okay. They'll understand. Look at how much their lives have changed this year. Caleb's getting married. He and Jessie have made good headway on building their new house. Matt and Mark have found Bridget. They'll have this place crawling with kids before we know it. Where does that leave me? I don't want to be the eccentric brother who lives upstairs forever. I want my own life, my own place in the world."

Rodney picked at the straw beneath him. "New York is an awesome place. I'd love to show it to you."

Jacob tried not to get too excited by Rodney's comment. "You don't have to tell me. I've always wanted to go there. I want to see the Statue of Liberty, the Empire State Building. I have a list of Broadway shows I want to go to as long as my arm. I want to hit Canal Street for the bargains and see the Macy's windows at Christmas."

Rodney winced, though the look wasn't sincerely pained.

"Fuck, man. You're not really going to make me do all that shit, are you? Play the tourist in my own hometown."

"Damn right, you're doing it all with me."

They were quiet for several moments. Rodney's face was still uncertain, something was holding him back.

When the silence became too much, Jacob nudged his knee against Rodney's. "Say something."

"It feels like you're the only one making all the sacrifices here. Moving away from your home, your family. What the hell do I have to offer that's worth you giving up so much?"

"You'd be giving me you. Jesus, Rod. That's all I want."

"I've never been in a real relationship, Jake. I don't want to fuck things up."

"In what way?"

Rodney shrugged. "Something tells me I'm going to be jealous and possessive."

Jacob grinned. "I already feel that way. You mentioned getting those phone numbers last night and it took everything in me not to hunt down the guys and beat the crap out of them."

Rodney didn't smile. "You've never had a real boyfriend either, have you?"

Jacob shook his head. "Rod, if you think we're moving too fast, I'll understand if you go home alone. Last night was our first time together. It's stupid of me to press for more, for a commitment when—"

"Don't even finish that, Jake. In my mind, we've been together for months. The sex was the last piece of a relationship that's been building since February. All of this was inevitable. I'm just fucking terrified of hurting you."

Jacob was confused by Rodney's tone. He sounded upset when it was taking all the strength in Jacob's body not to do a few handsprings in the yard. Rodney cared about him. "What's wrong? Why aren't you happy about this?"

Rodney sighed. "I'm a cop, Jake. My job is dangerous."

Suddenly, Rodney's hesitance made sense. "I know that."

"Do you honestly think you'll be okay with me leaving every day knowing that I could get killed? How could I ask you to go through that day after day? If the shoe were on the other foot, I don't think I could. I mean, those last few weeks on the run with Bridget nearly killed me. I love that girl and knowing there was someone out there who wanted to hurt her ate at me like a cancer. I walked around every day feeling like I was waiting for the other shoe to drop."

Jacob swallowed heavily as a memory he'd carefully tucked deep inside rose to the surface. "I saw you shot, Rod. I was fucking standing there when that bullet went into you."

"Then you know what I'm talking about. I can't guarantee you a nice long happily ever after, Jacob. And that's what you deserve. What I want to be able to give you. More than anything. It feels like the only thing I have to offer in the face of everything you're sacrificing and...I don't have it to give. The reality is I can't promise you I won't be injured, even killed."

"No one can make a promise like that. I don't care what job they do. I'm studying to be a journalist. Look how that relatively safe career path turned out for Bridget. An informant gives her details about a crooked judge and she ends up getting chased all over the country by a hit man."

"I know that, but most people don't leave for work with the knowledge they could be shot and killed. Every day I put on that uniform and strap that gun to my waist, I run that risk. How can I ask you to live with that?"

Jacob moved over to Rodney's hay bale, sitting close to him. "I know what you do for a living. I also know it's a part of you that you can't give up. I'd never ask you to. That's something I'll have to learn to deal with. I'd rather have a few days in heaven with you than a lifetime in hell alone. You choose to be a cop, to put your life on the line. I choose to be in love with a cop. That decision's made and I won't regret it. Not ever."

"You're in love with me?"

Jacob nodded. "Yeah. I sort of planned to spring that on you with this big romantic speech, but—"

Rodney laughed and wrapped his arm around Jacob's shoulder. "Going to warn you right now, I'm about as romantic as a coffee pot."

"Coffee's sexy. I like anything that's black and hot and gets me up in the morning."

Rodney kissed him lightly. "You're crazy, Jacob James, but I love you anyway."

"I like the sound of that."

Rodney narrowed his eyes. "You're also a hard man to argue with. Not sure this bodes well for my future."

Jacob ran a hand through his dirty blond hair, pushing a stray strand away from his face. "Just let me win all the fights and you'll be fine."

Rodney glanced around the barn as if trying to make a decision. Then he turned back to face him. "You're sure you want to come to New York with me? Give this thing a real shot?"

Jacob nodded. "I want that more than anything in the world. So what do you say, Mr. Hot Cop?"

Rodney took Jacob's hand in his, looking at their linked fingers. Then he gazed at Jacob's face, his smile growing, his eyes twinkling with glee. "I say Yee Haw."

EPILOGUE

Rodney winked at Jacob as Jake stood next to his brother, Caleb. When the wedding music began, Rodney rose with the rest of the family and watched Jessie walk from the barn to the ranch house. Jessie, a widow, claimed she'd already had her big white wedding. This time around she wanted a simple ceremony with only her family and closest friends.

She and Caleb decided to wed on the steps of the front porch of the home Caleb had grown up in. It was dusk, that beautiful time when the sun lost its potency, casting the world in muted, softer light. Rodney had to hand it to her. Jessie had selected the perfect moment.

Rodney sat next to Todd and Stephen while Bridget and Mark shared the row in front of them. Matt sat off to one side of the porch playing ABBA's "I Do" on the guitar. Rodney chuckled at the song choice, recalling his duet with Jacob.

Jessie looked beautiful as she walked toward her groom in a simple white sundress. She carried a bouquet of bright purple wildflowers and her hair—normally worn in a ponytail—lay long and loose against her shoulders. Her eyes as she looked at Caleb spoke volumes about how she felt in that moment. Rodney was overwhelmed by the pure love, happiness, and hope written on her face. He recognized the emotions well now. They were the same ones he saw when he looked in the mirror every morning.

"Dearly beloved," the minister began the ceremony. While Rodney heard the words, listened as Caleb and Jessie made their vows to each other, his attention was solely focused on Jake. He imagined what it would feel like to make that same pledge to him.

When it came time to exchange the rings, Jacob stepped forward and handed them to the minister, taking Jessie's bouquet from her. Given the limited space on the porch, he was serving as best man and maid of honor for the event.

Rodney joined the rest of the family as they stood and cheered when the minister gave Caleb permission to kiss his bride. It had been the perfect wedding. A beautiful beginning to the new chapter in Caleb and Jessie's lives together.

Jacob walked toward him. "Hiya handsome."

"Let me guess, weddings make you all sentimental and shit."

His lover nodded. "Yep. This one put me in a completely romantic mood."

"Me too."

Jacob's eyes widened in surprise. "Why, Mr. Jackson, I never thought I'd see the day."

"Don't get used to it."

Jacob laughed and took his hand. "Come on. It's party time."

The wedding reception was going to be a small dinner

party for nine. The minister had been invited to stay, but had double booked his weekend with weddings. He said his good-byes and congratulations to Caleb and Jessie, then dashed off to a wedding rehearsal.

The dinner wasn't merely a celebration, but a going-away party. He and Jacob had packed all their stuff and were flying to New York tomorrow afternoon. Tonight would be the last time the family would be together until Christmas. Bridget had only agreed to let them both leave if they promised to return for the holidays. It hadn't been a hard vow to make. Rodney wasn't looking forward to leaving her.

Stephen helped Todd serve the dinner they'd prepared before they joined everyone at the table.

Mark lifted his glass. "To Caleb and Jessie. Here's wishing you both a lifetime of happiness and lots of little rugrats. I'm looking forward to being an uncle."

Jessie laughed and rubbed her stomach. "You might be getting that wish a little sooner than you realize."

Matt whooped loudly, then quickly took the glass of cham-pagne out of Jessie's hand.

Jessie laughed. "I wasn't going to drink it. I swear."

Caleb kissed Jessie on the cheek. "Jessie didn't want to tell you all until she was a bit further along."

Jacob's face reflected pure joy. "What's the due date, Jess? Rodney and I will make plans to come back for it."

"Early March."

Jacob high-fived Caleb. "Hot damn. A baby. Too cool."

Rodney looked at Bridget and tugged on her hair. "Careful you don't drink the water around here, Bridge. Might be a baby epidemic going on."

"Don't you worry about me, Rodney. I have these amazing little magic pills that take care of that issue. I'm perfectly safe."

"For now," Matt added.

Bridget grinned, but didn't disagree. Rodney looked around the table. A year ago, he'd never met any of these people. Now he couldn't imagine his life without them.

He lifted his own glass. "I'd like to propose a toast to the James family. You took me in this year when I was at my lowest point. You picked up, dusted me off, and set me on my feet again. Thank you for that."

Mark reached over and squeezed his shoulder. "You brought us Bridget, man, kept her safe and alive. There aren't words to say how much that means to me and Matt."

"And now you're taking Jake off our hands," Matt joked. "Definitely feels like we should be the ones thanking you."

Jacob pitched a piece of bread at Matt's forehead. "Way to spoil the moment, idiot."

Caleb raised his hand. "Our lives have changed a lot in the past year. Last summer we were four bachelors stumbling through life. Now we have Jessie and a baby on the way, Todd and Stephen, the greatest neighbors on the planet, and the city slickers, Rodney and Bridget, in our lives. Our house has become a home and I'm very grateful. To family."

Everyone lifted their glasses.

Rodney took Jacob's hand and smiled. "To family," he whispered. Then he leaned closer. "And going wild."

If you're hot for Mari Carr's cowboys, why not give the Sparks in Texas series a spin as well.

Waiting for Us (prequel)
Waiting for You
Waiting for Her

Waiting for Him
Waiting for Them
Waiting for Love
Waiting for Snow

ABOUT THE AUTHOR

Virginia native Mari Carr is a New York Times and USA TODAY bestseller of contemporary romance novels. With over two million copies of her books sold, Mari was the winner of the Romance Writers of America's Passionate Plume award for her novella, Erotic Research. She has over a hundred published works, including her popular Wild Irish and Compass books, along with the Trinity Masters series she writes with Lila Dubois.

Follow Mari:

www.maricarr.com

mari@maricarr.com

Join her newsletter so you don't miss new releases and for exclusive subscriber-only content.

www.ingramcontent.com/pod-product-compliance
Lightning Source LLC
Chambersburg PA
CBHW061619210726
48287CB00001B/196